Price of a Thousand Blessings

Volume One

Ginn Hale

Price of a Thousand Blessings

Volume One

Ginn Hale

BLIND EYE BOOKS

Price of a Thousand Blessings
Volume One
By Ginn Hale
Published by Blind Eye Books
315 Prospect Street #5393
Bellingham WA 98227
www.blindeyebooks.com

Edited by Nicole Kimberling
Copyedit by Audrey Salo
Proofreading by Mary Evangeline Couling
Book Design by Dawn Kimberling
Ebook design by Michael DeLuca
Cover Illustration by Ginn Hale

print ISBN: 978-1-956422-12-2
ebook ISBN: 978-1-956422-13-9
Library of Congress Control Number: 2024944912
Printed in the United States of America

CONTENTS

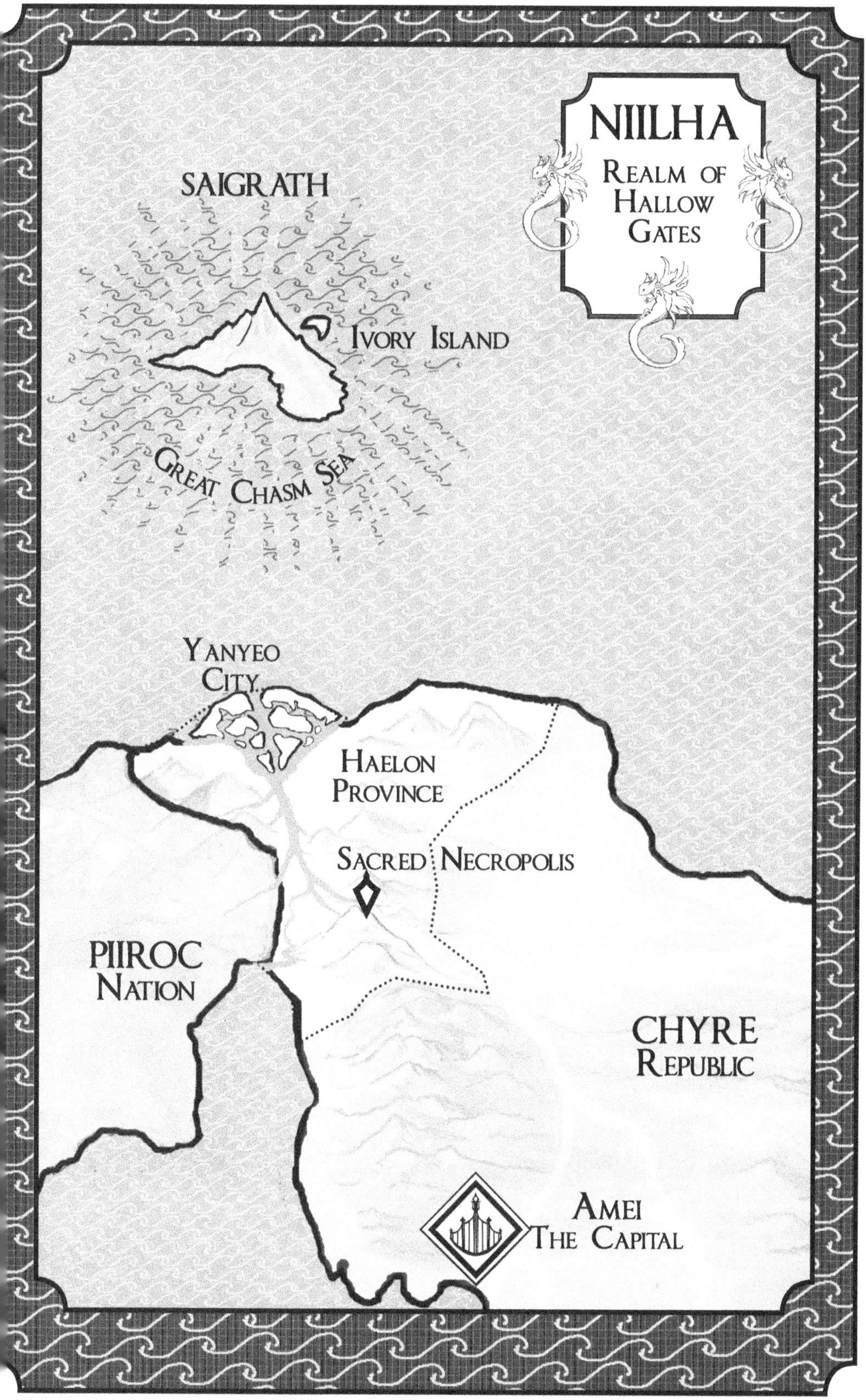
NIILHA
Realm of Hallow Gates
Saigrath
Ivory Island
Great Chasm Sea
Yanyeo City
Haelon Province
Sacred Necropolis
Piiroc Nation
Chyre Republic
Amei The Capital

Chapter 1

Cool morning light streamed over the high walls of the Lux Temple, while the vast city outside its gates fell strangely silent. In the temple courtyard, Cymin took a deep breath and prepared to begin the most important procession he would ever lead. He wore the pearl mask of the aloof East Deity for the occasion. His sister Yinni's face was hidden behind the gold mask of the benevolent West Deity. Wigs crafted from raw silk threads covered their shaved heads. The richly embroidered gold robes of their costumes billowed and fluttered, exposing their bare feet.

Behind them, sixty of their fellow tuteli clerics filled the narrow stone space, all standing in formation and waiting for the morning bells to announce the opening of Lux Temple's Spring Exhibition. Brilliant regalia, archaic weapons and beautiful musical instruments abounded. Ahead of them all rose the temple's huge ironwood gates, and beyond that, the secular world, filled with fascinating people, forbidden delights and all their future challenges.

Cymin bounced on his toes and rolled his shoulders, attempting to shake off a little of his nervous anticipation. This year's procession was expected to draw more spectators than any in the last twenty years, and the exhibition matches afterwards would be attended by the top combatants from the Five Mage Schools. Cymin's final year defending the honor of East Deity could be his most triumphant yet.

Or an utter humiliation—but Cymin didn't allow himself to think about that. Instead, he stole a glance to his sister. At twenty, Yinni was two years older than him but still three inches shorter. She tapped her graceful fingers along the Black Staff in her right hand. Only that betrayed her nervousness. Noticing Cymin's gaze, her fingers stilled.

"We'll astound the crowd and trounce all challengers," Yinni assured him. "By the end of the exhibition, thousands of new worshipers will flood the temple with donations and come begging for blessings from us."

"Only if all the people out on the street forget that we're just their local tuteli under these costumes," Cymin teased her, though in truth he wished to the Heavens that she could be right. "Once they remember that, they'll go back to looking down on us."

"Shut up and let me bask in my glorious delusion," Yinni responded. She then gestured grandly to the tuteli assembled behind them. "We're all beautiful today."

Cymin couldn't argue with that, and he didn't want to, in any case.

"Today we're divine!" he agreed, loudly enough for his voice to carry across the entire gathering—from the twenty costumed performers to the vast retinue of musicians behind them. Cheers and a few giggles met his proclamation.

All three of the tuteli adepts standing directly behind Cymin and Yinni laughed and patted each other's backs encouragingly. They were all close to twenty years of age and specifically selected for this year's procession on account of their grace as well as their skill in tempering fei'lux to power the spells embedded in their ancient weapons. They, like Cymin and Yinni, wore refined deity masks and moved with practiced finesse, transforming displays of swords, staves and spears into elegant dances.

Together, the five of them represented the nation's most revered and recognizable deities, the Five Guardians who had defended the Hallow Gates during the creation of the world and later subdued the Carnal Gods. While Cymin and Yinni represented the deities of the day and night, respectively, their three fellow tuteli adepts were costumed as the deities of the earth, sky and water.

If this had been 200 years earlier, during the reign of mage-kings, hundreds more deities would have filled out their ranks—at least one for every occupation, location or interest anyone could think of—but in the century since the People's Revolution, most of the expansive pantheon had been abolished.

Five deities were enough for the revolutionaries; any more than that constituted excess.

Behind Cymin and the other adepts came fifteen novice tuteli ranging in ages from six to twelve. They struggled to contain their excitement, several of them spontaneously performing the cartwheels and somersaults they'd be expected to display along the parade route. Others waved their hands in the air and struck poses as ferocious beasts. Strings of brass bells tinkled from their wrists and ankles, and bright ribbons adorned most of their headdresses.

These children were meant to evoke the deadly adversaries of the deities. Those dressed like dragons, sea serpents and other mythical beasts represented the defeated Carnal Gods who were still worshiped in the nation of Piiroc. Novices wearing floating ribbons and layers of colorful gauze were sharwae, guardian spells that had been corrupted from their original protective purposes so much that the deities had to fight and defeat them.

And last came the children adorned in chaotic splashes of body paint and riots of flowers, reeds and seashells. They played chuuraun, chimeric monsters born of creatures and spells that supposedly had been fused together by the savage fei'lux storms of the archaic days before the Storm Towers had been built.

Of course, all those mythic horrors and wonders were long gone. Or at least, they should have been—though this year might change that. Cymin turned his long black staff over in his hands and stared at the gates ahead of him, willing them to open.

At last, the city clock towers resounded with nine bells. The iron-wood doors of the Lux Temple's Sun Gate swung open and Cymin bounded out. He landed gracefully on the open street at the start of the parade route. Hordes of onlookers lined the roadside, and at the sight of him, countless excited voices suddenly roared. There were so many more spectators than he'd expected that Cymin nearly missed his second leap. Behind him, the temple musicians commenced to play, and for a moment the clamor of drums, horns and gongs of the procession nearly drowned out the shrill whistles and cheers of the assembled crowd. But not for long.

Everywhere Cymin looked, he saw more and more people. Shop-keepers, clerks and bike couriers gossiped with workers still wearing their factory overalls. Students dressed in bright green school jackets clustered around their instructors while little children waved from their parents' shoulders. Beggars and street vendors wove through the throngs while radio reporters and even a film newsreel crew jostled for good positions. He met the gazes of hundreds of strangers in a single glance. They filled the walkways, crouched atop newsstands, leaned from the windows and balconies of nearby teahouses and even perched on the tile rooftops.

Had all seven million of the capital's residents actually come out to watch the temple parade this year?

For the briefest of instants Cymin froze with shock. Then his four-teen years of training took over. In his right hand he raised his long staff. The gold teardrop-shaped finial at the top of it glinted in the sun, looking a little like a candle flame. Beside him, Yinni lifted her match-ing staff. Deep inside the Black Staves lay rods of goldwork, each etched with a treasury of ancient spells—the Thousand Blessings that once shielded entire cities from droughts, plagues and sieges. Though with-out fei'lux coursing through them the staves were little more than very heavy sticks.

Cymin flexed his left hand and began to draw fei'lux down from the seemingly tranquil air. A tingling current shot through the spell filaments—gold threads implanted into his hands and arms—and then spread across his chest. He spun in a circle, letting the fei'lux circulate through his body—tempering its erratic currents to match his heartbeat. In the time it took for him to complete one rotation, he calmed the torrent of blazing fei'lux to a steady stream of energy.

Then with his right hand he released that gentle flow of power into the Black Staff and channeled it to the gold rods at the core. Tiny gold sigils all along the shaft began to glow. Each sigil was itself powerless, but when grouped together they made up spells. The gold finial capping the staff flashed nearly as bright as the morning sun. Its light flickered across the gathered crowd while wisps of a silvery vapor coiled around the crown of the staff like steam.

Cymin leapt and spun again, twirling the staff as he went. Beside him, Yinni did the same. What appeared to be a playful dance was in reality a precise discipline, every step, leap and turn relating to the exact position of one of the thousand spells hidden within the staff. Those spells combined to make a larger spell array. Years of constant training and practice ensured that Cymin and Yinni not only roused the right spells but that they did so in perfect synchrony, their matched dance steps mirroring the flows of fei'lux they released. Cymin swept to the right, Yinni to the left. Sigils all along their staves glinted in time to the swelling music. Today they gently woke the sequence of spells that created a vast floating veil.

Plumes of silver vapor poured from their staves and coalesced in midair. One plume after another took on translucent floral shapes. Luminous petals as long as Cymin's arms unfurled. As the blossoms rose they interlocked like clockwork, spinning and spreading above the onlookers. Warm breezes stirred and fragrances of jasmine and rose drifted down. Steadily, the sky filled with bright silver spells—each evoking one of the Sacred Blossoms that seeded the world with the first blessings of life: warmth, sustenance, health, protection, joy and a multitude of other kindnesses.

Cymin and Yinni danced forward and the Veil of a Thousand Blessings stretched behind them, sheltering the rest of the procession. A warm breeze perfumed with the fragrance of spring blossoms spread over the crowd, driving back the morning chill.

The resounding applause, hoots and cheers that followed seemed out of proportion to Cymin. The subdued selection they'd conjured from the complete Thousand Blessings wasn't that impressive to him. A heavy rain would wash it away, and even fireworks could distort it.

This small array of spells was certainly nothing when compared to the magecraft required to serve in the Storm Towers. There, entire teams of tuteli battled onslaughts of wild fei'lux that surged down from the Hallow Gates far across the Great Chasm Sea. Those ancient, battered Storm Towers shielded their nation as well as the rest of the continent by capturing eruptions of fei'lux that could have scoured away both land and life and tempering them into sedate streams. The tempered fei'lux that the Storm Towers released became a steady flow of energy, one that drove electrical turbines, powered public trams and illuminated the newly built streetlamps all across the nation of Chyre. It was that tamed flow of energy that Cymin and Yinni tapped into now.

Surrounded by cheers and applause, Cymin gave silent thanks to all the older tuteli serving in the Storm Towers. And as he and Yinni led the procession onward, Cymin occasionally glimpsed the youngest tuteli dancing behind them. Despite their villainous costumes, several of the novices were too intimidated by the throngs of strangers surrounding them to be mistaken for anything but children. One scrawny boy actually clung to an adept tuteli's leg, hiding his face in the gold silk. His timidity was balanced out by a plump little girl—with a malevolent violet sigil painted on her brow—who forgot her role as a corrupt sharwae completely and began waving at onlookers and throwing kisses like the star of a moving picture.

Cymin smiled behind his mask.

Perhaps something good could come of so very many people watching the parade this year. Maybe a family would take a liking to that little girl, pay off her temple debt and adopt her. Or someone might take the shy boy on as an apprentice and give him a chance to earn enough money to buy his own debt back.

For grown adepts like himself and Yinni, adoption or apprenticeship weren't likely—after more than a decade of training and living in the temple, their debts were far too great—but a scout might hire one of them for stunt work on a moving picture. Or perhaps they could find side work performing blessings at a wedding or for the opening of a new business.

Cymin had recently been entertaining the fantasy that he might earn a little secular money before the end of the Spring Festival. After that he would begin his conscription maintaining the Storm Towers.

He often daydreamed about what it would be like to freely meet and mingle with the fascinating people who lived outside the Lux Temple. Though how many of them would be interested in him, he wasn't certain. Most people looked upon Lux Temple's tuteli as impoverished, celibate ascetics whose existences were entirely dedicated to refining the magecraft bestowed upon humanity by the deities.

As it was, the majority of secular people who Cymin interacted with were students from one of the five state-approved mage schools. Those encounters were largely confined to battles meant to hone the prowess of the Five Schools' mages and were therefore mostly unfriendly exchanges.

But what would it be like to lounge on silk cushions and converse with people on whatever subject crossed his mind?

His gaze swept across the crowd to a group of young scholars sitting on the roof of a winehouse. They exchanged relaxed smiles and toasted one another. Their long dark hair hung loose, and their green university robes fluttered in the spring breeze, exposing bare dangling legs. A sandal slipped from one young man's foot. A newsgirl on the walkway below caught it and hurled it back up to the roof. The scholars laughed and sang out some poem in response, but Cymin was already too far away to hear it clearly.

He smirked at his own wistful imagination. Master Tam would smack him until he saw stars if he knew of the absurdly shallow fantasies Cymin entertained while representing East Deity on this sacred day.

But after years of performing before lackluster gatherings of schoolchildren on day trips, bored government officials and dazed tourists, he felt a little giddy to see awe and appreciation in so many faces.

Still, as he manifested a shining veil of blessings over Grand Avenue, Cymin resisted the urge to display his genuine prowess. Tempting wisps of fei'lux curled around him as if summoned by his desire to show off. His left hand tingled and an excited hum stirred in his chest. It would be so easy to awaken the true power of the countless sigils etched into the core of this staff. Instead of faint silver flowers, this crowd could see the real invocations blaze to life. They'd be astounded—one of those rooftop scholars might even drop his wine cup.

But this year, of all years, the Temple Grand Master and the organizers in the Prime Minister's office would be furious if he rashly deviated from the plan, so he absolutely shouldn't screw around. He could not afford to add any fines to his massive temple debt. He was already facing seven years in the Storm Towers to work off his current balance.

Plus Yinni would probably slap the mask off his face for messing around and embarrassing her.

Cymin flicked his hand, releasing the stream of fei'lux back into the atmosphere.

I am East Deity, the light of the sun and guardian of creation. I do not show off just to impress pretty scholars in loose robes . . . at least not when anyone can catch me doing so.

As Yinni and Cymin crossed staves and circled each other. Yinni rolled her dark eyes meaningfully at a balcony on the right and said, "Hey! That's Una Bayan, isn't it?"

Cymin stole a sidelong glance at the group of people Yinni indicated. He recognized the screen actress at once. Her short-cropped dark hair, scarlet-stained lips and long silk trousers all evoked the vivacious, revolutionary roles that had won her many ardent admirers as well as a fair number of vitriolic critics. Two men in modern clothes lounged against the balcony railing on either side of her. One of them seemed rather mousy, with dull brown hair and a meek posture. But the second man rivaled Una Bayan in looks, with jet-black hair, a rich complexion and handsome features. He held a Bluecloud cigarette in between two of his long fingers. Then he suddenly looked down at Cymin and Yinni. His dark gaze seemed to bore right through Cymin's mask.

The man flexed his empty right hand, casting a spell directly. Cymin's eyes stung, and his vision wavered. The man had to be a master mage. Probably a graduate from the elite Boshyin School.

Embarrassed to have been caught gawking, Cymin lifted his chin and shrugged his shoulders. With every motion he attempted to convey: *East Deity is indifferent to beauty and cares nothing about screen stars or handsome men with cigarettes. He is simply studying the crowd. There are many more impressive people than you for him to observe.*

He maintained the pretense as they paraded on, making a steady circuit around the 800 acres of the sprawling Lux Temple Complex. At last, they neared the towering red walls of the exhibition grounds. Here, faces and figures Cymin had previously only seen in weekly newsreels suddenly became as plentiful as mice in a granary.

Clothed in resplendent silk robes and lounging in auto-carriages or pedicabs drawn by giant carriage birds, the governing elite and idle rich occupied long swaths of the walkways. Walls of dark-uniformed attendants, private security and city police insulated them from the surrounding rabble.

Then some dumb photographer dashed out into the street and lit off a burst of flash powder right in Cymin's face.

"You fucker!" Cymin's nerves hummed as the rush of white heat caught him unprepared. He barely had enough time to release his staff. The faint scars marking his hands and fingers gleamed for an instant—then the current dissipated. Cymin caught his staff again. He'd barely managed to expel the burst of energy before it polluted the stream of blessings. This year, of all years, was not the time to befoul the elegant Veil of a Thousand Blessings with ugly splotches that reeked of saltpeter.

Next to him Yinni's arms shook and twitched, but she didn't release her staff. Instead, she channeled the burst of power into her muscles to suppress it. Cymin winced in sympathy at the burning needles of pain spearing her every nerve.

He started for the photographer, but Yinni elbowed him and he regained his senses. Obviously, she hadn't endured blistering pain just to have him slap a random photographer on the open street in front of thousands of people.

Still, Cymin couldn't just let it go. He raised a finger from the Black Staff and ignited a wisp of fei'lux near the photographer's face.

"Heaven decrees that the wicked shall be struck down," Cymin's voice boomed out.

The burst of energy wasn't enough to even kill a horsefly, but it flashed bright and intimidating. The man yelped then fled towards the surrounding crowd. However, the instant the photographer reached the walkway, three women in police uniforms grabbed him and slammed him against the wall of a teahouse.

"And the Heavens' punishment comes swiftly," Yinni intoned.

They continued ahead.

Moments later, they reached the towering walls of the exhibition grounds. The huge scarlet doors were hauled open. Cymin kept his head up and his eyes focused ahead of him, maintaining East Deity's assured, indifferent demeanor the same way he had for the past five years. When their procession passed through the gateway, cheers rose from the wooden stands like thunder, and petals of cut paper stamped with blessings fluttered down like drifts of snow. He, Yinni and the other tuteli quickly found their places near the center of the exhibition grounds and stood facing the gate, ready to welcome the guests who would come to challenge them. Over the years, they'd welcomed adepts and masters from all corners and defeated the majority of them. Very few mages even qualified to test their prowess against the Lux Temple tuteli. Fewer still ever won a prestigious champion's ring from them.

Previously, he and his fellow tuteli had always outshone even the most promising and favored children from the Five Schools, so normally Cymin felt at ease here. Everything from the brilliant bas-relief carvings of deities and devils that adorned the surrounding walls to the pale flagstones beneath his bare feet was familiar to him.

But this year was different, and for the first time since he'd achieved the rank of adept, Cymin felt uncertain about the outcome of today's battles.

In his unease, even the exhibition grounds felt foreign. He glanced to the indifferent faces of the Five Deities that decorated the stone walls. The gilt and ivory inlay adorning their figures looked newer than he remembered. Beneath his feet, at the center of the grounds, the mosaic depicting the constellations, which had always been off by a few degrees, had been fixed. Cymin's favorite cluster of homely, worn-down and crooked stars had been replaced by gleaming gold perfection. Even the line of rusting iron vases along the outer wall, which normally sported inexpensive incense, had been re-glazed in vivid scarlet and now displayed vast bouquets of unlit fireworks.

The people filling the stands and the costly box seats had changed significantly too. Gone were the usual groups of devout grannies, as were the clusters of impoverished parents and relatives who'd come either to assure themselves that the children they'd sold to Lux Temple were thriving or to convince children being offered up to quietly submit to their exciting future as tuteli. Nor did Cymin recognize any of the trinket and food vendors who regularly worked the lower levels. Instead those benches were filled with well-dressed merchants, eye-catching entertainers, bureaucrats, bodyguards and a scattering of radio reporters wearing state official emblems on their jackets.

For the first time ever, the sleek, silver-haired prime minister and several famous members of his cabinet had deigned to attend the ceremony. Of course, they and their various attendants laid claim to the sheltered high seats. In their midst, Lux Temple's Grand Master Ryn appeared out of place with her shaved head and modest brown vestments. The gaunt and infamous Minister of National Security, Lui Dane, leaned close to the Grand Master. He whispered something to her. She nodded, but her tense expression made Cymin suspect that she would rather have endured a viper flicking its tongue in her ear than share Lui Dane's confidences.

Old Master Tam, who normally oversaw the ceremonies while Grand Master Ryn took part in the challenges, had been banished to a lower stand. Alongside him sat Lux Temple's wiry old physician, Master Shuun, and six uneasy-looking volunteer nurses.

"Does something feel wrong to you?" Cymin whispered to Yinni.

She gave an almost imperceptible nod. "Maybe it's the obscurity spells on the National Security agents."

"Probably," Cymin said. It was a good theory. People in blue NS uniforms dotted the crowd, though many more probably hid within obscurity spells. Cymin had no doubt that they'd deployed numerous other spells as well. He squinted up to where a gray shadow flickered in the clouds and guessed that it was a surveillance device of some kind. Still, Cymin's attention was drawn back down to the cobblestones. He really didn't like the feeling of the new mosaic against his bare feet.

The trumpeters at the gates blew out a cascade of resounding notes, heralding the arrival of competitors from the Five Schools, and Cymin's wandering attention jolted back to the gates. His pulse quickened and an absurd nervousness flooded him—as if he hadn't been greeting competitors from the Five Schools since he was seven years old. Yinni bounced anxiously on the balls of her feet. A plump little novice tuteli clutched at Cymin and Yinni's belt sashes, trying to pull herself a little higher to see past them. Yinni nudged the girl back into formation.

Cymin and Yinni again raised their staves, manifesting the Veil of a Thousand Blessings, as adepts and masters from the Five Schools marched through the gates. The visiting mages' silk clothes fluttered, and many of them smiled and bowed to the cheering crowds before lining up in their traditional positions.

Dressed in black, the elite mages of the prestigious Boshyin School took first position. They were followed by Chohe Institute's cosseted eccentrics, all dressed in luxurious violets. The cunning, cream-clad academics from Guishuun College stood in the third position. Orae Academy's all-male student body wore red uniforms. They jogged and joked into the fourth post. The yellow uniforms of the female students from the fledgling Ryde Academy shone bright as sunflowers. The young women swept into the fifth position with an air of excitement.

As always, Cymin tried to focus on reviewing his competitors and choosing one or two who seemed particularly self-important to thrash during the competitions. But he couldn't concentrate on the usual attendees as he had in past years. Instead he kept glancing to the open gates.

The final guests had yet to arrive: the Wraiths of Saigrath.

In some corner of his mind, Cymin wasn't entirely convinced that they would ever appear—or that they existed at all. But if they did, he wanted to be the first to lay eyes on them. The first to step forward and meet them.

"It's going to be all right," Yinni whispered. "No matter what happens, we can handle it."

Cymin nodded. He tried to ease his rising tension, reminding himself that it had been more than 200 years since Wraiths last crossed the Great Chasm Sea and appeared in the mortal world.

What's another few minutes?

Then the sky above them shuddered and five brilliant lights blazed through the clouds like stars falling to earth.

CHAPTER 2

The Wraiths were the reason that so many of the capital's politicians, newshounds and perpetually jaded citizens had so enthusiastically flooded the streets.

The importance of the Wraiths' arrival could also be seen in the heavy police presence.

Folktales and myths about the Wraiths abounded. Many claimed that the Wraiths weren't living humans at all but were vessels of pure fei'lux bound to the furious souls of ancient warriors and tyrants.

Late-night radio plays often featured ghostly Wraiths as villains. The previous year, Cymin had seen a moving picture starring Una Bayan that depicted Wraiths as pale mist that enveloped and possessed people. Despite being abducted to a lovestruck Wraith's lair, the revolutionary heroine of the film had valiantly resisted the Wraith's corruption by belting out the Chyrenese National Anthem. Her pure love of their nation and its hardworking labor force had burned the Wraith to ashes. Unfortunately, at the showing Cymin attended, the record that provided the film's audio had been old and scratched, so at the climactic moment it skipped and repeated the same warped little warble over and over.

Cymin had laughed so hard that he'd gotten thrown out of the theater.

Now he felt less confident in his amusement. Even historical records in the Lux Temple described Wraiths strangely. Deathly silent, pale as bones—descending upon battlefields like falling stars and laying waste to every living thing within miles.

Of course, those descriptions had been written centuries ago. Hyperbole abounded in books from the mythic ages.

But it was a fact that the Wraiths had once passed judgment over all known nations and then without warning they'd withdrawn all contact. They'd sealed themselves away and obscured all routes to their island realm. No one knew why.

Now, after a 200-year absence, the Wraiths had deigned to enter the city and observe the Lux Temple's Spring Exhibition. More than that, they'd consented to choose foreign disciples to train with them in the far north. Saigrath lay beyond the security of the Storm Towers, where dangerous storms of fei'lux flowed from the Hallow Gates to change and mold the landscape. From all of the talented and skilled people who stood ready now on the exhibition grounds, only ten mage adepts would be allowed to journey with them to learn their secrets.

Just imagining the raging ferocity of fei'lux in Saigrath sent a shudder through Cymin's body. But at the same time it filled him with a nervous excitement. How would it feel to have an endless stream of wild fei'lux coursing through him? How complex and immense could his spells become? What new type of magecraft might he learn from the Wraiths if he were chosen? Would it be something altogether different from what he'd already mastered? Could they possess an entirely different means of manipulating fei'lux?

Whether they were secular students from the Five Schools or tuteli of Lux Temple, all Chyrenese mages only practiced two methods of spell casting: ancillary or direct.

The vast majority of masters and adepts preferred an ancillary method wherein fei'lux was channeled through their bodies into an implement that housed one or more spells. The Black Staves that Cymin and Yinni wielded were ancillary implements of great renown; the blessings etched into them were the only remains of the long-lost *Heavenly Spring* scrolls.

But nearly any inanimate object could be employed so long as it had been properly etched and could withstand the force of fei'lux searing through it. For daily needs within the Lux Temple, Cymin and his fellow tuteli regularly resorted to carving spells into old broomsticks and even reeds. Adepts and masters from the Five Schools most often wielded beautifully crafted swords and spears as their ancillaries, though there were some who used more unassuming devices like compasses or even paintbrushes.

Regardless of their prestige, the advantage of ancillary objects lay in the fact that mages using them didn't have to be practiced or even all that familiar with a spell to cast it. They only had to attract and temper the fei'lux, then flow it through the ancillary. Even second-year novices could manage that. The disadvantages lay in the fact that ancillary objects carried a limited number of spells and the process of channeling and tempering fei'lux into those spells could be inefficient and slow.

Direct spell casting, on the other hand, offered immediate results even when very little atmospheric fei'lux was available. A mage only needed to grasp free-floating fei'lux, shape it into the sigils of the spell they wished to manifest and then release it—little more than drawing a symbol in the air. Except the *symbol* had to be perfectly conceived and shaped while channeling wild currents of fei'lux through the mage's own body, and then released at just the perfect instant and intensity. Any error, and the spell might wrongly manifest within the mage's flesh. Or the raw power churning through them could tear free or consume them.

But if mages were willing to risk burning themselves hollow, direct spells could manifest immediately and were only limited by the capacity of one's own mind.

Events like this one, where mages sparred and exchanged knowledge, weren't the best environments to cast a spell directly. Cymin had only ever competed against two mages who used direct methods for combat, but in both cases the mages had eventually collapsed. One spat out a mouthful of bloody sigils before crumpling to the ground. The other had howled as if possessed, then pissed himself and dropped like a stone.

Because of that, Cymin had always wondered about the stories of Wraiths being able to directly create massive spell arrays with only hand gestures.

All at once, Cymin felt a powerful gust of wind slice through the air. Overhead, currents of fei'lux rippled like the surface of a pond struck by stone after stone. Then high in the clear blue sky, five white points of light flashed. The noise of the surrounding city and even nearby conversations suddenly hushed. Alarm showed on the faces of people as they tried to speak but were unable to make a sound. Cymin himself gave a shout, but his words dissipated and only a silent breath escaped him.

Again the fei'lux that floated in the atmosphere around them shuddered. This time the ripple rushed down onto the exhibition grounds. Adepts and masters throughout the crowd all raised their heads. Cymin and Yinni, too, stared as the Veil of a Thousand Blessings shredded apart under the intense pressure. The gentle perfume of spring blossoms turned acidic, and a biting chill washed over them. The hazy white remains of the spell array sank to the ground, forming a cold fog.

Through the open gate, Cymin watched the same white mist descend over all of Grand Avenue. The Thousand Blessings wasn't the only spell disintegrating. Spells everywhere dissolved. Little green ones intended to soothe teahouse patrons and orange ones that suppressed pests, as well as the multitude of colorful good luck charms that adorned the doorways of offices and shops—they all scattered into wisps of vapor.

The five lights in the sky continued their descent. Cymin shielded his eyes against their brilliance. He could barely make out shadows moving within the blazing light. As they struck the cobblestones of the exhibition grounds, a shearing wind blew off of them, knocking several people off their feet and sending banners flying from the stands. Cymin gripped his staff and tried to pull in enough fei'lux to raise a sheltering blessing but could do nothing.

Then, an instant later, everything was still.

Five shockingly tall figures stood inside the red gates. Thick mists of broken spells rolled behind them as they strode forward.

They could be none other than the Wraiths.

People in the stands and even masters and adepts on the grounds gasped and shouted in alarm—their voices deafening after the previous silence. Cymin squared his shoulders, relieved that his mask concealed his own stunned expression. At least he and his fellow tuteli adepts could retain the illusion of poise and dignity. Though two little novices openly wailing while a third clung to Yinni's leg somewhat undermined their image. Still, Cymin knew his part. He forced himself to march forward to meet the Wraiths.

"On this holy day, the Lux Temple welcomes all free mages who come to test their skills and exchange knowledge," Cymin called out.

You may be terrifying motherfuckers, but East Deity doesn't cringe or cry . . . in public.

At first glance, Cymin thought that the Wraiths also wore deity masks and headdresses. But as he drew closer, he realized that their deathly pale faces were bare and their thick braids of white and gold hair weren't costumes. Their long, angular bodies were clothed in pale gray and fawn-colored leather. The two men in the lead seemed to be in their twenties. Each man held a white staff and wore a collar of bones around his neck. Sword belts supporting ornate scabbards hung from each man's hip. Cymin supposed both the staves and the swords were ancillaries.

The three women following behind appeared about the same age, and all carried spears. None of them offered the slightest smile, much less any greeting. Their gazes raked across their surroundings with the cold appraisal of lions selecting prey from a herd of gazelles.

Cymin stopped at the center of the grounds and braced his own Black Staff against the mosaic of newly installed gold stars. The Wraiths said nothing but continued to advance towards him. The fog preceded them, rolling over Cymin's bare feet and coiling around his calves like icy fingers. His hand trembled as he gripped his staff, but he held his ground.

In that instant, all the violent, murderous and horrific scenes involving Wraiths that populated so many cheap novels and late-night radio plays tumbled through Cymin's mind. His heart raced and a bead of cold sweat slipped down the back of his neck. He didn't know if he could fight one of them, much less five.

He nearly backed away, but then he realized that there was something fundamentally familiar about the way they approached him: two in the lead carrying staves and three others following. It was just like he and Yinni, acting as the East and West Deities, guiding three other tuteli and blessing their way. The Wraiths had even spread a kind of veil of spells out around them. It wasn't anything like the Thousand Blessings, but could this drifting fog be a Wraith equivalent? Perhaps the reason it had dispersed all the surrounding spells was to eradicate curses or magical traps? That, too, would be a means to ensure a safe passage.

Cymin considered the Wraiths, trying to forget all the myths and fiction surrounding them. If they had been just five mages from some strange school entering the exhibition grounds, what would he have made of them?

Physically, they were strikingly foreign and particularly tall. But nothing about them was beyond human proportions. Cymin just wasn't used to encountering people taller and even more toned than himself. Studying them more closely, he noted that one of the three women was actually rather young-looking, proportioned more like a girl in her early teens.

The two leading Wraiths stopped when they reached the edge of the mosaic. Now that they were closer, Cymin could see that though they both possessed the lean musculature of adult men, they probably weren't much older than himself. Their faces were sharp and hard-featured, but then the shorter of the two actually offered him the slightest smile. The other considered Cymin's masked face with a curious gaze. The three women in the back were all clearly nervous. They kept stealing quick glances to the throngs of people gathered in the stands as if the audience was the last thing in the world that any of them had expected to see.

All at once, Cymin considered how frightening it would be for these five young foreigners to enter a strange city and discover thousands of people gathered and watching them.

You're not monsters or tyrannical ghosts at all, are you?

They, like the students from the Five Schools, were simply five talented young people who'd traveled far from their home to attend the Lux Temple's Spring Exhibition.

Cymin relaxed.

"You've come from far away and must be tire—" Cymin began, but at the same time sensed a spark flare to life in much the same way he'd felt the photographer's flash powder ignite earlier. This blazed like a lit fuse.

Cymin wondered in horror if the bouquets of fireworks meant for the closing ceremony had been accidentally lit.

Except this sizzling spark didn't shoot towards the fireworks. Instead it blazed under the cobbles, rushing towards Cymin—towards the Wraiths.

Cymin recalled the new sections of mosaic as well as the obscurity spell both he and Yinni sensed as they crossed the grounds. With a shock of terror, he realized exactly what must lie waiting below him. At the same time, he felt the spark sizzling directly beneath his heels.

He sensed it flare and ignite a far greater force. Molten heat expanded through soil and polished stone.

Cymin swung his staff down, slamming the gold finial into the mosaic stars—but too late. The bomb hidden beneath the mosaic floor detonated, roaring to life like a fiery blossom bursting through the earth.

For one astounding moment, Cymin managed to contain the bomb's explosive force entirely within his staff. The spells etched into the shaft glowed white-hot, and a frenzy of red cords unfurled. The wood smoldered, searing Cymin's palms, but he gripped the staff like his life depended upon it—because it did. And his wasn't the only life at stake.

He spun in a dizzying pirouette as he channeled the power of the bomb into the spells housed in the Black Staff. Every one of the Thousand Blessings burst forth, but with a force far beyond the pattern of floral lacework they'd displayed during the parade. Now those fragrant blossoms interlocked like chainmail, forming radiant shields to shelter the entire exhibition grounds and surrounding streets.

He barely registered the startled expressions on the Wraiths' pallid faces or heard Yinni gasp out his name. The audience gathered in the stands and adepts and masters on the grounds all became a blur.

Powered by such explosive force, the Thousand Blessings continued to burst forth with the might of their original purpose: shields crafted to defend entire cities from armies of mages and Wraiths. Millions of sigils crackled and flashed like lightning as they fused into more and more immense translucent walls. It was as if the waters of an icy lake separated Cymin from everything surrounding him. Sigils flashed and sparkled in the depths like schools of silver fish.

Elation flooded him, and he glanced to the shadows where the two Wraiths nearest to him stood. He couldn't see them clearly through the Thousand Blessings, but one of them seemed to reach forward, slamming his hand into the shimmering wall rising between them.

"Be unafraid," Cymin gasped. "The East Deity is ever undaunted—" He couldn't complete the hollow boast. A jolt rocked him as the Black Staff cracked. It hadn't been crafted to channel the raw, relentless force of a bomb. It couldn't hold out against it. The hot wood under his fingers shuddered as fissures of steam splintered through it. Cymin released the staff just as the gold work of its finial melted and the wood shattered apart.

All the power Cymin had drawn into the staff surged back, and suddenly the force of an explosion raged into his body. It burned through his nerves, twisted his muscles and tore through his mind with a terrible heat.

Cymin knew he had to directly temper and diffuse the raging energy. He knew that. And he'd practiced tempering hundreds of seasonal storms of fei'lux before this. Simply circulate the power through his body, slowly and steadily releasing it in a stream of calm, cooling spells.

But the chaotic inferno of exploding chemicals was nothing like the swift sleek flow of fei'lux. His nerves were on fire. His left hand felt like it was plunged in boiling oil. His muscles jerked and twitched so violently that he could hardly drag in a breath. Flames seemed to invade his bones, melting the very marrow. His vision dissolved into spatters of light and darkness.

Cymin could hardly stay conscious, much less recall the precise sigils that made up any given spell. He choked but clung to his training. Reflex alone allowed him to keep pouring the explosive power out in long spirals of spells. He grasped onto any spell he could. The simple spells he'd practiced since childhood came immediately.

Wreaths of red, gold and green spells flew from his hands. Bursts of twinkling stars escaped his lips. Starlight to illuminate the temple paths at night. Hundred-petaled flowers to adorn the gardens in winter. Fragrant breezes to drive back the summer heat. Wards to drive pests from the kitchen storehouse. Myriad charms in the shapes of lucky beasts poured from his body: song crickets, firebats, flying fish, turtles, carriage birds and house snakes. Cymin filled the sky with immense banners of vivid magic.

But he couldn't form the spells as quickly as he needed to expel the energy surging through him. It hurt too much. His concentration wavered and desperation distorted his sigils, turning the spells strange and wild. They poured from his hands and mouth like gushing fires. He couldn't hold onto the fragrance of spring blossoms, gentle morning light, the melodies of birdsongs or the infinite calm of East Deity.

He could only think of escape and howl for release from the torment consuming his body and mind. Warped spells gushed from him and swept around him, encircling him in burning trails. As Cymin poured more of them out, they grew into a cyclone of wind, flames and smoke.

The whirling storm of spells tore Cymin from the ground and pulled him hurtling upwards. Wind whistled in his ears as he soared higher and higher. He whipped past a flagpole, startling a nest of parakeets. Beneath him, the walls of the exhibition grounds and then the entire Lux Temple complex—no, the whole of Grand Avenue—receded. Ringed in burning scarlet spells, Cymin twirled into the sky like a brilliant firework. The air grew frigid and felt thin in his lungs. He struggled for a breath as his blazing body tore through drifting clouds.

Gazing down from the Heavens, he was terrified and at the same time, filled with awe. The whole capital spread out beneath him like a map. He took in bustling thoroughfares, ornate buildings and hundreds of bridges spanning the long, silky river. The bright tents erected for the Spring Festival looked as tiny as a sack of spilled pinwheel candies. The gilded domes of the Palace Complex glittered like baubles. Directly below Cymin, the Lux Temple's thick red walls became graceful strokes of cinnabar. The Thousand Blessings he'd cast over the exhibition grounds looked like a tiny opalescent blossom floating in a red dish.

It was unreal and yet strangely familiar, like one of the disturbing dreams of flying that had haunted Cymin since he'd been a child. Now, just like in those old nightmares, he soared far too high and fast. He reached the apex of his journey up, and momentarily the blazing spells balanced perfectly against the drag of gravity. Cymin floated as if weightless. Then the rings of bright spells spiraling around him dimmed. Brilliant red and orange flames fluttered and extinguished into trails of smoke. The bomb's force drained from his stunned body almost as suddenly as it had invaded.

Bizarrely, the first thought that shot through Cymin's mind was simply: *this again*?

Then terror seized him. He reached out reflexively for anything to stop his fall. His outstretched hand brushed through the frigid vapor of a cloud. He plunged down. The cold air rushing past him threw his alarmed shout back into his throat as it lashed him.

He groped madly for any trace of fei'lux drifting through the air. This high up it swirled in abundance, but the instant Cymin dragged in a wisp, jarring pain knifed through his hands. For the first time since he'd felt the bomb detonate, he looked at his trembling fingers. Cymin felt nauseated. The gold spell filaments that had lain beneath the skin on his left hand had burned to open bloody wounds. His right hand was blistered, the fingernails cracked and blackened, and his second and third fingers felt dislocated.

He couldn't draw in a single wisp of fei'lux, much less cast a spell powerful enough to stop his fall.

Directly below him, the Thousand Blessings he'd cast already grew hazy. Individual blessings and sigils dissolved into rolling pale masses. They billowed up like clouds of steam obscuring the details of the fast-approaching city below.

"Fuck, fuck, fuck . . ." Cymin hissed his frustration as he plunged through the cold embrace of another cloud. Icy white tendrils curled around his legs and arms. After so much fire and radiant heat, the chill felt soothing and the cold numbed his mangled hands.

He forced himself to calm down again. He wasn't dead, so he wouldn't give up.

Think, think. The East Deity can't just spatter on the ground in front of everyone, for fuck's sake.

Then he realized the obvious. Yinni! The Thousand Blessings had protected her, so she could still use her Black Staff to manipulate fei'lux. If she knew where Cymin was now—that he was still alive—she could definitely save him. The same was true assuredly of Grand Master Ryn and even Master Tam. No matter how often Master Tam threatened to knock his head in, Cymin knew the old man wouldn't allow him to die publicly like this.

He just had to alert them to the fact that he was still alive and returning to the ground much, much too quickly. But very little fei'lux remained in his body, certainly not enough to cast a spell. At most, he could illuminate a single sigil. *Only one sigil*, Cymin thought for a moment, and then he realized exactly which one to choose. He grinned despite his fear and pain.

He clenched his eyes shut, blocking out the blue sky and ignoring the sensations of the shearing wind and icy mist washing over his skin. He pictured a single, simple sigil. The first one he'd ever drawn, scratching it in the dirt over and over. One horizontal stroke and three vertical strokes descending from it.

In old Imperial script it represented "spring rain" and was pronounced *"Min."* The same Min made up the second half of Cymin's own name.

It had always vexed Master Tam that Cymin incessantly used an Imperial sigil in place of modern letters to sign his name. In addition, Cymin had retained his childhood habit of absently scratching the sigil into any and every surface he could reach. Over the years he'd defaced desktops, dining tables, bathroom walls, temple columns and even the backs of a few temple statues with his personal sigil. Master Tam always roared with fury when he discovered one of Cymin's sigils in a new—often irreverent—location. When and where another of Cymin's sigils would inspire Master Tam's outrage was the subject of numerous wagers among the residents of Lux Temple.

There was no way Master Tam, Yinni or Grand Master Ryn wouldn't associate the sigil with Cymin. They'd know he'd survived and needed their help.

Cymin extended his mangled right hand and forced searing threads of fei'lux through his shaking fingers as he traced out the lines of the sigil. He felt like he was dragging a hot blade across his tendons, scraping them from his bones. The gold filaments beneath his skin sizzled. Cymin gritted his teeth against a howl of pain. He clenched his eyes shut, focusing all his will on keeping the four simple strokes shining with brilliant gold radiance.

Endure it, and someone will notice. They will notice. They'll reach out. Someone will help . . .

Cymin tried to expand his awareness further through the air, searching for any way to save himself. Despite the cold wind racing over him, sweat beaded his brow and back. He couldn't have much time left. He was too scared to open his eyes and see how very near the ground was now.

Then he felt a subtle ripple of fei'lux swirl past him. Instinctively, he extended his left arm.

Long, cold fingers clasped his wrist.

Cymin startled, opening his eyes to see a Wraith floating directly in front of him. Between his pale gray clothes and wind-tossed white hair, he looked like he'd been carved from the surrounding clouds. The Wraith cradled Cymin's left wrist in one hand and held his glassy staff in the other. Fei'lux streamed around the staff and radiated from the Wraith's long body in serene waves.

The wind buffeting Cymin calmed, and the wisps of cloud at his feet seemed to grow more dense, slowly easing his fall into a gentle descent.

Glancing past the Wraith's broad shoulders, Cymin glimpsed the pinnacle of the Starwatch Radio Tower. They couldn't be more than 700 feet high now.

The air felt warmer, and the noise of industry and busy streets grew louder. Lights flashed from the carriages of the Spring Festival ferris wheel. As they sank even lower, the newly constructed Citizens' News Building obscured much of Cymin's view of the sprawling city. He heard people shouting about the unexpected display of fireworks.

Someone in the stands gave a cry and pointed up to Cymin and the Wraith as they slowly glided down from the Heavens. The stunned quiet hanging over the exhibition grounds erupted into cheers and wild applause. A group of young women in the lower stands leapt to their feet screaming with excitement while men hooted and roared.

Cymin heard a radio announcer crowing into his microphone, "Spectacular! Our Lux Temple and the Saigrath Wraiths are setting the sky alight with fireworks and images of every lucky beast you could imagine. What a show! What a show, folks!"

The black eye of a film camera tracked their descent.

In the high seats, a group of NS officers gripped their weapons. Other officers who had mage training circulated eddies of fei'lux through ancillaries to create spells shielding the ministry elites. Cymin was certain that most of the NS officers realized that his improvised spectacle had hidden a mishap—but he wasn't certain how many had sensed the full power of the bomb. Hopefully no one in the ministries would blame Lux Temple for the breach in security. The temple was already struggling to retain government support. At least the prime minister and his cabinet members appeared delighted rather than disturbed. They all clapped heartily and even toasted Cymin and the Wraith.

NS Minister Lui Dane leaned forward in his chair, bringing his thin lips to rest on his slender, steepled fingers. He studied the Wraith holding Cymin's wrist as if he were a cobra contemplating a mongoose pup. Beside him, Grand Master Ryn gazed directly at Cymin. Her eyes were bright, and a broad, relieved smile spread across her tanned face. Cymin repressed his urge to abandon the dignity of East Deity and wave to her like a six-year-old. Thankfully, the six sigils securing his mask and headdress had withstood the tumult. Cymin's stupid grin remained hidden from the public.

Glancing down to the grounds, Cymin noted that a crack split through the central mosaic and a seam of ash and gold filled it—the remains of his staff. That, however, appeared to be the full extent of the damage done by the explosive. Yinni and the rest of the tuteli stood unscathed, as did the Wraiths and gathered competitors from the Five Schools. Relief welled up and flooded Cymin like the sudden rush of melt-water overflowing a river bank.

Everyone was safe, and he hadn't died!

Cymin turned his attention to the Wraith still gripping his wrist. Overwhelming gratitude surged through him. So what if the man was pale as a boiled egg, built like a ceiling post and dressed himself as if ditchwater was his favorite color? Even if those *were* human finger bones hanging around the man's neck, Cymin forgave it all. His knife-sharp features and distant expression were beautiful. His out-of-date clothes, the pungent smell of sweat, bergamot and birch oil drifting from his body, his chapped lips—everything about him was perfect. Because not only had he saved Cymin's life, but by doing so he'd protected Lux Temple and the tuteli from being publicly humiliated in front of powerful politicians and the populace of the capital.

You literally rose to the occasion. Cymin grinned at his own childish pun as his relief blossomed to a giddy joy. *East Deity will not judge you unkindly. He will repay your courage.*

Cymin wondered if he should offer to assist the Wraith and his companions in navigating the capital. Take them to the Spring Festival? Could he afford to treat them all to a meal?

Maybe not . . . they looked like they could eat a lot.

And they didn't even know each other's names.

Cymin considered how to belatedly introduce himself to the Wraith, given the awkwardness of the situation, but the other man's attention appeared to be focused entirely upon the Min sigil still glowing above Cymin's raised right hand. Belatedly, Cymin released his hold on the shining symbol. It flickered and then dissipated into the surrounding mist. Only then did the Wraith's gaze shift to Cymin. He bowed his head slightly, bringing his face closer to Cymin's.

"Why did you cast Min?" The Wraith's breath was surprisingly warm as it brushed over Cymin's ear. But the words were so quiet and oddly accented that if Cymin hadn't grown up speaking mage-tongues in Lux Temple, he might not have understood the question at all.

Admitting that he'd staked his life on being an unforgettably annoying jackass was not something Cymin wanted to disclose.

"To call you to me, what else?" Cymin felt the haughty response suited East Deity—even if his bloody, smoldering appearance didn't.

The Wraith drew back, scowling at the answer. He pinned Cymin with a suspicious glower. His blue eyes appeared surprisingly dark and looked very strange framed by thick white lashes.

"Who are you?" The Wraith's voice remained quiet, but the tone betrayed his agitation. The way he studied Cymin's mask and then shifted his grip on Cymin's wrist warned Cymin that the Wraith meant to reveal Cymin's naked face. At the same time, Cymin's toes touched the polished cobbles of the mosaic. He immediately pulled free from the Wraith's grasp.

"I'm East Deity." Cymin didn't hide his delight in outmaneuvering the other man. "Undaunted, righteous and ever-victorious."

The Wraith surprised him with a low laugh.

"Then who do you think *I* am?" With a flick of his hand he dissipated the spells that made up his glassy staff, turning it to mist. Then he turned and strode back across the cracked mosaic to rejoin his companions.

CHAPTER 3

Yinni swept to Cymin's side at once. She remained poised, but beneath the shadows of her gold mask, worry showed clearly in her eyes.

"Are you all right?" she whispered.

"Well, I'm not dead, but I don't know how much longer I can keep standing up," Cymin responded honestly. "The mob here today might panic if—"

"I know. But don't worry about them." Yinni stood shoulder to shoulder with him, supporting him without making it obvious. "I can handle everything, so long as you're all right." She reached to take his left hand in hers to properly salute the officials in the high seats.

Cymin flinched and braced himself to endure the pain. Then he was startled by how comfortable Yinni's grip felt. He stole a glance to his hands. Streaks of dried blood and sooty stains still dirtied his skin, but the charred, torn skin and fissures of exposed tendons were gone. Bruises and a few red streaks were all that remained of his previous injuries.

That had to have been the Wraith's doing, since Cymin certainly wasn't in any condition to heal himself. He suppressed the urge to look over his shoulder at his rescuer, instead focusing on maintaining his poise beside Yinni. Together they raised their clasped hands. Cymin's arm trembled from exhaustion, but Yinni kept him steady.

"Lux Temple welcomes our fellow mages and honored guests. We salute our honored judges. May the Heavens bless you all!" they called out in unison and then paused as thunderous applause and resounding cheers reverberated across the grounds. The muscles of Cymin's back and legs shook and he felt lightheaded.

"Now in the name of accomplishment and camaraderie, let the Spring Exhibition tournaments commence!" Yinni shouted the last words alone, but no one seemed to notice Cymin's silence.

Again a cacophony of cheers rose up. Yinni and Cymin lowered their arms, but Yinni kept hold of Cymin, leading him quickly into the midst of their fellow tuteli.

As a group they marched to the side doors beneath the stands. As they withdrew from the grounds, Cymin heard representatives from the

Five Schools drawing lots to decide which of them would first stand on the mosaic to issue the ceremonial challenge to the tuteli of Lux Temple. Before any of them settled on anyone, a group of resplendently dressed honor guards descended from the high seats to invite the Wraiths to join the judges.

Cymin tried to glance back to the group of Wraiths, but two tuteli novices hefted their shields up over their shoulders, blocking his view. Though he thought that perhaps his Wraith had looked in his direction. But then Yinni rushed him through the black carved doors, down a humid corridor leading to the washroom, and into the dressing rooms reserved for the tuteli.

In the locker room, Master Tam was already waiting for them.

Even at sixty years of age, Master Tam moved with a dancer's agility and maintained a meticulously neat appearance. Crisp folds delineated the collar, lapel and cuffs of his brown robe. Whereas most tuteli, including Cymin and Grand Master Ryn, indulged in crowns of fuzzy black stubble, he kept his head shaved to gleaming perfection.

On his wrists he wore long strings of etched amber prayer beads that he'd crafted into his ancillaries. They glowed faintly. Then with a motion of his gnarled fingers Master Tam broke the sigils securing Cymin's deity mask. Yinni caught the pearly mask as it fell, while a younger tuteli snatched up the scorched black ribbons of Cymin's headdress before it hit the ground.

Yinni handed off Cymin's mask as well as her own to an attendant novice. She and Cymin could wear the guises of deities while welcoming guests, but no tuteli would chance losing a battle—not even the mock combat of an exhibition—while representing the glory of the deities.

Normally, the moment Yinni freed herself from her headdress she would race Cymin to the water basins. There, the two of them and the other tuteli who'd been chosen to spar that day would splash and tease each other as they cleaned up. But today Yinni stood beside Cymin with an almost lost expression on her face. For just an instant Cymin thought he saw tears welling in her dark eyes. She reached out to touch his shoulder again, but before her hand landed Master Tam spoke.

"Yinni, I can look after him. You have your own duties." Master Tam cast a meaningful glance to the washbasins where the remaining tuteli had gathered in apprehensive silence. Then he lowered his voice. "Without Grand Master Ryn or Adept Cymin competing in today's match, your leadership is more vital than ever for Lux Temple."

Yinni straightened immediately and gave Master Tam an almost imperceptible nod. Then she reclaimed her normal calm expression and strode to join the others with composure befitting the West Deity. Out of habit Cymin started after her, but Master Tam blocked him.

Yinni cast him a sympathetic glance over her shoulder. One of the other tuteli whispered something to her and she passed him a hand towel. Then they set to cleaning up. Normally they would have gossiped and teased each other as they washed away road dust and sweat, but in the presence of Master Tam they restrained themselves.

Cymin noticed one of the other tuteli considering him with concern. Cymin stole a glance at himself in the mirror. Most days he presented an assured, handsome figure. Nature and years of relentless training had imbued him with a lithe, muscular body, and his face rivaled the deity mask he regularly wore. His deep black eyes curved slightly upward, as did his arched brows and lips, lending him an overall appearance of refined amusement, even when he was picking wax from his ears. But in Lux Temple his charm wasn't particularly notable.

The temple didn't buy children lacking in holy bearing any more than they accepted those devoid of sensitivity to fei'lux. And no tuteli chosen to represent a deity could be less than beautiful. Yinni and the three other tuteli washing at the basins were more than equal to Cymin. Even Master Tam, who had been stunning in his youth, retained a weathered elegance.

But just now, Cymin looked a wreck. A mass of dried blood spread from his nostrils down to his split lower lip. Another gash marked his cheek and the bridge of his nose, where his mask had cut into his face during his rough ascent. The dark beginning of a large bruise ran from his hairline down to his right eyebrow, giving his forehead an unlovely asymmetry, and half-dry scabs caked his left ear and the side of his neck.

Cymin lifted his hand to touch his throat. Then he noticed Master Tam's reproachful stare and stilled.

"Do you realize what you just did?" Master Tam demanded.

"About the Black Staff—I know it was a treasure entrusted to the temple, but at least there are two of them." Cymin pulled a sheepish smile and tensed, preparing to feel the old man's hand smack the back of his head.

"Shut up," Master Tam snapped. Then to Cymin's complete surprise Master Tam threw his arms around him and hugged him. Stunned and shocked, Cymin hung unmoving in the old man's embrace for several moments before he returned the hug.

"You scared me so much," Master Tam muttered. "Are you badly hurt?"

"I'm sore all over and really, really tired. But I think I'm fine." Cymin drew back from Master Tam's arms. He never would have expected the old Master to express so much emotion, so much affection for anyone, much less himself. Cymin beamed at him, flattered and foolishly happy.

"What on earth are you so pleased about?" Master Tam demanded. "You could have died!"

"I know, but I had to do something, otherwise all of you—" Cymin was too embarrassed of his own sentimentality to go on. Caring about the people around him enough to die for them was one thing, but saying it aloud . . . his fellow tuteli would never let him live it down if he made such a grandiose declaration. Instead, Cymin offered Master Tam a crooked grin. "If I hadn't acted, how else could you all have witnessed how truly amazing I am?"

Only then did Master Tam deign to slap the back of his head, but just lightly. "Clean up. Then I'm taking you to the temple infirmary. Master Shuun will do what he can with your spell filaments there."

Hours later, as the sun sank, the jubilant clamor of firecrackers filled the streets surrounding the Lux Temple Complex. But behind the shelter of the thick walls, deep blue shadows and quietness pervaded. Song crickets chirped while the murmur of prayers floated through the grounds like moonlight. In the temple infirmary, Cymin tossed on his medical cot. Despite an earlier course of sedatives and anesthetic, he jolted awake, gasping and drenched with sweat.

His heart hammered as if he was still plunging from the sky. He tasted the tang of hot iron and salt as if blood really was pouring from between his lips. He clenched his fists, desperately gripping the cold weight of the corpse in his arms.

I won't let go. Not even if it kills me. I'll never let go. Never let go . . .

Of who?

Cymin stared blearily at his empty hands. Black stitches seamed his fingers where the physician, Master Shuun, had removed his burnt-out golden spell filaments. The tight ache running along the left side of his scalp and cheekbone made him suspect those gashes now sported bristling stitches as well. Between the bruising, swelling and stitches, he probably looked a wreck. Nearly as unlovely as he'd appeared when he and Yinni had first been brought to Lux Temple from the refugee camp to begin their training. Back then, he'd been underfed and missing a front tooth, in addition to all the stitches and bruises. His battered hands had hurt in exactly the same way. No wonder an old nightmare from his childhood revisited him now.

As always, the details of his dream scattered as soon as he woke. He couldn't clearly recall why he'd been hurtling through the air or what he'd been trying so desperately to hold onto. Something that had dragged him down—something he both loved and resented and couldn't give up but had already lost.

Dreams were such strange things. Though, he supposed that after this morning's grand plummet from the Heavens, a relapse into his old nightmare wasn't all that remarkable. Except . . . he'd suffered from nightmares of plunging from the sky years before it happened in reality. When he considered it, wasn't that the wrong way around? He supposed that Master Tam would tell him he'd failed to recognize the omens in his nightmares. The old master believed devoutly in portents and constantly monitored constellations and the weather, searching for Fate's warnings for his young, arrogant charges. Cymin in particular received regular admonitions whenever any atmospheric disturbance stirred up from the east.

Well, screw you, Fate. The East Deity has once again escaped your clutches.

Cymin surveyed the clean infirmary room with a sense of profound relief.

The noise of distant celebration coupled with the calm within the temple assured him that another catastrophe hadn't occurred while he slept. He supposed that NS marshals were already investigating the bombing. Hopefully they would capture the culprits right away and spare Cymin a drawn-out interrogation.

He wondered how the competitions had played out in his absence. How many spoiled mages from the Five Schools had Yinni knocked on their asses with a calm sweep of her Black Staff? Who among all those mages from the Five Schools had the Wraiths chosen to invite back to the north? Envy filled his chest like an ache. If he and Yinni hadn't been tuteli, then they would have been in the running—he was certain. Who knew what mysteries the Wraiths could teach them, or what strange wonders thrived in the fei'lux-ravaged northlands? Moldering old tomes on the subject abounded with mythical creatures and godly beasts.

But then they were also filled with tales of demonic serpents the size of freight trains turning themselves into impish children and serious assertions that a school of 88,888 jellyfish could spontaneously fuse into a sea deity. Not to mention copious recipes for panaceas that called for dragon urine and phoenix droppings. So all that was best taken with a grain of salt.

Still, how fascinating would it be to see Saigrath in person?

Cymin sighed and forced himself to let that longing go. No good came from irritating himself over a matter so completely beyond his control.

An evening breeze rolled over his damp body, making him shiver. He stripped off his sweat-soaked undershirt, clumsily tossing it to the foot of the medical cot. He ought to go to the washbasin and rinse himself clean, but his muscles ached with fatigue and his bones felt leaden. He wasn't certain if he could use his hands to open the taps yet. The local anesthetic that had diminished the pain of his lacerated fingers to dull throbbing had also rendered his hands clumsy and weak. After brief consideration, he haphazardly wiped himself dry with a corner of his bed sheet. Then he lay back against the herb-filled pillow.

Through the infirmary's circular window, Cymin could hear the muted conversation of a group of novices as they hurried along the fragrant path through the apricot orchard below. Dense clusters of white blossoms packed the leafless branches, obscuring the passing figures. But their excited voices carried to him clearly. They speculated about the Wraith who had dared to follow the East Deity into the Heavens and how he'd been forced to descend holding their deity's hand like a servant swearing obedience.

Cymin grinned at the loyal novices' misreading of the situation and then laughed, imagining how greatly it would annoy that haughty Wraith if he knew how his actions had been misconstrued.

Another gust swept through the room, carrying with it the scent of flowers and spent firecrackers. Cymin thought he ought to get up and draw the screen to block the night breezes, but he still felt too tired to move. Instead, he watched stars slowly light in the darkening sky. In the gardens below, yellow lamps mirrored the Heavens' lights, turning garden paths into serpentine constellations. Cymin teetered on the edge of sleep.

Then he saw a pale gray form passing among the flowering apricot trees. A garden lamp illuminated broad shoulders, sharp features and white hair—the unmistakable figure of a Wraith.

Had Grand Master Ryn ignored the political danger and brought them into the inner courtyards of Lux Temple as honored guests? It would be like the Grand Master to do so, especially if she feared there would be another bombing attempt against them at the Palace Complex, where National Security had originally planned to house them. If so, then Cymin might see them. Perhaps he could even discover a bit more about the Wraith who'd saved him. He wanted to know the man's name at the very least.

After merely touching East Deity's wrist, were you so overcome that you can neither eat nor sleep, but must search for him hopelessly?

Cymin snickered at his absurd conceit. It was much more likely that the Wraith was searching desperately for the toilet. Most of the buildings in Lux Temple were hundreds of years old, and only a few possessed anything close to modern plumbing. The infirmary building was a happy exception, but the ornate, gilded guesthouse was not. At this hour every available bath and toilet would be packed with grubby novices.

The poor bastard is probably searching hopelessly for an inconspicuous tree to piss on. East Deity forgives your trespass.

Then, as quiet as a leopard moth, the gray-clothed figure bounded up from between the trees and alighted on Cymin's second-floor window ledge. If Cymin hadn't been sedated and exhausted, he would have bolted off the cot. As it was, he stared wide-eyed, so dazed that he could hardly sense the fei'lux rippling around the Wraith.

Garden lamps outside illuminated the Wraith's long body and stern profile. Even crouched with his absurdly long limbs folded, he filled the whole window. His joints appeared oversized, and his larynx formed a prominent kink in his long neck. His facial features were stark, nearly gaunt: his jaw was sharp, his cheekbones jutting and the bridge of his nose high. Only his very large, dark eyes lent him any of the softness of a youth. "Ox-eyes," Master Tam would have called them: deep and gentle-looking with thick lashes. But the white eyebrows above them angled up as if in perpetual anger. Truly an unforgettable face.

This really was the Wraith who followed him into the clouds. The one who came when he cast the sigil, Min. A disconcerting excitement fluttered through Cymin. His face flushed for no good reason whatsoever.

Fortunately, the infirmary room was dark. From the way the Wraith cocked his head and peered toward the bed, Cymin guessed that he could see the Wraith far better than the other man could see him. They both remained unmoving, studying one another for some time. The protracted silence gnawed at Cymin, and he wracked his dazed mind for something to say.

"Do you remember me?" the Wraith asked just as Cymin, too, spoke.

"Looking for the toilet?" Cymin blurted. Then registering the Wraith's question, he added, "How could I have possibly forgotten you?"

"Why would I seek you out to find a *toilet*?" The Wraith appeared to be affronted.

They both lapsed into silence again, staring at one another with equally skeptical expressions. Then the Wraith sat down on the windowsill and crossed his arms over his chest. He turned his face away as if to study the stars. To Cymin, the Wraith's posture seemed self-conscious. Was he offended? Or . . . was it possible that he was embarrassed?

During this interval, far-off city clocks rang out over the crackle of firecrackers. Then the night fell very quiet.

"I wasn't certain that you would recognize me in the dark," the Wraith said at last.

"Oh." That explained the odd question, but hardly elucidated the Wraith's weird choice of entrance. Was it somehow normal to leap in through people's windows in Saigrath? Perhaps they didn't have infirmaries and the Wraith hadn't understood how to visit. He recalled his earlier decision to treat the Wraith kindly.

"In the future, if you want to visit the infirmary, the front doors are on the west side of the building. You can go straight in and ask a nurse to bring you up," Cymin informed him.

"Or better yet," the Wraith replied. "I could directly approach the NS agents watching us, tell them that I'm hoping to recruit a spy for Saigrath and then ask for directions to your room. If I'm going to cast suspicion on you, I might as well go all the way with it, don't you think?"

Cymin arched a brow.

I see. They may not have infirmaries in the north, but they've certainly been introduced to the concept of sarcasm.

"Oh, yes, that makes sense." Cymin smiled gamely at the Wraith. "Sneaking in through a window is definitely the best way to quell suspicion. What perfectly innocent visit isn't conducted through a garden window in the dead of night?"

The Wraith scowled and Cymin took some satisfaction in his vexed silence, thinking, *We, Chyrenese, invented sarcasm. You're welcome to a lesson in its implementation.*

However, as the silence once again stretched on, his satisfaction soured, and his curiosity overtook it. Was the Wraith truly going to lounge in his window, wordlessly gazing at the stars all damn night? That couldn't be all he'd come here to do. How to get him talking again without lowering himself?

"Fine," Cymin stated. "I accept your apology." Cymin enjoyed the fleeting expression of confusion on the Wraith's face before continuing. "So, let's start again, shall we? What brought you through the window looking for me?"

"Assuming it wasn't an inability to recognize a door or locate a toilet, you mean?" the Wraith replied.

Cymin grinned, considering and then discarding several retorts that would have resulted in another protracted silence. He sighed. Perhaps his first questions *could* have been construed as offensive.

"I wasn't fully awake when you arrived. I honestly didn't mean any insult." Cymin offered his most serene smile.

East Deity is so gracious, you have no idea.

The Wraith studied him, then with an almost reluctant expression he ducked fully into the dim room.

"What the deities regret, the Heavens forgive," he said at last.

The Heavens? Really? Cymin silently applauded the other man's arrogance. He so effortlessly put Cymin's own audacity to shame.

"Since the Heavens are feeling so generous, won't they do me the kindness of offering a name I might use to address them?" Cymin asked.

"I'm Laithondi, Guardian of the Sun Gate and Defender of Creation." The Wraith gave a shrug. "Isn't it obvious?"

Cymin gaped at him a moment before realizing that he was serious. The Wraith had actually taken East Deity's given name for his own.

We Chyrenese may have invented sarcasm, but arrogance definitely belongs to you Wraiths.

"You're called Min?" Laithondi asked. "For the spring rain?"

"Cymin. Written in imperial sigils it means 'Abundant Spring Rain,'" Cymin corrected, and a little of his amusement dulled.

To those who didn't know better, his was an auspicious name. Just as the sigils of "Exalted Treasure" given to Yinni seemed loving. But both their names had been bestowed after floodwaters had trapped and drowned the rest of their family in the ancient tomb they'd been looting. The same spring flood had displaced and orphaned hundreds of other children from law-abiding backgrounds as well. So, the offspring of grave robbers won little sympathy from the righteous administrators of their refugee camp. One director in particular—a man named Soa—had wanted to ensure that they never forgot how the Heavens punished their kinsmen's shameful crimes. So, he'd bestowed new names on them like curses.

But Cymin refused to allow one bitter old bastard's spite to define him. First, he didn't believe that the Heavens would drown and displace thousands of innocent citizens just to kill a dozen grave robbers. Second, he'd made those imperial sigils his own, growing gleefully attached to their power to capture and provoke Master Tam's attention. And third, he took satisfaction in imagining Director Soa's red-faced consternation every time he heard Cymin's and Yinni's names announced as the best of the tuteli adepts in radio reports of the Lux Temple Exhibitions.

The sanctimonious fucker would probably choke on his own spit if he knew that this morning crowds of thousands had cheered the Abundant Spring Rain and Exalted Treasure he'd so relentlessly disparaged.

"Cymin." Laithondi repeated his name and snapped Cymin out of his reverie. Laithondi took a step farther into the room, though he seemed hesitant to come too close to Cymin's bedside. His uneasiness reminded Cymin of the feral cat that Master Tam regularly coaxed inside during heavy rainstorms. Could it be that Laithondi was unused to living indoors as well?

The Wraith glanced to the window and went perfectly still as the girlish voices of two passing novices drifted from the garden. They speculated on opportunities to spy on the visiting Wraiths up close and teased each other for lacking the courage to lay in wait at the baths. A soft laugh escaped Laithondi, and Cymin suppressed his urge to justify the novices' curiosity. Only after the girls were far beyond hearing did Laithondi return his attention to Cymin.

"I came to reward your courage in protecting us. Even if it was foolish and unnecessary, you did well." Laithondi reached into the pocket of his gray leather coat and produced a white orb, no larger than a salt plum. "So, I've brought you a balm for your wounds."

At least a hundred retorts to the Wraith's backhanded compliment sprang to mind, but as soon as he saw the pale orb in the other man's hand Cymin forgot them all. At first he wasn't certain if it was merely the play of the moonlight streaming through the open window, but the orb seemed to throw off a soft lustrous glow. Faint patterns flowed across its luminous surface. Studying it, Cymin could only think of the celestial pearls from children's stories and old myths. In books, they always contained magical wonders like the mesmerizing voices of sirens or the chilling wind of a winter gale.

Cymin watched light and shadows move through the sphere as a weird sense of familiarity whispered through his mind. He felt certain he'd seen this orb before. Under better light the patterns of clouds swirling across its pearly surface would be clear. If he turned the orb over in his hands, he'd find a hairline crack that had been repaired with a thin seam of gold. It left the impression of a single bolt of lightning lancing through storm clouds.

Cymin frowned at his recollection. How could he have seen this object before?

Was it possible that this orb had numbered among the imperial treasures his parents had looted from the lost tomb of some mage-king? Could he possibly have remembered it so clearly as a three-year-old?

Even if that was the case, most of those stolen treasures had been seized by National Security. So how would it have ended up in the hands of a Wraith?

More likely he'd seen an illustration of something like it in one of the temple history books. But the sense of familiarity and ownership struck him with such intensity that he found it disconcerting. Hazy images and sensations fluttered through his mind so quickly that he felt dizzy.

Mayhap East Deity hasn't shaken off his sedatives yet.

"Is this a celestial pearl?" Cymin asked.

Laithondi nodded. "Flawed, but not without value."

"You're offering to share the treasure from a celestial pearl with me?" Cymin couldn't help his incredulity. Wasn't this too much like something from a children's book? Even in those stories, there was always some kind of test or trial to be passed before a magical gift could be bestowed.

"If you can guess how to open it," Laithondi went on, "then naturally it's yours."

Naturally. Cymin rolled his eyes. *What could be more normal?*

"Does everyone from Saigrath wander the night with celestial pearls, requiring the injured they encounter to solve riddles before administering medicines?" Cymin asked. "Or is this quirk unique to you?"

Laithondi's pale lips twitched as if he was suppressing a laugh. Then he shrugged. He didn't offer Cymin any further explanation. Maybe he didn't want to chance dropping a clue to unlocking the celestial pearl.

I didn't even ask for your mystical salve, but now you expect me to work to get it. So annoying.

At the same time, Cymin *did* want to know how to open the luminous orb. What person wouldn't? He had nothing to lose, in any case. He wracked his brain, recollecting everything he could about celestial pearls.

"In stories," Cymin thought aloud, "celestial pearls only open for their owners. This one is yours, so the key ought to be your—"

He cut himself off. How could the solution be that easy or obvious? He didn't know much about this Laithondi fellow, but Cymin felt certain that he wouldn't tell him his name if it was the answer to a challenge he planned to issue with his next breath. There had to be something more to accessing the balm inside the celestial pearl.

He pondered Laithondi. What kind of riddle would a man who used East Deity's given name issue? Cymin studied him, but when Laithondi stared back at him, Cymin felt irrationally flustered, as if he'd been caught flipping through a book of erotic paintings. He averted his gaze to the glowing pearl. The cloud designs swirling over its surface cast stormy shadows across Laithondi's chest and outstretched hand.

Clouds and East Deity . . . Cymin thought. Then an invocation flashed through his mind.

Lost and wounded, clouds obscure my way.

Clouds obscured the contents of the jar, so perhaps the way past them . . .

"To open this celestial pearl, cast the archaic sigil for the sun," Cymin decided. "A circle ringed with five sacred flames. *Ondi.* The archaic form of the second sigil of your name."

Laithondi's fingers clenched around the pearl, making the flowing shadows quiver like startled snakes.

"I'm right, aren't I?" Cymin grinned and then, just to show off, quoted the complete invocation. "*I am lost and wounded, clouds obscure my way. I entreat the east sun, disperse them with the light of day.* Laithondi's Invocation."

"You truly—" Laithondi's pale lips remained parted, but he said nothing more and then closed his mouth. He stared at Cymin, his expression stricken.

"You're the one who set the terms, not me," Cymin pointed out. "If you couldn't stand to lose, you shouldn't have made the wager."

"I'm not troubled by the loss of a pearl." Laithondi turned the object over in his hand and peered at Cymin through the gloom. "Is the entreaty all you remember about it?"

"The entreaty was just a guess, actually," Cymin admitted.

"A guess?" Laithondi went very still.

"Yeah, sorry, if you thought it was something more." Cymin offered a guilty smile. "Lux Temple safeguards records and texts that survived the Age of Mage-Kings and the People's Revolution. I think I saw an illustration and description of your pearl, or one very like it, a few years back. It's supposed to contain . . . medical balm? I don't remember that part exactly, but the drifting cloud pattern stuck with me."

Laithondi shook his head, his expression unconvinced.

"I'm not lying. I truly have seen it before. If I remember correctly, there's a gold seam that runs down one side of the pearl. It looks like a bolt of lightning. Am I right?"

Laithondi's brows lifted. He nodded but didn't move a muscle otherwise.

"Come on, let me see for myself." Cymin wheedled. "Even if I only guessed the answer, I still got it right, didn't I? Didn't I?"

"You did," Laithondi admitted. He crossed the room in three steps, bringing the celestial pearl directly to Cymin's bedside. No trace of his earlier apprehension showed as he crouched down next to the cot and offered it. The pearl's glow lit his face, exposing the blue tint of his dark eyes and the dark lines of fatigue below them.

"It's yours," Laithondi said.

Cymin smiled and shook his head. He didn't intend to take the pearl. It was far too striking for the volunteer nurses in the infirmary not to notice, and he knew that several of them regularly passed information to National Security. If meeting with a Wraith could cast suspicion on Cymin, he feared that actually possessing a Wraith's ancillary—even a small, flawed one—might send him directly to an NS interrogation crypt for the remainder of his life. Or worse, it could implicate Lux Temple as a hotbed of imperial reactionaries and justify Lui Dane in purging the entire place.

"Just turn it so I can look, will you?" Cymin's hands were too battered to grasp it, but he still wanted to examine the pearl and see the gold seam at the back. As for the medicine inside, Cymin felt he could pass on any *mystic* remedy stored in a mysterious and unlabeled container.

Laithondi held the pearl between his long fingers and rotated it slowly between them.

Silver-gray patterns of clouds drifted before Cymin. Soft light streamed between them like moonlight. Then the fine line of goldwork flickered before Cymin's eyes. A pleased admiration filled him as he imagined the ancient mage who'd found this cracked pearl and, instead of discarding it, had recognized a greater beauty within its flaw. He imagined stroking the silky surface of the pearl and running his fingertip over the sharp edge of the fine crack as inspiration flashed.

"It's exactly like I remember." Cymin couldn't resist his urge to touch the gold seam with just the tip of his finger.

Laithondi's serene expression turned to horror. His large eyes seemed fixed on Cymin's fingers.

"What have they done to you?" Laithondi demanded. "Your hands . . ."

"Very ugly. I know," Cymin dropped his right hand back down, hiding it in the shadows of the bed sheet. "The gold spell filaments had to be excised. Once my tendons and nerves have recovered enough to support them, new spell filaments can be threaded in again."

Cymin didn't want to think about, much less discuss, how much a second set of spell-etched gold filaments would add to his temple debt. But without them, he wouldn't be capable of managing the truly heavy loads of fei'lux that flowed over the Storm Towers, and only by serving in the Storm Towers could he earn enough to ever be free. So, only by taking on further debt could he hope to pay off all that he owed.

Alas, even East Deity has debts to pay in this secular world of ours.

Were things different in Saigrath, where Laithondi served as East Deity? After all, Wraiths had been manipulating fei'lux long before advances in medicine allowed for successful grafts of spell filaments. He couldn't see any trace of the fine white surgical scars that all registered Chyrenese mages bore.

"How do you all acquire your spell filaments?" Cymin asked.

Laithondi appeared confused by the question.

Then Cymin realized that Laithondi probably didn't know the modern term "spell filament" since they only came into common use seventy years ago. None of the old tomes used the term, but some texts did mention threads similar to spell filaments in descriptions of Wraiths. They were often referred to as fei'thallus and understood to be fine strings of some specialized species of microscopic organism native to Saigrath. Modern historians and scientists still debated whether the old texts were actually describing fungi, algae, slime molds or some other common microscopic life. But most felt that any improvement in manipulating fei'lux bestowed by fei'thallus had been thanks to a placebo effect rather than some mystical symbiosis. All of them agreed that, if it had ever existed, the magical strain of fei'thallus described in legends had died out before the last of the mage-kings.

However, it was the closest archaic term Cymin could think of at the moment.

"Your fei'thallus, I mean." Cymin said. "How do you acquire and remove it?"

"They stripped the fei'thallus from your hands?" Laithondi didn't seem to register Cymin's question in his horror. He reached out as if he wanted to seize Cymin's hand but then drew back from the mess of Cymin's fingers. His expression was truly ugly, even a little sickened. "Why would they punish you like this? They can't have thought their little bomb would keep us from reclaiming what is ours." Laithondi lifted his gaze to Cymin's face. His eyes were wide with dismay. "You shielded them and yet they do this to your hands? How can you bear it?"

"No. It's not a punishment. Just a normal surgical procedure. And modern anesthetic is an amazing innovation," Cymin responded quickly to calm Laithondi down. "Don't you use anything like it when you receive your filamen—er—fei'thallus?"

Laithondi shook his head, or perhaps a shudder passed through his body.

"We are surrounded by a world of fei'thallus, but as Waethir we were blessed by the Sea of Eternity with the sovereign filaments of the Fei'suul Scepter," Laithondi answered as if he expected Cymin to be intimately familiar with such archaic terms.

The Sea of Eternity? Fei'suul Scepter? Waethir?

Like the celestial pearl, Cymin had encountered those words in old tomes and records. But the descriptions and explanations of them were riddled with contradictions and superstitions. He had no idea what they translated to in real, physical terms. He wasn't certain how to ask for clarification without causing offense.

"This should be put right," Laithondi said. Then he added, "I won't hurt you."

"Odd statement to open with, but I appreciate the sentiment," Cymin replied. "I, too, harbor no intentions to cause you—" The rest of his teasing response caught in his throat as Laithondi reached out and ran his hand down Cymin's bare chest. His skin felt surprisingly warm but roused tingling shivers as streams of fei'lux washed across Cymin's bare skin.

"What . . . what are you doing?" Cymin's question came out far breathier than he'd intended.

"Rousing fei'thallus." Laithondi closed his eyes as he stroked fei'lux down Cymin's abdomen. The hairs all across Cymin's body stood on end and Cymin instinctively tensed. Laithondi frowned and paused.

"Even fragmented fei'thallus in your body should respond to a pure stream of fei'lux. In turn they will stimulate the ignis. So long as it's intact." Laithondi scowled. "It will be best to know the truth either way."

Cymin almost laughed out loud.

The ignis? You're groping me, hoping to find the mythical ignis gland? You're going to be feeling me up for a while.

Though it made a kind of sense because the same archaic texts that described fei'thallus also claimed that ignis glands spontaneously developed in young mages once they were inoculated with certain mystical varieties of fei'thallus. Then the resulting ignis gland became the bodily repository for stores of more fei'thallus, which in turn allowed them to control greater loads of fei'lux. Modern mage-scholars speculated that in the unsanitary conditions of the past, mages might have mistaken anything from cysts, hernias or even clusters of worms for the magical, fei'thallus-rich ignis glands.

Of course you Wraiths still believe in that.

He should have guessed as much, but he'd been too startled and perhaps too excited to think clearly at first. But now he remembered. The sorts of outdated "medical" volumes that recommended boiled ice and dragon urine as an eye-rinse also contained numerous recipes calling for ignis glands harvested from the still-warm bodies of mages. Never mind that no modern physician had ever discovered any such organ; quacks and frauds of all kinds still hawked elixirs claiming to restore or even contain ignis glands.

While Cymin contemplated, Laithondi returned to his search, slipping his fingers beneath the waistband of Cymin's underwear.

"Whoa!" Cymin gave a shout and his heart tripled its rhythm as all the blood in his body seemed to rush after the sensation of Laithondi's callused fingertips. Cymin's loins twitched, and his breath caught in his chest.

"Wrong organ," Cymin gasped.

But Laithondi's expression remained focused. His hand stilled, and he pressed his first two fingers down hard against the muscles of Cymin's lower abdomen. A warm shock of fei'lux shot from Laithondi's fingertips, penetrating deep into Cymin's body.

Cymin jolted in surprise at the weird buzzing sensation, but it didn't actually hurt. He almost said as much. The words never came out because an instant later that little buzz grew into an intense hum that rippled through the core of his body in waves of heat. Cymin felt as if fei'lux was somehow pouring into his organs like a summer wind shaking through tree branches.

What the fuck?

Laithondi lifted his hand away, and the hot, shivering sensation ceased. Cymin struggled to catch his breath and work out what weird spell the Wraith had just cast. If it hadn't been such a bizarre sensation, Cymin would have suspected Laithondi of attempting to seduce him. The Wraith's expression didn't seem to match that theory, though.

"A little weak but fully developed and intact." Laithondi's tense expression relaxed. He opened his eyes and offered Cymin a slight smile. "The balm will help you heal and nourish the ignis."

"Balm? Ah, yes. Right." Cymin belatedly recalled where this strangeness had all begun—the riddle of the celestial pearl.

Laithondi lifted the celestial pearl and drew the shining golden lines of the sun sigil through the swirling clouds on its surface. The small gold sigil flared and the clouds dispersed, revealing a lustrous gold droplet. Laithondi swept two fingers through the droplet, scooping out a glistening curl. A honey scent filled the air, like that of the sweet water-jellies sold in the Flower Market.

But when Laithondi spread the balm across Cymin's chest and abdomen it felt both hot and icy, almost like camphor oil. Though the most disconcerting thing about it was the way it slithered into glowing shapes—very like lightning sigils—and then immediately soaked through his skin. Laithondi brushed a little more balm across the backs of Cymin's hands and the side of his face.

Again, warmth flared through Cymin's body, but this time it was gentle as it rushed all the way to the crown of his skull and the soles of his feet. Then it died away, leaving Cymin feeling cool and languid. His sore muscles eased, and the dull throbbing ache that had haunted his stitched fingers and head melted away.

"Better?" Laithondi asked.

Cymin nodded.

Laithondi rose to his feet and stepped back from the bedside. Then he lifted the shining pearl to his lips and blew over it. The gold sun sigil extinguished like a candle flame, and the puff of smoke left in its wake curled around the orb. It once again became a sphere of rolling clouds, interrupted by a single stroke of lightning.

Cymin gazed at it. He didn't really believe all that about rousing his ignis or stimulating fragments of fei'thallus, but he couldn't deny that Laithondi's balm—if it could even be called that—had worked.

And seeing the celestial pearl open had been beautiful. Worth the momentary indignity of what appeared to be a sincere attempt at rousing his imaginary organ, he supposed.

"Thank you," Cymin said belatedly.

Laithondi shrugged.

"The bomb was meant to stop us. You shouldn't have been caught up—" Laithondi cut himself off and spun on his heel. He strode to the window. Cymin peered past him, searching for the disturbance.

An apricot blossom wafted into the room on a current of fei'lux. The white petals fluttered like butterfly wings. Laithondi caught it between his thumb and forefinger. The green sepal leaves at the base of the blossom unfurled like five verdant tentacles and gripped his finger. Cymin squinted at the flower, suddenly uncertain of what it was that he was truly looking at.

Flower, butterfly, jellyfish?

"Security officers just entered the infirmary," a woman's voice rose from between the fluttering petals. "And Vessreid is going to notice if you're gone much longer."

Laithondi sighed heavily at the mention of the West Deity's name, but he gave no other response.

"If you can't get to the boy who devoured the bomb, just come back. We've found several others," the woman stated. "It's not worth it to have Vessreid pitch a fit right now."

"I found him." Laithondi glanced over his shoulder to Cymin.

"You did? Good." The woman's voice dropped to a whisper. "So, is he a candidate?"

Candidate? A spark of excitement lit in Cymin's chest. Could his action this morning have inspired the Wraiths to take him to study? Could that be the reason Laithondi had sought him out?

"No. He's not," Laithondi stated, crushing Cymin's tentative hope. Laithondi scowled at the blossom. "I'm already done here. I'll be back before Vess completes his meditation. Don't worry."

Laithondi clenched his hand, and Cymin felt him drain the delicate stream of fei'lux from the trembling blossom. The tentacles shriveled and the petals wilted. It dropped to the floor.

"From here on, you'd be wise to stay away from us, Cymin." Almost off-handedly, the Wraith tossed the celestial pearl back over his shoulder. Cymin caught it. Then Laithondi strode to the window and, as silently as he'd entered the room, he vaulted out, dropping beneath the apricot trees like a shadow.

"You're the one who came looking for me," Cymin protested, but the darkness offered him no reply.

CHAPTER 4

Cymin rolled the glowing celestial pearl over in his palm. The balm had reduced the stiffness and swelling in his injured fingers enough for him to easily pick it up and study it now. Silver clouds curled in the wake of his touch, and tiny currents beneath the smooth shell fluttered against his fingertips. The warm sensation reminded him of Master Tam's feral cat purring as it circled his legs. Cymin stroked the crooked line of the gold lightning bolt, and inexplicable fondness filled him.

Where do I remember you from, little treasure?

For a time, he sat, simply marveling that something so precious and beautiful had come into his possession. Despite his tendency to deride the myths and hyperbole surrounding many moldering ancillary artifacts, Cymin recognized that this celestial pearl truly was remarkable and, against all odds, contained an exceptionally magical balm.

Then he sighed. Neither the pearl nor the medicine was something he could claim to have casually picked up in a charm shop or found on the roadside. If the wrong person took notice, he'd be suspected of collaboration or, at worst, treason. What NS agent would believe that a Wraith had given him something so precious as a reward, asking nothing in return? No one. Cymin hardly believed it himself.

No, as soon as the pearl was discovered, Cymin would be suspected of accepting bribes from foreigners.

Briefly, he considered sneaking the pearl into the temple's collection of ancillary artifacts, but every item there was so meticulously stored, catalogued and maintained by the resident scholars that he couldn't imagine slipping anything past them. He didn't even want to think of how incensed the scholars were going to be when they found out that he'd destroyed one of only two staves containing the remains of the *Thousand Blessings to the Sea of Eternity* scroll. No doubt, the sudden appearance of a celestial pearl would alarm them and lead to an immediate investigation.

No, there was no getting around it. He had to get rid of it, he knew that. If he had any common sense, he should get up and toss the pearl out the window. He'd recovered enough of his grip that he should be able to land it in the mulch under the trees even if he couldn't chuck it all the way into the garden stream.

And yet, it was so very lovely and the contents so powerful. How could he just throw it away?

This balm might ease Master Tam's arthritic knee and shoulder, and if Yinni broke her ankle again, the balm might save her from another surgery. So many of the novices suffered injuries during their early training. Think of all the pain—and whining—the balm could prevent.

Except word would surely get out if he started flitting about the temple complex with a celestial pearl, slathering magical balm on every scratch and bruise.

Most of the novices can't keep a secret in the face of a tempting bag of candy, never mind NS marshals. East Deity should know better than to rely on the discretion of a bunch of six-year-olds.

Cymin sighed again. No matter how miraculous the medicine was, if it endangered the entire temple, then it wasn't worth the risk.

So.

It had to go.

Unconsciously, his fingers stroked the gold lightning bolt again.

Should he hide it and then dispose of it outside of the temple grounds to be absolutely safe? Maybe leave it on one of the cluttered shelves of an apothecary shop and hope it could someday do some good for someone? Or just toss it into the river and be done with it altogether?

The clatter of hard-soled shoes striking the wooden floorboards in the hallway outside his room snapped him out of his contemplation. Members of the Lux Temple went barefoot all year round, so those loud footsteps rang with a distinctly secular sound. They approached Cymin's door at a fast, even clip, betraying the martial rhythm trained into the police and NS officers.

Fear shot through Cymin, setting his heart racing. His fingers clenched around the pearl. *Where to hide it?*

No knock sounded from his door. Instead, the latch gave a quiet click.

Cymin dropped his hand to his abdomen, folding the waistband of his underwear over the pearl. The overhead lights flared, and Cymin narrowed his eyes against their intensity. He didn't have to put any effort into appearing startled by the intrusion of light and people.

The four NS officers weren't common agents, but full-fledged NS marshals, Cymin realized in horror. They dressed in blue uniforms, complete with holstered ancillary pistols, and invaded his room without a word of greeting. All four possessed sturdy builds and sported clean-cropped dark hair. They appeared to be two women and two men. The woman nearest Cymin held up an NS badge—as if the unnerving uniformity of the marshals' faces wasn't enough to identify them all in an instant.

The anonymity spell NS marshals employed was infamous and unmistakable. It rendered eyes, mouths, nostrils and even ears as narrow black slits carved deep into smooth skin the color of cement. The only detailed features on their gray faces were the shining blue national security seals—a four-winged hawk encircled by a ring of protective sigils—that lay like brands between their brows.

Their inhumanly simple features were impossible to read and quite unnerving. The female marshal returned her badge to the pocket of her jacket, and Cymin noted that her hands, like her face, appeared unnaturally uniform and smooth. Devoid of fingernails, knuckles and even wrinkles, her paste-gray fingers took on a disturbingly worm-like quality.

Please do not touch me with those tapeworms.

Cymin didn't need to feign his uneasy vulnerability as he drew the sheet up over the lower half of his body, further hiding the pearl.

"Good evening, Tuteli Adept Cymin." The words projected from the female marshal standing nearest Cymin, but her voice sounded as if a crowd of other people spoke in perfect unison with her.

"Greetings, marshals." Cymin tried to meet the marshal's eyes, but the two flat black lines conveyed nothing of a human gaze. He wasn't even certain of where she might actually be looking. The celestial pearl lying against his abdomen felt hard and hot. Cymin resisted the urge to cover it with his hand. There were too many people watching him right now, and he couldn't afford to attract any attention to the illicit artifact.

Four monsters walk into the room, and East Deity jams his hands into his underwear—they'd suspect me of something for certain.

"You're not all looking for the toilets by any chance, are you?" He made the joke to himself just to alleviate his own dread.

The marshals' faces betrayed no response, but at least one of the men cocked his head in a slightly confused manner. Cymin felt somewhat reassured to know that there were real human beings—capable of being flummoxed—somewhere under those disguises.

"You need to complete an interview about today's events, immediately," the woman nearest Cymin stated. "In consideration for your condition, however, your interrogator has kindly agreed to debrief you at Benevolence Hall."

Cymin relaxed a bit more. Benevolence Hall lay within the grounds of Lux Temple compound, so they weren't planning to drag him off to an interrogation crypt right away. That was something.

"Thank you for the kindness," Cymin responded. "Would it be possible for me to return to my dormitory for my clothes and then join you at the hall in half an hour?"

"Not necessary," the female marshal told him. "Your fellow clerics brought appropriate vestments."

One of the male marshals turned around and opened the door. Just past his bulky uniformed figure, Cymin caught sight of Yinni and Master Tam out in the hall, alongside two more marshals. Yinni hurried into the room, carrying a bundle of clay-brown clothes. She set them down on the bed.

"How are you feeling?" Yinni asked. Cymin recognized the tension belying her tight smile and upright posture.

"Popular." Cymin offered her a playful grin. "You think I could charge for my autograph?"

"*That's* what you're thinking about at a time like this?" The hard lines at the corners of Yinni's full lips relaxed, and her eyes lit with a hidden laughter. "You're so ridiculous."

Even as little children they'd been like this: her anxious for his sake, and him playing off the trouble he'd landed in as amusing. Hardly two years his elder, she sometimes acted more like a mother to him than a sister. Yinni glanced down at Cymin's stitched hands. A concerned furrow appeared on her brow.

"How did the exhibition matches go?" Cymin inquired before Yinni could worry too much over the cost of replacing all his spell filaments or ask him if they hurt. "Who did the Wraiths choose?"

"Waethir, not Wraiths," the female marshal interjected. "They are foreign nationals, not supernatural beings."

Cymin and Yinni both turned toward the marshal.

Everyone and their mother calls them Wraiths, Cymin thought.

And, if anything, the word "Waethir"—written in the original archaic sigils—was even more supernatural.

Originally the sigil *Wae* designated ancient guardian spells, so complex and powerful that they resembled living beings. The sigil *Thir* belonged to creatures of the Heavens, deities in particular.

Cymin considered enlightening the marshal about the derivation of the word, then he caught Yinni narrowing her gaze in his direction. Arguing with a member of National Security wasn't a wise choice under normal circumstances, but it would be particularly idiotic just now.

"Right you are. I misspoke." Cymin forced a smile up at the marshal's eerie face. "Thank you for reminding me."

She nodded, and Cymin returned his attention to Yinni.

"Did the *Waethir* say which ten mages they chose?" he asked.

"They observed the competitions, then withdrew to the guesthouse without a word. But the prime minister said that there would be an announcement early next week." Yinni handed him his undershirt. With clumsy motions, Cymin worked it over his shoulders. Yinni continued, "I think Paeth, Ovelah and Saum from Ryde Academy are likely to receive invitations."

"That's good news," Cymin said.

Yinni regularly exchanged letters with the twin sisters, Paeth and Ovelah, and they had even invited her to their townhouse once. They were a pretty pair with long curly brown hair, freckled noses and willowy figures. During the exhibition matches, they excelled at defensive maneuvers and normally won. But where they truly stood out from most other mages was in their skill at designing and building their own ancillaries.

The third girl, Saum, was short, black-haired and round-eyed with a deeply dimpled grin. She reminded Cymin of an adorable dumpling; plump, warm and packed with surprises. She used her ancillary hammers to toss out spells like a relentless wind-up toy bashing away on a drum: no grace whatsoever but astounding stamina. Her only weakness, in Cymin's opinion, was a tendency to fall into a predictable—almost playful—rhythm when she pounded out her resounding attacks. Even so, she could crush nearly any opponent's defenses, all while looking as happy as a honeybee in a field of sunflowers.

Yinni knew them all far better than he did, but Cymin liked them well enough to be happy for them.

"Did anyone win any champion rings off us?" Cymin pulled on his light trousers. For a moment, he considered palming the pearl and trying to shift it to a pocket, but there were too many people surrounding him. Instead, he secured the knot of his sash over the pearl and hoped it would help disguise it further.

"Saum and Nyle." Yinni betrayed only a moment of distaste speaking the second name, but Cymin scowled outright.

For the last two years, he'd taken a smug pleasure in denying Nyle an undefeated sweep in his matches.

Blade-thin and fine-boned, Nyle dressed in archaic black robes, wore his waist-length black hair in two neat braids and generally comported himself with the cool disdain of a twice-named noble from the

Age of Mage-Kings. Unsurprisingly, he attended the affluent Boshyin School, which infamously selected students from privileged, powerful families. Cymin didn't know Nyle's actual background, but it was widely rumored that the only single-named students Boshyin admitted were the descendants of mage-kings whose lineage names held so much power that they'd been banned.

"But we wiped the grounds with the rest of his snotty Boshyin chums," Yinni added.

"Good." Cymin pulled on his outer robe and made a crude attempt to fold the cuffs of the wide sleeves and the collar. Seeing this, Yinni took over arranging his sleeves for him while continuing to relate the details of several matches. Apparently, an owl-faced adept mage named Kimrin had mistakenly unleashed a wind spell so powerful that it sent him flying all the way around the arena. His impromptu launch so stunned his opponent that he'd actually won the match.

"I swear, he was flapping his arms and hooting 'Whooo, whooo, whooo' the entire time. Like an owlet on a merry-go-round." Yinni grinned and shook her head. "I had to fight so hard not to laugh that I could hardly stand up and chase after him."

"I wish I could have seen that." Cymin swung off the cot, rising to his feet. Muscles all along his legs and back shuddered at the sudden strain, and he swayed. Yinni caught him by the elbow.

Cymin steadied himself. "I'm good."

"Sure you are. It's not as if you barely survived a bombing this morning and are still recovering from surgery. You've never been better." Yinni cast a hard look at the female marshal. "I'll join you in escorting my brother to Benevolence Hall."

To Cymin's surprise, the marshal simply nodded and indicated that Yinni should lead Cymin out. In the hallway, Master Tam took hold of Cymin's right arm while Yinni continued to support him on the left, with the NS marshals bringing up the rear.

The nurses on duty bowed their heads as the marshals passed.

In spite of the oppressive presence of the marshals trailing them, Cymin enjoyed his evening stroll across the temple grounds. Cool breezes washed over him as Yinni and Master Tam chatted about soothingly mundane concerns. A large flock of arctic wigeons had descended upon the temple lake this afternoon and triggered an uproar among the temple ducks as well as the novices who tended them.

"You don't think they followed the Wrai—" Cymin caught himself, remembering the marshal's earlier chastisement. "—the *Waethir*, do you?"

"I can't imagine why they would. Though for them to migrate this time of year and to fly so far south . . ." Master Tam glanced up at the stars overhead as if seeking an answer to the curious appearance of the foreign birds. "Wigeons used to be considered omens of the Hallow Gates fail—" Seeming to suddenly recall the marshals trailing them, Master Tam abandoned his comment and simply added, "No point in stirring up superstitious nonsense over a few dozen birds."

"Better to stir up soup with them," Cymin said.

Yinni laughed and Master Tam smiled.

They passed below rows of fig trees. Here moon moths swarmed several of the lanterns, blocking the light with their large wings. The night's darkness seemed to close in and, suddenly, Cymin noticed a faint glow seeping from between the folds of his belt. He quickly placed a hand over the pearl lying against his abdomen, covering it.

"Cramp?" Yinni asked.

"That time of the month, you know," Cymin responded.

"Ah, they grow up so fast, don't they, Master?" Yinni grinned and Master Tam sighed. Cymin wasn't certain if he was pained or simply resigned to their childish humor.

"But seriously. Are you hurt?" Yinni asked.

"A little sore. I think I pulled a muscle this morning or . . ." Cymin glanced sidelong to Master Tam and whispered, "Maybe my ignis gland is coming in at long last."

Yinni snorted, and even Master Tam gave a chuckle.

"You look pained now, Master," Yinni said. "But you're going to miss us when we're gone."

As they left the deep shadows of the fig trees, the sky seemed to blossom with lights from the surrounding lamps and far-flung city towers. A few fireworks sparkled and, far off, the Spring Festival ferris wheel turned in a bright circle.

"You don't have to go, you know," Master Tam lowered his voice. "Shuun and I could arrange for you both to stay in the temple with medical reprieves and serve your civic duty here."

Cymin knew exemptions could be arranged. But as a rule, the tuteli permitted to remain in the temple for their civic service were those deemed far too mentally or physically frail to even venture into the surrounding city. On top of that, safe, local work rarely paid enough to clear temple debts, which meant that Lux Temple—and those of the staff who, like Master Tam, *had* cleared their personal debts—continued to shoulder the burden of the interest owed to the state.

"But I've found a very lucrative offer." Yinni glanced between Cymin and Master Tam, her eyes gleaming with delight. "After the exhibition, I received a handwritten letter from a certain starlet, who has a new film project that she could use my assistance with."

"You're going to be in a moving picture?" Cymin shared Yinni's elation. They both loved films, but Yinni excelled in acting. Even burdened with the long, tedious scripts meant to educate tourists and school groups, she engrossed and charmed most onlookers when she performed on the small stage in Benevolence Hall. She was as engaging and poised as any of the stars he'd seen up on a motion picture screen.

"It's going to be a documentary. But yes." Excitement radiated from Yinni's smile. Master Tam appeared somewhat troubled.

"I've heard stories about secular theater," Master Tam said. "Some of the people involved may not be reliable, and some take advantage—"

"I know. I know. But in this case, the person who contacted me is very well respected, and her project is something I think the temple would be quite proud of," Yinni responded. "Also, I brought the contract for you and Grand Master Ryn to look over before I sign it. Rest assured, I haven't lost my good sense."

"What is the project, then?" Master Tam asked.

"As I said, it's to be a documentary," Yinni lowered her voice. "About life in the Northlands and the return of the Wraiths—er. . . ."

"Waethir," Cymin supplied the proper word with a too-pious smile, causing Yinni to roll her eyes.

But then Cymin wondered if perhaps "Waethir" was a better way to address Laithondi and his companions, after all. Even if everyone in Chyre used the term "Wraiths," could it be a little insulting? They weren't actually ghosts or ghouls. Cymin tried and failed to imagine Laithondi referring to himself as a Wraith. That seemed less likely than Cymin calling himself or Yinni "Members of the Lux Temple Militia"—as the tuteli were often branded in newspapers and on radio broadcasts.

"My contract even guarantees me reimbursement for all my travel expenses. Even my secular shoes," Yinni stated.

"I'm so jealous! I want to get paid to wear shoes and visit Saigrath, too!" Cymin felt happiness and envy for Yinni in equal measure. If only he hadn't been injured, perhaps he would have been invited to join the film crew as well. At the same time, he couldn't regret the choice he'd made. If he hadn't stopped the bombing, then both he and Yinni would be dead. Now, at least one of them would be taking part in a film.

"The Ministry of Culture already approved funding. We've secured travel permits all the way to Yanyeo—"

"Yanyeo?" Cymin spoke up, recalling the salacious, late-night radio drama he and most of the other tuteli surreptitiously followed. "The Sinful City of Canals, Casinos and Carnal—"

"Yes. Chyre's northern port." Yinni cut him off with a glance at the marshals. Then she added, "I'll tell you both more about it later."

If the marshals thought anything of the matter, they didn't comment, and Master Tam changed the subject to the duty roster for the Spring Festival. For the first time in a decade, neither Yinni nor Cymin was expected to attend to or escort the temple's guests from the Five Schools. Cymin's injuries had won him a reprieve from his regular duties as well. He danced in a circle around Master Tam, all but crowing in delight at the promise of five days free.

"You keep fooling around like that, and I might change my mind about your condition," Master Tam warned. That inspired Cymin to fake an exaggerated limp for a few steps. But he gave up soon after realizing he was too tired to maintain the charade.

Too weak to feign weakness. Is that ironic or just pathetic?

Happily, above the glossy leaves of the temple's hundred-year-old mango trees, the pavilion tower of Benevolence Hall came into view. Cymin admired the familiar gilded building with an easy smile until he remembered that, inside, an interrogation awaited him.

CHAPTER 5

In the night gloom, the five stories of Benevolence Hall blazed like a giant, ornate paper lantern. Its light seemed to draw as many groups of well-dressed people as it did moon moths and star bees. The vivid insects flocked to cascades of night-blooming jasmine that garlanded the balconies, which jutted from the four upper floors. On the ground level, human silhouettes backlit by gold lamplight fluttered across paper window screens. Gilded statues of mythic three-eyed deer knelt, lining the steps leading to Benevolence Hall's vivid red doors, keeping a stony watch.

The hall shared a courtyard with the temple's lavish guesthouse. In the Age of Mage-Kings, visiting nobles had enjoyed the worldly amenities of both locales, while pursuing advances in their mage work as well as spiritual education from tuteli masters. Even now the two-story guesthouse, with its hot spring bath and luxurious suites, continued to indulge visitors important to the temple, while the grand stage and boisterous kitchen of Benevolence Hall provided sustenance, entertainment and debate—all at rather reasonable rates.

Even from outside, Cymin caught the sounds of rowdy conversation and laughter rolling out from the ground level. Up on the second- and third-story balconies, he spied Lux Temple novices serving guests delicacies and drinks, though the fourth and fifth floors appeared uncharacteristically sedate, especially for the exhibition day when Lux Temple hosted instructors and competitors from the Five Schools.

Cymin peered past the shining hall to the more sedate guesthouse. A couple of lights glowed from circular windows on the second floor; otherwise, the place appeared empty. He wondered if Laithondi and his fellow Waethir numbered among the few people who'd already retired for the night or if some of them might venture into Benevolence Hall to find company. If Laithondi was inside, Cymin wondered if he could use the bustle of the crowd to furtively return the celestial pearl to him. Then he glanced back at the six NS marshals following him, Yinni and Master Tam and abandoned the notion.

Cymin patted the sigil-engraved shoulder of one of the three-eyed deer protecting the steps.

The marshals have even more eyes on us than you do, Cymin joked to himself. Yinni and Master Tam, too, rubbed the statues in passing for luck. At the top of the steps, Master Tam reached out and caught the brass pull of the red lacquered door.

"Master, tuteli—my thanks for guiding us here." The female NS Marshal strode forward at a quick clip, catching Cymin's elbow in a firm grip. She angled her head at Master Tam and then to Yinni. "There should be no need for anyone other than us to escort Adept Tuteli Cymin further."

Yinni glanced to Cymin, and he recognized the determination in her expression. She was frightened of the marshals, but if Cymin objected to being left alone with them, Yinni would do anything in her means to stay beside him. Just knowing that, Cymin felt reassured enough to offer Yinni a cocky smile. She shook her head at him but relaxed enough to wish the marshals a good evening before hurrying inside the hall—no doubt to join her friends, Paeth and Ovelah. After his interrogation, Cymin would likely find her waiting for him at a table on the first floor.

Master Tam stepped aside for the marshals and turned in the direction of the masters' dormitories, but he didn't descend the steps. Instead, he turned his prayer beads through his hands, mumbling blessings, as if this was a perfectly normal place and time to indulge in a spate of meditation. One of the marshals cocked his head in Master Tam's direction but didn't attempt to clear the old master away. Rather, he stepped up beside Cymin and pulled the door open.

"We will go directly to the fifth floor." The female marshal continued to grip Cymin's elbow as she led him into the hall. "Refrain from engaging in any unnecessary conversation until after your debriefing."

"Of course," Cymin replied. They must have hated all the trivial chatter he, Yinni and Master Tam had enjoyed on the way over.

With marshals flanking him on either side, Cymin strode through the strings of lucky bells hung across the scarlet entry and into the bustling activity of the first floor. Humid warmth, the smell of onion cakes and a cacophony of voices washed over him. Fragrant steam poured out from the kitchen doors at the back of the hall. Wisps of incense rolled up the carved staircase and clung to the overhanging balconies like mist. Looking up past the interior balconies of the second, third and fourth stories, Cymin glimpsed stars shining through the huge circular skylight at the stairwell's top.

Much of the ground floor was an open space filled with tables surrounding a raised dais where performances would be staged. Along the far wall there were some private rooms, but tonight all of the wooden dividers had been packed away, leaving all the alcoves wide open. Every table and private room was crammed with adepts and masters from the Five Schools. Several of the tuteli who had been assigned service duties called out greetings in passing and Cymin flashed them friendly hand signs. But the instant the tuteli glimpsed the marshals, they swiftly returned to serving food and drinks to the crowded tables.

As they strode to the staircase, the crowd parted before the marshals, offering Cymin largely unobstructed views of the tables. He didn't catch any sign of Laithondi or his fellow Waethir. He did, however, recognize Nyle's slim, straight figure and long black braids. The young man's elegant expression remained impassive as a boisterous gang of Boshyin students cheered him and their school's accomplishments. The pretty girls and handsome boys surrounding Nyle took turns admiring the champion ring on his hand.

Like none of you have ever seen a gold ring before.

Cymin's first instinct was to silently deride the press of admirers surrounding Nyle, but he stopped himself. Because not only was winning a champion ring a remarkable feat, but he'd also just spotted Yinni three tables away exclaiming over the ring that adorable little Saum proudly displayed, her cheeks flushed red. Sitting across from them, with tumbling curls of brown hair cascading down their shoulders, Paeth and her twin sister Ovelah both lifted their wine cups in salute to their classmate.

Then, from a different table, two muscular young men wearing scarlet Orae Academy uniforms, one sporting a trimmed black beard and the other a crop of astoundingly red hair, bellowed out a toast to both Saum and Nyle.

Saum blushed even harder, and Cymin even caught a flicker of incredulous delight as it passed over Nyle's staid and refined features.

Cymin sighed. He couldn't continue to feel such petty and envious rancor in the face of this awestruck, pure happiness. No doubt, Nyle had trained and fought just as hard as Saum; they both deserved to enjoy celebration and congratulations. It wasn't their fault that they had parents and he and Yinni didn't.

Likely both champions would be invited to study in Saigrath as well. It was good for them and maybe good for everyone in Chyre. Maybe one of them would even discover some innovation in Saigrath that could make his own tenure in the Storm Towers easier or more survivable.

Cymin bounded up the stairs, and the marshals followed him like four unfriendly shadows. On the second and third floors, instructors, chaperones and wealthy guests all appeared to be as excited and celebratory as the competitors below. Gazing down as he continued up the next flight of stairs, Cymin spotted none other than rising starlet Una Bayan. She leaned over the carved railing, studying a table below. Then he realized that she'd been watching Yinni and the mages from Ryde Academy. As she pushed her bobbed hair back from her face, Cymin had a clear view of her pleased expression. Could it have been Una Bayan who'd approached Yinni to travel to the north and film the Waethir? He stared, not quite believing his eyes. Could Yinni be that lucky?

"Fifth story," the male marshal's discordant voice reminded Cymin to keep moving.

The fourth floor appeared devoid of guests and cheer. Two lines of uniformed security officers occupied the entire story. The first group stood at the windows scrutinizing the grounds below with largely bored expressions. The other set of officers surveyed the revelers beneath them with a variety of interest and amusement. Though the moment the marshals came into sight, the regular officers schooled their expressions to stern indifference. Three of the marshals escorting Cymin stopped at the foot of the staircase.

A single female marshal led him up the last flight of stairs and escorted him along the empty, quiet corridor of the fifth story. Perfumed oil lamps illuminated faded murals, depicting deities at play with an assortment of divine and lucky creatures. Here and there images of guardian wae appeared ringed in haloes of gilded sigils: a blazing phoenix, a winged salamander, an icy blue sea serpent and more than a dozen others that Cymin knew well enough to find them comfortingly mundane.

Normally, business moguls, government officials and celebrities reserved the fourth and fifth floors for banquets or private performances. As a novice, Cymin had toddled between gilded tables serving sweets from silver platters—occasionally sneaking one himself. And a mere month ago, he'd commanded the center of attention, adorned in East Deity's regalia and reciting the newly declassified *Six-Hundred Sacred Sigils* to a gathering of ecstatic mage-scholars from far-flung provinces. He naturally associated the fifth floor with conversation, applause and cheer. But this evening, the narrow corridor leading to the four banquet rooms seemed disconcertingly abandoned and silent, making even the celebration and clamor on the floors below feel worlds away.

Though he supposed that National Security taking up two whole floors at least saved the tuteli serving in the hall from having to lug heavy trays of food so many flights of stairs. So, as bleak as the fifth floor seemed, there was still something to be gained for Lux Temple. The thought cheered Cymin, and he even managed a smile when the female marshal stopped at the door of the lavish Splendid Fragrances Chamber.

She knocked once, and Cymin straightened as if preparing to represent East Deity on yet another stage.

"Come in," a man called in a relaxed tone.

Cymin pushed the door open.

The harsh white arc-lamp—normally only ignited for cleaning—blazed from the high ceiling. Its intense light seemed to strip the luxurious textures from the silk tapestries on the walls and revealed every stained detail of the floor's marquetry as well as the gnarled age of the balcony carvings and the jasmine blooms entwining them. The five giant brass incense braziers—each one cast in the shape of a famous guardian wae—hunched along the walls, looking rather cold and sooty. Though Cymin's favorite, a three-headed winged salamander, retained its wide, smug smile, despite the smoke streaks darkening its nostrils and broad mouth.

In the center of the room, Grand Master Ryn sat at a low amber table across from Lui Dane. The two contrasted each other in every aspect. Grand Master Ryn was a broad-boned, curvaceous woman in her mid-forties. Her round, tanned face seemed made for warm smiles and her rumpled vestments and fuzzy tonsure projected an indifference towards affectation. At a glance, her bearing seemed gentle and compassionate, very much in keeping with the manner of a woman who'd worn the West Deity's mask in her early life. But Grand Master Ryn was no pushover. She'd personally butchered a rapist who'd broken into the women's dormitory two years before. And on the practice grounds she reigned supreme. Cymin had been hauled off his feet and hurled several yards by her spells on numerous occasions.

Lui Dane, on the other hand, gave the impression of a man who'd been born in a pressed indigo uniform and, despite living some sixty years, had never smiled or encountered a meal he wanted to eat. Despite his age, his fair skin stretched taut and weirdly smooth across the hard angles of his skull. He wore his glossy black hair swept back in a stylish cut, and his blue uniform fit his thin frame with crisp perfection.

Both the clay teapot and dish of nuts and seeds sitting on the table between the Lux Temple Grand Master and the Minister of National Security appeared to have been, so far, untouched by either of them. The only sound that interrupted their mutual silence was the soft click of the NS marshal closing the door behind Cymin and no doubt scampering back to the far more welcoming company of her fellow gash-faced monsters.

Oh, so I can be trusted all on my own now, can I? What a courageous escort you turned out to be.

Though considering the palpable tension in the room, Cymin didn't truly blame her. If he could have, he'd have fled from the cool, almost predatory attention of these two as well. He suddenly imagined himself as a hapless mouse tossed into a room occupied by a smiling cat and a coiled snake.

"Come Cymin, sit here." Grand Master Ryn patted the embroidered cushion beside her own.

I'd rather save myself the trouble of being torn in half by the two of you and just throw myself off the five-story balcony.

Instead Cymin forced himself to trudge to the low table and then sank down alongside the Grand Master.

Lui Dane studied him over his long, steepled fingers. Like Cymin, Lui Dane bore multiple white scars on his fingers from multiple spell filament implant surgeries. A thick folder embossed with the National Security seal lay near the minister's elbow.

"Help yourself, Adept Tuteli." Lui Dane indicated the tea and nuts.

Cymin considered a polite refusal, but it had been nearly twelve hours since he'd last had anything to eat or drink.

"Thank you, kind benefactor." Cymin started to reach for the teapot when he felt Grand Master Ryn nudge him. He recalled his manners adding, "Though first, may I serve either of you?"

Lui Dane nodded.

"Go ahead," Grand Master Ryn agreed.

Cymin gingerly took up the teapot and filled cups for Grand Master Ryn and Lui Dane. They observed his movements in silence. Between the appearance of his scabbed and stitched hands and the knowledge that he was hiding a celestial pearl on his body, he found himself growing more and more self-conscious with each motion. A bead of sweat trickled down his abdomen from where the celestial pearl dug into his belly, and his hands trembled by the time he poured tea for himself. He suddenly felt too nervous to eat, so he just took a drink of the tea, only to discover it was a bitter medicinal brew that had gone cold.

Neither the Grand Master nor Lui Dane touched their own cups.

Cymin picked up one of the thumb-sized waterseeds but didn't bite into the oily flesh. Instead, he glanced between Grand Master Ryn and Lui Dane.

"The marshals said that there were questions for me concerning this morning," Cymin said.

"Among other things," Lui Dane replied. "But let us begin with the bomb this morning. How and when did you become aware of it?"

"I felt something was off about the mosaic when we entered the grounds, but I didn't know what it was." Cymin almost added that Yinni had also expressed uneasiness about the grounds but decided against it, not wanting to embroil her in this if he could help it.

"But you said nothing at that point," Lui Dane stated.

"I thought it might just be my imagination." Cymin shrugged. "The crowds were so much larger than we were expecting, and there was so much noise and activity. And then the Wrai—Waethir arrived, and the blessings they used were so strange I barely recognized them." Cymin glanced first to the Grand Master, then Lui Dane, searching for a sign that they understood how stunned he'd felt in the midst of all those people and spells. Grand Master Ryn nodded to him, but Lui Dane's expression remained impassive.

"With all that, the repairs to the mosaic didn't strike me as suspicious so much as . . . I don't know." The absence of any easy language to convey what he'd experienced frustrated Cymin. "It just wasn't what I was used to feeling under my feet. But everything seemed different this year."

"Then, when *exactly* did you realize what was wrong?" Lui Dane asked.

"I only recognized that it was a bomb under me when I felt the ignition spark racing under the mosaic. Then the bomb began to detonate," Cymin admitted.

Lui Dane studied him in silence for a moment.

"You responded very quickly for someone taken completely by surprise," Lui Dane's words might have been commending, but suspicion permeated his tone.

"You'd have moved fast too, if it had been your balls over that bomb," Cymin snapped.

Lui Dane's black brows rose at the crude remark.

Belatedly, Cymin registered Grand Master Ryn's leg bumping against his own. She gave him a sidelong look and didn't have to open her mouth for him to hear her reprimand in his head.

If you can't be polite in the presence of someone who could kill you, at least keep silent.

It was a gem of wisdom she'd often repeated to him on the training grounds.

A guilty flush heated Cymin's face, and he quickly filled his mouth with more of the tepid, bitter tea.

Grand Master Ryn gave a resigned sigh and smiled at Lui Dane.

"Didn't I say that Adept Cymin's reflexes are much faster than his sense of self-preservation?"

"You did, indeed," Lui Dane replied.

Grand Master Ryn, at last, took a sip of the tea. She frowned. "I don't know how you can stand the brew from these bitter eastern leaves."

"Without the bitter, we cannot appreciate the sweet," Lui Dane replied. He, too, drank but then returned his attention to Cymin. "Who would you guess is responsible for the bomb?"

"I don't know." The default answer would be anarchists or imperialists. But neither group seemed likely to possess the connections or sophistication to plant a bomb within the Lux Temple grounds while they were being guarded by National Security. "Maybe Piiroc Extremists, hoping to derail any alliance between us and the Waethir?"

As Master Shuun always says, when in doubt, just blame the Piirocs. They're always up to something, somewhere.

In mythic times, it had supposedly been the tyranny of the Piiroc Holy Royals and their Carnal Gods that united the Wraiths and first mage-kings to rise up against them. And the fact that their Holy Royals had used sigils of subjugation to bond people to them in lifelong servitude—and to some extent still did—struck Cymin as reason enough to oppose them.

Eons had passed since the Piiroc's Carnal Gods had been destroyed, but, like a tumultuous couple locked in an arranged marriage, Piiroc and Chyre still endlessly battled, allied, supported and then undermined each other. The border between them moved like an ocean tide. Invasions, truces, intermarriages of ruling families and assassinations abounded on both sides. Currently, Chyre's republic and the constitutional monarchy of Piiroc maintained a tense peace treaty, while covertly prodding one another for potential weaknesses. Though, recently, a surge in the popularity of the Royal Flame Apotheosis had inspired a rash of Piiroc religious fanatics and militias, intent on overthrowing the secular governments of both nations.

At least, that was how they were lampooned in the newspaper.

Lui Dane inclined his head in the very slightest of nods.

"Are you aware of the value of the staff you destroyed?" Lui Dane asked.

The sudden change of subject gave Cymin a moment's pause, but then horror swept through him. Were they really going to hold him responsible for the cost of the Black Staff?

"If I hadn't used it, people would have died," Cymin protested. "Not just me but my fellow tuteli, students from The Five Schools, the Wraiths—"

"Adept Cymin, I did not ask you who you felt was endangered," Lui Dane broke in. "Only if you understood the value of the staff you destroyed."

Cymin sucked in a deep breath. He wanted to abide by Grand Master Ryn's advice, but in this case, he couldn't remain silent, either. He suppressed his frustration and tried to think of how he would respond if he were wearing East Deity's mask. Unconsciously, he straightened and lifted his chin to look Lui Dane directly in the face.

"As an ancillary artifact the staff is—was—a treasure. Modern scholars studying its spells are still making discoveries that they hope will lead to greater innovations in fei'lux technology. As a piece of Chyrenese heritage, it was a priceless artifact," Cymin replied. "But the lives of Chyre's people are still more valuable."

"You spout propaganda with such conviction. Tourists must enjoy your holiday performances to no end." Lui Dane's thin mouth curved in a sneer. "However, as a tuteli, you know that people's lives are far from priceless. They can be bought up at bargain rates twice a year right here at Lux Temple. As for East Deity's Thousand Blessings staff, it, too, has a set value. The cost of constructing a replica is approximately thirty times your personal temple debt . . . if we don't include the cost of a second set of spell filaments."

Cymin scowled at Lui Dane. *Since you already know all this, then why the fuck did you ask me?*

But of course, he knew why the security minister had baited him like that—to belittle him and remind him of the loans Lux Temple had secured and guaranteed to pay for his education and upbringing. Cymin's debt wasn't his alone but had been taken on by the entirety of Lux Temple. Now that he'd destroyed an artifact belonging to the state, he'd burdened the temple even further. Perhaps beyond any amount he could hope to earn back, even if he spent the next fifty years serving National Security in a Storm Tower. Cymin slugged back another mouthful of bitter tea and bowed his head.

"Everything has a price," Lui Dane stated.

Then he picked up the folder and took out two large black-and-white photographs. He spread them out in front of Cymin. They captured an ornately engraved scepter from a variety of angles. Judging by the size of the cigarette case in both photographs, the scepter was about as large as a grown man's thigh bone and of a very similar texture. A teardrop-shaped finial crowned one end. The other sported an oddly ragged band of silver wires that made Cymin wonder if they hadn't been broken off from something else earlier.

The shaft reminded Cymin of the carved ivory lamps he'd seen in the charm market—only the engraving looked much, much more finely detailed and costly. Metallic filigree edged the thousands of intricate carvings, creating a gleaming lacework. Cymin leaned closer to the photos, peering into the hollows of the carved patterns. He realized that etched spheres, rings and cogs cut from smaller bones lay interlocked like clockwork within the scepter's shaft and finial. Cymin wasn't certain, but he thought he recognized archaic sigils representing the Hallow Gates and the Five Deities carved into numerous cogs.

"Is this some kind of ancillary clock?" Cymin wondered. The more he studied the scepter, the more intricate it seemed to become.

"You don't recognize it?" Lui Dane asked.

"No. Should I?" Cymin looked to Grand Master Ryn, but she, too, seemed surprised and fascinated by the photographs.

"Unlike the staff you destroyed, *this* ancillary scepter is one of a kind. We know from the sigils that it originally belonged to the Waethir. Reclaiming it is a large part of their sudden willingness to visit us and take on Chyrenese students." Lui Dane paused to fix Cymin with an intent gaze. Cymin had no idea why. Then Lui Dane went on. "It was rescued from tomb robbers fourteen years ago. Since then, it's been studied by numerous Master Mage-Scholars, but none of them have been able to unlock its true function."

"Maybe it's broken," Cymin said. Though the mention of grave robbers made him uneasy.

Lui Dane shook his head at the suggestion. Then he pulled a third photograph out from beneath the other two.

"You're certain you don't remember *anything* about it?" he asked.

The photograph showed a partly flooded stone crypt. The soft mounds of moldering human bodies were scattered in the dank water, while numerous polished sarcophagi broke the dark surface like islands. Tangles of jewelry and embroidered shrouds hung across many of the sarcophagi. On the lid of the sarcophagus nearest the camera, a drenched toddler hunched. The scepter clenched in his arms was unmistakable, as were the human bones scattered all around him. The child stared straight into the camera with an expression nearly as vacant as that of the skull next to his foot.

"That's you, is it not?" Lui Dane asked.

Cymin stared down at the hollow-eyed, filthy child in the photograph. Snot glistened beneath the boy's nose, and dark stains crusted one of his scrawny thighs—maybe mud, maybe shit, Cymin couldn't say. What he did know was that he'd been alone in that dark, flooded crypt for days before rescuers discovered him. And this was what they'd found. Shame and sorrow stirred in his chest. He looked so helpless. So pathetic.

The comforting sensation of Grand Master Ryn gently patting his leg pulled Cymin back from his shock. He looked up from the photograph to Lui Dane.

"If you say so. I've never seen this picture before." Cymin didn't want to think about that, and he absolutely didn't want someone like Lui Dane to witness his distress.

He shifted his gaze from the little boy's hopeless stare, searching the photograph for anything to distract him from the intensity of his emotions.

He focused on the details of the scepter clutched to his bony bare chest. Cymin glanced to the other photographs of the scepter, then returned his study to the image of the flooded crypt. The teardrop finial at the top of the scepter had opened into spiraling rings of sigil-etched petals like the blossom of a lotus. A very faint glow even appeared to emanate from the scepter. It cast an odd light across the boy clutching it.

"Any thoughts?" Lui Dane inquired.

What kind of parents settle a toddler on a pile of bones? Cymin thought to himself. But, studying the photograph, he recognized that he'd been placed on the high ground—atop sarcophagi on a raised stone dais. Who knew? Maybe the bones, like much of the jewel-studded debris, had been washed up later by the flood waters.

"Who comes across this scene and thinks that the first thing to do is to take a picture?" Cymin asked at last.

An asshole, obviously, but I'm curious if you know that, sir.

Grand Master Ryn shook her head, while Lui Dane lowered his gaze to the photograph. His brow wrinkled for just a moment, then he looked back up at Cymin.

"You and the scepter were discovered in the deepest section of the necropolis. It took seven days for the floodwaters to recede to the point that the chamber could be accessed. By then, no one expected, nor was prepared, to discover a survivor. The photograph was taken while the antiquities team located a float they could use to reach you," Lui Dane said.

Seven days. Cymin stole an uneasy glance down to the child in the photograph. He shouldn't have survived. Then he reconsidered the way the child in the photograph clung to the scepter and the faint luminous glow that swathed the boy. He probably owed his life to the Waethir relic. Cymin almost dropped his hand to his abdomen to touch the pearl. But he stopped himself in time.

"Any thoughts about the scepter?" Lui Dane prompted.

I absolutely was not old enough to be financially responsible if it's broken now. Cymin pressed his lips closed on the comment and just shook his head, thinking: *See, Grand Master, I can learn.*

"It clearly holds a number of powerful spells, at least one of which Cymin was able to manifest," Grand Master Ryn said. "Though no doubt the Waethir possess a far greater understanding of the scepter and its capacities."

But they aren't about to share their secrets, Cymin thought, and it occurred to him that the reason for returning this scepter to the Waethir was probably much more complicated than simply returning an antiquity to its people or building friendly relations with Saigrath. One of the best ways to understand a spell—and later recreate it—was to witness it being manifested. To do that, the Chyrenese government would have to turn the scepter over to the Waethir and then observe them. Spy on them.

But why involve me?

"Would you like the opportunity to pay off the entirety of your temple debt in one fell swoop?" Lui Dane asked.

Cymin started at the offer and reflexively looked to Grand Master Ryn. She gave him a gentle smile and an encouraging nod. Cymin emulated her, nodding his agreement, though he wasn't actually certain at all.

"Would you like the opportunity to reclaim and master the spells that saved your life so long ago?" Lui Dane tapped the photograph, and Cymin briefly met that pathetic little boy's desperate stare. "What about seeing the mysteries of the Waethir's homeland for yourself?" Lui Dane coaxed.

Cymin thought of Laithondi, and his fingers grazed the warm pearl pressed against his abdomen. He recalled that strange and wondrous flower drifting in through his window.

Cymin met Lui Dane's cold gaze. These offers weren't without a catch—they were bait—tempting delicacies scattered across the barbs of a fishhook, and if he accepted any one of them, he'd be caught. He understood that the instant he saw Lui Dane's thin lips curve in the slightest smile.

Even knowing as much, Cymin still said, "Yes."

CHAPTER 6

The rest of the night passed in an exhausted daze for Cymin. From signing a number of contracts and stumbling downstairs to his discovery that the throngs of patrons in the Benevolence Hall had multiplied to a raucous chaos of close-packed bodies, Cymin registered almost nothing beyond bone-deep weariness. He managed to find Yinni's table and smiled vacantly at Paeth, Ovelah and Saum. All of them chatted excitedly, and Yinni beamed as she again mentioned joining the crew of a documentary. Saum effused about film stars while Ovelah mumbled and stuttered too quietly for Cymin to even guess her intent. Paeth and Yinni mentioned the Waethir, but beyond that, the details of the girls' conversations flowed past him like a burbling stream rushing over a torpid pebble. Slowly he drifted to sleep.

At some point, he came back to his senses enough to realize that he'd lolled over and flopped his head onto Paeth's slender shoulder. Yinni, Saum and Ovelah seemed to have joined the boisterous crowd, cheering two muscular Orae students as they danced and stripped off their bright red jackets. He jolted upright and self-consciously wiped at the corner of his mouth, hoping that he hadn't been drooling on Paeth as well as using her for a pillow.

"Did all the shouting wake you?" Paeth asked softly. "I tried to cover your ears."

"Sorry." Cymin offered her a groggy apology—not even registering her words. His ears rang and his head ached. "I didn't mean to—"

"It's fine," Paeth assured him with a very kind smile. Then she leaned closer and lowered her voice. "Yinni told me that the explosion this morning hadn't been a planned part of the exhibition but a terrible accident. You were so incredibly brave to step in like that. Thank you."

"You're always quite welcome." In his stupor, Cymin responded automatically as if he'd been waiting on her table. That won him a laugh from Paeth. This close, he could see that her teeth were quite small and that three of the freckles scattered across her nose and cheeks spilled over to her upper lip.

"You must be so tired," Paeth commented. "I don't mind if you lie back against me and rest."

Lolling across someone in a public hall was unseemly enough, but a tuteli man sprawled over a pretty young woman—that ventured into the realm of a punishable offense. Cymin had already had more than enough of fines and battering for one day.

"That's very kind, but I really should get back to my dormitory." Cymin hauled himself from the bench seat and ambled back to tuteli quarters in a daze. He didn't recall undressing or even climbing up into his bunk. He simply fell into the darkness of sleep where his old, chaotic dreams engulfed him.

Screams and smoke filled the air around him. Invading mages in gleaming black armor slaughtered their way up into the mountain stronghold where he stood bleeding. At any moment, they would break through the last defense and ascend to the Heights. Cymin dragged himself up to an immense altar of silverwork and carved bone. His bloody fingers left trails across the silver, while the bone absorbed his blood as if it were its own. Reaching out, he grasped the white scepter that stood integrated into the heart of the altar. As he tore the scepter free, blackened blood spilled from his mouth. It stank of uumthal poison. He swayed on his feet, feeling his life fading with every breath.

He needed to flee with the scepter while he still possessed the strength—before they found him. Battering rams crashed against the gates and his heart hammered in time. His life was almost gone. He had to escape now. And yet he crouched down and wrapped his arms around the limp body slumped against the altar.

I won't let go. I won't. . . .

Cymin woke with a leg dangling over the edge of the top bunk bed and his face pressed into his dormitory pillow. He gasped in a breath of fresh air and flopped onto his back, frowning up at the sigil he'd scraped into the wooden ceiling years ago. Min. The clean, simple strokes reassured him. The jumbled images and agony of his nightmare faded from his mind, leaving him dazed and languid. In his groggy state, all his recollections of the previous day felt unreal. The explosion, meeting Laithondi, agreeing to spy for Lui Dane: all that seemed outrageous and bizarre to him now. Nothing like the familiar and mundane ceiling above him, or the lumpy, herb-stuffed pillow lying next to his face.

Had any of that really occurred?

Then dormitory bells rang and Cymin bolted upright. Nine in the morning? He should have reported to the kitchens two hours ago for his duties. Why hadn't his dorm mates woken him?

He felt oddly clumsy as he struggled to throw off his blanket. His arm brushed the waistband of his underwear, and he felt the celestial pearl hum at his touch. Then he took in the black stitches seaming his fingers and came fully awake.

Yesterday hadn't been a dream. . . .

Not only had he agreed to work for National Security, but he'd signed the contract while hiding a Waethir's celestial pearl on his body. A very uneasy feeling fluttered through his stomach, but he forced himself to ignore it. It was too late for regret or fear—and, in any case, how else could he ever hope to free himself and the temple of his immense debt? He just had to accept the commitment he'd made. Last night, he'd truly said "yes" to Lui Dane and assured him that he could meet his contact the next day at ten.

The next day . . . being today.

Crap!

He was in danger of missing the appointment Lui Dane had arranged. Cymin bounded from his bed, grabbed his wash-kit, snatched up his clothes and sprinted for the dormitory bath. Thankfully, this late in the morning only a few thirsty sparrows populated the place. They flitted out the open windows when Cymin raced in, leaving him his choice of tiled stalls. The only inconvenience in washing after everyone else was the tepid trickle of water left in the shower cisterns. Still, by racing from one stall to another, he managed to shave and completely rinse himself clean before the taps dried up entirely.

He threw on his underclothes and robe, then quickly hid the pearl in the inner pocket of his robe along with his pouch of holy salt and his prayer beads. He secured his work knife and empty coin purse to his sash.

He glanced to the dressing mirror and was momentarily shocked by the line of black stitches running up the side of his head. Thanks to the celestial pearl, his wounds had largely healed, but the long lines of stitches gave the impression of half his face being roughly sewn to his skull.

Not exactly inconspicuous for my first day as a spy.

Cymin quickly snipped the threads and pulled them out with a set of tweezers. Then he considered his hands, briefly wondering how suspicious a complete recovery from surgical incisions in less than a day might seem. The temple's physician, Master Shuun, would certainly raise an eyebrow. However, Cymin was known to be an exceptionally gifted mage, and since only a fool wouldn't attempt to heal himself in this situation, a quick recovery wasn't so remarkable. If he retained some stitches, he could probably even avoid questions about which healing sigils he used to seamlessly mend so many of his wounds. After a moment, he settled on removing the stitches from his fingers, while leaving those on the backs of his hands that had closed the deepest cuts. This way, he could use his hands more freely while still retaining the impression of several lingering, deep wounds.

That done, Cymin ran from the dormitory. The morning breeze retained a shiver of the tropical winter's damp chill. But as Cymin pelted across the temple gardens, he noted signs of summer's fast approach. Quick-growing wildflowers seized upon long dark stretches of freshly tilled soil while countless honeybees swathed the fragrant blossoms festooning trees and shrubs in buzzing gold. The plum trees near the less trafficked Bronze Gate even bore small green drupes that promised an abundance of autumn fruit.

While pretending to observe the trees, Cymin stole more than one glance to the guesthouse where the Waethir were staying. He refused to acknowledge whom he hoped to see. At the Bronze Gate, a fellow tuteli adept waved him through, and Cymin at last abandoned his secret hope of another chance encounter.

You missed your opportunity to dissuade East Deity from meeting his other obligations. Don't blame him in the future, all right?

He rushed into the crowded streets of the rambling Scholars' District.

On this side of Lux Temple, tiny print shops and bookstores dotted nearly every block, filling the gaps between busy restaurants, sprawling winehouses and a multitude of upper-story garrets. Chyre National University students jostled along the sidewalks debating the minutiae of everything from law to fashionable haircuts. The streets rang with bicycle bells as couriers and pedicab drivers shouted at each other. Occasionally, Cymin heard the low whistles of the huge flightless carriage-birds that pulled the glossy carriages of elite citizens through the throngs of bicycles. Even as harried as he was, Cymin always paused to gawk at the towering carriage-birds with their brilliant red crests and long silver-spurred legs.

A particularly striking pair of birds strutted past just when Cymin reached the doors of the Clever Crickets Teahouse. The red carriage they drew behind them glinted with silver filigree, and Cymin noted that two men followed it on bicycles, each balancing a compact moving picture camera on his shoulder like a steel parrot. The carriage stopped further up the street, and as Cymin watched, Una Bayan handed the carriage reins to a young man and jumped down from the driver's seat. She glanced to the two cameramen with an amused smile before reaching out to help someone out of the carriage. Even with a crowd of students passing between them, Cymin couldn't fail to recognize Yinni. She beamed at Una Bayan and said something that made the starlet laugh and pat her shoulder.

So, it had been Una Bayan who'd hired Yinni after all. How fantastic for Yinni! But could his own luck be any worse than to encounter her here, right now? If Yinni spotted him, how would he explain meeting some strange secular man at a teahouse? Worse, how would he explain the presence of his sister to his National Security contact? Cymin hunched behind a painted signboard and peered at the group.

He didn't think Yinni had seen him, so entranced was she with Una Bayan's attention. The cameramen bicycled around the women, one filming their conversation while the other captured the surrounding street scene. Cymin wondered if they were practicing a technique or filming for the actual documentary.

Should he simply bluff it? Greet his sister as he normally would, then just head into the teashop? He decided against it. Not only could that put Yinni in the awkward position of having to introduce him to her employer, but he really didn't want to risk his exchange with Lui Dane's operative being filmed.

Instead, he waited until her back was turned and quickly ducked into the crowded teashop. From somewhere near the back came the sound of an excited radio news announcer reporting on the progress of the Waethir's tour of the capital city. Apparently, they'd spent most of the morning meeting with the heads of various government ministries, exchanging greetings and gifts.

No chance of running into Laithondi at Lux Temple today—either to offer him a meal or to return his celestial pearl to him—he supposed.

Cymin pulled his attention back to his surroundings. The smells of herbal concoctions and old textbooks wafted over him as usual, but what caught his notice today were the stagnant pools of fei'lux drifting near the floor. Overhead, he saw the spell banners hanging limp. In addition, the dozen mechanical crickets in sandalwood cages dangling from the rafters all lay stiff and silent. These must have numbered among the countless fei'lux-driven ancillaries that shut down after the Waethir had dissipated so many fei'lux streams when they descended upon the city yesterday. Even knowing that the brass crickets were merely ancillary devices, Cymin felt a pang of sympathy seeing them toppled onto their backs and sides as if dead.

Without his spell filaments, he didn't know if he could even summon fei'lux, much less restart the spells within the crickets, and he felt hesitant to have an audience for his attempt and possible failure. But at the same time, he wanted some sense of how much magecraft he retained before he met Lui Dane's other agent.

Cymin stole a glance around the teashop, checking if anyone was watching him in the surrounding hustle. The angular young woman working at the tea counter glanced up at him, but she seemed lost in her own thoughts as she exhaled a cloud of cigarette smoke and returned her attention to the booklet she'd been leafing through.

The clientele of students and academics seemed to share the teahouse attendant's preoccupation with the written word. Many gathered around battered tables scattered with newspapers or else perused the floor-to-ceiling bookshelves that lined the far wall and filled much of the overhanging second-story loft.

So, no one was watching. Time to wake the crickets up.

Cymin flexed his hands, and the stagnant fei'lux slowly whirled around his feet and ankles like sluggish water. Cymin felt it pooling around him but couldn't seem to call it to him. He focused more intently, tensing his muscles. But today the fei'lux felt slick as sesame oil. It sloshed over his hand and slipped through his fingers. Only on his third attempt could Cymin draw a stream of fei'lux to his left palm and hold it. It pooled there, feeling thicker than he was used to, but Cymin was relieved to find that he could move fei'lux at all without his spell filaments.

As he drew the fei'lux into his body and circulated it, an odd sensation crept through his gut. Not painful so much as itchy—like a scab about to fall away. He channeled the fei'lux up to the spells etched into the brass crickets and overhanging banners. A fragrant breeze wafted from the banners, and the little guardians popped up, chirping sweet notes. The fei'lux drained from Cymin's body, and the uneasy feeling in his abdomen dissipated, leaving him a little tired. He swayed on his feet but caught himself and glanced nervously around to see if anyone had glimpsed his momentary light-headedness.

No one in the teashop took note of him or the blessings. The crickets' chirps hardly carried over the radio and surrounding conversations, and any passing gusts could have filled the banners. But Cymin felt secretly pleased. The flies, wasps and bees buzzing around dishes of cut fruit and honey jars would soon be banished, and the odors of sweat, sour breath and moldering texts would wash away. In half an hour the slight differences would accumulate to create a subtle air of comfort throughout the space.

East Deity is still compassionate. He just has to take work for National Security, all right?

As he approached the young woman working at the tea counter, he continued to observe the gathered crowd. Most of the clientele were men in their twenties and thirties clothed in green scholar robes—though a few daring, educated women gathered in small groups to study and debate as well.

No one appeared to note Cymin's presence, much less step forward to greet him. Despite Lui Dane's assurance that he only needed to reach the Clever Crickets by ten and the agent would find him, Cymin tried to work out who in the crowd might be observing him. It certainly wasn't the woman at the counter. She looked only at the booklet laid out flat before her. Absently, she extended her hand and stubbed her cigarette out against a concrete ashtray and continued reading.

Cymin glanced to the open booklet. The cheap pulp pages were crammed with smudged text, supposedly revealing the suppressed history from the Age of Wraiths. Cymin skimmed a few passages. This section focused on the old-time practice of offering the excess children of mage-kings to the Wraiths as "diplomatic emissaries," which, in reality, had been a nice term for exchanging hostages, but in this booklet seemed to be code for being stolen away into a mystical harem.

The booklet went on to describe gorgeous Wraiths swooping down on the backs of giant hawks and carrying nubile girls and boys away in nets woven from starlight. Then his gaze caught on three imperial sigils that made up an ancient name. Min and *Roa* were the first two. The third sigil was *Haeyi*, the family name of the most powerful line of mage-kings in Chyre. They had founded the nation and ruled it until the People's Revolution annihilated the entire family. The Haeyi name alone had once commanded so much power and influence that revolutionary leaders banned it as a threat to the nation. In modern texts—if the name had to be mentioned—the sigil was always over-printed by a shroud of thin gray ink, so that its form could barely be discerned. The registry of second-name sigils, which a select few descendants of twice-named nobles were permitted to use, didn't mention it at all.

No one could ever claim the Haeyi sigil as theirs again.

So, printed in its uncensored form on a page, the sigil lent a sense of subversive danger to what otherwise appeared to be historically inspired erotica.

Maybe that was why Cymin couldn't seem to stop staring at the name. Minroa Haeyi. He read the few sentences surrounding it.

Born of the mage-king's third captive courtesan, Minroa was said to be as seductive as his Piiroc mother and as talented in magecraft as his infamous brother, Mage-King Xondir Haeyi. He numbered among the last youths presented to the Wraiths of Saigrath. As a boy of fifteen he was taken and trained in their ways. He soon became infamous for his cunning nature and perverse appetites—

The young woman turned the page, leaving Cymin to wonder what sort of appetites this Minroa fellow had developed among the Wraiths.

Cannibalism? Candied flies? Blue cheeses? Before he could further amuse himself with other absurd possibilities, the illustration that filled the next page seized his attention. A dark-haired, sly-eyed youth stretched languidly across a background of stylized poppy blossoms. He held a wine cup in his right hand, while the long dagger in his left barely disguised his supple nudity.

"He looks like he has interesting plans for his evening," Cymin remarked.

Startling at the sound of Cymin's voice, the young woman working the counter flipped her booklet closed and looked up. A flush colored her cheeks as she met Cymin's gaze, then she glanced down to his brown robes and her expression turned pitying.

"Welcome, tuteli. Charity water is in the jug. Help yourself." She pointed to the left of the counter where a large gray crock stood with a dipper and a small stack of wax-leaf cups. She returned to her booklet.

"Blessings to you, kind benefactor, and my thanks," Cymin murmured.

He would have chided her for assuming, after only a glance, that he couldn't afford to buy anything. But he had to admit that she wasn't wrong. He didn't possess a single paper scrap of secular money. And he didn't actually want to disturb her reading, either.

So, he strolled to the crock and ladled himself a little cup of the water. He was pleased to note that someone had flavored it with lemon peels and scattered mint leaves across the surface. A few bees rested on the floating leaves, also partaking of the teashop's charity water.

Outside the teashop, clock towers rang out ten. Inside, an announcer on the radio reminded listeners that northern storms in Yanyeo had delayed several passenger trains and that curfew in the capital had been lifted for the Spring Festival, but fireworks required permits. At the same time, a group of people came through the doors. The woman at the counter straightened and hid her booklet away under the counter. To Cymin's horror, Yinni, Una Bayan and the two cameramen strode in. The shorter man still filmed, but the taller of the two men had stowed his camera away and now simply carried a cigarette in his hand.

The instant after Una Bayan swept through the doors, the entire teashop quieted. People all around stared at the actress, some openly gawking, while others studied her more surreptitiously from behind their books and teacups. The sharp contrast of her pale complexion, black bobbed hair and vivid red pin-striped suit made her quite eye-catching. Her trademark scarlet lips quirked in a small pleased smile. She stopped beneath the sandalwood cricket cages, directing Yinni's attention up to the guardian crickets.

Though Yinni's hair was shaved to stubble and she wore plain brown tuteli robes, her height and athletic grace made her as striking a figure as the actress. An almost radiant beauty suffused her clear features and sweeping dark eyes.

"Whenever I begin a new project, I come here to listen to the crickets, drink a cup of Red Fortune tea and purchase a book," Una Bayan pronounced. "It's one of my favorite rituals. I'm so happy you can join me."

The shorter cameraman shadowed the actress and Cymin's sister, while the taller man crushed the ember of his cigarette between two fingers and scanned the shop with an indifferent expression. He was dark-haired, fit and very well groomed and, like Una, he seemed to be in his thirties. As they locked eyes, Cymin realized he was the same handsome man who'd stung Cymin's eyes with an obscurity spell during the procession the previous day.

Cymin averted his gaze before he suffered another spell, but not before Yinni caught sight of him. Her expression brightened. As she and Una Bayan strode to a long common table, Yinni beckoned him to join them. Cymin smiled but hesitated.

"I'll get the drinks," the tall cameraman announced. Then he strode towards Cymin. "Come, give me a hand, will you?"

As a tuteli, Cymin had been groomed to respond to requests for assistance. So, out of reflex, he moved to the man's side at the tea counter.

"Cymin, right?" The man asked, but he didn't wait for confirmation. "Your temple sister, Yinni, has had nothing but good things to say about you."

"Oh . . . well, I've got nothing but good to say about her, too." Cymin was a little at a loss for what to do. There was no way he could meet with an NS agent while rubbing shoulders with Una Bayan and being filmed.

Lui Dane had only given him one order so far, and he was already screwing it up.

"I'm Mazilane," the cameraman supplied. Then he turned a winning smile on the young woman at the counter and ordered a variety of teas as well as a few dishes of snacks. He glanced to Cymin. "Waterseeds and Three Bitters tea for you?"

Cymin blinked at him for a dazed instant.

Those were the exact code words.

Was it possible that the man just happened to use the code words that Lui Dane's agent was supposed to say to him?

Was it?

No, Cymin decided it couldn't be a coincidence. But the man played the entire exchange off so casually that Cymin felt taken aback. The fact that Mazilane seemed to be an intimate of Una Bayan's struck Cymin as even more bewildering. National Security had an agent so close to Una Bayan? Their most outspoken critic?

But of course they did. That was the point of spies, wasn't it? To infiltrate and secretly undermine enemies, while appearing to be on their side. He knew that, but somehow he hadn't really considered what it could mean in terms of the real world.

Cymin forced himself to smile at Mazilane. He remembered the words he'd been instructed to give in response. "I am fond of waterseeds, but I'll pass on the bitters for a cup of Glad Meeting. Thank you."

"Of course," Mazilane agreed, and then he handed a colorful selection of secular money to the woman behind the counter. She sorted it away into a register, then hustled from the counter to fill clay teapots and gather the dishes of seeds and fruit. As she placed the dishes on the counter, Mazilane passed them along to Cymin, who neatly stacked them up his arm. Serving in the Benevolence Hall had long ago prepared Cymin to balance any number of dishes. If called upon to do so, he could even spin a few on his fingertips.

Though he restrained himself to simply transporting the dishes this morning.

"Well done," Mazilane commented, then he took a teapot in each hand and headed to the long table with Cymin trailing him.

Mazilane plonked the teapots on the table with little ceremony before dropping into the chair across from Una Bayan. With his foot, he pushed the seat next to his out for Cymin. As he sat down, still wrestling with his uncertainty about the entire situation, it suddenly occurred to Cymin that he didn't know if Mazilane alone was Lui Dane's agent or if others in the documentary crew were also NS agents. Was it possible that Una Bayan herself was a spy?

Given her well-established campaigns against National Security's restrictions of the press and public speech, that seemed very unlikely. The shorter cameraman—who appeared star-struck every time he looked at Una Bayan—seemed too unaware of everyone else to be much of a spy. And as for Yinni, her admiration for Una Bayan stemmed from the starlet's fearless opposition to National Security. Lui Dane could never have recruited his sister.

So, likely Mazilane alone was his contact. Cymin bowed his head and bit into a waterseed. He had no idea of what else he should do.

"We were just talking about you," Una Bayan informed Cymin. "Yinni said that those assholes in NS added some absurd property fines to your temple debt in order to force decades more of service in their Storm Towers out of you."

Cymin nodded, and Yinni offered him an encouraging smile. He bowed his head and ate another seed.

"Well, Minister Dane can go and fu—" Una Bayan began but Mazilane cut her off, clearing his throat.

Una Bayan laughed. "What? I was only going to say that the minister could go and fuuu-und someone else to do that work. NS already exploits temple debts to take criminal advantage of the tuteli. After Yinni told us what you did yesterday, Cymin, it's obvious that you deserve better than being worked to death in an isolated Storm Tower."

Yinni glowed with delight at these words. They moved Cymin as well. Not many Chyrenese paid attention to how many tuteli were sent to serve the Storm Towers or how few returned. Those who did survive often suffered terrible spell-burns and lifelong disabilities. On the rare occasions the matter was publicized, the tuteli were generally depicted as either brave stoics or as object lessons, demonstrating the tragedies that befell the children of citizens who succumbed to gambling, drug addiction and other vices leading to debt.

"Well—" Una Bayan leaned forward and offered Cymin a charming and conspiratorial smile. "It turns out that Mazilane is short an assistant, and we're looking for someone with mage training. And since, legally, working for the Ministry of Culture is a valid form of National Service, how about you throw your lot in with a bunch of actors? Join us to follow the Wraiths into the north instead of letting NS officers drag you off to the Storm Towers? I can't promise that the work will be glamorous or easy, but it should be an adventure, and you won't have to suppress your fellow citizens or suffer alone in some far-off tower. All the funding has already been secured, so it's just a matter of saying yes. How about it?"

Across the table Yinni nodded at him, and her eyes lit with glee. She must have spent much of last night and this morning convincing Una Bayan and her associates to find a place for him. Gratitude welled up within him, but the feeling was bittersweet.

For a moment, Cymin really wished that he'd heard this offer before he'd met with Lui Dane. But then Cymin stole a sidelong glance at Mazilane. The other man met his gaze with a sardonic smile, and Cymin realized that the matter probably wasn't so simple. Everything from the need for another assistant to Cymin arriving here at the Clever Crickets just in time to bump into Una Bayan had likely been arranged on Lui Dane's orders.

Cymin felt a sudden terrible guilt.

Was he now going to be spying on Una Bayan as well as the Waethir? He'd always enjoyed her acting and respected her outspoken politics. The fact that she'd given his sister a means to escape the Storm Towers made him admire her even further. Cymin felt a sharp pang of remorse just looking at Yinni and knowing that he had sold himself to the enemy of her personal hero.

He opened his mouth and very nearly refused the offer.

But then he recalled the reason he agreed to work for Lui Dane in the first place. First, he would escape the danger of serving in a Storm Tower for decades without spell filaments. But beyond that, he'd brought a monumental debt on Lux Temple. If Cymin couldn't clear it himself, then others in the temple would be forced to take up the burden in the form of yearly interest. The people who'd raised him and cared for him—Master Tam, Master Shuun, Grand Master Ryn and, most of all, Yinni—would all suffer for his rash decision.

"You could do worse, kid, believe me." Mazilane spoke lightly as if teasing him. But Cymin felt certain there was a warning in his easy words. The other man must have recognized Cymin's ambivalence.

"Yes, I'd love to join you," Cymin told Una Bayan. "Thank you so much."

Una Bayan lifted her chin as if filled with pride, while Yinni gave a quiet cheer, all but dancing in her seat. Even the other cameraman nodded happily. Cymin didn't know if he shared Una Bayan's and Yinni's pleasure in saving him from the Storm Towers or if he was just glad for another body to lug equipment. Either way, Cymin lifted his hands in thanks to each of them in turn.

"Welcome to our troupe." Una Bayan pushed another dish of salted seeds to Cymin. "We've got an adventure ahead of us, and I'm glad you'll be part of it!"

"I am as well," Cymin replied, and he didn't feel like he was lying. It seemed so much better to accept Una Bayan's proposal than the one Lui Dane had offered, though he knew that in reality they were one and the same thing.

CHAPTER 7

In an odd reiteration of the previous evening with Lui Dane, Cymin again sipped tea and chewed waterseeds as he signed a binding work contract. But this morning, his surroundings were relaxed. The teashop was filled with diffuse light, mechanical cricket songs and easy conversation. The people sharing his table smiled and raised their cups, toasting their shared enterprise.

Yinni's voice rang as if she were cheering a great conquest, while Mazilane's tone sounded more sardonic. Una Bayan elbowed him, then folded Cymin's contract away into her neat red purse. At the same time, the shorter, more plain-faced cameraman introduced himself as Hiral and pointed out the basic mechanisms of the ancillary film camera perched on his shoulder. Yinni, too, studied the camera with fascination.

It was smaller than Cymin had imagined a motion picture camera to be, only a little larger than the hunting falcon that obviously inspired its overall design. The steel-gray housing that resembled its head stared at Cymin with two large black lenses. Though as he looked more closely, Cymin realized that numerous smaller lenses and whisker-like antennae studded the head and ran all the way down the dull gray body to the neat fan of its tail. Thin metal plates protected the camera's folded wings much like a beetle's carapace, but Cymin could just discern the gleam of tiny gold spells shining up from the crevices between the planes of metal. The weathered impression of the sigil *Soir* which represented "human thought" marked the camera's chest. At its base were two powerful black clasps that Cymin imagined could grip almost any surface, be it a tripod, rocky promontory or slender twig.

Cymin found the ingenuity of the ancillary so distracting and delightful that much of his earlier trepidation faded. He didn't know how to be a spy, nor was he certain that he wanted to learn, but when it came to matters of magecraft, he felt entirely comfortable.

If only being on the film crew could really be my job. I'd be great at it.

Then, taking a sip of his tea, he decided that he ought to just pretend that he truly was part of this film crew. He'd feel much better and probably behave more naturally if he allowed himself to be immersed in the illusion.

"Soir is Mazilane's ancillary. He's a real beauty," Hiral explained. "Most of the cameras you, I and Yinni will be using won't be so finicky or sophisticated."

Mazilane cast the camera, and Cymin, a rather amused smile. Cymin had no idea why. Before he could give it much thought, Una Bayan called their little party back to order and began to work out the day's schedule.

"Yinni, I'd like you and Hiral to join me for a visit to the Grand Rail Train Office. I've heard rumors about problems with the northern lines to Yanyeo. I want to be absolutely sure that all our travel permits are in order, just in case we have to make a sudden change in our route."

"What's happened to the northern lines?" Cymin asked.

"I'm not certain," Una Bayan replied. "I've overheard my father complaining to his security officers recently. It might be excess fei'lux overwhelming the Storm Towers again, or it may be Piiroc extremists sabotaging the Haelon Rail Lines. With the Waethir visiting, security is tight, so it's difficult to know what's real and what's a smoke screen. Still, better to pull a few strings and be a little extra prepared."

Cymin didn't need to ask about Una Bayan's connections in the Ministry of Transportation. Everyone knew both her parents and her eldest brother held leading positions there, while her aunt and uncle directed departments in the National Treasury and the Ministry of Culture and Education, respectively. It was easy to forget because the actress herself was so publicly outspoken against the centralized power of the ministries and their chronic nepotism. Cymin wondered if their family dinners were wildly fractious or largely silent.

"Mazi, your plans for filming today are . . . ?" Una Bayan cast Mazilane a speculative look.

"I'll take Adept Cymin with me to the Palace Complex to capture footage of the Wraiths touring the place. Even if NS shuts us down, it'll be a good opportunity to introduce Cymin to the camera equipment and the fine art of dodging police."

"Police?" Cymin and Yinni objected in almost the same breath. The threat of police and security had never been something to joke about for her or Cymin.

"Mazi's just teasing you." Una Bayan shot Mazilane a chastising glance. He responded with a shrug. "We have all the film permits we need. What I'm actually concerned about right now is how we approach the Wraiths. I don't want to alienate them by shoving cameras in their faces and barraging them with questions. They need to be treated with respect and be given time to get comfortable being filmed." Una Bayan sipped her tea. "We need them on our side when it comes to crossing the border from Yanyeo into Saigrath. We should treat them quite carefully."

"I had the same thought at first, but last night I managed to chat two of them up, and they weren't exactly shy creatures of exquisite sensitivity." Mazilane paused to frown at his tea. Cymin noted the sharp tang of bitters drifting from the cup. Mazilane slugged back a second drink. "They were both very interested in my cameras, photography and moving pictures. They seemed disappointed when I told them it was too dark to take their photos, but I promised that I'd do it if I ran into them again. So, if we contrive to come across them at the palace compound, I'm certain those two at least will be delighted to be filmed. If the other three are more nervous, then I'll use the excuse of teaching Cymin here about how the equipment works to introduce the Wraiths to the technology too. Maybe they can take turns filming each other and get comfortable having the camera around that way."

"Which two of the Wraiths did you talk to?" Una Bayan set her teacup down and studied Mazilane with interest. "How did you get past security to meet them?"

Cymin wondered the same thing—though he suspected that he knew how Mazilane had gotten around the security officers. He was one of their own, after all.

"It's all down to charm, patience and relentless distribution of sexual favors," Mazilane said offhandedly.

The other cameraman appeared both scandalized and awed. Yinni frowned, but Una Bayan rolled her eyes and laughed.

"Don't scare my new hires, Mazi," Una Bayan chided. "They aren't used to your sense of humor yet."

Mazilane sighed. "Alright, I admit it. Credit for the encounter actually goes to Lux Temple's lack of certain amenities." Mazilane shook his head, and a lock of his dark hair fell over his right eye. He swept it back in a motion that seemed both naturally graceful and practiced at the same time. "I ran into them when we were all looking for the toilets. After locating the facilities, we all had a laugh and then struck up a conversation on the way back to the guesthouse courtyard. They call themselves Bailon and Eirjiri."

Bailon was the name of the Deity of the Sky, while the name Eirjiri belonged to the Deity of the Earth.

Yinni's brows rose at the audacity of mortals claiming the names of deities for their own.

"Not exactly demure, these Waethir," Mazilane remarked.

"That is rather bold," Una Bayan commented.

Cymin smiled to himself thinking: *Just wait until you meet Laithondi.*

Una Bayan took a mechanical pencil and small notebook from her red silk handbag and wrote down the names. Cymin noted that she didn't use the imperial sigils taught to mages, but instead penned them in common phonetic script that most anyone could read. She glanced to Mazilane. "Impressions?"

"Both girls have strong features and great laughs. Eirjiri looks like a teenager, but from the way she interacted with Bailon, I think she must be older—at least in her twenties. They weren't particularly formal, but they still managed to shut down any inquiries I made about the border and crossing it," Mazilane provided. "As for filming them, as long as we soften the lighting and don't put them in full profile, they'll look good. They're not shy but a bit . . . eccentric. Definitely eccentric."

"Eccentric is good on film." Una Bayan flipped back a page in her notebook. Cymin glimpsed a list of names. He recognized several and guessed that Una Bayan was already compiling a list of the adept mages whom the Waethir were most likely to take with them to Saigrath. He wasn't surprised that Saum and Nyle were the first two candidates penciled in. Paeth and Ovelah appeared below them. Una Bayan tapped her pencil beside Ovelah's name.

"I don't know what we're going to do if that Ovelah is chosen," Una Bayan said. "How can she be so dull? The girl Paeth is her sister, isn't she?"

"They're twins," Yinni provided quickly. "Ovelah is half an hour younger."

"She's like a worn-out carbon copy. So meek. It's like pulling teeth to get her to utter a sentence. When she finally does, it's half-stutters and whispers." Una Bayan shook her head.

"She takes a little time to warm up to strangers," Yinni put in, quick to defend her friend. "Once she's comfortable with you, she can actually be fun and insightful. Isn't that right, Cy?"

Cymin nodded but refrained from adding his own impression of Ovelah. Once she grew comfortable, her conversation style became a barrage of half-formed but relentless questions. At times, it felt like being interrogated by a friendly ghost.

Una Bayan considered Yinni and then Cymin.

"You're probably right that I should give her a chance. My Boshyin school bias is just getting the better of me." Una Bayan's expression turned rueful. "Ryde Academy girls were always the toughest to beat, back in the day. Mazi, do you remember that absolute beast who thrashed us every year?"

"No," Mazilane stated, and there was something about his sour tone and Una Bayan's amused expression that made Cymin think there was a larger private story behind the interaction, something Una Bayan enjoyed needling Mazilane over.

"You do!" Una Bayan said. "During the Spring Exhibition our final year, she nearly cut Mazi's head off."

Cymin glanced to Mazilane and noticed that a fine scar really did run from just below his jaw to his larynx. The cameraman, Hiral, peered at the scar as well.

"And whose fault was that, actually?" Mazilane responded.

"I'm not to blame for her lack of good humor," Una Bayan responded. She gave Yinni a conspiratorial glance and added under her breath, "One moment you're harmlessly teasing a Ryde Academy girl about where her boyfriend spent the night, and the next second, she's attempting to decapitate your best friend. Really. You can see how I got a poor first impression. But that said, I do like Saum. She's like a little keg of cream cakes and gunpowder."

Yinni and Cymin exchanged a knowing smile. Saum was a tireless machine in a fight, but off the field of battle, she was the single most starstruck girl either of them had ever encountered. She was an ardent fan of an ever-changing constellation of handsome actors. Just in passing conversations with her, Cymin had learned the horoscopes, heights, shoe sizes and dessert preferences of all top five of this season's leading heartthrobs.

"She's incredibly energetic," Yinni said. "But no one who's fought her has lost their head, so there's nothing to worry about there." She cast a glance to Mazilane, and he gave a dry laugh in response.

"What about the tall red-haired boy? Xaon?" Una Bayan asked. She tapped her pencil next to the name. Cymin perked up, recalling the genial and muscular redhead who'd toasted Nyle and Saum for winning champion rings the previous night in Benevolence Hall.

"Nineteen. Extremely skilled with a sword," Mazilane replied. "Definitely not shy—after Hiral commented on his hair color, he offered to show us his pubic hair to prove it was natural. He's very likely to be chosen along with his classmate, Jeshri."

"And do we know anything about the classmate?" Una Bayan inquired as she jotted down notes next to Xaon's name.

"Jeshri, also nineteen years old. Hails from Yanyeo's upper class but has boarded in the capital since he was six." Again, Mazilane supplied an answer. "Brawny swordsman. Black hair and a thick beard. The beard makes him seem more mature . . . up until he opens his mouth, that is."

"Oh yes, him I remember!" Una Bayan nodded and jotted down a note. "He stayed late at the hall, laughed a lot and tried to give us all a strip show after he got really drunk. What is it about the boys from Orae Academy that they can never keep their clothes on? We'll have to watch for that while filming. We don't want footage cut by censors because one of them is running around in the background with his dick hanging out."

Cymin suppressed a laugh, and Yinni covered her smile with her hand.

"Any others that seem likely to be picked?" Una Bayan asked.

None of them answered right away, but all of them looked thoughtful

"This might sound strange," Yinni spoke up before Cymin could. "But I think there's a possibility that the student from Chohe Institute might be picked. Kimrin—"

"*Whooo, Whooo*, the owl-boy?" Cymin wasn't certain how likely of a candidate he could be. Not unless the Waethir were looking for comedic relief.

Hiral snorted at Cymin's description and Mazilane just shook his head, but Una Bayan grinned.

"The flying boy with the thick spectacles and bright feathered cap." Una Bayan tapped her lower lip with her mechanical pencil. "You're right, he did look a little like an owl."

"His fight was absurd," Yinni admitted. "But afterwards, I kept thinking about how he managed to keep fei'lux flowing while he was tumbling around in a whirlwind, and the fact that he recovered right away when he touched the ground. Everyone was laughing, including his opponent, but he won the match."

"You have a good point," Mazilane commented. "Owl-boy might not have been as out of control of the situation as he pretended to be."

"Or even if he was, he kept his fighting spirit up." Una Bayan added Kimrin's name to her notebook.

"Did a girl named Ife attend this year? She was part of a scythe team." Cymin asked. He remembered Ife's name particularly because it was written with the same sigil as the crescent moon, which was the shape of her scythe blade. Her speed and the clean quality of her viridian-tinged spells had actually reminded him a great deal of Yinni's magecraft.

"Yes," Yinni responded, but her lip curled like he'd farted in her face.

Cymin shot her a questioning glance.

"I'm a little biased against her because she's a complete bitch. She probably sleeps with a know-it-all expression on her face. And even when she says something that seems nice, it's a little too nice to be sincere, if you know what I mean." Yinni sipped her tea and then sighed. "But you're right to mention her. She and that snotty friend of hers, Zevlyn, both tore through their opponents when they fought in the doubles. The only combatant who came close to beating them was a really tiny girl from Chohe Institute. She was almost too fast and small to target."

"Quin," Mazilane supplied the name, then looked to Una Bayan. "Director Berd's niece. We met her at the Rose Festival. You called her a human hummingbird."

"The sugar drinker who never sat still." Una Bayan appeared theatrically aghast. "We'll never get her in focus. She's going to be a quivering blur throughout the entire film. You don't really think she'll be picked, do you?"

"Nearly certain of it," Mazilane replied. "The two Wraiths I met last night were talking about her as well as the scythe team Cymin mentioned."

Una Bayan frowned but then jotted the three names down in her notebook and crossed another two off. She stared down at her list, and Cymin peered at the ten names and odd notations.

"So, if we're correct," Una Bayan said. "We will be filming the following: Saum, a powder keg of sweet cream. Two muscular strippers—"

"Xaon and Jeshri," Mazilane supplied the names.

"An owl and a hummingbird—"

"Kimrin and Quin," Mazilane added.

"A matched set of mean girls with scythes—"

"Ife and Zevlyn."

"Bright and dim twins—" Una Bayan put a tick mark in her book.

"Paeth and Ovelah," Mazilane responded.

"Ovelah isn't dim," Yinni objected.

"I don't mean to insult your friend, my dear. Think of it like the Mirror Constellation; one a bright star, another more . . . distant." Una Bayan drew a large and small star beside their names. "It's just a device to help me remember everyone more easily. We have to come up with things like this all the time to remember lines for films."

Yinni nodded, though Cymin knew she wasn't entirely convinced.

"And last is the Porcelain Prince," Una Bayan snapped her notebook closed.

"Who?" Cymin asked.

"Nyle, obviously," Yinni informed him.

"How is he a Porcelain Prince?" Cymin objected.

"Gorgeous face, perfect body, elegant superior expression and hardly ever speaks a word to riffraff like us. He's the best of Boshyin's schoolyard kingdom," Yinni replied as if it was obvious.

Cymin scowled. He couldn't refute any of that, though he wished he could. He popped a waterseed into his mouth to keep from saying something petty. He felt certain that if he and Yinni had possessed the money or connections to enter Boshyin, or any of the other mage schools, they would have numbered among the candidates. But focusing on that wouldn't do any good. It would just make him feel more bitter and envious.

We're both still going to Saigrath. What's there to sulk about?

"I'll ask a couple of friends at the Department of Census and Records to dig around and see what more we can find for interview questions later," Mazilane addressed this to Una Bayan, who nodded in agreement. Mazilane then set his tea aside and fished a cigarette case out of his pocket but didn't open it. He looked to Cymin. "In the meantime, we need to get moving if we're going to catch the Wraiths at the Palace Complex."

"Oh. Right." Cymin had really hoped he could get in a meal, but now didn't seem like the time. Hungry as he was, he stuffed the remaining waterseeds into the outer pocket of his robe and slugged back the last of his tea.

Mazilane motioned to Hiral, and the other man immediately handed his camera over. Mazilane swung it onto his shoulder, and even at a distance, Cymin felt the rush of fei'lux that flared between the man and the machine. The camera's dark lenses rotated, and golden sparks seemed to light up their depths. Its steel clasps flexed like a cat's claws kneading Mazilane's broad shoulder. Then without a further word, Mazilane started for the door.

After offering a respectful nod to Una Bayan and Hiral and exchanging a quick hug with Yinni, Cymin raced after Mazilane. He caught up to the man half a block down the street, just in time to feel the fei'lux all around them surge to Mazilane's left hand. Then he caught hold of the camera with his right hand. In an instant, he saturated the camera's spells with perfectly tempered fei'lux and then hurled it straight up into the air. Golden spells all across it flared, and Cymin had to narrow his eyes against the glare. The gray casing of the camera unfolded into long sliver wings as it soared high above them.

"What are we filming?"

"Nothing. It's just a pain in the ass to carry Soir on a public tram," Mazilane stated.

"Will Soir follow us?" Cymin craned his head back, following the camera as it glided in slow circles overhead. If he hadn't known better, he might have mistaken its silhouette for that of a hawk or eagle.

"I have it tethered." Mazilane tapped a metallic band on his wrist. Cymin had taken it for an ancillary wristwatch previously, but now he noticed that the steel casing housed two circular displays. One looked like a compass, while the second flickered like it was reflecting patches of the sky. "If you stick around, I'll teach you how to use it. For now, don't worry about it."

Mazilane strode ahead, and again Cymin followed him. After two blocks, they caught the public tram. Mazilane bought his ticket with secular bills, while Cymin held up his prayer beads. The conductor waved Cymin to the back of the tram with the postal sacks. Mazilane scowled and followed him. They both stood, leaving the canvas seats for those younger or older than themselves. Though at this hour only a few passengers occupied the tram, and all of them were seated at the front where the wind screens protected them from gusts and road dust.

"Here." Mazilane handed Cymin a wad of colorful paper bills. Cymin accepted them with awed delight. He rarely saw, much less held, secular money. The elaborate designs printed across the colored paper lent the humble red bills and the torn yellow ones the beauty of small treasures.

"Don't look so happy," Mazilane snapped. "It's not much, and I'm only giving it to you because I don't want to waste the rest of my day playing daddy, trailing you around and paying your way."

"A jackal is always grateful for a meal, whether a rabbit provides it gladly or not." Cymin emulated Master Tam's benevolent tone as he continued to smile at Mazilane.

Mazilane shook his head and muttered, "Great, another wiseass to add to the company."

They rode in silence. Cymin counted his money. Three red bills, a torn yellow and half a green bill. A total of thirty-six credits, more than he'd ever had at one time in his life. He carefully tucked the secular money away into the inner pocket of his robe.

Mazilane tapped a cigarette from his case and lifted it to his lips, then he gave Cymin an expectant look. Cymin stared back at him, feeling like he'd missed something.

"Can you light it?" Mazilane asked. His gaze dropped meaningfully to Cymin's stitched hands.

"Assuredly," Cymin responded, though he did wonder why Mazilane hadn't just made the request outright.

Maybe he's lost track of what he needs to be tight-lipped about and what he doesn't.

Using fei'lux to light incense, candles and lamps was a common practice in Lux Temple. Cymin just hadn't ever considered manifesting a flame—even a small one—so near another person's face. But now he guessed that Mazilane wanted to test how well he could manipulate fei'lux while stripped of his spell filaments.

He was glad he'd practiced on the little brass crickets earlier.

Cymin raised his left hand and stared intently at Mazilane's mouth. He found he was actually rather nervous. It would be so easy to burn him if he wasn't very, very careful. After hesitating a few moments, he noticed Mazilane's arched brow.

"It's fine if you can't." Mazilane's lips curled in a smile. "I'm told lots of men have trouble performing under pressure."

Cymin scowled at him.

It's not me that's the problem. It's you. I'm not certain your face will withstand the force of East Deity's prowess.

Cymin suppressed the retort—it was really beneath him to let Mazilane bait him.

His fingers shook with the effort, but after a moment, Cymin managed to capture a wisp of fei'lux with his left hand. He drew the sigil for fire with his right and sent the fei'lux rushing into it. With a flick of his fingers, he tossed the hot white spark to the tip of the cigarette.

The pandan-perfumed paper and blended tobacco caught light at once. There was another scent as well—one Cymin could only identify as fungal. Mazilane drew in a deep breath but turned his head when he exhaled, so that none of the smoke rolled over Cymin's face.

A moment later, he pinched out the ember and returned the partially smoked cigarette to his silver case.

"So, you still have some control over fei'lux. Good," Mazilane said. "Have you used any sort of camera before?"

"No," Cymin admitted.

"Recording equipment?"

"Never." Cymin shook his head.

Mazilane frowned, then asked, "Any good with machines?"

"I've repaired temple bicycles and patched up the water pump once."

This seemed to hearten Mazilane somewhat. He checked his watch, or rather the tether to the camera soaring overhead. The compass needle followed the tram's route through the Scholars' District and into the business center of the city. The second display fluttered with images of the upper stories of buildings as well as brief glimpses of the street below and the roof of the tram. Mazilane pulled his cuff down over the tether, covering both displays from Cymin's curious gaze.

His attention returned to Cymin.

"Ever used a pistol?" Mazilane asked.

"Never."

"Rifle?"

"I've never even held any gun," Cymin said.

"Ever thrown a fight?" Mazilane raised his brows.

"No." Cymin couldn't suppress the offense in his voice. When he fought, it had always been for the honor and pride of Lux Temple and the tuteli. "Have you?"

"Plenty of times," Mazilane responded. "Sometimes the smartest move is to let someone else think they've won."

Again he paused, studying Cymin's face closely, then he asked quietly, "Ever killed anyone?"

"No!" Cymin's indignation turned to horror at just the thought. At most, he'd bruised his opponents, but he'd never fought any of them with the intention of doing them genuine harm. Not even Nyle or the other snotty students from the Boshyin School.

Cymin opened his mouth to ask Mazilane if he'd ever taken a life, but then didn't dare. Mazilane continued to stare into his eyes for a while, as if waiting for the question. Cymin found the cold quality of his expression almost as unnerving as the inhuman faces of NS Marshals.

The tram rumbled to a stop and a cluster of tourists hurried on, excitedly chattering about their next destination. Several children showed off postcards to an older couple, who Cymin guessed were their grandparents. A little girl peered at Cymin's robes and offered a shy wave. He waved back but didn't take offense when the older woman drew her attention away from him to the view outside. The children hooted and whooped as the tram swooped down the steep hills, descending to the riverside avenues that lead to the Palace Complex.

"So, fourteen years ago you were the kid in the flooded necropolis," Mazilane said quietly.

Cymin frowned, recalling the humiliating photograph and knowing that Mazilane must have seen it even before meeting him. He nodded.

"If I can get it back into your hands," Mazilane asked, "will the Wraiths' scepter respond to you again?"

"I have no idea," Cymin admitted, though for just an instant the feeling of gripping the bone-white scepter seemed to flicker at the edge of his memory. Then it vanished. "I was too young to remember touching it the first time. But even if it doesn't, we only need to witness the Waethir manifesting its spells to eventually understand how it works. That shouldn't be too difficult, should it?"

"Yeah. Maybe they'll hand over their state secrets and the keys to the Hallow Gates while they're being so generous to us." Mazilane gave an acerbic snort and looked out at the street as if he couldn't bear the sight of Cymin's naïve face.

Cymin shrugged. Laithondi had gifted him a celestial pearl just the night before. "You never know."

Pink and white blossoms of flowering cherry and apricot trees lined the sidewalks, while stark gray government buildings rose behind them.

"Look, you're cute, and I'm sure your can-do attitude has gotten you plenty of head pats from the fair-minded codgers at the temple. But what you're signing on for now isn't a game, so let me give you a last chance to step back." Mazilane kept his voice low, despite the hum of surrounding spells and excited conversations. "Because if you stay with me, then from this point on, there will be no way out. And you may end up changing every answer you just gave me. You understand?"

Cymin nodded, though he knew for certain that he'd never kill anyone. Understanding didn't mean agreeing. Mazilane narrowed his eyes at him as if he sensed Cymin's rebellious thoughts.

"You do not want to test me, fresh meat," Mazilane said. "It won't be a fight you'll win or get back up from. I promise you."

"I understand," Cymin stated firmly.

"No. You sure as shit don't understand." Mazilane swore softly under his breath. "If you did, you wouldn't be giving me that fresh-faced hopeful attitude."

Cymin understood why Mazilane didn't want to work with him. Cymin wasn't naturally suited to be a spy, nor had he been trained for the work. But he also couldn't afford to refuse the job. He'd already signed a contract with Lui Dane. He just had to make the best he could of the situation and hope that he could find a way to pay his debts and keep his conscience clean at the same time. So far, just not thinking about it too much seemed the best choice. Cymin watched the cityscape roll past. The modern buildings thinned, and more and more ornate, gilded structures from the ruinous Age of the Mage-Kings came into view.

"All right, then," Mazilane said at last. "From here on out, you work for me. You learn what I teach you and keep up with me. When the time comes, you do *exactly* as I say."

Cymin just nodded.

"Ministry officials handed the scepter over to the Wraiths early this morning," Mazilane went on. "So right now, your objective is to keep a close watch on them—and it. Be sweet, soppy, sexy or stupid. Whatever it takes, make them want to keep you around."

The tram slowed to a stop in front of a rolling landscape of blooming azaleas and granite-paved footpaths. Beyond the azalea gardens, gold gates topped with finials of divine wae and heavenly beasts rose up. The bell of an ancient clock tower rang out the eleventh hour of morning as Cymin and Mazilane hopped off the tram at the Palace Complex.

"Right on time," Mazilane murmured.

Just ahead of them, four NS marshals escorted the five Waethir past clots of gawking tourists and through the ornate gold gates of the ticket office. Cymin instantly picked Laithondi's tall figure out from among his companions. It was probably a matter of mere chance, but Laithondi glanced back over his shoulder at the same moment. When their gaze met, Laithondi immediately turned his attention away and strode after the marshals. Cymin's heart sank.

Laithondi had already rejected him as a candidate last night. What if he objected to Cymin joining the film crew on the journey north? What would he do then?

Mazilane pushed Cymin into the ticket line. "It's too late to fret now, little jackal. Time to go get your meat."

CHAPTER 8

During the course of his work as a tuteli, Cymin had visited the Palace Complex several times to perform blessings, demonstrate archaic temple ceremonies and serve at fundraising banquets. He knew that if he walked to the staff entry in the east wall and showed his prayer beads, he'd be free to wander the general grounds, gawking at the ornate buildings and observing the extravaganza of tourists flooding in and out of them.

But today he didn't have to surreptitiously peer into windows or pretend to be working in some distant hall.

Today he possessed secular money. Enough to purchase a "Royal Key" ticket, which entitled him to stay the entire day and enter all the exhibits, shows and gardens. For a moment, he imagined exploring the complex at his leisure. He'd search out paintings from an age before Lux Temple fell under NS management, back when tuteli Grand Masters commanded enough power to pose genuine threats to the mage-kings. He could explore the vast armory filled with Hundred Deaths Armor, which he'd only ever darted into one time, after giving a holiday performance.

And then, after a meal, he'd climb to the peak of the palace roof and stand in the spot where a revolutionary tuteli archer was said to have felled half the last mage-king's personal guards.

Or he might come across an adult-only exhibit featuring relics of illicit love affairs between princes, mage-warriors and poets. There were rumors that the historians at the palace kept a secret trove of such things stored in the back rooms, far from the eyes of children and government ministers.

The thought alone thrilled Cymin.

However, a glance at Mazilane, who stood ahead of him in line, quashed his fantasy itinerary. He wasn't here to enjoy himself, and the money he handed over to the elderly woman in the ticket booth wasn't his to begin with. Still, Cymin didn't want to crumple under Mazilane's prognostications concerning his inevitable moral downfall. Instead, he chose to cling to his excitement and hope. After all, who knew where they'd find the Waethir? Or where they might wander after that.

Passing through the entry gates, Cymin took a moment to get his bearings and absorb his surroundings.

During the reign of the Haeyi mage-kings, only the most privileged elite of Chyre would have had permission to roam freely throughout the grand promenades, magnificent gardens and resplendent architecture of the Palace Complex. But now, a hundred years after the People's Revolution, the Palace Complex was a working museum. Anyone with five secular red bills could explore the grounds and still have half a red note left to buy themselves a ride on the ferris wheel at the fairgrounds across the way.

Cymin turned in a slow circle, observing the swooping rooflines with their lavish gilding and intricate carving. Architecturally, the Palace Complex resembled Lux Temple, though the majority of carvings and statues here were luxurious depictions of the golden phoenix, the personal emblem of Chyre's most powerful and infamous mage-king, Xondir Haeyi.

Xondir had risen from a lowly position—he'd been the son of a captive Piiroc consort—to seize the Chyrenese throne and expand the nation's dominion across half the continent. Though the sigils of his family name were now banned, his personal emblem still held pride of place, reminding everyone of Chyre's strength at the height of its power.

A sea of brightly painted kites and paper banners filled the sky, advertising everything from tiny noodle shops to the National Agricultural Trade Show, which was apparently taking place in some far-flung exhibition hall. Heritage scholars and tour guides had to shout to make themselves heard over bursts of radio music and the cajoling calls of all the vendors hawking souvenirs and countless fragrantly alluring foods.

Many of the people working in the Palace Complex attempted to dress in a somewhat historic manner, though there was no consensus as to which period of history. For numerous young men, that simply meant stripping down to an old-fashioned breech cloth or smock, while most women either hid their dark hair beneath colorful, translucent veils or wore the blue star vests of the first revolutionaries. No one appeared to be game enough to attempt to totter around on the carved tall-shoes so often pictured in ancient portraits. Nor did anyone sport anything like the Hundred Deaths ancillary armor that Chyre's most dangerous mages had once worn into battle.

Though on various raised pavilions scattered throughout the grounds, very properly costumed performers reenacted thrilling scenes from history on a two-hour schedule—or so the elderly woman in the ticket office had informed him. Assassinations, infamous affairs, revolutionary plots and several duels could all be witnessed, with time left to follow a guided tour through the inner chambers of the palace itself. She'd pushed a guide booklet that explained it all into Cymin's hands, and he'd thanked her before making way for a large family.

As he and Mazilane crossed the grand courtyard, Cymin noticed two men wearing bald caps as well as robes that were not too different from his own. From the scar drawn on the side of one of their faces and the theatrically decorated moon-bow strapped across the other's back, Cymin guessed these two were portraying the tuteli insurrectionists who stood against the mage-kings during the People's Revolution. Their roles in the final battles had ensured that Lux Temple was spared when so many other temples were purged by the new government.

Though just now, both of them seemed occupied with the contents of a leaf-paper bowl brimming with fried dumplings. The scent of sizzling chives and spices drifted over Cymin as he passed the performers and their lunch. His mouth watered and his stomach growled.

Next to him, Mazilane paused and narrowed his pale amber eyes, but his attention focused on the tether on his wrist. Cymin fished a fistful of waterseeds from his pocket. He tossed them into his mouth and chewed them, shells and all. Mazilane adjusted a dial on the tether and then pushed a small button. The camera soaring above them circled in a steadily descending spiral, then it dropped onto Mazilane's outstretched forearm like a hunting hawk returning to its trainer. Surprisingly few people seemed to notice it, but then, hundreds of kites and banners swirled through the air above them. Distractions abounded.

Not the least of which was the presence of five towering pale Waethir and four worm-fingered, gash-faced NS Marshals.

The group stood out conspicuously from the loud, vibrant crowds. The marshals' stark blue uniforms represented the only hint of color in the otherwise gray expanse of their presence. The Waethir had abandoned their bulky winter coats and left behind their larger ancillary weapons, but they still appeared strikingly foreign with their ghostly complexions, long pale hair and archaic gray leather clothes. Tourists gave them a wide berth, occasionally stealing nervous glances towards them but immediately averting their gazes at the sight of the marshals.

The five Waethir lingered beneath the huge gold statue of yet another phoenix. Sunlight glinted off the statue's outstretched wings and threw off pools of reflected light like bright embers.

Spotting Laithondi wasn't difficult, given his height. Even among his fellow Waethir, he stood out. The bone-white scepter that Cymin had been found with when he was a child now hung like a short sword from Laithondi's belt.

A foolish urge to simply race over and snatch the scepter up rippled through Cymin, but he suppressed it at once.

Not the most subtle opening for a would-be spy. But then again, does East Deity truly want to be a good little agent for Lui Dane?

Cymin stole a glance to Mazilane. The man had put on a gentle smile, but his gaze tracked the Waethir with a predatory focus. Cymin didn't wonder if he'd ever really murdered anyone, but rather how many people he'd killed.

If I don't pull my weight as an agent, will Mazilane strangle me to death in a bathroom stall? How did my life get so complicated in just two days?

He shook his head at the absurdity of his situation. But unwilling to think too deeply about it, he turned his attention to Laithondi's companions.

Two of the three women circled the statue with curious expressions. Mazilane nodded toward the taller of the two.

"That one is Bailon," Mazilane whispered.

Mazilane hadn't lied when he described her as "strong-featured." Bailon's jaw and brow were as sharply angled as Laithondi's, and her shoulders looked nearly as square. She wore her silver hair up in an old-fashioned crown of braids, which emphasized the sharpness of her jawline. At a glance, Cymin could have mistaken her for a handsome young man, but her overvest and three-layer robe were all in women's cuts—with the closures running down the center instead of being offset to the left. On top of that, the distinctive gold locket of a daughter-talisman hung from her belt like a watch fob.

Cymin recognized the archaic accessory from old illustrations of Piiroc queens and princesses, as well as from the tacky replicas that cluttered cheap charm shops in the shanty section of town. Even if they no longer worshipped the Carnal Gods, women of Piiroc descent often kept fragments of their parent's bones inside the ornamental lockets. Even Yinni kept a daughter-talisman—albeit a humble version she'd carved from soapstone. She hid it beneath her robes to avoid remarks about the "Piiroc corruption of modern women."

Though Cymin did wonder why a Waethir would wear a Piiroc-style adornment. The Waethir obviously shared Lux Temple's pantheon of the

Five Deities, but they appeared to have also incorporated the Piiroc idea of bones being sacred. Or did it go the other way? Could both Chyrenese and Piiroc rituals have shared roots with an older faith from Saigrath?

Cymin's gaze lingered on Bailon's daughter-talisman.

Maybe he was overthinking this, and religion played a very small role in the matter. Perhaps she kept the charm for the same reason Yinni kept one. She had nothing else left of her parents.

After the flood killed their parents, when he and Yinni were still in the refugee camp, his sister had pleaded with a camp administrator for weeks just to win the few fragments of their parents' skulls that she so treasured. One of the only times she ever lost her temper with Cymin in the camp had been when he'd mistaken one of those bits of bone for rock sugar and tried to eat it.

Cymin didn't want to think about that; he shifted his gaze to admire the graceful pattern of white clouds embroidered across Bailon's gray vest and robes. Quite fitting for Sky Deity.

"The golden-haired girl beside her is Eirjiri," Mazilane informed him.

Eirjiri was more fine-boned and younger-looking than Bailon—maybe fourteen or fifteen. Her eyes, like her hair, were gold, and a sharp nose dominated her pale face like an aquiline promontory. Her vest, robes and loose-fitting trousers were studded with white stitchwork that resembled mountains: fitting for her Earth Deity namesake. She, too, sported a daughter-talisman, but hers had been carved with the impish face of a woman sticking her tongue out at the world. Studying the gold locket hanging from her belt, Cymin couldn't help but recall all those comedic stories of shy young brides summoning their grandmothers' crafty ghosts to aid them in confounding their overbearing in-laws.

The third woman hung back near Laithondi and the other male Waethir. She leafed through a copy of the Palace Complex souvenir guidebook with a quietly inquisitive expression. Her silver braids hung in loops, and her eyes, like Laithondi's, were wide set and such a deep blue that they seemed black. Her sharp brows also resembled his. In fact, as he studied her, Cymin felt certain that she and Laithondi were related by blood, most likely siblings. A motif of cresting waves decorated her vest, robes and trousers: clearly Sea Deity.

Curious waves forever reaching out to explore foreign shores.

Wasn't that how she was always described?

"I'm going to go out on a limb and guess she's named after Arnaith," Cymin remarked.

"Correct. The women are named for the deities of the Three Realms: Sky, Earth and Sea. Or the three states of matter: gas, solid and liquid, as every first-year science instructor likes to point out." Mazilane considered Cymin with an assessing expression. "The two men are the Deities of Time: Day and Night—the rising sun of the east and the setting moon of the west. Laithondi and Vessreid. But which is which?"

Mazilane clearly already knew the answer but meant to test Cymin's observational skills. So Cymin pretended to study them closely. Both of them wore necklaces of carved finger bones and kept their long white hair braided back from their faces in two thick plaits. The same pattern of suns and moons decorated their clothes.

The man beside Laithondi wasn't as tall, but his straight posture and raised chin lent him the illusion of standing shoulder-to-shoulder. Like Laithondi, he was clean-shaven, but where Laithondi's features appeared sharp to the point of seeming menacing, his companion possessed a more gentle countenance. When he frowned, he gave an impression of concern rather than annoyance.

"The shorter of the two is Vessreid, and the one with the scepter is Laithondi," Cymin stated. "I'd put money on it."

"And what makes you so certain of that?" Mazilane studied them as well, frowning slightly.

"Because Laithondi introduced himself to me yesterday," Cymin replied with a grin. "You don't really forget a man you meet while falling through the middle of a cloud."

So busy testing me, you forgot the obvious . . .

Then Cymin strode ahead through the surrounding crowds, edging up on Laithondi's right. He started to raise his hand to wave, but a male NS marshal turned an inhuman stare on him, and Cymin froze where he was. He felt slightly unwell just being in the marshal's proximity. He knew that part of his queasy fear was being actively provoked by the spell at the center of the blue seal that shone on the marshal's brow, but being aware of that didn't alter the sickening sensation of cold, sticky worms slithering over his skin. He diverted his gaze, pretending to study the towering golden statue of the phoenix.

Let Mazilane handle his fellow security agents.

He noticed that the Waethir also averted their gazes when they fell on the NS marshals, and he felt sorry for them. He'd only had to endure the company of the marshals for half an hour last night, and it had filled him with dread. He couldn't imagine how dispiriting it must be for the Waethir, who were already far from their homes, to find themselves hemmed in by these disturbing figures.

In the quiet, uncertain moment, Mazilane stepped forward, breezing between the marshal and Bailon with a handsome smile. Cymin noticed all the marshals begin to drift back from around the Waethir.

Mazilane beamed at Bailon and then waved to Eirjiri.

"Didn't I promise to find you two again? I've brought my camera, so you can see how it works for yourselves." Mazilane hefted the gray ancillary up into the air. Then, with a casual gesture to Cymin, he added, "I don't know if you remember this young fellow from the parade yesterday. He's a tuteli adept. Goes by the name Cymin."

"It's an honor to meet you." Cymin followed Mazilane's cue. To his relief, Bailon offered him and Mazilane a broad smile. Eirjiri sidled up on Mazilane's right side with an excited expression and beckoned for the other three Waethir's attention.

"This is Mazilane," Eirjiri said. "He's the ancillary mage we were telling you about last night."

Arnaith strode forward. She held her open hand up in greeting, then took the lead, introducing herself and each of the Waethir in turn. Cymin half expected Laithondi to give some sign that he recognized him—even if it was only to acknowledge that he'd saved Cymin from plummeting to his death—but instead he hung back and kept silent. Vessreid, on the other hand, offered him a warm smile. But as he continued to study Cymin's face, his expression slowly took on an uneasy edge.

"You're the tuteli who first greeted us yesterday," Vessreid said. "The one who contained the explosion."

"That's right." Cymin nodded. He noted that one of the NS marshals turned sharply toward Vessreid at the casual mention of the bomb in public.

Vessreid ignored the marshal, instead taking a step closer to Cymin. He looked very serious—almost hostile.

"While you were in the air, you invoked the sigil Min," Vessreid made the statement almost as if it was an accusation. "Why did you do such a thing?"

Yesterday Laithondi had asked him about that as well and with the same terse tone. Now, Cymin guessed that the sigil carried some larger association for the Waethir—and not a good one. He didn't want to be deemed guilty by association, so he immediately launched into self-deprecation, cheerfully explaining his bad habit of defacing his surroundings with the sigil that made up half his name.

"The sigil for Cy is harder to draw quickly, and as a rule I try not to get caught vandalizing the area. So I just write 'Min.' That also leaves a little room for me to claim innocence," Cymin admitted with a smile. To his surprise, Bailon laughed and clapped him on the back.

"At last, we meet up with someone who isn't too clever to show his true personality or too cultured to have fun," she said. "How delightful."

"Thank you," Cymin replied automatically, though he wasn't certain it was a compliment, really.

Bailon nodded to him, then looked Mazilane up and down. "Or I suppose we've met two delightful people, but Cymin here is clearly more daring and less sly."

Mazilane inclined his head in acknowledgement, and a very handsome smile flitted across his full lips. "Right you are. But you don't strike me as a woman who's opposed to more cunning amusements when it comes to cultural exchange."

"Yes! That's just what we've been missing!" Eirjiri stated with a gleeful smile. "Wagers and weighted dice and games where the loser must drink, dance and strip! Then we could truly get to know each other. We should start things off right!"

Cymin raised his brows. It wasn't even noon yet.

"Absolutely! We'll also find Xondir's grave and dance on it," Bailon agreed. "But first, I want to collect my silver cask. It contains the finest cloud liquor you could wish for."

"Your cask?" Mazilane furrowed his brow.

"Yes, it's here along with about a million other treasures that slimy shit Xondir stole." Bailon flipped through her guidebook to the Palace Complex and found the page. She held the booklet open for Cymin and Mazilane to see the photograph of the sumptuous silver cask sitting in a display case.

The description beneath the photograph read: *Silver cloud liquor cask of the Sky Deity, Bailon. Buried beneath the statue of the Summer Phoenix in the year 1704, after "Wraiths" defeated the previous mage-king's rebellion and enthroned his Piiroc consort's son, Xondir Haeyi. The flask commemorated the new peace treaty forged between the nations of Saigrath and Chyre at that time. It's believed that the dictates of that treaty fueled dissatisfaction among Chyrenese nobles and led to the attempted coup against Xondir Haeyi in 1705. Xondir Haeyi ruthlessly suppressed the rebellion. However, after the "Wraiths" departed four years later, he discarded many of the social reforms imposed by the treaty. This cask is one of the few artifacts that remain from the earliest period of Xondir Haeyi's reign.*

"Yes, that's it!" Eirjiri leaned forward and tapped the page in the booklet.

"And already out of the ground, no less." Bailon smiled fondly at the picture.

Cymin warmed to her enthusiasm, though he found it strange that Bailon would claim to personally own an offering left beneath an ancient statue more than 200 years prior. She couldn't be more than twenty-five years old. But maybe in Saigrath the tuteli appointed to embody the Five Deities were encouraged to inhabit the characters more completely than Cymin or any of his fellow Chyrenese tuteli would ever have dared. Considering that they answered to the deities' names at all times, their duties obviously went beyond merely wearing a mask and reciting scripture for events and ceremonies. They certainly took historical dress much more seriously . . .

As he pondered the life of a Saigrath tuteli, Cymin felt a shadow fall over his shoulder. He glanced to his left and noted that Laithondi had stepped behind him to look at the guidebook. Laithondi met his gaze and held it. Cymin didn't know if it was just his imagination or not, but fei'lux seemed to stir and twine between their bodies. Or perhaps that was an effect of standing so near the scepter.

Mazilane reached out, very casually gripped Cymin's elbow, and drew him a little away from Laithondi. He released Cymin's arm but brushed his fingers across Cymin's hand. As he did so, he manifested a very faint ward spell from his tether. It glinted briefly like a bracelet locked around Cymin's wrist, then disappeared.

"Wouldn't want to lose you so soon after finding you again, would I?" Mazilane commented.

Had it been someone else, Cymin might have thought Mazilane was flirting with him, and he felt anxious about the responses of the surrounding crowd. Same-sex relationships had been decriminalized twenty years before but were still sometimes viewed as vestiges of the mage-kings' vices. In addition to that, tuteli were expected to uphold the virtues of austerity and abstinence—at least in public.

So what was Mazilane doing? Testing the Waethir's tolerance to public displays of interest?

Cymin doubted that. Because throughout lore the Waethir were infamous for imposing legal protections for same-sex marriages—even between women—upon various kingdoms. The first time Cymin had come across one such mention, he'd felt thrilled to uncover historical proof that his own desires weren't inherently tied to the decadent corruption of mage-kings or his mixed Piiroc ancestry; he'd never forgotten it.

Mazilane probably wasn't thinking of any such matter. His interest lay with National Security and the spells hidden away in the Waethir's scepter. Maybe he feared Cymin getting too near the scepter would accidentally set off a spell, as it had done when he was four years old?

Until just this instant, Cymin hadn't considered that, but now he realized that Mazilane's concern—and his warding spell—might be justified.

The fei'lux between Cymin and Laithondi still fluttered and twisted as if searching for an outlet. Cymin edged just a little nearer to Mazilane. The warm feeling of fei'lux caressing his skin died away.

"Rather attractive, isn't it?" Mazilane glanced at Laithondi and nodded at the photograph in the booklet.

Laithondi's eyes narrowed, but Cymin wasn't certain if that was in response to Mazilane or the growing intensity of the noonday sun.

"Hmm, says here," Mazilane went on as he read from the booklet, "the cask can be found on the second floor of the palace, in the silver rooms. The cloud liquor it contained is long gone. Though, according to this guide, a modern, far less hallucinogenic version can be bought in the garden pavilions at a reasonable price."

"Asshole," Bailon muttered. "He breaks the treaty and then he has the gall to exhume my cask and drink my liquor."

"Did you truly expect better from the likes of Minroa and Xondir Haeyi?" Vessreid asked. "I told you looking for it was a waste of time."

Cymin stole a glance to Vessreid. He sounded so personally aggrieved when he spoke those ancient names, it was strange. The temple in Saigrath truly must have groomed the chosen tuteli to personify their deities. Then he wondered how often they were required to perform publicly. Were the schoolchildren on day trips as snotty and inattentive in Saigrath as they were in Chyre? Laithondi didn't seem like the type who'd put up with some public official's brat flicking spit wads at him, that was for certain.

Though Cymin supposed he'd have a chance to see for himself when they got there.

"I doubt Minroa drank any of your cloud liquor," Laithondi told Bailon. "He hated the stuff."

"Let Minroa drink hot piss in hell," Vessreid responded, and he spat on the ground. Bailon and Arnaith also spat. Eirjiri sighed and Laithondi looked suddenly tired.

The entire exchange mystified Cymin. How did an ancient, obscure figure like Minroa Haeyi garner such hatred? His name wouldn't have meant anything to even Cymin if he hadn't seen that sensual illustration of the young man just that morning. Yet the Waethir spoke as if he were more infamous than his older brother, Xondir Haeyi.

And it was weird enough that they responded so strongly to Xondir.

After all, his infamy and renown had only truly flourished years after the Waethir withdrew across the Great Chasm Sea into the north. It had been their retreat that freed Xondir Haeyi to break the truces they'd brokered and seize countless small temples and kingdoms. He'd raised the

Storm Towers and founded the first secular mage school. Other than his own sister, his forty-year rule had been largely free of powerful adversaries, due to the absence of Wraiths.

And during that time, he'd forged a multitude of squabbling nations into the vast unified kingdom of Chyre—though the cost had been merciless warfare and the ruthless oppression of thousands upon thousands of souls. Thankfully, the brutal absolute monarchy that he founded eventually fell to the uprising of the People's Revolution.

But how could any of that have affected modern Waethir, living far across the Great Chasm Sea?

Cymin stole a sidelong glance to Laithondi, only to realize that Laithondi was studying him in return. Laithondi's dark gaze flickered to where Mazilane had placed the ward on Cymin's wrist. Once again, his eyes narrowed. Cymin's curiosity about historical figures vanished immediately.

Could Laithondi already suspect that he and Mazilane were in collusion? Cymin felt a guilty heat rise in his face.

"I sense watchful eyes," Arnaith pronounced suddenly, and Cymin almost flinched.

Then she pointed up to Mazilane's camera, and Cymin relaxed.

"That's the camera I was telling Bailon and Eirjiri about last night. Its name is Soir." Mazilane tapped the tether on his wrist, and the camera descended in dramatic wheeling swoops. At last, it alighted on Mazilane's wrist. He gamely offered Soir to Arnaith.

"There's an ambitious mind and soaring spirit moving in it, as well. But it's so small." Arnaith studied the camera. Her dark blue eyes lit up with fascination. "How have you fit so many spell arrays inside it?"

"Machine etching can cram a surprising number of sigils into a small space. Just the flight instructions inside the housing contain 72,000 individual sigils that make up 640 spells, which can be arranged into eight different arrays. In addition to that, the tether system allows me to augment the spells etched inside the camera. That way, it doesn't have to carry thousands of different spells for exploring, mapping or tracking a subject, and I don't have to waste too much thought on keeping it airborne." Mazilane stroked the camera as if it were a pet.

"Didn't I say that the camera sounded very clever, Vessreid?" Eirjiri spoke up. Then to Arnaith, "I knew you'd love it."

"You did. And you were quite right," Arnaith replied. "It's beautiful."

"Bai and I weren't just wasting our time talking to this one." Eirjiri gave Mazilane a grin.

"No, you weren't. We should never have doubted you," Vessreid replied with an indulgent smile. He nudged Laithondi, who turned his attention to Eirjiri.

He offered her an approving nod. "You have impeccable taste in conversation partners."

Cymin relaxed. No one suspected him. But of course they didn't. How could Laithondi possibly know that he'd agreed to become Lui Dane's agent? His own guilt was making him far too edgy, he realized.

Mazilane, in comparison, seemed utterly at ease. He tossed Soir back up into the air, directing it to weave and swoop between kite strings and fluttering banners. Then he extended his wrist, displaying the tether to the Waethir. "Would any of you care to give it a try?"

Both Bailon and Eirjiri looked excited by the prospect. But it was Arnaith who gazed at the images moving across the twin dials of Mazilane's tether with an expression bordering on infatuation. Her fingers twitched and cold eddies of fei'lux curled around her. Her quiet but intense curiosity reminded Cymin of Ovelah, when she became so focused on an ancillary that she seemed half in love with it. Because she was so much like Yinni's friend, Cymin couldn't help but anticipate Arnaith's delight at being offered an opportunity to fly Soir.

So he was a little dismayed an instant later, when Arnaith schooled her expression into mere interest. She crossed her arms behind her back and stepped away from Mazilane.

"It's meant to fly, and the sky is Bailon's realm. She should play with it first," Arnaith responded. "I'll observe."

"But—but I want to fly it as well!" Eirjiri bounced on the balls of her feet, seeming quite childlike, despite her stature. She cast Laithondi a pleading look.

"The earth is perfect for landing on," Laithondi said. "Or crashing into, as the case may be. So, Eirjiri's realm is relevant as well. Maybe they should have a go together."

Laithondi offered Mazilane a smile, but something about it seemed unfriendly.

"Right. Let's try it together." Bailon threw an arm around Eirjiri's shoulders and pulled her to Mazilane's side. Eirjiri poked the silvery housing, then frowned at the tether on Mazilane's wrist.

"Are there hawk bones hidden inside your bracelet?" Eirjiri asked. "Do you use them to imbue your camera with the memories and reflexes of flight?"

"No. No hawk bones involved at all," Mazilane replied.

"Insect skulls?" Eirjiri peered at the tether. "Dragonflies are brilliant in the air. Is a dragonfly's mind locked inside?"

Cymin and Mazilane both stared at Eirjiri in stupefied silence for a moment. Did she truly understand so little about science that she thought the ghosts of birds or bugs served as a navigation system for Mazilane's camera?

What did that say about the state of Waethir technology, overall?

"A camera and tether filled with the aspirations of dragonflies would be awfully poetic," Mazilane replied. "Sadly, the reality is mostly made from rings of acid-etched copper and steel, with a few transmission wires and resonance crystals thrown in."

"Oh. So, instead of trading on spirits with wings, you Chyrenese taught metal to fly?" Eirjiri cocked her head and gave a soft laugh. "That's what I adore about you people. You're so unexpected and imaginative! I love visiting here."

You're rather unexpected yourself, Cymin thought, but not unkindly. He actually found Eirjiri charming. Her exuberance reminded him of Saum's joyful and bubbly personality. He wondered if Eirjiri would also turn out to be boy-crazy. Maybe she and Saum could share magazines.

"I'm excited to see how it works now!" Eirjiri continued to bounce on her toes, nearly dancing with excitement. "You must show me!"

"I'll direct the fei'lux through the air," Bailon decided. "You two play with the dials and buttons."

Cymin dropped back, making room for Bailon and Eirjiri. Arnaith remained at Mazilane's back, peering over his shoulder. Cymin noted that only two of the NS marshals remained close enough that he could spot them through the surrounding throng of tourists. Where the others had gone, Cymin had no idea, but he knew better than to try and search them out. He returned his attention to Mazilane and the Waethir.

As Mazilane demonstrated the settings on the tether, breezes of fei'lux whipped up around the group of them. Cymin listened to the instructions, and his hands tingled with the rushes of fei'lux that Bailon and Eirjiri manipulated.

Fei'lux that had already been tamed by the Storm Towers as well as the city's shields felt largely uniform. However, after being tempered, it inevitably took on a little of the mage's character. Even after burning through a spell, a residue of that character often lingered. Master Tam had compared the residues to the perfume remaining after incense burned out. But Cymin always thought of it as the smell of someone's breath—or farts—depending on how badly the fei'lux flowed into the spells it was meant to power.

His own spell residues tended to be warm and a little woody, while both Master Tam and Yinni tended to leave a minty coolness after they'd powered a spell. Of course, ancillaries themselves could flavor a spell residue, as could the character of the spell. So it wasn't a perfect way to recognize exactly who had manifested any given spell.

Even so, Cymin noted that the Waethir left very unusual residues. First, they were exceptionally faint, which meant the Waethir were extremely efficient when they channeled fei'lux into spells, wasting almost no power to carry a residue. But the subtlety didn't disguise the uniquely tactile quality of their spell residues.

Where Cymin would have described Chyrenese spell residues in terms of scents and flavors, the Waethir's seemed like textures. A bouncy resilience bubbled through the residue of fei'lux that Bailon tempered. Eirjiri's manipulation seemed to bake the fei'lux to the pebbled quality of a dry riverbed. What Cymin could sense of Arnaith's effect was a slick frigid pressure making streams of fei'lux feel like a slurry of ice and oil.

Cymin stole a glance to Laithondi, only to have the man meet his gaze with an arched brow. Caught out, Cymin immediately looked away.

Nothing to be suspicious of, here. East Deity is simply curious and observant of the whole world.

Cymin refocused himself on the camera. Very soon, he'd be expected to operate one himself. He rarely encountered an ancillary he couldn't master, but without spell filaments, he currently struggled to catch a firm grasp on any of the fei'lux whipping around him.

His curiosity about Laithondi and Waethir spell residues faded. He concentrated more intently on fei'lux that hadn't already been tempered or channeled into an ancillary. His fingers ached, and that weird grinding sensation again flared low in his abdomen.

Is this what I get for joking about growing an ignis gland?

If he hoped to control the camera, then not only would he need to understand its workings, but he'd have to reclaim more of his previous grasp over fei'lux. Though for the moment, he satisfied himself listening and watching as Bailon and Eirjiri sent the camera up among the jumble of kites and banners. Tiny images flickered on the tether as Soir rose above the grounds of the Palace. The perspective from the air was so much more vast and fascinating. Not only could he pick out the winding gardens and grand statues, but the rows of food stalls also came into view.

The itchy sensation in his gut began to grow into a gnawing hunger. He snatched another handful of seeds and ate them, but it really wasn't enough. His stomach let out an aggrieved growl.

At the same time, the camera banked between a flurry of windswept kites and then clipped a flagpole. Suddenly, it spun out of control and plunged into an azalea hedge.

"No! No, no, no!" Bailon winced at the impact. Beside her, Eirjiri clapped her hands over her mouth, then gave a nervous laugh as she looked to Mazilane.

"Sorry," Eirjiri said. "I was sure I could pull it up in time. Is Soir hurt?"

Mazilane assured them that the camera had been designed to withstand far more violent impacts. Though Cymin had noticed his expression tighten when the camera plunged, and he felt certain that the man had used all his willpower to resist taking control of the tether.

From behind him, Cymin heard a soft laugh, but when he glanced back, he wasn't certain if it had come from Laithondi or Vessreid.

"It's fine." Mazilane fished the camera out from the hedge. "Shall we try again, or would you all prefer to continue touring the Palace Complex?"

"I'm hungry," Laithondi announced.

Vessreid and Arnaith both shot him curious looks, but then Vessreid smiled.

"After our last meal, I've lost all confidence in my ability to engage Chyrenese courses. And I've no idea how to judge the quality of the vendors here." Vessreid glanced around as he commented, clearly searching the surrounding crowd of tourists.

"Our government escorts seem to have taken their leave," Arnaith informed him. "So there'll be no advice from them."

"Thank the Heavens for that small mercy," Vessreid murmured, and Arnaith smiled briefly in response.

Then Vessreid raised his voice just enough to carry clearly to Cymin and Mazilane. "Would our companions be willing to make recommendations?"

On the few occasions Cymin ate outside the temple, he could only indulge in charity offerings handed over to him after he'd repaired a spell or cleaned up worn sigils. Those meals mostly consisted of steam cart buns stuffed with peanuts and peppergreens or, occasionally, a bun filled with sweet folly-custard. Both were delicious in his opinion, but he couldn't suggest that the Waethir eat the food restaurants set aside for tuteli handouts.

Though just thinking of any food right now made Cymin's stomach gurgle and snarl at him. He stuffed the last of his waterseeds into his mouth.

"Weren't we talking about this before we reached the city?" Eirjiri suddenly spoke up. "I wanted to eat crispy duck with banana flowers. Bailon, you wanted—"

"Ginger rice and crab." Bailon nodded. "Oh, and those cakes. The little ones that are drenched in orange liquor, then set on fire! Let's have those . . . and peaches."

"Oh yes!" Eirjiri's gold eyes lit up like flames. "Peaches! It's been so long since I've tasted peaches."

"Perhaps one of you knows of an eatery that offers these things?" Arnaith glanced first to Mazilane and then Cymin before adding, "For myself, I'd like ribbon noodles in gold truffle sauce. Both Vess and Laith enjoy buttered pheasant with pearl mushrooms."

Cymin thought his pulse actually picked up a little at the mention of so much costly food. He would be happy if he could just cram a couple dumplings down his throat.

"Gold truffle, crispy duck and buttered pheasant." Mazilane shook his head with a chagrined expression. "I can only assume that all of you were reading an ancient prince's memoir when you came across those dishes. Though I do know of a courtyard pavilion not too far from here that offers ginger rice as well as ribbon noodles. And cloud liquor as well. Although, it will certainly be a pale imitation of what was once in your cask, Mage Bailon, it's very readily available."

"Today, I might just be in the mood for something readily available," Bailon responded with a wink to Mazilane. They both laughed, seeming very much at ease with each other already. Cymin envied and admired them. He stole a quick glance to Laithondi and wondered if the Waethir's decision not to accept him as a student might have been different if he'd possessed more of Mazilane's glib charisma.

"Let's go, then!" Eirjiri smiled and hooked her arm around Mazilane's elbow. "Along the way, you should tell us about all the things you people have accomplished since you killed off the Haeyi mage-kings."

"I didn't personally kill any of them, but it would be my pleasure to trade historical gossip." Mazilane offered her a smile.

"Good. I'm already sick to death of hearing about Chyre's upright revolutionary martyrs. I don't care how handsome they were. They bore me." Bailon stood on the other side of Mazilane. "Let's talk about hilarious scandals and unfortunate fashion trends."

Cymin couldn't help but wonder what a woman who wore clothing that was hundreds of years out of date would consider unfortunate but warmed to her for her interest in drama and humor.

"And, and—" Eirjiri broke in "—the moving pictures films you were describing. Tell us more about those too. I want to see one."

Arnaith followed close behind the three of them, her attention still fixed only on the camera now perched on Mazilane's shoulder. Her fingers flicked and flexed around strings of fei'lux.

Cymin followed her, and after a few steps, he noted that Laithondi and Vessreid had taken up positions on either side of him. Cymin tried to think of something to say to either of them but felt oddly distracted as another warm rush of fei'lux swept over him. He glanced in the direction it was coming from and found himself staring at the scepter swinging from Laithondi's hip.

Should he ask about it? That would be a normal thing to do, wouldn't it? Or would his interest seem suspicious? He hadn't inquired about any other ancillaries the Waethir carried or wore. Should he ask about one of those first? He stole several furtive glances to Laithondi's towering figure.

How many finger bones was he wearing around his neck? More than enough to make up two entire hands.

"Is it true that Chyrenese tuteli are now under the control of some security department?" Vessreid asked.

"What? Oh. Yes and no." Cymin attempted not to sound nervous at the mention of security. "The temple grounds have to be maintained within historic regulations designated by the Ministry of Information and Education. But weapons, spells and mages are all controlled by National Security. But we aren't NS agents."

At least, his fellow tuteli weren't.

"Their National Security minister already told you that this morning." Laithondi shot Vessreid an annoyed look. "Do you think a battered tuteli adept is going to refute him for you?"

"I wanted to hear what a tuteli would say about it. Chyre is supposed to be a nation of revolutionaries now, isn't it?" Vessreid shrugged. "And what's the harm in chatting when those bandimander marshals aren't on hand?"

"You just want an excuse to air your complaints about the minister. And, in any case, a bandimander being out of sight doesn't mean it's gone," Laithondi responded. He met Cymin's gaze for a moment. Then he aimed a glower at a distant figure moving between the various painted stalls selling souvenirs and light refreshments.

Cymin followed Laithondi's gaze but couldn't pick out a marshal from the passing crowd. Though, if they'd simply removed their anonymity spells and uniforms, the marshals would look no different from anyone else. They could trail the Waethir far more discreetly that way.

"I suppose you're right," Vessreid replied. He spared Cymin a smile. "Though I do think that your perspective of the relationship must differ from what your National Security minister described."

"It's not exactly a relationship, so much as a debt that I can't . . ." Cymin trailed off before he could say anything truly foolish. He managed a tired smile. "We just do what we can to get along."

Vessreid frowned at Cymin, but in a sympathetic way, as if contemplating a person of very diminished prospects. Cymin peeked to Laithondi and noted that he, too, considered Cymin with a slightly concerned expression.

"You must be quite tired of all the niceties and lies," Vessreid commented in a gentle tone. "The world would be a better place if only we all could be honest."

Cymin nodded, though he wasn't sure that honesty would improve his current situation. In fact, lying to himself about the seriousness of his position was about the only thing keeping him from succumbing to a fit of panic whenever he contemplated the Waethir and their scepter too long.

Fortunately, their surroundings were distracting and boisterous enough that Cymin didn't brood on the thought of his—or the other tuteli's—powerlessness. Instead, he pointed out a rack of bright kites all painted like brilliant birds and butterflies. Laithondi asked which of them Cymin liked best, while Vessreid attempted to identify the real animals they were meant to resemble.

As they wended their way toward their destination, other visitors gawked and whispered, but they largely kept their distance. The few children who toddled near were quickly swept back from the Waethir by alarmed parents or siblings. Cymin caught sight of several different groups of young mages who'd participated in the Spring Exhibition also touring the Palace Complex. Saum, Paeth and Ovelah dashed into one of the palace buildings, following a tour guide. A few minutes later, Cymin spied Yinni walking with Una Bayan and the cameraman, Hiral.

Just glimpsing his sister, Cymin at once felt like a shipwreck survivor sighting a sail on the distant horizon.

Rescue might be on hand!

If Yinni and Una Bayan and Hiral all joined the group, they would take a little pressure off of Cymin and let him relax. Or, at the very least, they could give him a better sense of how he ought to be acting. Because, right now, he was so self-conscious that he couldn't tell if his actions seemed friendly, suspicious or just unimaginably stupid.

He really didn't want the Waethir to think he was stupid—or suspicious.

It was all fine for Mazilane to tell him to charm the Waethir and cozy up to their scepter, but in reality, Cymin had no experience acting in any role other than that of East Deity. Even then, he hardly did more than put on a dignified air while remaining largely silent. But Yinni could smile and chat warmly with even the most offensive of the temple patrons. That wasn't even considering Una Bayan's charm, which was literally on a professional level.

But just as Cymin lifted his hand to wave to his would-be rescuers, the three of them disappeared into a distant building. With his attention following them and not his own steps, Cymin's foot caught on a rough flagstone, and he stumbled.

A powerful grip caught him, and Cymin looked up to see Laithondi nearly bowed over him. Cymin wasn't small, and yet Laithondi supported him as if it required no effort at all. Laithondi's head was so close that Cymin felt his warm breath rush over his ear. The scent of birch oil and something else—a fragrance like lemons and ferns—filled Cymin's lungs. His expression seemed fixed. Unblinkingly intense. The heat of his hands seemed to soak into Cymin's clothes, making his entire body feel flushed.

For an instant, they stood, almost embracing.

Then Laithondi jerked Cymin upright and quickly stepped back as if he were worried Cymin had fleas.

"What were you thinking, coming out today?" Laithondi demanded. "Are you in any condition to be wandering around?"

A little taken aback by the outburst, Cymin stared at him in silence for a moment.

I see that I'm not the only one who doesn't know how to be charming.

But Cymin didn't say as much. Instead, he pretended to brush dust from Laithondi's hands off his robe.

"You did just undergo some sort of surgery, didn't you?" Vessreid looked up from the postcard he'd been studying. "Laith mentioned it earlier. Your hands . . ."

"They're almost completely healed." Cymin lifted his hand and fluttered his fingers for Vessreid to see. Then he flashed his brightest smile. "I'm just a little hungry and tired. And also distracted by all the brilliant collectibles on sale."

"It's fascinating, isn't it?" Eirjiri glanced back at them. "It wouldn't hurt to explore a little, would it?"

"We should eat first," Laithondi stated.

"It's hardly been two hours since those ministers stuffed cakes and fried fish down our throats," Bailon responded, then she took ahold of Mazilane's arm. "And Mazilane has just explained the value of all the pretty Chyrenese paper they gave us, in exchange for a gold ingot."

Laithondi gave an irritated grumble, but in a matter of seconds Bailon and Eirjiri had ducked into a shop with Mazilane. Arnaith shrugged, and then she, too, veered to a stand selling clockwork toys.

Along with the numerous memorabilia stands, the people in bright costumes kept all of them distracted and made for an entertaining journey. Mazilane amused both Bailon and Eirjiri by pointing out the most fashionable clothes while discussing celebrity scandals, per Bailon's request. Arnaith nodded along, but clearly cared far more about the inner workings of commemorative wristwatches and radios. Potted plants, packs of seeds and postcards caught Vessreid's attention more.

Laithondi eyed a number of the brass charms on sale in tatty little stalls but only stopped to actually look at a display of fountain pens, and he didn't buy one. He only reminded his companions that he wanted to eat.

Cymin agreed with him heartily but wasn't in a position to say as much.

Even so, the other Waethir kept stopping to study various delights and make small purchases. And the interest of one always drew the others.

At one point, while Laithondi stalked ahead and the rest of the party all clustered around a framed blueprint of an early railway engine, Cymin suddenly felt a sickening sourness creep from the surrounding fei'lux. He stilled, trying to identify this particular spell residue. He'd encountered this same sensation in a hidden spell yesterday when he'd stepped onto the mosaicked grounds of the Lux Temple arena.

A jolt of horror shot through Cymin's entire body. His heartbeat hammered in his chest and cold sweat beaded on his brow.

No. Not again!

Then Cymin felt another terribly familiar spell flicker to life like the crackle of a firecracker—or a spark igniting along a fuse.

Chapter 9

Long rows of bright tents and painted stalls packed with historical replicas and other souvenirs wound around Cymin like a maze. The perfume of fried foods and floral beverages drifted from pavilions far across the rolling green lawns while the crowds of tourists and sightseers filled the air with a symphony of conversation, bartering and laughter. Cymin hardly registered any of it.

The unique sensation of a sparking fuse spell seized his mind and petrified his body, pulling him back to the vivid memory of the previous day's explosion. Visceral terror sent his heart hammering and sweat pouring down his back. His entire body shook as the tender scars all along his hands and arms seared with intense pain, as if once again caught in an inferno of power.

Yesterday, when he'd leapt into the blast, he hadn't known how much agony he'd endure when he absorbed the bomb's force. Ignorance had gifted him with reckless courage. But now, he'd experienced molten spell filaments sizzling through his flesh while a cyclone of power tore through his mind and organs. He'd howled and burned and then plummeted, helplessly.

Now, he understood the consequences—the pain and terror—intimately. The memory alone froze him in place.

I can't. I can't do that again . . .

And yet there was no time to call out to anyone else. The fuse was already lit, the blast inescapable. He had to act. Freezing up would doom him, along with the multitude of people surrounding him.

Cymin reflexively raised his right hand to his brow as if securing his deity mask. At the same time, he opened his trembling left hand and prepared to absorb as much of the furious explosion as he could. He clenched his eyes closed to hold back the tears of pain. The sizzling sensation buzzing through the surrounding fei'lux surged so near Cymin, he almost smelled black powder.

Then, nothing.

Cymin remained tensed with his hand raised for a moment longer. Then, slowly, he lowered his hand and looked around in confusion.

A few feet away, a circle of children in moss-gray school uniforms squealed and giggled. The crackling sensation that had alarmed Cymin zipped through the air again, fizzing around them. The children wriggled as if being tickled, then burst into laughter. The spark-spell again sputtered to nothing.

At last, Cymin claimed enough control over his fear to notice that several of the children gripped lighters. Rudimentary sigils marked the bodies of the lighters—just enough to excite fei'lux but not truly shape it; most of the lighters only spat out tiny yellow flames. But one of them sported a shoddy imitation of a Piiroc fire sigil. As the little girl holding it spun the flint, the crude spell buzzed to life along with a vivid blue flame. That disturbing tingle rushed over Cymin's hands once more. At the same time, the more fei'lux-sensitive children shivered and giggled wildly. The other children laughed at their jumps and shivers. Cymin remembered playing with broken spells in the same manner when he'd been much younger.

He had mistaken a children's game for the presence of the bomber.

Stupefying relief flooded Cymin, seeming to wash away all his strength and concentration.

He hardly registered it when two teachers jostled past him to swoop down on the young students and confiscate the lighters. Protests and excuses sounded as the errant children were hustled back to their educational tour. Cymin remained in place, feeling stupid and exhausted.

"You look terrible." Laithondi's voice startled Cymin from his daze.

Cymin spun to find the Waethir towering much closer to him than he expected and gripping a cardboard box painted with honeybees and poppy flowers.

Cymin started back a step.

Laithondi frowned, then glanced down at the box. Cheery phonetic script declared the seed crackers inside "a timeless indulgence." Laithondi held the box out as if he were searching for a place to discard it.

"You're hungry, aren't you?" Laithondi asked.

East Deity isn't a trash receptacle.

Cymin scowled at him. Though, in truth, even ten minutes ago Cymin would gladly have relieved him of the sweet, seed-studded crackers. But at this moment, his stomach still flipped inside him like a landed fish. He felt certain that anything he ate would immediately need to evacuate his body.

"Is something the matter?" Laithondi asked. "You truly do look unwell."

"No. I was just . . ." Cymin caught himself before he could admit that he'd been so utterly shaken by nothing. Laithondi already seemed to regard him as feeble and had issues with bringing him along on their walk through the palace grounds—never mind the greater journey to

Saigrath. The last thing Cymin wanted was to disassemble in front of Laithondi. At the same time, he felt like he truly did need to sit down somewhere and calm himself.

"I was looking for a public toilet," Cymin stated. "I just remembered that we passed one a little way back. You and the others should go on ahead. I'll catch up with you in a few minutes."

Cymin turned away, and though his legs felt disconcertingly weak, he fled into the crowd. To be certain that Laithondi couldn't see him, he darted between a pair of bright blue tents. And then, to his horror, he felt another sensation from the bombing floating on the fei'lux around him once again. A spell residue, sharp and tangy as a tangerine peel. He'd caught a hint of the same residue during the explosion.

Cymin spun in a circle to make certain that another group of children weren't toying with broken spells. None of the people passing him or loitering near the stalls were manifesting spells of any kind. And yet, the residue continued to drift to Cymin.

What the fuck? Am I going insane?

As much as he wanted that thought to be a joke, he knew that it wasn't entirely impossible. He'd lost his grip on reality once before.

In the wake of the Haelon Flood, his mind had descended into a chaotic turmoil. He'd been unable to discern his bizarre nightmares of misty lands and terrible battles from his waking life in the refugee camp. That was when he'd first begun to scrawl the sigil Min on everything.

The bouts had taken him like fevers and left him unable to remember much, other than Yinni protecting him so camp authorities wouldn't lock him away in an institution. Even after he regained his sanity and Grand Master Ryn brought him and Yinni to Lux Temple, Cymin never reclaimed the memories of his parents or his time in the tomb.

For a while, Yinni tried to prompt him to remember by sharing her own recollections and telling him stories. But nothing came of these efforts, except that Cymin learned very well how much Yinni had loved and missed their parents, while he felt only the absence of that sorrow.

For him, the memories of a four-year-old represented only hazy recollections from a life he'd left behind. Cymin had built an entirely new life for himself in Lux Temple. But if he again descended into delusion—and if he lost his identity—once again . . .

Cymin had no idea what he'd become or how he'd cope. The possibility frightened him more than another bomb.

Thinking that, Cymin focused on the spell residue like it was his salvation. The crowds here were vast, and it wasn't impossible that the bomber had followed the Waethir to the Palace Complex after failing in a first attempt to destroy relations between Chyre and Saigrath. Just because he'd been wrong about the fuse spell didn't mean this spell residue was a delusion as well.

Taking a deep breath, Cymin calmed and turned in a slow circle, searching for the tangerine fragrance of the spell residue.

This time, he caught a clear sense of the residue drifting on the breeze. Definitely not a trick of his imagination.

Cymin shot after the residue before it could dissipate. He darted between couples and dashed past beckoning merchants. At last, he reached a squat yellow tent painted with green stripes. He ducked in through the low opening.

A middle-aged man with a droopy mustache stood beside a register, surrounded by a mix of secondhand books and colorful souvenirs. Hats and smocks emblazoned with Palace Complex logos cluttered sheet metal shelves, as did figurines and stuffed animals. A random assortment of books and postcards filled spinning wire racks. All very flashy and cheap—probably the only things Cymin could actually afford to buy.

Cymin peered at the merchant, and the other man cast Cymin a dubious glance in return. Was the unfriendly expression because Cymin had thwarted the man's plans yesterday or was it because tuteli rarely purchased anything?

"Need help finding anything?" the merchant inquired.

You don't happen to have a Piiroc bomber on hand, do you?

"Just looking," Cymin responded. However, as he approached the merchant, Cymin found that the intensity of the spell residue actually waned to nothing.

"Of course you are." The merchant shrugged.

Cymin turned slowly and found that the citric scent of the spell residue emanated from deeper inside the tent. He gave the merchant a quick smile and a gesture of blessing before striding after the spell residue. It led him to an unimpressive wire book rack.

Scanning the books, Cymin rolled his eyes at the titles. Awkward innuendo, forced alliteration and fumbling wordplay such as *Plunder of the Piiroc Priestess*, *The Conqueror's Constant Conquest* and *Going Down on History* figured heavily. Most of the covers presented illustrations of busty women being stripped of flimsy, quasi-historical garb. Though a few volumes featured brawny, bare-chested men with a variety of large furs, swords or hunting hawks obscuring their groins.

Cymin stared at the rack, feeling both disappointed and deeply confounded.

Had the bomber really been hanging around, thumbing through selections of historical erotica? And then what? Left a spell residue here, like some kind of ejaculate stain? Could that even happen? If so, did Cymin really want to continue sniffing after the spell residue?

Cymin sighed. There was no denying that the remains of some spell wafted over the books. In all likelihood, it had been an anonymity spell, maybe even one that featured a citric-scented Piiroc sigil—like that shoddy lighter. But wasn't it highly probable that the anonymity spell had served to hide the purchase and perusal of one of these books, rather than obscuring a would-be bomber?

It wasn't as if Cymin and a multitude of other tuteli hadn't attempted to sneak contraband into the temple that very same way. Over the years, tuteli novices had crafted any number of anonymity spells to hide everything from pornography to pets and even prostitutes in their dormitories. In fact, Master Tam's ability to instantly sniff them out had been the very thing that alerted Cymin to the existence of spell residues and how they could lead back to a particular object or mage.

At last, the absurdity of the situation forced Cymin to acknowledge that, after he'd panicked in the face of that tiny Piiroc fire spell, he'd allowed lingering fear and agitation to stoke all his buried anxieties until they led him to this. Now, he could either try to convince himself that this book rack of used erotica somehow played a crucial role in a Piiroc terrorist plot, or he could admit that he was exhausted and out of his depth and scared.

Yes, all right. East Deity isn't used to being so uncertain of himself. He got scared and acted a little stupid.

Years earlier, when he'd still been a novice in Lux Temple, he'd defeated his sparring partners so often and so ferociously that one day a scrawny novice had collapsed sobbing just at the sight of him. Master Tam had comforted the weepy boy and, at the time, Cymin stood to the side, trying not to openly scoff at the master's coddling words. But now he thought he actually understood them.

"Your fear is perfectly natural, just like feeling anger, sorrow or desire. We all experience these things. And it's only after experiencing the power of those emotions that we have the opportunity to master ourselves and rise above them. That is the true measure of your strength."

Today, Cymin had truly had the opportunity to experience the power his fear held over him. He hadn't exactly mastered it. But he'd managed to calm himself down before he'd done anything truly embarrassing and foolish.

Thank the Heavens, he'd kept all his suspicions to himself. How humiliating would it have been if he'd led either Mazilane or Laithondi along with him on his chase and ended up here with one or both of them?

East Deity has maintained his dignity . . . aside from responding to a box of fancy crackers by suddenly racing away.

Cymin smiled wryly, feeling better for being able to see the humor in his situation. He again studied the book rack, feeling relieved and even a little thankful that its contents were ridiculous enough to rouse him from the thrall of paranoia. Pretty women and muscular men in awkward poses fluttered past as he turned the rack.

Then he noticed a familiar image at the bottom of a wire book rack. Unlike the surrounding books, this battered pulp paperback sported a rather dispassionate title: *The Forgotten Agent*. However, its cover boasted a color reproduction of the portrait of Minroa Haeyi that Cymin had seen at the teahouse that morning.

Encountering the obscure fellow's image twice in one day seemed like a sign from the Heavens. At the very least, Master Tam would have told him it was a portent he shouldn't ignore.

Cymin snatched the book up and stared at the portrait. If the real Minroa Haeyi had looked anything like this sun-kissed, dark-haired young man, he must have been stunning. Even as a flat illustration, the alluring quality of his amber gaze made Cymin feel a little embarrassed and self-conscious. He started to trace the line of the man's chest and then stopped.

What was he doing? And in public too. Cymin stole a glance back to the merchant at the register. The man regarded him with an expression that was both unsurprised and unimpressed. Cymin felt his face flush. No wonder the mage who'd last handled this volume had cast that tangerine-scented anonymity spell. It was too late for Cymin to attempt the same thing so he pretended not to see the merchant instead.

Cymin flipped the book open and noticed that someone had penciled a brief note on the title page. *Dear little cousin, I leave this to you. May it help you find me and remember yourself.* Cymin pondered the cryptic dedication. He had no way of knowing what it really meant, but he hoped that everything had worked out for the cousins. In any case, it wasn't the book's previous owner that truly interested Cymin.

He flipped past the title pages and skimmed the introduction, which explained that this volume collected the letters the Chyrenese prince, Minroa Haeyi, had penned to his sister. The author noted that the letters could not be authenticated, but if the contents were true, then this mere youth had, in fact, overturned two great kingdoms.

Cymin frowned at the grandiose claim. Still, he couldn't resist turning the page and reading the editor's statement on the explosive new secret history.

The youngest son of the Chyrenese mage-king and his captive Piiroc consort, Minroa Haeyi spent his early years in the palace, entertaining favored courtiers. However, his mother's role in an assassination plot against his father cost him what moderate status he possessed. He and both his two older siblings were imprisoned. For three years, they languished while their fates were debated in the king's court. Eventually, all three children would be banished to remote lands in lieu of execution. The first to be exiled was the fifteen-year-old Minroa. Sent into Saigrath with a diplomatic party, his true purpose was to seek out the secret to the Wraiths' immortality.

Minroa, however, had plans of his own and soon forged an exceptionally intimate relationship with a Wraith known as Laithondi (referred to as Ondi in the collected letters and editorial commentary, henceforth.) Exploiting his deep connection to Ondi, Minroa was able to trick his mage-king father into believing the Wraiths had grown weak and that their stronghold, the Heights, was ripe for plundering.

Minroa then lured his father and 4,000 troops into the Heights and set a deadly trap at the Black Gates. He personally participated in the battle, slaughtering the warrior-mages of his own homeland.

In doing so, Minroa won the Wraiths' complete trust and support.

Not only did Ondi secretly gift Minroa with a celestial pearl filled with magical essences, but he took Minroa as his lover.

(The extensive and explicit details of this have not been excised from this printing, for the sake of historical accuracy.)

Ondi also ensured that rulership of Chyre was handed over to Minroa's elder brother, Xondir Haeyi. But while Xondir sat on the gilded throne in Chyre, it was Minroa who actually ruled from the northern wilds of Saigrath.

However, rebellion and unrest plagued the early years of Xondir's reign.

In the end, proving himself to be no one's pawn, Xondir Haeyi took the bold course of building the Storm Towers and breaking his treaties and ties with the Wraiths. He rode north with an elite force of his chosen mages, and three months later the Wraiths mysteriously withdrew from mortal lands.

In the years that followed, Xondir Haeyi conquered hundreds of other kingdoms and rose to become Chyre's most powerful mage-king. Minroa, on the other hand, would fall into obscurity, a trivial footnote in Chyre's glorious history: a pretty, half-Piiroc catamite prince, sent to appease the strange appetites of the mythical Wraiths of Saigrath.

Only now can Minroa's role in securing Xondir Haeyi's victory over the Wraiths and ensuring Chyre's brilliant future be revealed in all its naked truth.

Cymin eyed the introduction with profound skepticism. Yet, he couldn't quite bring himself to set the book aside. The sentence assuring that none of the explicit material had been removed particularly compelled him.

Cymin stole another, more furtive glance back to the merchant and was relieved to see the man's attention swing to a couple of young women who'd just stepped into the tent, searching for souvenir aprons.

Cymin immediately returned to his book, leafing ahead to a random page. The interior print was smudged, and numerous penciled notes marked many of the margins, but the text remained legible.

Dear Sister,

Should you be so unfortunate as to be exiled to my side, I advise you to bring more coats, gloves and socks than you could imagine anyone ever needing. Pack a charcoal burner, a sled and a snow shovel as well. For, in addition to the three-day sleet storm that turned my clothes to ice sculptures and froze my bathwater, we've now experienced such an immense deluge of snow that the front doors of the ambassador's guesthouse were completely buried. After a week, we began to fear that we'd been abandoned here to starve—what an irony to escape a cold prison in Chyre and travel hundreds of miles, only to die trapped in an icehouse in Saigrath!

Thankfully, young Ondi returned—that same youth whose brother dragged him away after we spent a day running across rooftops all through the city—he descended from the Waethir Heights to dispel the storm and free the city's population.

As it turns out, the daring tuteli scamp was a deity in disguise!

And not just any deity, but one of the five Waethir—the East Deity!

If I had known at the time, I would have taken more care to spoil and flatter him during our adventures. I certainly wouldn't have teased him for cutting his foot and then carried him on my back through the gambling alleys. But, in truth, I'm glad I didn't know; it would have ruined the joy of that day. And now that he's met the true me, it's too late for me to play the fawning sychophant. So, there's relief as well.

Ondi walked on the wind, soaring up over the snow drifts to our second-story windows as if he weighed nothing. His skin and hair were flashes of pale gold, shining through the flurries like sunlight, and his smile was so very warm. I will admit it only to you, but I was so relieved to see him that I nearly wept. But how would I ever again taunt him for being childish if I had? He brought food and cast the most astounding spells that allowed us to fly up with him to the stronghold above the city.

Here in the Waethir's Heights, it is ever summer. Pools of hot springs abound, and there are entire orchards in flower, all sheltered beneath immense pavilions of glass. The walls and roofs are faceted like dragonfly wings, and the fei'lux is so strong here that it saturates the air like the fragrance of a thousand blossoms.

For the first time in two months, I fell asleep feeling warm.

Cymin tried to picture the Heights as Minroa described them. Verdant trees blooming beneath giant dragonfly wings while mountains of snow fell outside.

Mountains of snow . . .

. . . frozen bathwater.

He had experienced chilly nights in the refugee camp, and he knew about snow; he'd seen pictures and read about it. But he would never have imagined it burying a building up to the windows of a second story.

Minroa's advice about securing a coat, socks and gloves was much appreciated. Who could say what other insights the book might contain. Cymin flipped through the yellowed pages feeling their volume while absently scanning a word here and there. Then a phrase—*his lips on my naked*—flashed past. Cymin jolted, completely losing his place. He hurriedly leafed back through the thin pages but couldn't easily locate the passage again. Still, he was certain he hadn't misread it.

He glanced at the cover and decided that he had to buy the book.

If anyone caught him with it, he could explain that he needed it for research, to better prepare for his journey to the north. Couldn't he? A very naked Minroa Haeyi stared back at him with a knowing gaze.

Cymin decided that he'd need to hide the book cover somehow. Maybe not going so far as to cast a spell on it. A sheet of paper would work. Plenty of students made protective paper covers for fragile tomes, so it wouldn't seem too suspicious. And then he could read at his leisure.

Having decided that, Cymin grinned at the book. He felt almost as if it were already his, or at least meant to be. He thumbed past a few pages of the editor's commentary to another excerpt from a letter:

The fei'lux blazes so intensely here that some nights the entire sky is filled with displays of brilliant light. Those nights, if raindrops fall, they sizzle like firecrackers. I've learned that several plants only flower, and breeds of insects and fish only hatch, during such storms. The Waethir believe that these creatures can resonate with them through the fei'thallus and even retain their memories for them after they die. Last night, Ondi brought me to a tide pool where some of them had just hatched. They looked like little jellyfish to me, but very bright. I watched Ondi feed them, and then we carried them by hand into the sea.

This may sound strange, but the jellyfish truly did seem to know Ondi; they never once stung him. They were right little bastards to me though, and I—

"Hey tuteli, this isn't a lending library!" The middle-aged merchant called out and, at the same time, Cymin felt a stinging sensation flit around his wrist where Mazilane had secured the ward. Cymin snapped the book shut mid-sentence, nerves jangling. He'd clearly been away from the group too long for Mazilane's liking.

"I'm going to buy it," Cymin decided. He straightened and strode to the counter with the book gripped in his hand.

Cymin handed the book to the merchant.

"I'd like it wrapped," Cymin stated.

The vendor glanced at the artistically drawn nude figure and smirked.

"Of course you would." The merchant accepted Cymin's money and then wrapped the book up in a vermilion paper. Just as the merchant shoved it back towards Cymin, a low voice sounded from outside the tent.

"Cymin?"

"Yes, on my way!" Cymin snatched up his wrapped book and turned to see Laithondi bow to step through the low entry into the tent. As Laithondi straightened and drew closer, Cymin heard the merchant gasp.

Laithondi presented a particularly unearthly figure in the low shade of the tent. His height lent him a looming presence, while his pallid hair and skin seemed to almost glow. And then there were the bones hanging from around his neck. Even in a place where staff regularly dressed in a variety of historical costumes, donning actual human finger bones was bound to make an impression.

"Heavens protect me! A fucking Wraith . . ." the merchant whispered. "A real . . . fucking Wraith . . ."

Glancing between the horror-struck merchant and Laithondi, Cymin suddenly forgot his embarrassment about the book. Instead, he thought he recognized a flicker of disappointment in Laithondi's expression. How tiring must it be for him and the other Waethir to constantly be greeted as inhuman portents of death? In reality, they seemed rather friendly and certainly more accepting of the Chyrenese than this merchant was of them.

"He's no such thing," Cymin informed the merchant quietly. "Laithondi is an honored Waethir from Saigrath, and a guest of our nation."

The merchant cast Cymin a skeptical look and continued to cringe back beside his register. Cymin ignored him and strode to Laithondi.

"Still need me to polish off your crackers?" Cymin asked. Though he noted that the cardboard box was nowhere to be seen now.

"I found a pigeon that seemed happy to take on the work for me," Laithondi replied.

Cymin smiled.

Laithondi glanced at the red-wrapped book in Cymin's hands. His sharp brows lifted speculatively. "Who is the gift for?"

"Me," Cymin replied with a laugh.

But, as he quickly pocketed the book, he realized that he actually did owe Laithondi a gift. Laithondi had given him a celestial pearl. He doubted that celestial pearls were so common that people just handed them over to anyone injured—the way Chyrenese visitors piled jasmine flowers and moon wafers on bedside tables in hospitals.

Earlier, Cymin had thought he should return the celestial pearl to Laithondi at the first opportunity. He even began to fish amongst the contents of his pocket for it now. But just as he did, it occurred to him that the gesture could seem insulting, both to the pearl itself and to Laithondi. The last thing he wanted was to offend Laithondi, especially with the merchant gawking at them.

Cymin's fingers brushed over the emberwood prayer beads in his pocket. He'd polished and carved each bead himself, and they were the most precious things he possessed. Still, he held the string of red beads out to Laithondi.

"These are for you." Cymin decided before he could regret it. "I carved the sigils myself, so they aren't exquisite treasures. But they're very lucky."

Laithondi's large eyes widened in surprise as Cymin dropped the beads into his hand. Then he simply stood there staring at the plain string of simple sigils cupped in his palm. Did he think they were so flimsy that they couldn't withstand his grip? Or were they simply too clumsy and worn for Laithondi to want to accept them?

Cymin felt his face heating with more and more embarrassment the longer he stared at the sad assemblage of roughly carved beads. Hunger and romanticism had made him momentarily impulsive and delusional enough to think that a man who, according to the book he'd just been reading, lived in a glass dome of eternal summer surrounded by beauty and splendor would be impressed by a homemade gift of no monetary, or even aesthetic, value.

"You made these for—" Laithondi began.

Just then, Mazilane swept into the tent, looking ready to skin Cymin. However, his glower vanished when he saw Laithondi. The stinging sensation prickling around Cymin's wrist stopped. When Cymin glanced over, he noted that Laithondi had already hidden the homely prayer beads away.

"Wasn't one or the other of you dying of hunger?" Mazilane inquired. He considered the tacky merchandise and then the rack of trashy novels with a disdainful glance before settling his gaze once again on Cymin. "What's so interesting in here?"

"Nothing at all." Cymin hurried past both Laithondi and Mazilane as he rushed out of the tent. He was afraid to see more of Laithondi's response to his poor gift. To hide his shame, he brashly called over his shoulder, "Linger too long and a certain jackal might eat your dinner before you can sit down."

Chapter 10

The Eighty-Nine Feasts Pavilion overlooked a lush garden maze where mage-kings had once secured their consorts behind shimmering walls of murderous spells and pretty, but dangerously deep, moats. In modern times, the maze had been stripped of spells and opened up into wide, wandering garden paths, while the moats became a string of languorous lily pools. A few outdoor stages marked areas where tour guides and reenactors attempted to remind the hungry crowds on their way to the pavilion of the historical significance of their surroundings.

Normally, Cymin would've paid the costumed women on the nearest stage more attention, especially since they threw so much drama into their roles as gossiping maids serving the infamous mage-king Xondir Haeyi at the end of his reign.

The performers speculated with great relish about how constant war with his own sister, who had become a Piiroc Apotheosis, had driven the mage-king to madness. His paranoia of her assassins, combined with his own treacherous courtiers, led him to wear Hundred Deaths Armor at all times—even when he dragged hapless boys and girls to his bed and performed forbidden Piiroc rites upon them for days on end. The actresses agreed that Xondir Haeyi, like his father before him, had become obsessed with attaining immortality at any cost. They assured one another, and any passers-by, that it would be the ruin of him.

The melodrama of it should have captivated Cymin: a powerful, crazed mage-king as unreadable as the dark helm of his Hundred Deaths Armor, up against alliances of scheming courtiers seeking revenge for the abductions of their beloved siblings and beautiful servants. It sounded like the sort of historical pot-boiler that he would have stayed awake late into the night to hear on the radio.

But after the last half-hour of fear and false alarms, he felt so dazed and hungry that he was certain that Xondir Haeyi himself could appear on one of those stages and he wouldn't even notice. He just wanted somewhere to sit down and get something—anything—to eat.

The people ahead of him in the queue outside the Eighty-Nine Feasts Pavilion chatted about what they would order and how soon the pavilion host would escort them in to select a table. Cymin's eyelids drooped and his mouth watered as two middle-aged women listed all the dishes they'd enjoyed the last time they'd visited: flower salads, exquisite dumplings, rich soups, sweet and savory pies of all sorts, ginger rice scattered with herbs and fat ribbon noodles.

He was so absorbed in imagining the dishes that he barely registered Mazilane wrapping a strong arm around his shoulder. Cymin nodded absently as Mazilane went on explaining that the documentary the two of them had been hired to film was going to be a travelogue from Chyre to Saigrath.

"We want to foster better understanding between the Chyrenese people and your Waethir population," Mazilane stated.

Cymin nearly corrected Mazilane's gaffe; Waethir was obviously a holy title and not the name of the regular citizenry. However, Mazilane didn't seem like someone who'd make such a significant error—unless it was on purpose.

"Only we deities are Waethir," Arnaith immediately corrected Mazilane. "The common people of Saigrath call themselves Sai."

Mazilane smiled as if delighted by her admonishing tone.

"Now you see." He glanced to Cymin. "That's just the kind of information that natives know but we filmmakers could easily get wrong. Hopefully, the Sai people will be as forgiving as you Waethir and overlook our honest mistakes."

Cymin nodded along, but he was only half listening to the conversation. His attention was fixed on the big red double doors of the Eighty-Nine Feasts Pavilion. The smiling host, dressed in pretty gold robes, glided out and beckoned the middle-aged women inside. He, Mazilane and the Waethir would be seated next. It wouldn't be much longer. He just had to remain upright and vaguely awake a little longer.

"You can't truly think you will be able to reach Saigrath on your own," Arnaith responded.

At the same moment, both Laithondi and Eirjiri spoke.

Laithondi growled, "Cymin's hardly recovered enough to walk around a park, much less endure the journey to Yanyeo and across the Great Chasm Sea."

Eirjiri crowed over him, saying, "We should take them with us! It would be fun. The more the merrier!"

"Absolutely not!" Both Arnaith and Laithondi snapped.

"But—" Eirjirri looked pleadingly to Bailon and then Vessreid. "It's our duty to protect mortal lives—"

"Escorting additional mortals on a dangerous journey doesn't constitute protecting them," Laithondi stated. His gaze darted to Cymin but then flashed back to Eirjiri. "It will only distract us from safeguarding those whom we've already committed to protecting and endanger the documentary crew as well."

"There's already been a bombing," Bailon added as if the massive explosion might have slipped Eirjiri's memory. "You'd feel awful if something like that happened again and these two handsome fellows were hurt."

"I wouldn't let them be hurt," Eirjiri muttered and crossed her arms over her chest like a sulking child.

"It's fine, really," Mazilane put in before the argument could go further. "We've made our own arrangements. Our crew has no intention of imposing upon you."

Cymin lowered his gaze to his bare feet to hide his skepticism. Imposing on the Waethir was the entire reason that Una Bayan had sent Mazilane out to meet them.

"I've filmed in plenty of inhospitable places and under rough conditions over the years. I'm sure we'll muddle through just fine on our own." Mazilane squeezed Cymin's shoulder as he went on. "It's not as though we have any choice—at least Cymin here doesn't."

Cymin glanced up at the mention of his name and was surprised to catch the glower Laithondi shot at Mazilane.

But it was Vessreid who spoke up.

"What do you mean, he has no choice?" Only concern showed on Vessreid's attractive face, in contrast to the anger in Laithondi's expression. Bailon and Eirjiri, too, appeared discomfited. Only Arnaith's face remained impassive.

"Right, you Waethir don't know about the duties required of Chyrenese tuteli." Mazilane gave Cymin's shoulder another gentle squeeze.

Cymin thought he meant for him to explain the requirements of his civil service. Cymin really didn't feel up to it but tried to quickly organize his thoughts so that he wouldn't sound pathetic or desperate.

East Deity has his pride.

Before Cymin could say anything, Mazilane went on.

"It all started when Xondir Haeyi instituted the Spring Exhibition battles and compelled Lux Temple to tithe adept tuteli of his choosing to serve him or his Storm Towers. Ravishing temple orphans has fallen out of favor in our modern day, but the tuteli are still needed to safeguard the nation. So, all adept tuteli are required by law to repay the debts incurred in their upbringing and training by performing civil service. Normally, that means a five-year National Security conscription to serve in a Storm Tower."

Mazilane paused to gaze at Cymin. The pity in his face seemed a little contrived to Cymin, but Eirjiri and Vessreid both seemed moved by it. Bailon's brow wrinkled with alarm. Laithondi scowled. Only Arnaith maintained a detached expression.

"Cymin is an outstanding mage, and if it hadn't been for the bombing yesterday, I wouldn't be at all worried for him. But interceding the way he did cost him his spell filaments. Now he can hardly temper enough fei'lux to light a spark." Mazilane nodded to Cymin's stitched hands, and all five of the tall, willowy Waethir looked down at him. Cymin tucked his hands into his sleeves, feeling very self-conscious.

This was exactly what he hadn't wanted. But he didn't dare speak up and anger Mazilane. Instead, he focused on the pavilion doors and prayed for the host to appear and call them to a table.

"Even tuteli with intact spell filaments don't always come out of the Towers unscathed, so Cymin's chances . . . " Mazilane trailed off shaking his head.

At the same time, Mazilane dug a shockingly strong finger into Cymin's shoulder blade, making Cymin flinch and catch his breath. To onlookers it no doubt made him seem to be fighting back long-suffering emotion. Cymin wanted to knock Mazilane's hand away, but then realized that doing so would only make him appear even more frightened and fragile. As though merely hearing his situation described was too much for him to bear.

The briefest of glances also assured him that Mazilane's words had been effective. Bailon and Vessreid both regarded him with sympathy mixed with consideration. Bailon even reached out and rubbed Eirjiri's golden hair as if reassuring her that they were on the same side now.

Cymin suppressed his urge to swear as Mazilane went on speaking in a tone of sad resignation. "He only has a week to find another ministry job. If he can't do that, then NS will toss him in a Storm Tower to burn for the next five years."

"That's terrible," Vessreid snapped. "Does your National Security know no shame?"

You don't know the half of it. If you did, you wouldn't feel so sympathetic towards me or Mazilane here.

"Neither shame nor mercy," Mazilane responded. "But fortunately, not everyone is so heartless. As soon as our producer, Una Bayan, learned of Cymin's situation, she hired him. And because our documentary falls under the Ministry of Education's purview, it qualifies as civil service."

"After he was so brave yesterday, who wouldn't want to come to his rescue?" Bailon bowed her head slightly, as if attempting to meet

Cymin's gaze. Her silvery hair and long neck lent her the air of a mythical swan-maiden as she offered him a kind smile, as if he were a bashful novice who needed coaxing to talk to anyone.

It wasn't that anything Mazilane said was untrue, just that he made Cymin sound so pathetic. Cymin couldn't bring himself to look at any of the Waethir. After all, they were honored and elevated as deities in their homeland, while the people of his nation saw him as a sob-story at best and a parasite at worst. They only cheered when he wore East Deity's mask.

"So that's what I meant about Cymin not having another choice." Mazilane at last looked to Arnaith and then Laithondi. "Our documentary might seem meaningless to you. Maybe even annoying. But it's the only thing keeping Cymin out of a Storm Tower. We won't just give up on it."

At that moment, Cymin felt all the Waethir turn intense and compassionate gazes on him like fierce rays of sun burning a flush across his cheeks. Then, to his relief, the host at last appeared at the door of the pavilion and beckoned.

"They have room for us." Cymin hurried ahead.

Thankfully, the last words on the subject had nothing to do with him.

"So long as you can keep up," Laithondi's voice sounded from behind Cymin, addressing Mazilane, "you may accompany us to Saigrath."

This early in the spring, people largely dined inside at the low wooden tables surrounded by soft cushions. Three large brass stoves shaped like pot-bellied dragons radiated fragrant heat as they kept stock for Everlasting Broth simmering. Walking through a cloud of the savory steam, Cymin felt his stomach whimper like a famished street dog. Unconsciously, he drifted a few steps closer to one of the big brass stoves. The dragon's protruding flat-top belly supported several skillets of sizzling crab cakes as well as the traditional kettle of stock. Cymin drew in a deep breath of steam, tasting the sweet crab, sizzling onions and toasted sesame oil.

The host who'd brought them in offered the Waethir a large, ornately carved table near a group of green-robed scholars. Laithondi glanced to Cymin, and for just a moment, he wondered if the Waethir was hoping for him to offer his advice. But then Arnaith spoke up, eschewing the crowded cozy interior, with its warm air and comfortably cushioned seats as, "Best left for aged, ill, or infirm mortals who might need them."

Cymin, feeling ill and infirm, followed them out to the pavilion's courtyard, where gnarled wisteria trees shaded a series of lily pools. Here, the majority of cast iron tables and carved stone benches stood empty. The few diners who'd chosen to eat outdoors sat close together, sharing dishes and using the chilly weather as an excuse to snuggle close to one another.

Cymin lifted his own mood a little by briefly imagining Laithondi reenacting the same overtures by forcing Mazilane into an ungainly embrace and cramming a large steam bun into his big mouth.

Then he paused to seriously ponder how the Waethir would attempt to charm someone.

Give him a celestial pearl?

Cymin sneered at his own stupidity.

More like refuse to travel with him and constantly point out how inept and unwell he is. Truly, indicators of fervent romantic interest.

Arnaith chose a round table beneath the shadows of a wisteria tree, largely removed from the other diners. To Cymin, this seemed like a cold and gloomy spot, but he supposed that the Waethir, coming from a land of dark winters and snowfall deep enough to envelop a house, were probably feeling overheated—not that any of them were willing to say as much. The speed with which they stripped off their jackets and outer robes as soon as they settled on the circular bench gave them away.

Bailon beckoned Mazilane to sit between her and Eirjiri, close to the edge of the lily pool, while Laithondi quietly indicated for Cymin to settle between himself and Vessreid. Arnaith sat on the other side of Laithondi and eyed Mazilane's camera from over Eirjiri's shoulder.

"There are so many choices listed here," Eirjiri commented as she turned over the two pages of the pavilion's menu. "But what are the numbers beneath them?"

"The prices of each item," Mazilane responded. "Everything in Chyre has a price."

"Oh? What is yours, then?" Bailon asked with a playful smile.

"I'm far too costly for anyone to buy outright," Mazilane responded. "But I do offer free samples for discerning persons to enjoy."

Laughter followed the repartee. Though, as he laughed, Cymin suddenly realized that in his embarrassed haste to depart the souvenir tent earlier, he'd failed to collect the change for his purchase. Which meant that very little remained of the secular money Mazilane had bestowed upon him only a few hours ago. Cymin scrutinized the menu, focusing only on the prices. In a glance, it became obvious that the only dish he could afford was an appetizer. So, either another round of waterseeds or a dish of chilled persimmons, scattered over sorbet.

This day just won't let me win.

Cymin stole a glance to Laithondi, wondering what he would order from the rich menu and noticed that his cheeks were pink. The flush lent a touch of much-needed color to his pale face, but since a sunburn was likely to blame, Cymin felt a little guilty admiring the effect.

That thought settled Cymin on his choice.

"I'll order the persimmons and sorbet for us all to share," Cymin announced. It felt good to be magnanimous, particularly after Mazilane had painted him as such a sad creature earlier.

"Persimmons. How lovely!" Vessreid glanced to Cymin with an expression refreshingly devoid of pity. He had a nice smile—rather gentle and just a little shy. "They're my and Laithondi's favorite fruit, did you know?"

"I do now." Cymin gave Vessreid his best smile. Mazilane had told him to charm them, after all.

He stole a sidelong look to the far end of the table where Mazilane had traded seats with Eirjiri, so that he could better answer all Arnaith's questions concerning the spell-etched machinery that allowed power stations to tap into fei'lux tempered by the Storm Towers in Yanyeo. Arnaith listened with intense focus. Between her impassive face, pale complexion and still figure, she seemed more like a stone statue than a living woman. Only the flicker of her dark eyes and the sudden whirls of fei'lux around her betrayed her excitement about Mazilane's descriptions of acid-etching spell sigils for mass production. Both Eirjiri and Bailon had grown bored with the subject and turned their attention to the scarlet and gold fish swimming in the lily pool.

"They'd be easy enough to catch." Bailon leaned out over the water, her long, slim body moving with studied grace. She swept a silver braid back over her shoulder before it could brush its reflection in the still water. Beside her, Eirjiri crouched with the careless air of a child. The gold color of her hair made it look as if she were bathed in warm sunlight.

"But I'm dead tired of fish," Eirjiri said. "Besides, they look happy right now."

Bailon nodded and smiled at one of the big red fish.

Sandwiched between Laithondi and Vessreid, Cymin tried to think of a suitably charming topic of conversation. In his exhausted state, all he could think was that he shouldn't have sat down on Laithondi's discarded coat, but it made a nice cushion on the cold stone bench, and he didn't want to give it up. He studied Laithondi's weird white eyelashes, then looked quickly away. A moment later, his eyes drifted to the strings of hand bones that both men wore around their necks. Laithondi wore about twice as many, and some looked very old while others seemed disquietingly fresh.

Laithondi caught his gaze and gave Cymin an almost sinister smile.

"They're *my* bones," Laithondi stated.

They obviously are now, but they weren't always, were they?

Before Cymin could verbalize his mental reply, servers in old-fashioned yellow gauze robes arrived to deliver pots of Lucky Tea and take orders. Cymin provided his choice quickly and then left the rest to Mazilane and the Waethir. His eyes burned and his eyelids felt heavy, so he closed them. He listened as the list of rich, delicious dishes washed over him like an enticing song. It seemed to go on and on. He imagined the tantalizing flavors of shimmering fat ribbon noodles, fresh cress, crispy duck, pepper snake, ginger rice, peach dumplings and warm pots of fragrant cloud liquor.

Cymin forgot about being charming. Dappled sunlight and slight breezes fluttered over his skin. The conversations around him, as well as the noise of tourists and distant performers, drifted by without penetrating Cymin's mind. His aching muscles relaxed, and the pangs of discomfort in his new scars seemed to fade.

How nice it would be if he could locate a sunny patch in an herb garden and nap. Maybe he'd find an opportunity to flip through the book hidden in his pocket. The excerpts and the seductive image of Minroa Haeyi on the cover had piqued his interest. Plus, Minroa had agreed to work as a spy in Saigrath to escape imprisonment. Cymin felt sympathy for the young man; his own situation wasn't so different, after all.

A fish in the lily pool splashed, jumping after passing insects, and Cymin's thoughts drifted back to Minroa's description of carrying brilliantly colored jellyfish from a tide pool to the open water.

He imagined their scarlet bodies pulsing like tiny hearts. Delicate gold tentacles skimmed his cupped palms. In the book, Minroa had been stung but continued to help Ondi carry the small creatures to the ocean.

Cymin sighed, imagining two figures racing from a rocky outcropping of a beach to the surging waves.

Overhead, the full moon would shine like burning phosphorus while streams of fei'lux turned the night sky agate-blue. Flecks of moonlight and fei'lux would reflect and break across the dark water's surface.

He visualized Minroa moving with practiced elegance, while the wind threw his long black hair into his face and wet sand dragged his light steps and dirtied his silk clothes. Smiling at these details, Cymin slid unknowingly into a dream.

Minroa released a dozen of the tiny jellyfish into the cold seawater, quietly cursing them for stinging him all the while. Their scarlet bodies floated on the water like scattered flower petals. Then they washed away into a darkness far beneath the crashing waves.

Irritated red splotches covered Minroa's fingers, palms and even his wrists.

Beside him, Ondi, the lanky Waethir youth, grinned and steadied him as they returned to the rocky tide pools. They scooped up more jellyfish and raced back down the beach to the crashing tide. Ondi stepped in front of Minroa, shielding him from a powerful cresting wave. Icy water soaked the young man, but for some reason he looked incredibly happy.

The third time that they returned to the rocky tide pool, Ondi said, "Leave the rest for me. I won't get stung."

Minroa frowned at the remaining jellyfish and then considered the dripping wet young man beside him. Sand and bits of kelp spattered his white braids, and numerous bruises marked his face and bare arms.

Ondi was such an unrefined youth. Too trusting. And naïve as well.

Yet he possessed the key to so many things Minroa could not yet grasp.

Wasn't that a bit too frustrating?

"I'm being so nice to the little monsters, and they just won't let up! Are they biased against foreigners? What is your secret to charming the things?" Minroa asked. Despite the evening gloom, his face was beautiful and his pout just playful enough to pass for teasing. "Or did you say something to turn them against me?"

"I didn't! I would never speak ill of you," Ondi answered earnestly. He wiped the droplets of seawater back from his pale eyes. "It's just that they sense you aren't one of them."

"And you *are*?" Minroa arched his brows skeptically, then glanced to the Waethir's hips. "Wherever have you hidden your tentacles, Ondi?"

A nervous laugh escaped Ondi. However, he answered quite seriously, pointing up at the luminous blue clouds of fei'lux overhead. "When the fei'lux surges, it's easy to build connections between the different strands of wild fei'thallus, making them resonate with each other. Mine are particularly strong and easily bond to any strands that grow wild throughout Saigrath. Especially in sheltered places like caves or tide pools. So, I simply fed a stream of fei'lux to the wild fei'thallus in the jellies—like you would channel it into an ancillary. That creates a link between my fei'thallus and theirs, so from this point on I can reach into them, and they sense me as if I'm one of them."

"You could make them serve you like living ancillaries?"

"I suppose I could but . . . I'm not certain why I would. They're better off living their own lives in the ocean." Ondi shrugged as if indifferent to possessing such power over other creatures. "The facet of myself I left in them isn't anything much. Just enough that I can touch them without being stung."

"A facet of yourself left in them? They're not all going to spawn a generation of white giants now, are they?" Minroa teased, but not entirely without appreciation.

"No. They aren't so infused with my character or my fei'thallus that they could become chuuraun; I merely imparted an impression of this moment to them. So even if I die tomorrow, my memory of this moment will live on with them. You and I, standing together before a rising tide, under the full moon."

Hearing those words, Cymin felt a surge of sweetness and sorrow at once.

Then something nudged him from behind and the scene around him faded. Light burned through his closed eyelids. Cymin frowned and turned his face away, burying his head under a fold of cloth to block out the sudden intrusion of sun.

"Tuteli Adept Cymin?" a voice called him quietly.

"Jellyfish won't forget us . . ." Cymin murmured. He burrowed deeper into the blanket. It felt so warm and comfortable. A tempered current of fei'lux washed into him, soothing his aching hands and circulating through his bloodstream to saturate his body.

He wasn't ready to wake up yet. He'd undergone surgery last night. Couldn't he just sleep in a while longer?

"Tuteli Adept Cymin." This time he recognized Vessreid's voice. He felt a hand nudge his arm again. "If you are this tired, perhaps you should return to Lux Temple."

"*You* go," Cymin mumbled. Couldn't everyone leave him alone?

He pulled his eyes open to realize that he'd nuzzled his face up against a firm expanse of gray leather. The scent of sweat, bergamot and birch oil rolled over him. He glanced up to meet Laithondi's amused gaze. Then the full situation dawned upon him.

Cymin wasn't in a garden in Lux Temple, nor was he standing on the shore of a black sea with a cerulean aurora igniting the night sky in blue flames. Those surroundings had been the images in fleeting dreams. In reality, he occupied a stone bench where sunlight filtered through branches of an overhanging wisteria. Carp splashed in the nearby lily pool, and all the Waethir seated at the dining table eyed him. He was still in the Eighty-Nine Feasts Pavillion.

And at some point, he'd dozed off and slumped onto Laithondi's chest.

Chapter 11

"Shit!" Cymin bolted upright and made a clumsy attempt to straighten the folds of Laithondi's leather coat. He could hardly believe that he'd just floated into some absurd romantic dream in the middle of the day. And glancing at Laithondi now, Cymin realized that he must have conjured an approximation of this man into his dream as well. That lanky Waethir youth's white braids and dark blue eyes clearly arose from Cymin's impression of Laithondi.

Recalling how sentimental and trusting the Ondi in his dream had been embarrassed Cymin further. A flush spread across his face until even his ears burned.

"You've not yet recovered from your injuries, have you?" Laithondi asked.

"I have." Cymin didn't need or want to be treated like a sickly weakling. He already felt useless enough without spell filaments. "I'm just shockingly lazy. And you make a comfortable pillow."

Vessreid laughed, while Laithondi rolled his eyes, and Cymin felt much less self-conscious. They both seemed to understand his lingering exhaustion without needing to draw more attention to it.

But Mazilane shot him a curious glance, as if Cymin had done something particularly daring. Did Mazilane suspect he'd flopped onto Laithondi on purpose? Perhaps in a clumsy attempt to get closer to the scepter? Then Cymin recalled the sensation of tempered fei'lux flowing into his body. Had that been part of his dream or could it have been the scepter? If it was an effect of the scepter, why had it stopped?

Cymin desperately wanted to reach out and touch the thing. He just managed to restrain himself and instead gazed down at its intricately carved surface hanging against Laithondi's angular hip. Laithondi glanced to where Cymin's open hand lingered over his thigh. He raised one sharp white brow in question, and, belatedly, Cymin realized how inappropriate his gesture and stare might appear.

East Deity isn't so dazed and desperate that he'd grope a stranger . . . at least not while he's wide awake.

At the same time, he could hardly explain the truth.

The embarrassed flush already coloring his cheeks intensified to a fevered blaze.

Fortunately, at that moment, Mazilane raised his voice to shout a greeting across the pavilion grounds to the other side of the lily pond. Everyone's attention leapt to him and then to the group of people he called out to.

Una Bayan strolled at the head of the group while Yinni and three young women dressed in yellow jackets followed along. Even surrounded by bright sprays of spring flowers, Una Bayan's vivid red pinstripe suit and scarlet lips commanded attention. Yinni presented a far more sedate figure, clothed in clay-brown robes, and deprived of both hair and any cosmetics. But with her clear features and limber build, she exemplified that classic depiction of an ideal tuteli: dignity, grace and wisdom unsullied by the vanities of a mortal world.

The three young women who followed on Yinni's heels all wore cheery expressions. Cymin knew them at a glance. The curvy twins with long curls of brown hair flowing over their shoulders were Paeth and Ovelah. Paeth laughed and patted Yinni's shoulder, while Ovelah trailed a step behind with a more wan smile—like a muted reflection of her twin. Saum wore her black hair in a bobbed cut recently popularized by Una Bayan. She was much shorter and a little more plump than her companions, but she skipped along with enthusiastic steps, and when she laughed along with Yinni and Paeth, her voice carried all the way across the lily pond. She gripped a glossy magazine in one hand, and the gold champion ring she'd won the night before flashed on the other.

If he hadn't known that Hiral had accompanied Yinni and Una Bayan, Cymin might have overlooked the man entirely. Dressed in sedate russet clothes and a gray cap, the cameraman trailed far behind the rest of them, head lowered to study the tether on his wrist, while his gray camera glided above them all.

"Friends of yours?" Bailon asked Mazilane. She appraised the group of women with interest.

Cymin automatically nodded in response to the question but stopped himself from explaining further, since he wasn't certain what strategy Mazilane wanted to employ.

"The woman in red is the producer of our documentary, Una Bayan," Mazilane explained. "Beside her is another new hire for our film crew, Tuteli Yinni—"

"Tuteli Yinni?" Vessreid—who had hardly glanced to the women when Mazilane waved—now turned in his seat, his expression lifting with delight. Laithondi, too, looked across the pond, but he didn't appear nearly as happy as Vessreid.

Cymin frowned. Not that he wanted people to hate Yinni on sight, but when men who'd never met his sister responded with such excitement, it was rarely an indication of good intentions. Vessreid's expression, however, reminded Cymin far more of Master Tam's doting appraisal than that of the average ogling pervert.

"Her composure throughout the Spring Exhibition was quite impressive," Vessreid commented. "Even in Saigrath, such focused control of fei'lux is rare to see during a battle."

"If your Ministry of National Security hadn't barred us from selecting tuteli, Vess would have chosen her as his student right away," Bailon remarked. "He argued for quite some time with your officials, but they all claimed they were too powerless and their departments too poor to expunge her debts on their own. And, of course, Vess refused to stoop to bribing them, no matter how blatantly they hinted."

Vessreid drew himself up stiffly. "Why would I bestow gold on swine who are so ignorant and heartless towards the holy tuteli that they treat them as fodder to train pampered secular mages?"

"Because it would have worked?" Bailon muttered, and Eirjiri suppressed a grin.

Cymin was touched by Vessreid's outrage on the behalf of Chyrenese tuteli. At the same time, he knew Bailon had assessed the situation rightly. Bribery among petty officials was so commonplace that many inspectors and regulators actually posted their fees, calling them "handling charges." That doctrine of corruption allowed criminal organizations like Yanyeo's Ember Knife to easily elude prosecution, while impoverished tuteli languished in Storm Towers.

"Resorting to bribery would be an insult to Tuteli Yinni's skills," Vessreid stated. "Truly outstanding people, like her, will always rise above their lesser peers. They only need an opportunity."

"Una Bayan told me much the same thing when she decided to hire Yinni and Cymin, both. It seems that you two share a talent for spotting greatness," Mazilane told Vessreid. Then he squinted across the distance of the lily pond. "I'm not sure who the girls in Ryde Academy jackets are, but since Una Bayan has been putting together a list of your probable candidates, I'd guess that they were standouts in the exhibition as well. We're hoping for film interviews before you all set out—"

"Yes, that's my Saum!" Eirjiri's delighted whoop cut off the rest of Mazilane's words. "She's so low to the ground that I didn't see her at first. But look at her, zipping along like a fearless little honeybee."

Eirjiri waved, and Saum, seeing her broad gesture but obviously unable to hear her, looked momentarily surprised, but then waved back with friendly delight.

Bailon glanced to Arnaith and asked, "Those are the twins you liked, aren't they?"

"Paeth and Ovelah," Arnaith said.

She didn't actually answer Bailon's question, but Cymin guessed that she didn't need to. The fact that she recognized the twins at a glance and knew their names was telling enough. However, Arnaith's attention didn't remain on the girls. Instead, she cast Mazilane a harsh, assessing look. Cymin found her expression worrying—it was as if she could peer right through all Mazilane's charm and pretense to view the truth deep within him.

Mazilane returned her gaze with an unperturbed smile, then he turned his attention to Cymin.

"Sorry, little jackal, but it looks like your lunch is canceled. If Una Bayan tracked us down, then she wants our help with the interviews." Mazilane stood and drew his wallet from his coat pocket. He addressed Bailon. "Will it be all right if I leave the money for the food we ordered with you? I'm not sure how you calculate gratuities in Saigrath, but here—"

"No! We want you to stay," Eirjiri objected. She glanced first to Bailon and then to Laithondi. "How can we send Tuteli Cymin away when he's barely up from his sick-bed and hasn't had a thing to eat? And Mazilane was going to show us how to properly dip Chyrenese pepper snake in flower sauces!"

"It's fine. We'll do it another time." Mazilane touched the tether on his wrist, and his camera dived from the branches of wisteria to alight on his shoulder. Cymin sighed and started to rise as well. He'd really wanted to eat something—or to at least sit down for a little longer.

To his surprise, Laithondi caught his elbow and pulled him back down to the bench seat, but he didn't say a word.

"Just invite your producer and the others to come join us," Bailon said. She continued to study Una Bayan's eye-catching suit and bright red heels with interest. "They look entertaining at the very least."

"Yes! Let's do that," Eirjiri agreed. "I want to chat more with Saum. And Arnaith could talk to the twins about their past . . . "

Arnaith gave a shake of her head, and Eirjiri trailed off with a scowl. She shot Laithondi an obviously pleading look.

However, it was Vessreid who addressed Arnaith.

"We're all going to be traveling to the same destination soon," he said gently. "We might as well share a meal and get to know each other a little better. Isn't that so, Laith?"

Laithondi shrugged.

Arnaith sighed and, oddly, glanced to Cymin. Her deep blue gaze—so much like Laithondi's—fixed on him for a disconcertingly long time, then she looked away to where Paeth and Ovelah had come to a stop beside Saum.

"Fine," Arnaith said at last. "If they wish to, let them join us."

Only then did Laithondi's grip relax, and he released his hold on Cymin's elbow.

Mazilane beckoned to Una Bayan and called out to relay the Waethir's invitation to dine together.

At the same time, Eirjiri bounded up on the bench seat to flag down the group of women as if she were hailing a passing ship. The couples at the surrounding tables gawked, and a server edged towards their table. His expression was pinched and resolute, as if steadying his nerves to request that Eirjiri quiet down. But then another customer at a different table beckoned him over. Out of the corner of his eye, Cymin saw her flash something very much like a badge. The server nodded and returned to his duties inside the pavilion, leaving the Waethir to do as they pleased.

So the security detail following the Waethir hadn't simply abandoned them, after all. Cymin had to make a conscious decision not to stare at the older woman.

Mazilane strode around the lily pool, meeting Una Bayan and the others halfway. As he guided them back to the Waethir's table, Laithondi shifted toward Arnaith.

"You brought the pall?" Laithondi asked her quietly. He seemed certain enough of the answer to extend his arm out to her.

Arnaith reached into the pocket of her discarded coat and drew out a silky black cloth. Silver and gold threads woven through the delicate fabric glinted in the sunlight. Arnaith twisted the cloth between her palms, preparing for some kind of spell.

Even with Laithondi sitting between them, Cymin felt fei'lux surge to Arnaith. It didn't seem to him that Arnaith tempered the fei'lux through her body, but more like she crushed and compacted it with only a gesture. Dense, cold air swirled between her long fingers, and then the fei'lux suffused the cloth, rushing through the pall like ice water.

Arnaith tossed the roiling fabric into the air. Laithondi caught a corner of the material and sent his own surge of fei'lux through it.

Cymin had to shield his eyes from the sudden flare of light. An instant later, the cloth seemed to absorb the entire blaze. Its surface took on the leather texture of a briefcase as it unfolded into a narrow black box. It reminded Cymin of the carrying case for a very long flute, but the gold and silver sigils that glowed up from below the leathery skin were far more suited to the curses adorning Hundred Deaths Armor.

Then Laithondi opened the pall with a flick of two fingers. A murky gray smoke appeared to fill its interior, and a scent like copal incense drifted from it.

Laithondi drew the scepter from his hip. Again, Cymin felt tingling warmth rush over his body as the scepter swept past him. He resisted the urge to catch it.

Instead he folded his hands in his lap and watched as Laithondi pushed the bone-white scepter down into the smoky darkness of the pall. Ropey muscles along Laithondi's forearm flexed and tensed as if the scepter somehow resisted him. Laithondi glowered down at the scepter, and at last it dropped into the smoky depths of the pall. At the same time, a gush of fei'lux surged through the black walls of the pall, briefly illuminating the hundreds of beautiful, deadly sigils. Laithondi withdrew his hand. The pall snapped shut, going as dull as an ordinary leather case.

Laithondi sighed and then placed the case on the bench between himself and Arnaith. Cymin looked away before anyone noted his too-interested gaze.

Fortunately, at that moment, Mazilane returned with Una Bayan, Yinni and the girls from Ryde Academy. The other Waethir appeared more interested in the people Mazilane had summoned than in the pall or Cymin.

Mazilane made introductions and explained a little more about the documentary film that Una Bayan was producing. Halfway through, Una Bayan took over and Mazilane reclaimed his seat between Arnaith and Bailon.

This meeting between the two groups couldn't be a chance encounter, but Mazilane and Una Bayan played it out so naturally that it was easy to forget the contrivance. Cymin actually found it relieving to do so.

Paeth, Ovelah and Saum were certainly all fooled. They beamed and blushed and stared at the Waethir with genuine, nervous excitement. Eirjiri, Bailon and Vessreid returned their starstruck stares with kind and welcoming expressions, while Arnaith and Laithondi remained a little distant in demeanor, but not unfriendly.

"Our hope is to show the people of Chyre that the Sai and the Waethir aren't supernatural ghouls but simply the people of another nation, and our future allies," Una Bayan summed up her proposed documentary for both the Waethir and the young women from Ryde Academy. "At least, that's the plan, may the Heavens be willing."

At this, Cymin thought: *Well, the Ministry of National Security certainly wills it, so that's half the Heavens on your side already.*

"Ghouls? Really. Can you imagine any shambling, decayed ghoul with fashion sense as dazzling as mine?" Bailon laughed at her own question, then invited Una Bayan to sit next to her. Eirjiri called Saum over, and Vessreid immediately gestured for Yinni to come and sit between him and Cymin. Paeth followed Yinni. Ovelah trailed her sister. But when Cymin started to scoot away from Laithondi to make room for Paeth to sit beside him, Laithondi placed his hand on Cymin's thigh, stopping him.

"Arnaith would love to talk with the two of you, I think," Laithondi informed the twins. "She was fascinated by the ancillaries you used during the exhibition. Someone mentioned that they were of your own making."

Ovelah nodded in response and opened her mouth, but all that escaped her was a little gasp. Paeth offered Arnaith a very flattered smile but then turned back to Laithondi with an expression of hopeful entreaty.

"Do you think that you and Cymin could switch places so that . . ." Paeth trailed off suddenly after meeting the clear refusal in Lathondi's gaze. An instant later she shook her head and said, "Never mind."

Then she led Ovelah to the space Arnaith had made for the two of them. She sat beside Arnaith, leaving the place between herself and Laithondi for Ovelah. At the same time, Laithondi casually moved the black pall containing the scepter onto his lap and rather casually draped one hand over it.

The last person to be seated—or noticed at all—was Hiral. He stood to the side, looking shy, until Yinni waved to him. Alerted to his presence, Eirjiri quickly pointed out the open space for him between Saum and Vessreid.

Cymin gazed around the circular table, feeling amazed that everyone had managed to find a place. What had been a party of seven nearly doubled to thirteen in seconds. Going clockwise from Cymin's left, there was Laithondi, then Ovelah, Paeth and Arnaith. Mazilane, Una Bayan and Bailon occupied the seats directly across from Cymin. Next, came Eirjiri, Saum, Hiral and Vessreid, then finally Yinni sat on Cymin's right, closing the circle.

They seemed an incongruent mix of people at first glance but, considering them, Cymin picked out some similarities. Arnaith, Paeth and Ovelah all shared a fascination with machinery and ancillary magecraft. They also all possessed a willowy, understated grace in the way they moved and held themselves. Mazilane, Bailon and Una Bayan, on the other hand, were all outgoing, dark-eyed and well proportioned, with strong features and daring attitudes that drew attention to them. Physically, Eirjiri and Saum contrasted one another to an extreme. A lanky pale teenager with gold eyes and hair, Eirjiri towered over Saum's curvy petite figure. Where Eirjiri was deathly pale, Saum possessed a healthy brown complexion as well as lively dark eyes and glossy black hair. But in character they seemed as similar as sisters, both excitable, exuberant and optimistic. They even laughed with the same cadence.

Hiral was more difficult to gauge; he was so unassuming as to be almost invisible. In comparison, both Vessreid and Yinni were far too physically attractive to be easily overlooked—with lean, toned figures and perfectly shaped features—but they did seem to keep their own council, maintaining an attitude of benevolent, dispassionate dignity. At least until some injustice infuriated them. Perhaps the same could have been true of Hiral?

Cymin stole a sidelong glance to Laithondi, wondering what, if any, traits the two of them might share. Cymin was tall and strong, but not as imposing in height as Laithondi, nor were his features anywhere near as stark or harsh. The fact that they'd both been appointed to represent East Deity hinted at some similarity in their bearing and character, but Cymin couldn't really imagine what that was. He peered up at Laithondi's sharp profile and recalled the feeling of the man's callused hands on his abdomen. At the same time, Laithondi's dark blue eyes angled in his direction, catching him out. Cymin looked away quickly, but not before noting the flicker of an amused smile curving Laithondi's lips.

"This is perfect!" Eirjiri crowed from across the table. "The Heavens have contrived a way for us to bring Tuteli Yinni and Tuteli Cymin with us, despite all those stodgy officials!"

A few diners at neighboring tables startled as her voice rang out, but apart from the volume at which it was delivered, most seemed unfazed by Eirjiri's exuberant exclamation and returned to their own concerns. Eirjiri gestured broadly. "And it's all thanks to Mazilane and Una Bayan and . . ." Eirjiri peered at Hiral, then glanced to Saum, obviously expecting her to supply the man's name. Saum just shrugged.

"Hiral," Cymin provided.

The other man appeared startled that Cymin remembered. Cymin smiled at him. He wasn't bad-looking, just a bit plain, particularly when surrounded by so many striking companions. Hiral held his gaze for just a moment, offering him a quick, bashful smile.

"Ah, Hiral . . . Hiral . . ." Eirjiri repeated, as if attempting to memorize the name. "In Saigrath, we would write your name with the sigil that means 'a comet' . . ."

"Piirocs use the same sigil to represent the wandering eye of a flounder," Arnaith remarked. Both Paeth and Ovelah's faces lit with delight, learning this bit of trivia, but Hiral didn't seem all that happy. Cymin didn't blame him; it wasn't exactly flattering to be compared to a flounder or to have Piiroc origins connected with your name. But Eirjiri clapped and grinned.

"The wandering eye. Yes, that's it!" Eirjiri looked back to Hiral. "You wander with the eye of your camera! I'll remember from now on!"

"Indeed," Bailon batted her eyelashes at Hiral in playful flirtation. "And if I indulged your wandering eye, would you indulge my wandering hands?"

"Bailon—" Vessreid's reprimanding tone reminded Cymin of Master Tam when he neared the end of his patience.

"It was just wordplay, Vess." Bailon rolled her eyes, but then cast Hiral a friendly smile. "Don't worry, my dear. I'm a flirt, but I don't mean anything by it."

Hiral nodded, looking both flushed and shy. He half-hid behind his camera, fussing with one of its wings. At the same time, Arnaith eyed the camera itself, then looked to where Soir rested on Mazilane's shoulder. She was plainly making some private comparison. Of what, Cymin had no idea.

Vessreid cleared his throat and then, with a rather formal air, addressed Yinni. "I am gladdened that you've found a way to join us. I felt that you possess the greatest potential of any of the mages we observed yesterday. It's my hope that during the time that we are traveling together, you would allow me to offer you some instruction, even if I am not allowed to formally call you my disciple."

"Really? That would be so wonderful. I'm beyond honored. Thank you." Yinni bowed her head modestly, her cheeks flushed red. She wasn't unaware of her prowess, but such direct flattery was unusual for any tuteli to receive. Cymin didn't know how he'd take it if one of the Waethir suddenly praised his magecraft and asked to teach him.

Not that anything like that could happen now that his spell filaments were gone. Cymin curled his fingers into his palms self-consciously.

"I very nearly didn't get to come along, actually." Yinni's comment drew Cymin's attention back from his brooding.

"Trouble at the Grand Rail Station?" Cymin guessed from her expression that she'd run afoul of bureaucracy. Tuteli were allowed free movement within the capital, but traveling beyond the city required a work certificate or a ministry-issued waiver. Attempting to leave the capital without one or both would get a tuteli arrested and charged for deserting National Service conscription. Even with their paperwork and certificates in perfect order, young tuteli departing the capital for any reason other than serving the Storm Towers could expect to be detained and questioned.

"Yes. A petty little stamp-licker in ticketing thought he could make a move." Una Bayan's scarlet lip lifted in a dramatic sneer. "The slime wriggled right past Hiral and me to pull Yinni aside and inform her that the regular trains to Yanyeo had been suspended for repairs, due to these recent fei'lux storms, so there weren't any vacancies available to tuteli aboard the remaining Yanyeo Express. Then the creep went on to claim that *he* could arrange for a berth in a staff train car, if she made it worth his while."

A surge of outrage rushed through Cymin at the disgust and humiliation Yinni must have felt. It wasn't uncommon for minor officials to bully, harass and demean novice and even adept tuteli—he'd experienced it himself on occasion, but it was worse for attractive women. He looked to Yinni, half expecting to see rage smoldering in her gaze and fully prepared to go jump the ticketing bastard and beat him to a pulp.

But Yinni simply looked amused and shook her head.

"I was so furious and so amazed by Yinni's dignity in the face of such a repulsive little prick—excuse my language—but he deserved to be called worse." Una Bayan swept a lock of her hair back behind her ear and went on. "Anyway, I'd already cleared the use of my own private train cars with Father months ago. I had all the papers in hand. So I walked right up and told him as much. The little man nearly choked on his own tongue when he realized that he'd been caught out by Minister Bayan's daughter, attempting to extort bribes from her traveling companion."

"Got him fired?" Mazilane asked.

"Not just that, he's also being charged with breach of public trust, indecent conduct and extortion," Una Bayan replied. "Hiral filmed the entire exchange, Yinni signed the complaints against him, and I co-signed as a witness. I radioed Father from the ticketing office and had officers take him away right then and there. No other girl will have to deal with him again."

Yinni nodded, a rare expression of smug delight lighting her face. Having Una Bayan turn the tables on the man—especially in such a dramatic manner—must have been quite satisfying. Cymin wished he could have witnessed it himself.

"The spirit of justice worked through the three of you," Vessreid commended them.

"Alas, these days even the spirit of justice has to rely on nepotism to get the job done," Mazilane commented.

Cymin heard a snort of amusement escape one of the passing servers.

"The method matters little when the outcome is righteous. Only those who protect the powerless are worthy of power themselves," Vessreid stated.

At the same time, Bailon cocked her head, considering Una Bayan. "The way you wear your hair was strange to me at first, but I think I like it now."

"Oh, well, thank you," Una Bayan replied. "I like your hair as well."

Bailon nodded as if that went without saying.

At the same time, Laithondi nudged Cymin and asked, "Are you siblings?" He gestured in Yinni's direction.

"Absolutely. Don't believe her if she denies it," Cymin replied.

"Hiral as well?" Laithondi inquired.

Hiral? Cymin was so stunned by the idea that either he or Yinni could resemble so unremarkable a person as Hiral that he almost failed to answer.

"No. We're only coworkers," Cymin said at last. "Why would you think . . . ?"

"You have the same shape of notch in the helix of your ears—" The rest of Laithondi's reply was cut short by another of Eirjiri's excited hoots.

This time, Cymin fully shared her delight as he looked over to see six gold-clothed servers descending upon their table with a multitude of silver platters and beautiful serving dishes. Each brimmed with fragrant food. Crispy fried pepper snake, three different brilliant flower sauces, a heap of glistening ginger rice, scallion cakes, sesame cress scattered with tender herbs, tangles of fat ribbon noodles, sour pea soup, persimmon sorbet *and* peach dumplings filled the table. Still more servers arrived, these bearing small casks of cloud liquor as well as fresh pots of Lucky Tea. Young attendants flitted around the table distributing cups, cutlery and individual serving dishes. Lastly, the pavilion host himself brought them a gold platter boasting the shimmering perfect orbs of twenty-six perfectly candied egg yolks.

Cymin tore his gaze away from the tempting variety of dishes that the Waethir had ordered and focused on the only food he could actually claim. A small sorbet bowl resting in a slightly larger dish of crushed ice and mint leaves. The persimmon slices scattered over the sorbet had been trimmed to look like blossoms. *It might be cold, but it's still quite pretty,* he assured himself. It was all that he could afford, in any case, and more than he ought to have expected.

He noticed Yinni, too, averting her gaze from the tantalizing feast of other people's food spread across the table. She extended her forefinger to push a porcelain dish of butter mushrooms out of her line of sight.

"I'll share my—" Cymin began to assure her, but Eirjiri spoke over him.

"Everyone, enjoy as much as you want of everything. If there's more you'd like, simply order it. This will be my treat, in celebration of this fortuitous meeting with our future traveling companions as well as our chosen disciples." Eirjiri gave Saum a meaningful nudge and beamed at her.

"Disciples?" Saum's confused expression slowly changed to one of joy as she held Eirjiri's gaze. "Me? Truly?"

"Absolutely!" Eirjiri replied. Then she gestured to Paeth and Ovelah. "Obviously, Arnaith wants to teach the both of you."

"Indeed," Arnaith stated with a calm smile at each of the twins. "There is much I will learn from you as well, I'm certain."

The twins stared, wide-eyed, at Arnaith in stunned silence, then Paeth began to thank her with a hand pressed to her chest, as if she could hardly bear the pounding of her heart. Ovelah simply bowed her head and murmured her gratitude in stuttering whispers. Yinni beamed at her three friends.

Cymin, too, felt heartened to know that Paeth, Ovelah and Saum had been chosen. The long journey north would likely be much better for both himself and Yinni with their company.

"Well, this *is* a wonderfully dramatic announcement," Una Bayan commented. She glanced to Mazilane's camera, then Hiral's, and lowered her voice. "And in such lovely surroundings too. Though aren't the identities of the mages you've chosen to train supposed to be a secret?"

"Your government wants it kept quiet until they release an official announcement to the public on our final day here. But what's the point of that?" Eirjiri motioned as if brushing away a biting fly. "The sooner our chosen mages know they'll be leaving, the better they can prepare and the more time they'll have to say their goodbyes. Whisking them away in the dead of night without notice is too cruel."

Cymin noticed Mazilane's smile tighten for just an instant. He wondered why the man cared either way. Then he realized that planting a bomb wasn't the only way to undermine the tentative alliance between Saigrath and Chyre. Assassinating the outstanding mages who the Waethir planned to teach would also disrupt relations—particularly if the Waethir were blamed in any way for the deaths.

"We should still keep the matter to ourselves," Vessreid stated.

Laithondi and Arnaith both nodded their agreement, while Bailon smiled like she'd won a wager. Then Eirjiri actually rolled a small gold coin across the table to her.

"Fine. Pretend that I didn't tell you anything," Eirjiri commented to Saum. "Pretend that we randomly asked you to share our table. And later, we'll randomly explore this old palace together after sharing a feast for no reason whatsoever."

"Absolutely!" Saum agreed gamely, "I love random activities."

"All right, then," Eirjiri gestured to the platters, plates and bowls piled across the table. "Everyone help yourselves and don't hold back!"

CHAPTER 12

Despite Eirjiri's urging, Cymin did attempt to restrain himself—at least at first. But he'd been hungry for so long that now, with an abundance of rare, delicious and costly delights spread before him, he couldn't stop himself from sampling a little of everything. And then serving himself large portions of those dishes that surprised and gratified him most.

Who would have thought that slices of beef could be soft as butter melting in his mouth? Or that misty scenes of rolling green hills and fields of flowers could be evoked by the delicate fillings wrapped in translucent dumpling skins? He'd never before tasted fermented flower sauces so perfectly brewed that they bubbled and percolated on his tongue, leaving a sweet floral tang after he'd swallowed them.

The wonder of so many flavors, as well as the freedom to choose from among them, nearly overwhelmed Cymin. Never in his life had he been offered such an abundance of food that he could actually refuse to eat something he found unappealing.

The experience came as a sort of revelation to him.

Previously, he'd only thought of privilege in terms of how much any one person could obtain and possess—be that petty officials demanding hefty bribes or Boshyin mages clothed in gossamer silks and casually tossing around beautiful ancillaries, crafted just to suit them. What he hadn't considered was a more subtle but greater indication of power: the freedom to refuse.

On the surface, the two seemed like the same thing; by choosing to fill his porcelain bowl with butter mushrooms rather than sour pea soup, Cymin took what he wanted and, by default, rejected a less appealing option. But that didn't mean that an abundance of material comforts always represented freedom of choice, did it? Cymin suddenly remembered that portrait gracing the cover of the book hidden in his pocket.

Minroa Haeyi had been born to the title of prince and probably dined on delicacies finer than these Cymin now enjoyed. But when it came to controlling the direction of his life, did he have any freedom? Had he willingly posed for the provocative painting that represented him to modern generations? Was he given any option before being whisked away to the frigid realm of Saigrath? His letters made Cymin certain he had not.

Cymin, for all the poverty of his circumstances, had at least wanted to travel to Saigrath. Lui Dane had used his debt against him, but the fact was that he could only do so because Cymin had made the choice to sacrifice the Black Staff. He'd stepped into a trap, yes, but at least it had been one he'd played a role in making.

From that perspective, he could consider himself more advantaged than even a Haeyi prince, couldn't he? It just depended on how he chose to think of himself.

He stole glances at the others all around him and suddenly wondered who among them labored under unseen constraints and who controlled their own destinies. Were Mazilane's circumstances like his own or had he gladly joined National Security? Had the Waethir always aspired to their positions or had their status and responsibilities been conferred upon them as inescapable decrees?

His eyes drifted to Laithondi. The Waethir seemed momentarily lost in contemplation of his small spoonful of persimmon sorbet. Cymin couldn't imagine why he would give a dessert such a mournful gaze.

Did it reject your advances and break your cold Waethir heart?

"Don't you like it?" Cymin asked.

Laithondi startled at Cymin's intrusion into his thoughts. Then he shrugged.

"Vessreid said persimmons are your favorite fruit," Cymin added.

"The sorbet is perfect," Laithondi replied with a smile in Vessreid's direction. But then he lowered his voice. "But even deities sometimes regret their decisions and wish to change their minds and try new things."

"There are plenty of other options here," Cymin gestured to a plate of glassy green peeled citrons and then to the bowl of absurdly round red strawberries. "You don't have to limit yourself."

Laithondi's grim expression lightened, and Cymin suddenly thought that a smile truly brought out the best of his angular features and dark eyes. But then Laithondi shook his head.

"My reluctance is a passing cloud, my fidelity the blazing sun burning it away." Laithondi's words reminded Cymin of the designs carved into his celestial pearl. Laithondi offered him a truly arrogant grin and added, "I am ever faithful to the one I chose."

Then he ate the sorbet and helped himself to a short glass of the pearly cloud liquor.

Cymin studied his own serving of the sorbet. Had Laithondi actually been talking about Vessreid?

Or persimmons?

Or something entirely different?

Cymin had no idea, and his ignorance vexed him more than it should have. He contemplated the matter so long that the icy dessert melted to an overly sweet liquid in his spoon. Even so, it remained delicious and Cymin didn't waste it.

Fortunately, everyone around him appeared too pleasantly occupied with their meals and light conversations to notice his distraction, though Yinni did cast him a sidelong glance. But her attention was drawn away an instant later by Mazilane.

The man had kept his promise and demonstrated the most elegant manner in which to dip fried pepper snake in flower sauce—the solution was to fill a soup spoon with the sauce and use silver serving tongs to place a slice of pepper snake in the spoon. While they all emulated Mazilane's instructions, Saum told them about her failed attempts to make steamed buns in her dorm room. Her improvised gas burner very nearly incinerated the bunk bed and ceiling fan. Una Bayan shared stories of the horrifying concoctions that stood in for food on the sets of various films she'd worked on.

People laughed and chattered and passed around dishes. Steadily, pots of tea dried up and platter after platter of delicacies emptied. Cymin, at last, escaped the gnawing hunger that had churned through him all last night and today. He sighed, feeling truly sated for what seemed like the first time in his life. He didn't think he could possibly eat anything more.

But then his gaze fell on the pretty, gilded platter of luscious candied yolks. Only three remained, glinting in the afternoon sun. Ever since he'd overheard a group of Boshyin mages musing over candied yolks, he'd wanted to taste one. But they were exactly the sort of sweet, rich indulgence that tuteli were never allowed to partake in.

As casually as he could, Cymin took up the silver serving spoon and scooped up one of the candies. Yinni looked up at him, her expression filled with admonishment. Her lips parted, but before she could speak, Cymin dropped the golden yolk onto her plate. He grinned at her. She couldn't put it back on the platter, nor would she waste food—so she had no choice but to indulge along with him.

East Deity magnanimously makes you his accomplice. Enjoy!

Cymin felt Laithondi's shoulders move with a silent laugh, but he didn't know why. It wasn't possible that he'd read Cymin's thoughts in his expression, was it? Cymin didn't waste time wondering over it; only two candied yolks remained.

Cymin snatched one. The sweet yolk melted in his mouth like honey but tasted as luscious and rich as buffalo cream. The unexpectedly delicate tang of lemon and nutmeg elevated the candy to a delight. A slight moan escaped Cymin.

He glanced to the serving platter just as Laithondi scooped up the last yolk. *Damn it—too slow. Well, at least I've had the one in my lifetime—*

Then, to Cymin's shock, Laithondi placed the candied yolk on Cymin's plate.

At the same time, at the far end of the table, Saum brought out her magazine to share with Eirjiri and Bailon. Yinni's attention also turned to it, and then she laughed. Una Bayan and Mazilane looked on with amusement while Arnaith, Vessreid and Laithondi studied the splashy magazine cover in curiosity.

"This one is mostly photographs," Saum stated. "You have photographs in Saigrath, don't you?"

"We do not. However, Mazilane has explained the concept to us." Arnaith pushed a braided loop of her silver hair back from her face as she replied. "And we've seen several photographs in the palace guidebooks."

"But those were dull artifacts locked up in glass cabinets. This looks like a catalog of rather pretty people wearing coy expressions." Bailon nodded her head at the magazine. "Let's have a look at it. Are there naked photographs of comely concubines included as well?"

"Or maybe funny pictures of people in the midst of forcing out a hard poop?" Eirjiri suggested.

Momentary silence descended over the table. Paeth looked horrified, and Ovelah nervously turned her gaze down to her lap. The other Waethir exchanged long-suffering glances while Mazilane snapped his cigarette case closed without taking anything out.

Cymin suppressed his own snort of laughter as he imagined the uproar that such unbecoming photographs of film stars and radio idols would cause. The publishing company would probably be burnt to the ground—if not by the irate performers themselves, then by the vast throngs of their enraged fans. Though it did make him wonder what the entertainment industry was like in Saigrath.

Then he noticed Hiral panning his camera across them all. He was so unobtrusive that Cymin had almost forgotten that he was filming them. Fortunately, Hiral passed over Cymin quickly, turning the dark lenses of his camera back to Saum's oversized magazine.

"Nothing quite that—eh . . . thrilling?" Saum laughed. "No, they're portraits of film stars from all the *best* motion pictures." Saum grinned across the table at Una Bayan. "Present company included!"

She happily tapped the black and white photograph of Una Bayan's dewy face that graced the glossy cover. The image came from the film she'd starred in recently, in which her character had subdued ghostly Wraiths with the Chyrenese national anthem.

"You were a whopping success at the box office." Saum launched into a summary of the film's basic plot.

As she did, Cymin felt his shoulders tensing. The film's depiction of the Waethir had hardly been flattering—or even human. After only knowing this group of them for a few hours, Cymin felt ashamed of it.

He glanced to the glittering gold candied yolk on his plate and thought of the celestial pearl hidden in his pocket. Never would he have expected such generosity from strangers. In return, he had agreed to spy on them in hopes of stealing their ancillary spells. Cymin sighed; he now felt too guilty to eat the candied yolk.

But what else could he do? As one of Lui Dane's agents, perhaps he could ensure that no harm came to the Waethir themselves? At the very least, he would be expected to protect them from Piiroc agents' attempts to destroy an alliance between Chyre and Saigrath.

Cymin sliced the candy in his dish in two and placed a portion on Laithondi's plate, then ate his own half.

Laithondi looked briefly surprised but then ate his piece of the golden candy. A faint smile curved his mouth afterwards.

Saum wound up the sweeping conclusion of the film with a broad gesture of her arms, nearly knocking a teapot off the table. Fortunately, none of the Waethir seemed to take offense to their depiction—or at least not to Saum's exuberant descriptions of it. Bailon snickered at the idea of Wraiths being ghosts of long-dead mage-kings. And all of them burst into laughter upon hearing that the film's ghostly Wraiths were banished by a national anthem.

"It wasn't the most nuanced of scripts." Una Bayan had the grace to appear a little embarrassed.

"A bunch of sexist fuddy-duddies in the Ministry of Education still managed to misunderstand it, though." Saum shook her head. "They wrote all kinds of nasty protests."

"I remember that!" Paeth spoke up. "It was because the heroine defeats the ghosts using a song. So they argued that, technically, that represented her employing Piiroc magecraft because Piiroc magecraft is said to channel fei'lux through sound."

Cymin nodded automatically. The association between Piiroc magic and music was so strong that the manufacture and sale of ancillary musical instruments were closely monitored. Public purchases were legally limited to lucky crickets and weak ancillaries like blessing chimes and bells, whose range were limited to a twenty-foot capacity.

Though, oddly, the old tomes in Lux Temple didn't ascribe Piiroc magecraft to musical ancillaries. Rather, they described the Piirocs contorting fei'lux with their voices as well as a gruesome variety of body parts and blood.

"That's all true, of course. But Piirocs don't use musical spells to fight ghosts. Ghosts aren't real," Saum responded, then she looked quickly to Eirjiri with a slightly worried expression. "At least as far as I know."

"As far as I know, as well," Eirjiri replied happily. "Though I do like a good ghost story, myself."

"Wh . . . w. . . why did . . . people used to think . . . ghosts and . . .?" Ovelah trailed off, glancing to Paeth.

"Yes, why *did* people believe you Waethir were ghosts back then?" Paeth asked, understanding her sister's question implicitly. "They even call you Wraiths in most of the old texts."

"Because we were spooooooky!" Eirjiri grinned. "And we let women make their own choices and even serve as leaders."

A short bark of laughter escaped Arnaith, though she quickly regained her collected demeanor. Bailon snorted and continued to smile.

"It's probably because we Waethir don't forget our experiences from one lifetime to the next. Or our friends or enemies, or promises kept or broken," Bailon replied. "When we arise from the Sai tuteli to become Waethir, the wisdom of our past is always returned to us."

Cymin's attention turned fully to Bailon. Did she mean that the dying Waethir actually transferred their memories to the next generation, or that the chosen tuteli simply inherited heaps of ancient memoirs and diaries to memorize? The first option recalled Lux Temple's oldest myths of tuteli fully being possessed by deities, while the second struck him as more likely. In either case, it might explain why Bailon felt a sense of ownership over a liquor cask that was hundreds of years older than she was.

The announcement impressed Ovelah to no end. Her eyes widened, and she whispered something to Paeth.

"Does everyone in Saigrath remember their past lives?" Paeth inquired.

"Only the Waethir," Vessreid answered. "The rest of the Sai are mortals like yourselves. They, too, are unburdened by their pasts."

"Even we used to be better at forgetting, but—" Eirjiri's comment was cut short by Arnaith.

"No one wants to hear a list of everything we used to be better at." Arnaith pushed her empty teacup forward, and Paeth quickly refilled it for her.

"So you Wae . . . Wae . . . you remember . . . why . . .?" Ovelah's voice was so meek in the presence of the Waethir that it hardly carried past her lips. Still, Paeth seemed to easily grasp her sister's thoughts.

"Yes, we have all been wondering." Paeth looked to Eirjiri. "Why did the Wraiths withdraw across the Great Chasm Sea?"

"We—" Eirjiri's response was again cut short, but this time it was Bailon who spoke up.

"That was 209 years ago." Bailon shrugged. "Who knows why anyone did anything back then?"

Cymin found it suspicious that Bailon could know the exact location of a liquor cask that had been buried at the start of Xondir Haeyi's reign but then claim ignorance of the motive behind her entire nation abandoning the kingdoms they'd previously dominated. His gaze seemed drawn to the black pall resting on Laithondi's long legs. The scepter inside it had been discovered in an ancient crypt on the northern border between Chyre and Piiroc. Cymin suddenly wondered how it had come to be there, and how long ago the Waethir lost it. Could it have played as much of a role in their departure as it did now in their return?

Cymin didn't know why the thought occurred to him, but the longer he stared at the pall, the more a nagging uneasiness spread through him—as if he were attempting to recall some aspect of a dream, but the harder he tried to focus, the more vague and faint the entire thing became, until he wasn't certain of even a single detail.

At last, he gave up and simply rubbed his tired face. So the Waethir had secrets too. Who didn't?

"True. Too true. I hardly know why I do anything I do now," Eirjiri muttered. Then she nudged Saum. "What else is in this magazine of yours?"

Saum required no further encouragement to share her favorite subject. She launched into explaining the real value of this particular issue of the magazine. It contained the most recent list and photographs of the top twelve rising film stars. All were multi-talented, dashing and, most importantly—according to Saum—single.

"So they say," Una Bayan informed her with a conspiratorial wink. "Come share the pictures, and I'll tell you what's true and what's a pack of lies."

"Volunteering to destroy a girl's romantic dreams and the spotless reputations of twelve actors in one go." Mazilane arched his brows. "There's efficacy in action."

Despite the admonishment, he joined Una Bayan in gently mocking actors' love lives and personal habits. Nothing they revealed was particularly scandalous, mostly stories behind odd pet names or little rituals to ensure good luck. The most amusing was the story of how one strapping actor confessed to having eaten raw onions the day of filming a love scene, and Una Bayan had responded by devouring two cloves of raw garlic.

"We were together in a stinking hell then. Just like the lovers we played," Una Bayan quipped, and she won a round of laughs.

Listening to it all, and hearing Laithondi's soft laugh, Cymin felt all at once more relaxed. Despite the differences between everyone gathered at the table, he found the company harmonious and pleasant. A line from some old poem came to him: *Our friendship was a spring glade where pale birches sheltered bright azaleas and rabbits played, unaware of poachers.*

"Before we leave at the end of the week, you must take me to see these moving pictures," Eirjiri told Saum.

Saum nodded, her hand on her heart, as if agreeing to take on a task of sacred and profound importance.

"Even if we don't get to see all the best films this week, there are several famous cinemas in Yanyeo, too," Saum added.

"That's right, we'll be passing through Yanyeo!" Paeth said. "That will be our one chance to visit the infamous Pavilion of Twin Fates. We'll have to take you all there before we finally depart for Saigrath." Paeth suddenly caught her breath as if she had been startled. "I . . . I think it just sank in for me. Ovelah and I are really, truly going to be traveling with you and learning Saigrath magecraft! And Saum and Yinni and Cymin are coming as well. I can't believe we could be so lucky!"

"Dreamed . . . so long," Ovelah whispered. She clenched her eyes closed and seemed to tremble with excitement.

"I refuse to think about it too much, so as not to just fall on the ground squealing with joy," Saum stated. "I'm going to pretend that this is just a random meeting and we shared a feast for no reason in particular."

"That's my girl," Eirjiri replied.

"But since we have met," Bailon said, and she glanced to Mazilane meaningfully. "You must tell us about all the best, most salacious establishments to visit in the short week we have in the capital."

" . . . In all the papers . . . so many stories about . . ." Ovelah's voice faded out, but again Paeth seemed to know exactly what she wanted to suggest and picked up for her.

"The Secret Garden Winehouse!" Paeth twisted a curl of her hair around one finger. "We've heard they offer all sorts of exotic entertainments—many, barely legal. Someone claimed that they even employ a girl who dances naked with trained tigers! But it costs two and a half blue bills just to get inside."

Cymin hid his gasp, pretending to yawn, and Yinni shot him a somewhat helpless glance. Even more than him, Yinni was protective of the few scraps of secular money she'd obtained and careful to uphold her image as a tuteli. Certainly, neither of them could afford to even cross the threshold of a venue like the Secret Garden. Never mind that their reputations as tuteli would be ruined if they were so much as seen hanging around outside the infamous pleasure-house.

"Or perhaps we could show the Waethir the greater scope of the city," Yinni suggested. "If we visit the roof of the Grand Library at sunset, we can watch the whole city light up."

For free, Cymin added to himself.

Thankfully, the Waethir didn't dismiss suggestions of a river walk or visiting the Grand Library. Though the prospect of either clearly pained Bailon and bored Eirjiri.

"What about music in the capital?" Laithondi asked.

"You like music?" Cymin felt a little stupid as soon as he asked. Why would Laithondi ask if that wasn't the case? Just so he'd know what establishments to avoid?

Laithondi nodded, and Cymin wracked his mind for a good answer to make up for his earlier question.

Numerous radio halls featured state-certified musical performances, but the selections were mostly limited to nationalist ballads and anthems, since almost anything else might be accused of harboring Piiroc leanings. Then Cymin remembered the run-down little music hall Yinni had snuck him out to when he'd turned eight. It had been little more than a tin roof tossed over bamboo scaffolding near the waterfront, where slums of Piiroc expatriates intersected with those of Dajiryn Island diaspora. But the people had been kind, gifting Cymin with tamarind candies and tickling his ears. The musicians were treated with near reverence, though many played instruments improvised from little more than water glasses and wash tubs. The melodies had been so strange and sweet that even though he couldn't recall any one of them exactly, he did remember loving them.

"Sounds like a perfect location for the tone-deaf to get themselves pickpocketed," Mazilane stated after Cymin described the place. Then Mazilane advised a visit to the more exclusive Pangolin Winehouse instead.

Other suggestions came from Una Bayan as well as Paeth and Saum. Their discussion ranged from the People's Radio Broadcast Hall to private music clubs. While they debated the better points of each, the host of the Eighty-Nine Feasts Pavilion sidled to the table with the bill. He was a prim-looking man with pinched features. At the moment, he seemed unsure if he should present the bill to Laithondi or Vessreid. Then Eirjiri gestured, and fei'lux around her long fingers whirled out in a gold arc. The bill was snatched from the host's grip and drawn to Eirjiri's hand. She glanced at the long tabulation of large numbers with an amused expression. Then she fished two large yellow coins from her discarded coat and held them out to the host.

When the pavilion host accepted the coins, his hand dropped as if their weight was far more than he'd been prepared to support. His shocked expression inspired a laugh from Eirjiri and Bailon.

Cymin peered at the coins. Having hefted gold antiquities as East Deity, Cymin suddenly wondered if they could actually be solid gold, rather than plated alloys common to obsolete Chyrenese coins. In either case, they weren't normal Chyrenese currency. Who could say whether they amounted to too much or too little to cover the cost of the feast.

The host stood gripping the awkward coins and looking uncertain of how to proceed. Just as he seemed ready to issue some statement of dissatisfaction, the older woman—who Cymin had noticed instructing the waitstaff previously—beckoned him to her table. She made a request for more tea and said something else much more quietly. Cymin was now absolutely certain that she'd been one of the NS marshals who'd originally escorted the Waethir to the Palace Complex. Her words appeared to reassure the host of the genuine value of the coins. He departed looking jubilant, though not before thanking Eirjiri for her immense generosity.

"Were those real solid gold?" Saum asked in an awed whisper. "They were half the size of my fist."

"Of course," Eirjiri replied. "All the treasures of the earth belong to Eirjiri, so I can always afford to be generous to mortals. Soon enough, you'll be able to do the same—"

"But that should be a lesson for a later day, Jiri. No need to turn the occasion of your first meeting into a tedious classroom session." Arnaith rose from the bench. She collected her white leather coat and swung it over her shoulders in a graceful motion. "I've been sitting too long. I want to stretch my legs and learn more of the history that has passed since the last time Waethir visited this palace."

"Any particular branch of history?" Una Bayan, too, stood, as did Mazilane and Hiral.

"Please, not mathematics. They're deadly dull," Saum whispered. Paeth shot her such an aghast look that both Cymin and Yinni laughed.

"The ancillaries you Chyrenese now employ are very different than the ones we know in Saigrath. Laith has told me that they rely on something called spell filaments," Arnaith stated. "Where would you advise I begin to learn more of their development?"

"Well, if you're curious about the rise of modern Chyrenese mages and our ancillaries, the best place to begin is the armory," Una Bayan advised. "Sadly, many of our earliest advances were driven by conflict. Though I like to think that nowadays medicine, education and even the arts contribute just as much to innovations in our magecraft."

"It is a nice thought. But as you suggest, the armory is likely where I will find my answers." Arnaith inclined her head and glanced to Laithondi. He rose to his feet and nodded.

Paeth and Ovelah also hurried to stand, though neither of them appeared all that excited to visit the forbidding armory building.

"I'll skip the long grim walk through a world of war crimes," Bailon decided. She glanced to the twins, then to Saum and Eirjiri and, lastly, to Mazilane. "I don't suppose there's an exhibit of your nation's most laughable fashion trends or scandalous publications?"

"Not as such," Mazilane replied. "But I'd be happy to play guide and show you every bare ass hidden in the backgrounds of the portraits in the gallery arcade that bridges the consort gardens and the Mage-Kings' Proclamation Hall."

"Perfect." Bailon batted her eyelashes theatrically. "Throw in a few full-frontal nudes, and I might give you a tour of my own private collection."

"Count me in on that as well," Una Bayan decided.

"A threesome, how delightful," Bailon said, then she glanced to Hiral. "Will you be joining in or just watching from the side?"

Hiral flushed and bowed his head, hiding his face beneath the brim of his cap.

"Hiral can come along with me," Yinni spoke up, then she looked to Una Bayan. "If you don't mind. I'd really like to visit the palace gardens—"

"I would as well!" Vessreid stated. He glanced to Arnaith. "I have no desire to see the hateful weapons of those Haeyi bastards, not even after they're dead."

Arnaith shrugged. "Suit yourself."

"I was going to suggest the garden," Laithondi's tone was surprisingly gentle towards Vessreid. "I saw in the guidebook that the palace atrium still shelters your teaspice tree. The vanilla orchids survived the revolution as well."

Vessreid's tense expression relaxed at the mention of the tree and orchids.

"Who could resist the lure of blossoms and perfumes?" Paeth mused. Cymin wasn't certain from her wide doe-eyed gaze if she was addressing him or Yinni.

". . . s?," Ovelah whispered as she stared at Vessreid. "Can . . . t . . . oo?"

Vessreid was visibly confused. Cymin also struggled to figure out what she'd meant.

"It would be lovely if you'd both join us," Yinni told Ovelah before anyone else could ask her to repeat herself. "Maybe the five of us could try filming some of the flowers. We'll see who can get the worst shot."

Paeth and Ovelah drifted to join Vessreid, Hiral and Yinni, delighted at the invitation.

"So," Eirjiri surveyed the circle. "Our tour options are perverts, plants or . . ."

"Platoons!" Saum provided the third alliteration.

"Good one." Eirjiri clapped her on the back, then asked, "Which would you prefer to join?"

"Ummm." Saum briefly considered her classmates and Yinni, but then shook her head. "Sorry. I have to go with the perverts on this one."

Cymin was, himself, torn. He harbored both fascination with, and dread of, the malevolent ancillaries housed in the palace's notorious armory. But he was also very curious about all the secret titillations that Mazilane promised to expose.

"What about the rest of you?" Mazilane asked. His gaze slid over Laithondi to fix on Cymin.

Cymin took the hint—he would go wherever Laithondi went and keep the scepter in sight. Right now, Laithondi swung the pall across his back and stepped over to Arnaith's side.

"I'm following the platoon tour," Cymin announced. He stretched and then sauntered to where Arnaith and Laithondi waited for him.

"A wise choice," Arnaith stated. "Magecraft can be learned under any circumstance. But the true test is passed by facing death in the midst of war."

Laithondi looked pained by Arnaith's sweeping statement and hastened to add, "Combat also necessitates advances in medical treatments for those injured in battle." Laithondi's gaze dropped to the black stitches seaming the backs of Cymin's hands. "Which is a most noble endeavor."

Their parties separated outside the pavilion. Mazilane, Una Bayan, Bailon, Eirjiri and Saum strolled towards the airy gallery arcade that connected the sprawling three-story concubine manor to the domineering gold palace, where generations of mage-kings held court from their spell-encircled thrones. Yinni, Vessreid, Hiral and the twins started down a pebbled path that wandered through open gardens and past water features before reaching a large iron framework of a building. So many panes of glass festooned the structure that it took on a scaled appearance, like that of some giant translucent fish lying in the sun. Cymin could just make out the twisted silhouettes of old trees and wild vines growing inside it.

Then he, Laithondi and Arnaith turned west, walking past the open arenas and ironwood stables, where vast flocks of carriage birds had once been bred and trained as mounts for public parades as well as battle. The roof of the stables supported a sculpture of a resplendent gold phoenix with its wings spread wide.

Crowds of tourists and throngs of schoolchildren out on field trips swarmed around the arena's fence, watching six gawky red hatchlings trail their trainer. Cymin smiled at the fuzzy little bird at the back of the group. It veered off from its larger siblings to snap up dried fruit that children tossed to it and to chase a wind-tossed leaflet.

"In the past, the Haeyi kings would have chopped that little one up and fed it to its stronger siblings." Arnaith's grim proclamation startled Cymin. He hadn't realized that she'd stopped so near him to observe the birds as well. Laithondi stood a little behind her, also watching the chick's antics. He met Cymin's gaze with an almost apologetic expression, then nudged Arnaith.

"Good for it, being born into better times, then," Laithondi said.

Arnaith frowned and continued to observe the playful chick as well as the children tossing their sweets to it.

"You're right," Arnaith said at last. A subtle smile lifted the corners of her mouth. "Good for it."

Then she continued along the wide worn path that led to the hulking gray monolith that was the palace armory. Laithondi and Cymin fell in behind her. They walked side by side, but in silence.

Unlike most classic Chyrenese buildings, the armory hadn't been constructed on a pentagonal plan. Instead, the single-story stone mass had been carved from a domed hill and retained a roughly circular shape. The gray granite exterior stood unpolished and unadorned. Only the huge cast-iron gates, with their filigree of gilded blessings and acid-etched security spells, lent the armory any air of the ornate grandeur that marked the rest of the Palace Complex.

The gates stood open, and even at a distance, Cymin could feel smoky, charred spell residues seeping from the interior. A few sensitive tourists turned aside, wrinkling their noses like they'd whiffed a ghastly fart, and one young man, dressed in Chohe Institute's rich purple uniform, stopped in his tracks as a nauseous green pallor spread across his face. The two young women accompanying him quickly led him away to rest on a bench near the stables.

For his part, Cymin didn't enjoy the sensation of those rank corrosive residues, but somehow, he did find them compelling—almost familiar. They were like the pungent odor of machine oil that hung over the old water heater in the temple. Or the sour reek of sweat and liniment that always greeted him upon entering the locker room. Or the fish sauce and lime pickle that nearly choked him when he opened the fermentation pots in the kitchen but, after dispersing into vats of broken rice, became comforting flavors.

Cymin stole a glance at Laithondi and Arnaith, trying to gauge their responses.

Laithondi cocked his head slightly, then muttered, "Smells like Haeyi magecraft."

Arnaith snorted.

"I was going to say it stinks of betrayal," Arnaith replied. "But I suppose that's much the same."

Laithondi glanced to Cymin.

"We probably sound boring and bitter to you," Laithondi commented.

"I don't know enough of Saigrath's history to judge," Cymin replied. Though he did harbor a secret sort of sympathy for the figure of Minroa Haeyi, he wasn't about to admit as much. Cymin merely patted the book tucked away in his pocket.

The line of visitors at the armory gates was sparse and moved quickly. The single sleepy attendant barely glanced at Cymin's ticket before waving him inside. Cymin shivered as he passed through the gates, but once he stepped into the vast chamber, he felt a flush of excitement and his pulse started to speed up. He'd wanted to tour the armory since he was a boy.

Whoever designed the exhibits had taken full advantage of the armory's natural gloom and cavernous space for dramatic effect. As far as Cymin could see, sets of bright spotlights cut through the darkness to illuminate life-sized manikins dressed in recreations of Hundred Deaths

Armor and striking theatrical battle poses. On risers, looming behind the figures, massive cages built from spell-etched iron bars and layer upon layer of thick glass panels confined the genuine suits of armor as if they were dangerous prisoners.

Even through the thick protective cases, Cymin sensed the searing and poisonous spells etched into every link of chainmail. Merciless sigils glinted over sleek faceplates, and crushing spells adorned the perfectly articulated gauntlets. He shivered just walking past them.

A few feet ahead of him, a little boy suddenly let out a wail and burst into tears. The child's mother glowered at the father, then swept the boy up in her arms and carried him into a sheltering circle created by dozens of gold chains strung with blessing-bells and luminous panes of butterfly glass. The bells chimed softly, and the butterfly glass threw off gold and blue halos of light. Dozens of these shelters hung throughout the armory, each driving back the wisps of malevolent power seeping from the surrounding Hundred Deaths Armor like toxins. After a few moments, the little boy calmed down enough for his mother to walk him out.

"A stronger parent would let him cry and teach him to stand unwavering before the threat of death." Arnaith frowned at their retreating backs and shook her head.

"Would you really have wanted to listen to him howl and scream for however long that lesson took?" Laithondi asked her.

"Of course not." Arnaith cracked a sly smile. "I'm relieved they proved to be so weak-willed."

"What about you?" Laithondi asked Cymin.

"I'm glad they left for all our sakes," Cymin replied.

"I meant, how are you feeling?" Laithondi said. "In this place?"

"Fine." Cymin scowled at him. In truth, an angry twinge had begun to flicker through his chest and his hands ached, but he wasn't about to let Laithondi think he was as weak as a five-year old.

"Hmm." Laithondi scowled at the armor towering over them and stepped back. "It makes me a little sick."

"Overcome yourself," Arnaith told him. "Don't try to use Tuteli Cymin as your excuse for running away."

Laithondi gave a soft laugh at that, and Arnaith smiled. Observing their interactions, Cymin felt certain that they were close, but their exact relationship also seemed rather inexplicable. He couldn't tell which was the elder or how much of their repartee was serious at all. They remained largely quiet as they continued to explore the armory, taking in displays of weapons as well as the everyday provisions of Chyrenese armies from different ages. The first firearms wielded by common fighters appeared and, at the same time, the Hundred Deaths Armor of mage-warriors became more ornate and sinister. Soon, the suits stood between seven and eight feet tall. Many bristled with so many interlocking plates of cursed steel, folded wings and horned helmets that they almost took on the appearance of gigantic insects. Cymin stared at a particularly outlandish suit of armor, wondering how much of it was merely for display at court and what aspects had truly been brought to life on the battlefield through inundations of fei'lux.

As he pondered, he became aware of a reedy docent in demure historical garb, lecturing a group of strapping young men, all wearing red Orae Academy uniforms. Two of the men wore ancillary swords at their hips. The shorter of them wore a neat black beard, while the taller sported a shock of hair as bright red as his uniform. They struck Cymin as familiar. Then he remembered Una Bayan's list of candidates. Two had been swordsmen from Orae. Xaon and Jeshri. One red-haired and the other dark and bearded. Could these two be the *muscular strippers*, as Una Bayan had dubbed them?

Cymin peered at them through the gloom, but it was the docent who caught his attention.

"Myths and popular fiction attribute vast powers to the armor." The young docent straightened her spectacles in a rather theatrical manner. "But modern scholars speculate that, in reality, the mage-warriors of the past weren't capable of manifesting the vast majority of spells etched into their armor."

"Fuck me . . . no way!" the bearded swordsman objected from amidst his peers. The docent glanced to him and appeared briefly impressed by his affable smile. Then she cleared her throat and went on as if unperturbed.

"Without spell filaments, mages of the past had to rely on free-floating fei'lux to power their spells. So what we see in the Hundreds Deaths Armor is an overcompensation. Only by completely encasing themselves in literally thousands of curses could the mage-warriors increase the likelihood that any one of those spells would capture a stream of fei'lux and manifest during battle.

"And, of course, after the Storm Towers were raised, free-floating fei'lux no longer stormed through towns and cities, so the ancillary armor steadily lost its value. Nearly 150 years would pass before our modern spell filaments were invented. Now, Chyrenese magecraft has reached its modern pinnacle, far surpassing the age of all these suits of armor."

The Orae boys responded with hoots and self-congratulatory cheers. The red-haired swordsman even thrust his corded arms into the air to display the white scars marking him as a mage.

Cymin frowned at his own stitched hands and didn't linger to hear any more of the guided tour. Instead, he worked his way back towards an alcove Laithondi and Arnaith had wandered into.

It seemed that the towering displays of Hundred Deaths Armor that had held him enraptured hadn't captured the Waethir's attention. Instead, they'd sought out an exhibit of portraits and lightboxes with pieces of clothing laid out in them like corpses in caskets. Delicate and subtle spell residues drifted from the gleaming fabrics inside each one. Here and there, placards explained the significance of the displays.

Cymin studied the contents of the nearest glowing cask. At first glance, they resembled a pair of tattered gloves woven from the finest gold wire and encased in decayed silk. Bending over the case, Cymin noticed that the gold wires were embedded with sharp inward-facing barbs, which would have been driven into the skin if the gloves were actually worn.

He scowled at the torturous gloves.

But as he looked more closely, Cymin picked out weathered sigils engraved into several of the gold wires. Once he recognized a few, others became clear to him. The sigils cut into every gold wire were blessings. Many of the same blessings that modern spell filaments employed.

These must have been precursors to modern, surgically implanted filaments.

"They were attempting to make them that long ago?" Cymin wondered. He was so used to thinking of spell filaments as a modern surgical innovation that he'd never considered their ancient beginnings.

Curiosity piqued, Cymin studied the next display case. It held a long leather vest. Dull gray scale armor protected the chest and back of the vest. But the interior was stitched with so many gold wires and sigils that they resembled a bright silk lining. According to the posted placard, these ancillary garments—the gloves and vest—were believed to have belonged to Xondir Haeyi himself, which took Cymin by surprise.

He'd only ever seen the mage-king depicted in full armor—an imposing, almost inhuman giant, raising brutal weapons in the midst of bloody battle, or seated atop his radiant throne like an unfeeling machine. But from the proportions of these clothes, Cymin realized that the ancient mage-king must have actually been very thin, almost frail. Had he spent his life overcompensating for a diminutive stature, or had the weight of war and rulership worn him down over the decades?

Then Cymin noticed the needle-like spines jutting from the gold lining of the vest. Even worn loosely, the spines would have pierced deep into the flesh. It must have been agony to move while wearing the thing. Cymin suddenly realized that the stains demarking the weathered sigils on the wires were a residue of the mage-king's blood. The idea horrified him.

At the same time, a desperate part of him wondered if he could make something similar to regain the power that had been stripped from him.

He stared at the gold needles and bloodstained sigils, wondering which pain was greater: the agony of countless spines biting into his body with every breath he took, or the feeling of worthlessness now coiling through him. The despair that Cymin had struggled to suppress all day rose again. Would he ever again be capable of handling enough fei'lux to manifest more than flickering lights and faint fragrant blessings? Or had he ruined his future in a moment of reckless impulse?

Cymin scowled at his own morose turn of thought.

So what's there to regret? I stopped a bomb from killing my family. I'd do the same thing again. And even if I can't do more than light cigarettes and make fake crickets sing, I'll still have eaten candied yolks and visited the mysterious lands of Saigrath. What am I trying to mope about?

How many other tuteli would have sold their teeth for the opportunity before him? Less than an hour ago, hadn't he been thinking he was better off than even a Haeyi prince? What had changed since then? Nothing but his surroundings. He realized that he'd unknowingly let the dour atmosphere of this place get the better of him. He needed to heed Arnaith's advice and "overcome" himself.

He stepped back from the display case with its grotesque, torturous spell filaments and inadvertently bumped into Laithondi.

The contact seemed to startle the Waethir out of his own melancholic reverie.

"Sorry," Cymin said at once.

"Not your fault," Laithondi replied, but he hardly seemed aware of Cymin. He shook his head and moved away from the display of ancillary garments into the luminous circle of blessing-bells. Chimes whispered and the butterfly glass cast cerulean shadows over his pale figure. Moments later, he stepped out from the soothing light and strode to a miniature portrait hanging in a light box.

At the same time, Arnaith stepped up beside Cymin and then moved past him to the case containing the vest. She pressed her forehead against the glass display case. Loops of her silver hair fell across the glass. She scrutinized the stained vest with a fascinated expression.

"So, he didn't escape unscathed after all." Arnaith's quiet comment was probably meant for Laithondi, but she was so focused on the display that she hadn't noticed he'd gone. She continued, "How madly desperate must he have been to turn his own blood into a boiling sea of spells? He'd have burned and bled in a fiery hell every time." Arnaith smiled, but she didn't seem happy, so much as bitter. "And it still wouldn't have replaced the thallus he poisoned."

"Fei'thallus, you mean?" Cymin asked.

Arnaith started at his question and spun around to stare at him. Cymin took an involuntary step back.

"Laith said that none of you believe in fei'thallus anymore." Arnaith's gaze narrowed as she straightened to her full height, staring directly into Cymin's eyes as she studied him.

"Well, a few mage-scholars have isolated microscopic organisms that might have inspired the myths. But nothing they cultured turned out to conduct fei'lux very strongly. Definitely nothing like the stories." Cymin sighed. "More fantasy than real magecraft, just like the mythic ignis gland."

Arnaith blinked and then suddenly laughed. She looked surprisingly young and happy in that moment.

"Good for you all, putting myths and nonsense behind you." She patted Cymin's shoulder. "That's just perfect."

Cymin didn't know how to respond. He'd never encountered someone who seemed so happy to have another person not share her beliefs. It felt almost like she'd tricked him, but he couldn't think how.

Fortunately, Arnaith didn't seem to expect any reply. She strolled a little distance to where Laithoni stood, studying a small, gold-framed portrait. She, too, gazed at the painting in silence. Her expression shifted subtly from a brief delight to aggrieved disdain. Then she wandered back to continue observing every detail of Xondir Haeyi's ancient, blood-stained vestments.

Cymin went to join Laithondi, scrutinizing the small portrait that seemed to absorb his attention and repel Arnaith. A plaque declared the painting to be one of only three surviving portraits of Xondir Haeyi before he'd permanently withdrawn into his Hundred Deaths Armor. As such, it must have come from early in his reign. Definitely before he declared war against his Piiroc sister.

He appeared to be in his early thirties. An ancillary crown already held back the black locks of his hair as he glared directly out from his portrait. With his sweeping dark eyes and full lips, he truly did resemble the picture of Minroa that graced the book Cymin had purchased. The young mage-king's portrait, however, was far more detailed than that of Minroa. Cymin could even make out a scar on Xondir Haeyi's neck as well as a rather distinct notch in the top of his right ear.

He smiled at that.

He almost pointed it out to Laithondi, to ask him if he thought it proved that the infamous mage-king was a relative of his as well. But he didn't know Laithondi well enough to tease him.

At least, not yet.

As if feeling the weight of Cymin's attention, Laithondi looked at him.

"How are you feeling?" Laithondi asked.

Cymin very nearly assured him that he was fine. But then he recognized the exhaustion in Laithondi's face and remembered his harrowed expression as he sheltered among the blessing-bells.

"Honestly, I think I've seen enough of this place," Cymin admitted. "I'd rather go back and watch those little carriage birds run around. What about you?"

"Yes. Let's do that." Laithondi's smile was relieved. He waved to Arnaith, and she drifted to them. Cymin expected her to opt to continue touring the armory; she'd seemed so intensely fascinated with those first attempts at spell filaments. But to his surprise, she shook her head.

"I've seen what I wanted to see," she declared.

So the three of them returned to the stables. Cymin used the money he'd meant to spend on sorbet to purchase a paper bag of dried fruit and grain to toss out to the carriage birds. The three of them spent the next hour relaxing on the lawn, tossing out the occasional treat and observing the flocks of leggy little carriage birds racing around the arena. Cymin supposed that he ought to have used the time to attempt to get nearer to the scepter, but he didn't. Mazilane wasn't there to observe him, and it had just struck him that the longer he could manage to drag out his mission, the closer he would get to Saigrath.

No doubt, Mazilane would catch him out at some point. But that was a problem for another day.

Only a little later, Yinni, Vessreid, Hiral and the twins found them—thanks to Hiral's camera. Paeth ran to Cymin's side and handed him a delicate perfume card with a pressed vanilla orchid inside. It smelled lovely, but Cymin had no idea what he was supposed to do with it. All he could do to reciprocate was hand over a piece of dried apple from the bird-feed bag. Paeth popped it in her mouth, choking slightly at its coarse quality, before Cymin could stop her.

Fortunately, Mazilane's camera, Soir, swept down and landed on his shoulder, giving Cymin an excuse to escape the awkward exchange.

When Mazilane himself appeared moments later, Cymin handed the camera over to him and dropped back into the proper position of an assistant. Yinni and Hiral joined him.

Glancing back along the path, Cymin saw the rest of their party approaching, but the NS marshals had also made their reappearance. Grim and gray, they flanked the other party of Waethir.

Tourists parted around them, and all the laughter and conversation that had surrounded the stables muted to whispers.

"It would seem that our friends from Saigrath have appointments elsewhere," Mazilane stated. "So we'd best bid them a good afternoon."

Saum and Eirjiri took the prospect of parting the hardest, throwing themselves into each other's arms while fiercely declaring how wonderful it was to have met each other. Una Bayan and Bailon beamed at one another, and Cymin belatedly realized that Bailon was now wearing some of Una Bayan's scarlet lip color, while Una Bayan sported a woven leather bracelet that looked like it matched Bailon's cloud-studded vest.

Arnaith assured Paeth and Ovelah that she would seek them out tomorrow for their advice on ancillary construction. Vessreid thanked both Yinni and Hiral for their company, and the three of them agreed that they should find time in the next week to visit the botanical gardens if they could.

Across the crowd of their companions and gray-faced NS marshals, Laithondi gazed directly at Cymin. He smiled, and Cymin smiled back without knowing why. Then, all at once, Laithondi's easy smile faded and his gaze became distant. Without a word, he turned on his heel and took his leave. The other Waethir hurried after him, and the NS marshals chased behind them.

Standing a little ahead of Cymin, Mazilane too watched them withdraw, then he muttered, "And now the real work begins."

CHAPTER 13

The next day passed in a frantic rush to prepare for the journey ahead. Cymin hardly had time to hear the temple physician, Master Shuun, scold him for removing his own stitches before Yinni appeared with a list of provisions they needed to procure and whisked him away. Together they scoured the street markets for clothes and dry goods. Cymin joked with merchants and hauled goods while Yinni bargained for deep discounts with a serene but unyielding smile. She refused to waste a single one of the red bills Una Bayan had entrusted to her.

So, while students from the Five Schools cavorted through spring festivities and the Waethir were escorted to political appearances, Cymin and Yinni chased down wholesalers and Dock District traders. Eventually, Yinni found a riverside grocer who after hearing of their expedition, patriotically agreed to throw in a free case of fermented tea leaves along with their large purchases of honey and broken rice. And according to Minroa's letters, palm oil was a rarity in the north, so Cymin bought some to mark up and resell in Saigrath to further finance their journey.

The grocer simply laughed when Cymin bowed to him and then hefted all three sacks of broken rice onto his back to avoid the grocer's exorbitant delivery charge. Nothing less was expected of impoverished tuteli.

Later, a few pious women in a weavers' courtyard sold them discounted off-cuts of waterproofed cloth as well as batting for quilting. They also donated two patchwork wool coats.

Cymin offered the women blessings as well as heartfelt thanks and let several of them rub his fuzzy scalp for good luck. Just as they were taking their leave, a young girl rushed after them, stammered something too fast for Cymin to understand, and then shoved a bag of wax paper-wrapped malt candies into his arms. Flushing scarlet to her ears, the girl then pelted back to the other weavers.

"Thank you!" Cymin shouted after her, then he stuffed the bag into the deep pocket of his outer robe.

"I love street shopping with you," Yinni whispered as they left the courtyard laden with bulging bundles of fabric.

"Because I can carry twenty percent more than a carriage bird my same size?" Cymin swung a sack of waxed thread and pebble beads over the bundles strapped to his back. Yinni had been making this claim about him since childhood.

"No, because your smile means a reliable twenty percent discount on anything women are selling. As well as sacks of free sweets from shy admirers." Yinni shifted the weight of her own full pack on her back. Together they lugged their bounty of supplies back to the temple.

There, Cymin lugged the cloth to the temple's sewing rooms and plied the novices who worked there with beads and soft malt candies in order to persuade them to help him and Yinni sew all the blankets and clothes they would need. The elderly master in charge chided him for assuming a handful of polished soapstone and a few cheap sweets could get him so much work on such short notice. But then, before Cymin could even hang his head, she snatched two malt candies from his hand and set to work at her battered foot pedal sewing machine. In a matter of minutes, she and her crew of novices stitched up one of the frayed coats for Yinni and set about quilting a vest for Cymin. The master laughed at Cymin's amazed expression and waved aside his offer of more candy.

"Tam dropped by last night and told me everything," the elderly master informed him as her gnarled hands ran yard after yard of fabric through the teeth of the sewing machine.

"He did?" Cymin didn't know why he hadn't expected that.

"Of course." The master's smile seemed both teasing and benevolent at once. "That old fusspot can't decide whether he's more proud or worried for the two of you, but he certainly isn't going to send you off unprepared. Rest assured, we'll have everything made before the end of the week."

Cymin felt absurdly moved and ended up giving away all the candies that he'd originally intended to keep for himself. Despite the loss, he danced along happily as he left the building.

However, he very quickly regained the awareness that as much as he needed warm clothes and food for the journey ahead, it was far more urgent for him to reclaim his previous control over fei'lux. Right now, even the unremarkable Hiral could beat him out when it came to keeping an ancillary camera supplied with a stable flow of fei'lux. Never mind attempting to grasp the subtle workings hidden within the Waethir's scepter.

He had no idea what he would do if he had to defend himself or anyone else from another bomb.

Just give up and die? Run away? Cymin dismissed both ideas.

So the next morning, he rose before his dorm mates and slunk through the pre-dawn shadows to claim two hours alone on the sandy training grounds before the novices arrived. He didn't dare to practice with an ancillary of any value. Instead, he picked up a discarded broom handle, carved in just two sigils—Min, for rain and *Lyn*, for blossom—then as an afterthought tapped in two copper tacks to enhance conduction on contact. He felt a little embarrassed employing an ancillary more suited to a young child than an adept, but he wanted to focus on basics, and not much could be more basic than this.

He twirled the broom handle between his fingers like a baton. Then, out of habit, he turned clockwise and then anti-clockwise, tracing circles through the sand with his toes as if he still commanded so much power that he needed to set a shield-line to protect those around him. The motions helped him relax. He spun more quickly and tossed the broom handle from hand to hand. With each move, he expanded his awareness, focusing on the faint shining streams of fei'lux he felt radiating through the cold morning air like rays of warm sunlight.

He had grown so accustomed to fei'lux simply flowing into him—to the pull of his spell filaments—as if he were basking in sunshine that he'd almost forgotten what a struggle it had been to capture and hold a stream of fei'lux before he'd undergone surgery. When he and Yinni first entered Lux Temple, it had taken him hours to isolate a single stream of fei'lux, and days had passed before he'd managed to smoothly draw one into his body, never mind channeling it into an ancillary.

Thinking about it now, he felt a little awed by all the effort that mages must have gone through before spell filaments were invented. There was no end of absurd stories of long-lost secret techniques—everything from cannibalistic blood sacrifices and erotic Piiroc rituals to fasting in meditation beneath a lake for three years—that had supposedly imbued mages with supreme control of fei'lux.

A few might have been grounded in some reality, but even so, they seemed to involve pain and sacrifice. He scowled, remembering Xondir Haeyi's blood-stained garments in the armory. The mad mage-king's agonizing creations had to have been an isolated extreme undertaking; otherwise, Lux Temple's records would have been filled with descriptions of such terrible raiments. So, Cymin guessed that most mages in previous ages had simply worked harder or in larger groups than anyone acknowledged. It wasn't uncommon for the names of novices and even adepts in any field of work to be forgotten, leaving all credit to a select few masters.

Cymin himself wasn't really keen on sharing either hardship or glory. So, if he hoped to achieve anything, he needed to push himself as hard as mages who'd fought and bled to temper fei'lux and shape spells when magecraft had still been an unforgiving discipline.

His whole body shook—his muscles tensing and his nerves tingling—as he tossed the broom handle and flexed his fingers, grasping after currents of fei'lux only to feel them slip free, or worse, sizzle and snap at his skin like burning black powder.

Is it possible that I've gotten worse at this than I was as a snot-nosed four-year-old? No. I've just grown lazy. Come on, East Deity's greatness isn't just a bundle of spell filaments. Focus!

He took in a deep breath and imagined blowing all his frustration out as he exhaled. Then he began again, turning through the motions of calling down fei'lux. Streams poured over his bare arms and chest. Slowly, steadily, he caught one faint stream after another as if wrapping each of his fingers in delicate threads of spider silk. His muscles trembled and sweat poured down his back as he carefully restrained each of his motions while constantly channeling those fragile streams of fei'lux through his hands and into the wood fibers of the broom handle. At last, he felt the copper tacks heat against his fingertips. The simple two-sigil spell glowed in the pre-dawn gloom.

At last, the air surrounding the broom handle rippled. A milky haze floated from the two glowing sigils, unfurling like smoke drifting from burning incense. Cymin held the flow of fei'lux steady as he swung the broom handle around. The instant he closed the circle, the smoky haze coalesced into dozens of large translucent lotus blossoms. They hung in the air, shimmering for a moment before bursting apart in a shower of fragrant raindrops.

Cymin grinned as the perfumed water pelted his bare chest and shoulders and dribbled down his body.

Yes! Did it!

A wave of lightheadedness followed his exhilaration. He swayed, stumbled and just managed to keep from falling over. Then he regained his composure and wiped away the beads of sweat dripping down his brow before they could sting his eyes. His hands ached and discomfort throbbed through his gut like he'd been kicked in the belly, but he took heart. Even without spell filaments, he'd managed to control and channel fei'lux long enough to manifest a spell. Now he just needed to keep practicing.

If he was lucky, none of the Five Schools mages or the Waethir would realize how badly the loss of spell filaments had affected him. He could still hold his head up proudly in their company.

Then a quiet applause sounded from behind him, the slow, mechanical quality of the claps ringing with unmistakable derision.

Cymin turned to see Laithondi at the edge of the practice grounds, crouched in the shadow of a plum tree. He met Cymin's gaze with an oddly disapproving—almost disappointed—expression, as if he'd caught Cymin picking rotten prawns from the kitchen compost heap.

Cymin flushed, and the sweat trickling down his back felt suddenly cold. Or perhaps that was the remnant of the fragrant rain he'd manifested. Embarrassed at having his weakness observed, he wanted to put Laithondi on the defensive. He very nearly demanded Laithondi explain what he was doing hunched in the shadows like a creep. Then he caught sight of Master Tam's half-feral cat rubbing up against Laithondi's extended hand. Had he followed the cat out to the practice grounds? It did visit here regularly, coaxing and stealing treats from novices. Over the last few days, Cymin had fed it as well.

Laithondi stroked the cat's chin, and it purred so loudly that Cymin heard it from across the practice grounds.

Little traitor. See if East Deity sneaks prawns from the compost for you in the future.

Laithondi rose to his feet. The cat continued to lounge beneath the plum tree while Laithondi strode to Cymin. He studied the broom handle that Cymin held, clearly reading the sigils that made up the smoldering spell carved into it.

"MinLyn?" Laithondi shook his head. "Who begins with such an ostentatious display? Are you trying to wreck yourself?"

"It's only two sigils. Hardly even a spell." Cymin rolled his eyes. "I could manage it in my sleep."

Laithondi raised his brows at the obvious lie, and Cymin regretted his response instantly. After all, Laithondi had witnessed his struggle, had seen him nearly collapse after manifesting the spell for only a moment. MinLyn really had been too much for him. But Cymin wasn't used to thinking of himself or his skills as tenuous. Only days ago, he manifested that spell and hundreds more for the entire route of a city parade.

Now a spattering of fei'lux-infused raindrops nearly knocked him to his knees. Cymin frowned at the ground, where little puddles darkened the sand. Numerous leopard moths edged them, drinking in the fei'lux-saturated water drops like nectar.

"I'm just tired. There's so much to do before we leave that I haven't gotten a good night's sleep," Cymin said. It wasn't entirely a lie. Recently, his sleep had been restless, filled with strange dreams—some terrifying and others intoxicatingly luxurious—many inspired by what little he'd had time to read of Minroa Haeyi's letters. But he wasn't going to tell all of that to Laithondi. "But there isn't a spell I can't handle after I've had my breakfast."

"If you say so." Laithondi shrugged, not even bothering to challenge Cymin's claim. "But if you collapse while we're traveling, neither the time nor means to help you recover will be available. You should not be so reckless."

"Well . . . thanks for your concern, I guess," Cymin replied dryly. "Did you rise early and slip away from the NS marshals just to tell me that? Or are you skulking around in the shadows for some other reason?"

"No other reason," Laithondi responded.

Cymin stared at him, uncertain of how to respond. Laithondi closed the distance between them and flicked the carved broom handle like he was sounding it out for rot. Cymin pulled it back from his extended fingers.

"Yesterday, I happened to have a word with your temple physician, Master Shuun." Laithondi lifted his judicious gaze from the broom handle to Cymin's face.

"Just the one word?" Cymin asked, because Master Shuun wasn't the sort who enjoyed idle chitchat, particularly not with outsiders.

Laithondi rolled his eyes at the comment but then went on, "He felt that, given the extent of your injuries, you would definitely qualify for an exemption from having to serve in the Storm Towers. If you applied for one."

"It's possible," Cymin allowed. It wasn't as if he could explain to Laithondi that he'd already signed a contract with NS and wasn't going to get out of anything. "But I don't have to now. I'm working on Una Bayan's documentary project. I can leave the exemption for someone who needs it."

"But if the documentary is abandoned, you won't be without any other options," Laithondi stated.

Cymin frowned as he grasped exactly what Laithondi was hinting at. He'd changed his mind about the documentary. And had gone out of his way to find an excuse for dumping Cymin in particular.

You can be "ever faithful" to a dessert, but you can't keep a promise to a human being? Screw that! I won't let you squirm out of this. My freedom and my life depend on it.

"You agreed that our film crew could come along with you on the journey." Cymin gently, but firmly, nudged Laithondi's chest with the broom handle. "Why are you trying to break your word to us now?"

"I agreed that you could come along." Laithondi caught the broom handle between two fingers and sent such a startling current of fei'lux shooting through it to Cymin's fingers that he nearly dropped the thing. "But *only* if you could keep up with us."

Cymin jerked the handle back from Laithondi before the brass tacks melted.

"We'll keep up just fine," Cymin assured him.

"You were nearly killed," Laithondi snapped. "You've had no time to recover, and if we are attacked again, it could cost you your life. Don't you understand that?"

"It's not your business whether I do or not," Cymin snapped right back. "You gave your word. Are you going to keep it?"

Laithondi glowered at Cymin, and fei'lux surged around him like lightning building in a cloud. Cymin stared right back into his deep, blue-black eyes, refusing to back down. After a moment, Laithondi released the streams of fei'lux and looked away to where the cat sat, his expression somewhere between exhaustion and disappointment. Cymin expected him to turn his back and walk away.

Instead, he angled his head to consider Cymin askance. His gaze dropped to the broom handle, and he sighed.

"Since you insist on traveling with us in your current condition, I'll try to instruct you in the Waethir practice of drawing down fei'lux," Laithondi stated. "If you can master it, you won't have to rely on spell filaments."

Cymin was so prepared to fight that he almost launched into a further argument. Then Laithondi's words sank in.

He thought two things in that moment: The first was how strange it was that the Waethir truly could control immense currents of fei'lux without anything resembling spell filaments. Maybe those stories about the secret techniques of the mage-kings weren't just myths. Because, putting aside all Laithondi's earlier talk about microscopic fei'thallus and mythic ignis glands, his offer now made it clear that the Waethir's prowess was a skill to be learned rather than just a strange inoculation.

And secondly—most importantly—Laithondi was willing to teach him! Despite the fact that he hadn't been accepted as his student, Laithondi was still offering to teach him! The aspirations and hopes toward magecraft that had been stripped from him along with the spell filaments ignited within Cymin again . . .

Joy surged through him, and he beamed at Laithondi as he flipped the broom handle between his hands in excitement. It occurred to Cymin that, in spite of himself, Laithondi was once again going out of his way to do him a kindness. Cymin didn't understand why, but he was far too grateful to question the matter. He let go of his earlier irritation and offered Laithondi a brilliant smile.

Meeting his gleeful gaze, Laithondi seemed to grow a little embarrassed. He shifted his attention to the broom handle Cymin continued to twirl like a baton.

"Put that—your ancillary—aside for now," Laithondi instructed.

"The master instructs, and it is done!" Cymin tossed the carved broom handle onto the clover lawn at the edge of the practice grounds where it couldn't roll underfoot.

See how respectful East Deity is to you? Come. Teach me all your secrets! He turned back to Laithondi before the man could change his mind.

Then he noticed the flushed amusement in Laithondi's expression, and he realized that he was acting a little too obedient. Cymin schooled his features into a mask of dignified calm.

You've pleased East Deity, but there's no need to look so smug about it. Candied egg yolks have the same power to move his heart.

"What sigil would you like to begin with?" Cymin balanced on his left foot and absently ran his toes through the sand, tracing the first stroke of Min.

"No sigils for the time being. First, we'll rouse the fei'thallus," Laithondi said.

"Fei'thallus. Right."

Wake up, microscopic organism! Algae, slime molds, fungi, time to get to work.

Cymin didn't tease Laithondi aloud, but it took a little effort. Playfulness always pervaded his happiness, but it wasn't always appreciated, so he inclined his head respectfully and said, "Please instruct me."

Laithondi studied him in silence for a moment—almost as if waiting for a rejoinder—but Cymin controlled himself. At last, Laithondi held his hands out to Cymin, palms up.

"Place your hands on mine," he said.

Cymin reached out and rested his palms against Laithondi's. His hands were warm and even more callused than Cymin's. As the cuff of his coat fell back, Cymin saw that he wore the string of forty-two prayer beads that Cymin had given him wrapped around his right arm. In comparison to the smooth red beads, his wrist bones appeared particularly sharp, and his skin looked deathly pale.

"Chyrenese mages are trained to draw fei'lux with the left hand and direct it outwards with the right, correct?" Laithondi asked.

"Yes," Cymin nodded. "Isn't it the same for Waethir?"

Laithondi shook his head.

"We spread the intake of fei'lux across as much of our bodies as is possible. When we shape and manipulate it, most of us use our hands, but there are no set rules. Eirjiri likes to use her toes when she's feeling playful. Vess sometimes directs fei'lux wherever he's looking." Laithondi's fingers curled just a little against Cymin's hands. He didn't volunteer how he chose to manipulate the fei'lux he'd absorbed, but recalling his actions in the clouds, Cymin guessed that Laithondi employed his hands.

"For now," Laithondi went on, "let's use what you already know. Draw the fei'lux from my body with your left hand—"

"What? No!" Just the suggestion alarmed Cymin, and he pulled his hands back from Laithondi's. "I can't strip fei'lux directly from you. Draining another mage is strictly forbidden. One of the unforgivable trespasses of the Haeyi mage-kings."

In the face of Cymin's alarm, Laithondi simply sighed.

"Do you really believe that in your current condition you could *steal* anything from me?" Laithondi gave a dry laugh, but then his expression turned serious, and he caught Cymin's hands in his own. "That's not what I want to teach you, in any case. We're going to create a circuit of fei'lux that we will circulate between us. The more fei'lux that flows through you, the more it will stimulate and encourage fei'thallus within the ignis to actively draw fei'lux. It's a little like priming a water pump. Do you understand?"

Cymin didn't, but he nodded because he didn't think that esoteric descriptions of ignis glands and fei'thallus would mean much to him. It would be better just to dive in and try it.

"Let us begin then. Speak up if this becomes uncomfortable." As Laithondi spoke, Cymin felt the faintest stream of fei'lux already caressing the nerves all across his left hand. Steadily, the fei'lux penetrated his skin and trickled through his muscles and sinews. It flowed like a warm current through his chest and loins, tingled along his toes and then fluttered back up his body to rush along his right hand. As the fei'lux filled him, that scent—something between bergamot and birch oil—drifted through Cymin's senses.

"Don't return it to me immediately," Laithondi instructed. "Circulate the stream at least three times. As it moves through you, try to smooth and refine it, so that when you pass it back to me it flows like an even exhalation—like you're singing a note to me very softly. Do you understand?"

Return the fei'lux at a low, steady amperage, as Master Tam would have instructed, but Cymin still understood what Laithondi meant and nodded.

He circulated the stream of fei'lux, feeling it rush along his nerves, all the while focusing on slowing and stabilizing the flickering, sometimes almost stinging sensation. If it had been a musical note, as Laithondi suggested, Cymin thought it would be the low resonant sound of a bass drum. Imagining that sound helped him relax as his muscles tensed and his nerves shivered against the fei'lux racing through them. Only after circulating the fei'lux five times did Cymin feel comfortable releasing the stream back into Laithondi's palm. Even so, he used the greatest care. Laithondi wasn't an ancillary; his nerves and flesh could be damaged if the flow surged too fast or too strong.

"Good, but no need to be so timid in returning the fei'lux. I'm used to weathering the storms beyond your Chyrenese protective towers."

Timid? East Deity treats you with concern and you call him timid!

Cymin frowned, then asked, "Are you trying to tell me that you prefer it rough?"

To Cymin's surprise, Laithondi laughed.

"Concentrate," Laithondi told him, but his smile seemed to linger.

Laithondi continued to release warm currents of fei'lux into Cymin's open left hand. Smoky scents of cook fires and temple incense dulled in Cymin's perception, as did the songs of birds and crickets. Cymin's awareness focused entirely on the ever-growing streams of fei'lux circulating through his own body. He smoothed away the jittery, frantic qualities, refining each to a constant current—a calm, low note. Then he returned that to Laithondi. The exchange felt gentle and slow at first.

But Laithondi pulled more and more fei'lux from the air surrounding them and channeled it into Cymin. Droplets of perspiration slipped down Cymin's chest and back as the heat of so much fei'lux grew inside him. Streams rushed through his muscles, racing faster than his pounding pulse. His whole being seemed to hum with energy. Hairs on his arms stood on end, his muscles trembled and deep in his belly a feeling like a growing fire flared and roiled.

Still, Laithondi pulled down more fei'lux. Soon, dense bands of fei'lux whirled around them, forming luminous halos. Cymin's skin tingled as if he were standing too close to a power turbine. He lowered his gaze and noted fine arcs of light flickering between their interlocked fingers. It reminded him of the tiny bolts of lightning in the celestial pearl Laithondi had given him.

Then a flight of bright yellow honeybees buzzed past his face and dived down to loop around his and Laithondi's clasped hands. Out of the corner of his eye, he noticed a pair of dragonflies dart by. Clouds of silvery leopard moths and glinting green orchid bees flew through the veils of fei'lux surrounding them. Their wings shimmered with its light.

"Are we supposed to be attracting this many insects?" Cymin asked.

Laithondi blinked, then glanced to the clouds of bees circling their hands and the leopard moths fluttering overhead.

“The resonance of fei’lux passing between us has entangled them with us in this moment.” Numerous agate butterflies alighted on him, clinging to his hair and clothes like sapphire adornments. “It’s harmless. Don’t be distracted.”

Cymin continued to circulate and refine the fei’lux that Laithondi shared with him, but his mind began to wander as if on the verge of a fever.

He suddenly thought of Minroa’s writing about insects and fish responding to storms of fei’lux, and it occurred to him that the idea wasn’t actually absurd at all. Of course animals—even plants—would respond to such a powerful force in their environment. They weren’t so complex as to craft spells, but that didn’t mean that fei’lux couldn’t benefit them in other ways.

Unbidden, his dream of holding those pulsing scarlet jellyfish rushed over him. For an instant, it even seemed that his surroundings wavered and he once again gazed at dark cresting waves illuminated by hundreds of fiery red bodies.

Even if I die tomorrow, my memory of this moment will live on with them. You and I, standing together before a rising tide, under the full moon.

Cymin recalled Ondi’s claim that he’d imparted a memory to them and then considered Laithondi’s comment about the surrounding insects being caught by the fei’lux and sharing this moment with them. Was that just a Waethir belief? Or could something like that truly happen? Could the streams of fei’lux passing between him and Laithondi right now entangle the simple minds of the bees and butterflies swirling all around them? What would such a memory feel like to an insect?

Would they remember flashes of stunning blue wings fluttering past the pale finger bones hanging around Laithondi’s neck? Feel the rising heat of Cymin’s exhaled breath? How would they experience the sensation of sweat beading on Cymin’s upper lip or the scent of birch oil drifting from Laithondi’s clothes?

And someday, if another stream of fei’lux captured them, would the memory play back through them again, like a song etched into the shellac surface of a phonographic record?

Cymin’s gaze drifted to the etched surface of the scepter hanging from Laithondi’s belt, and he suddenly found himself wondering what memories and histories were captured in all those fine lines and delicate moving parts. What might they recall in the right stream of fei’lux?

Do you remember me holding you with the water rising all around us?

As Cymin thought about it, a faint stream of fei’lux escaped him, coursing to the scepter. A flash of gold flickered from within the depths of the carved bones. A faint voice seemed to whisper enticingly in Cymin's ear.

You could do so much more. The power to build worlds or destroy them is here in front of you. Aren't you tempted, East Deity?

"What do you mean?" Cymin murmured.

"That's enough." Laithondi pulled his hands free of Cymin's grip. A shocking chill hit him and reflexively he spread his fingers out to reclaim that intense heat.

I won't let go. Not even if it kills me. I'll never let go. Never—

Laithondi stepped back, eluding Cymin's grasp. As he pivoted away, he pulled the folds of his leather coat over the bone scepter, covering it entirely.

"I won't . . ." Cymin came back to his senses, realizing that he was standing, staring at Laithondi in a daze—almost as if he'd been sleep-walking.

"You aren't recovered enough," Laithondi stated.

"I have!" Cymin protested. "I was just distracted by all the bugs. There are *so* many of them—"

Just as he spoke, the moths, butterflies, bees and dragonflies seemed to awaken as well. All at once, they rose into the air, bright wings and metallic bodies fluttering and flashing as they dispersed into the greenery of the surrounding gardens. Cymin stared after them, feeling stunned.

"You can't say that's not a distracting sight," Cymin pointed out.

Laithondi sighed as if unable to argue but still unwilling to concede.

"They come and go like clouds and flowers. You remain steadfast as cliffs. Calm as mountain lakes," Laithondi spoke as if reciting a poem. "Placid waters reflecting frenzied colors, depths ever unmoved."

The words and the archaic phrasing struck Cymin as deeply familiar, like something Master Tam would have recited for esteemed guests in the Benevolence Hall.

"Is that a classic poem?" Cymin asked.

Laithondi shook his head.

"A Chyrenese guest to the Heights wrote it a long, long time ago." He frowned. "I don't recall the rest of it."

They come and go like waves wearing down stone.

You remain determined as cliffs. Isolated as mountain lakes.

Poison seeping into placid waters . . .

Cymin strained to remember the entire poem, but his thoughts were scattered by a loud shout.

"Laith!" Arnaith's voice bounced across the practice grounds as she strode into sight. Three NS marshals followed her, as did two men wearing slick suits and Ministry of Transportation badges. "Ministers and bandimanders want to discuss your new overland travel plans for their trains."

Bandimanders?

For some reason, the image of long blue-gray worms wriggling beneath sheets of ice flashed through Cymin's mind.

Had Minroa mentioned something like that in his letters?

Laithondi nodded. Almost absently, he patted Cymin's shoulder.

"What you lost will return to you soon enough. So there's no need to push yourself so hard," Laithondi said, then added, "Take care."

He strode across the sands to Arnaith's side. He didn't look back, much less invite Cymin to join them. Cymin offered Arnaith a smile, and she acknowledged him with a nod before turning to walk beside Laithondi. The entire group started off towards Benevolence Hall.

"I thought you didn't want him." Arnaith's words sounded a little teasing as they drifted to Cymin.

"I don't," Laithondi replied, and he cast a disapproving glance back over his shoulder.

Cymin scowled back at him, but then, catching sight of a pair of mating butterflies still clinging to Laithondi's hair like gaudy combs, he smirked.

"At least East Deity isn't covered in amorous insects," Cymin muttered in consolation to himself.

Laithondi gave him a rather odd look, and the corner of his mouth quirked up. Belatedly, Cymin noticed he also had a pair of lovestruck dragonflies clinging to his own robe.

Chapter 14

In the following days, Cymin continued to rise early and practice circulating fei'lux as Laithondi had instructed. He spent the rest of his mornings shadowing Mazilane and Hiral on outings to film establishing shots of the city's landmarks. After that, he and Yinni lit out across the city to purchase supplies the cameras and cameramen required for the journey north. The work was tiring, but it also gave him an opportunity to explore sections of the city he'd never visited before.

Magecraft engineering warehouses as pungent and crowded as any spice market did frantic trade in an endless assortment of screws, resonance crystals, transmission wires and fuses. The chemists at the industrial apothecary, on the other hand, moved at the slow, steady pace suited to people who regularly handled volatile and explosive compounds. They double-checked Cymin's lists and corrected his pronunciations of their many unfathomable concoctions before sending him on his way with a wooden crate stamped with more skulls than a case of rat poison.

In the midst of shopping, he happened to pass a travel agency. Posters of exotic locales hung from the agency's eaves like blessing-banners. Many depicted scenic panoramas of the canal city of Yanyeo with misty silhouettes of Storm Towers rising like giant lighthouses in the background. For perhaps the first time in his life, Cymin realized that he could admire the splendid scenes of floating markets and flower-strewn lagoons without dread gripping him. He paused to admire a poster depicting a nightscape of pleasure-houses and music halls all aglow with colorful lanterns. Their lights reflected in the dark canal waters like stars while a full moon hung high in the sky overhead.

Yanyeo is actually a very pretty place, isn't it? Then Cymin noticed the prices listed for a trip to the city and he broke into a wide grin. *And I'm being paid to go!*

After that, he took on more errands and outings with even greater relish. He even found it funny rather than eerie when after two hours of searching, he stepped into a dim, side-alley tinker shop and was greeted not by any living soul but by hundreds of disembodied lenses focusing on him from shelves like watchful eyes. A note on the counter informed him that the shop's owner would return from lunch in half an hour and to occupy himself until then.

Cymin nearly missed the temple's evening curfew that day, and the one after it too. Those same evenings he passed out still dressed and sitting on his cot with his face in the book about Minroa Haeyi. Every time, he jolted awake in the dead of night with his head full of confused, half-dreamed recollections of the man's observations of Saigrath.

Every day, he rose earlier than the sun and practiced the exercises Laithondi had taught him until he was dripping with sweat and plastered in dazed moths and honeybees. Despite the flurry of insects, his ability to draw down fei'lux truly seemed to improve. Maybe even a little too much. Sometimes the fei'lux streams rushing to him felt as if they would inundate his body to the point of overflowing. He released them steadily and carefully, but his nerves still remained raw and tingling half an hour later.

After four days of practice, he felt secure enough in his ability to risk working with a real ancillary.

Not that Mazilane cared whether he was prepared or not. He simply pulled Cymin onboard a public transport with him and then, after they'd found their way to the postal freight at the back, informed Cymin that they'd be filming a private ceremony at the exclusive Coronation Amphitheater just outside the Palace Complex. He thrust a press card into Cymin's hand. The thick cream paper bore his name in phonetic script, his employment number and an official vetting code on one side. On the other side a very recent photograph of Cymin stared out from the hazy surroundings of the Royal Stables. His expression appeared so wistful that Cymin was embarrassed just looking at it. He couldn't help but think that Mazilane had saddled him with this particular ID picture as a subtle kind of ridicule.

"So, what's the event?" Cymin quickly hid the card away in his pocket.

"The Waethir are announcing which mages they'll officially accept as disciples. For the sake of the students' security, the only people in attendance will be adepts and masters from the Five Schools and their closest relatives." Mazilane's expression turned sarcastic as he went on, "Oh, and half the nation's bureaucrats, their mistresses and flunkies, and some 700 private citizens with money enough to buy the amphitheater itself. But the official press won't be informed until the day after tomorrow. You know, because the organizers wouldn't want to risk the selections being leaked before the Waethir and their students have departed."

"Do you truly think the students will be in danger after the announcement?" Cymin asked quietly. He really didn't want to think of anything happening to Paeth, Ovelah or Saum.

"Personally, I don't believe our bombers give a steaming shit about the students or disrupting diplomatic relations between Chyre and

Saigrath. But I could be wrong." Mazilane shrugged. "In any case, you'll be filming today. You can do that much, right?"

"Of course," Cymin replied. Earlier, Hiral had mentioned picking up an old "bustard"-style camera from a defunct riverboat. Cymin assumed he'd be practicing on that, so he was shocked when Mazilane held his arm out, offering him Soir.

It was a beautiful, sleek ancillary that was likely a pleasure to control. Still, Cymin wavered. He'd seen how attentively Mazilane cared for and cleaned the machine. He didn't want to chance damaging it—especially not after he'd destroyed the Black Staff.

"I should probably wait," Cymin said quickly. "Hiral said he'd bought an older—"

"Great idea," Mazilane cut him off with a sarcastic smirk. "That way you can pick up a bunch of bad habits by handling a piece of trash bustard and then have to learn all over again with Soir. Genius."

"Fine, have it your way then." Cymin scowled at Mazilane as he snatched Soir from his forearm. Then he held out his left hand for the camera's tether.

Mazilane unstrapped the tether.

"I was trying to show a little respect and consideration," Cymin muttered as Mazilane buckled the tether around his wrist. The leather felt warm and just a little damp against his skin. "I noticed how distressed you were when Eirjiri and Bailon crashed Soir—"

Mazilane suddenly laughed, and Cymin frowned at him. He hadn't said anything funny. Or was Mazilane trying to cover up his embarrassment after Cymin exposed his sentimentality?

"That's the oldest con in the book." Mazilane was still grinning as he spoke. "You need to win a patsy's confidence quick? Entrust them with something valuable of yours—something they can tell you secretly love—then make them break it, lose it, drop it in the dirt. The more magnanimous you are after that, the more guilty they feel. And the more they believe that they've wronged you, then the less energy they have to be suspicious of you. All they're thinking about is how to make things up to you and how to win you over. Textbook infiltration."

Cymin frowned at Mazilane's handsome, smiling face. Then he glanced down at Soir.

"I really thought . . ." Cymin trailed off, not wanting to detail how easily he too had been taken in.

"And you have the audacity to call yourself a jackal." Mazilane snorted. Then his gaze dropped to the camera, and unmistakable pride filled his expression. "Soir is equipped with dozens of flight overrides. There's no way someone just fiddling with his tether could actually crash him—not even a Waethir. But he's also clever enough to know how to feign a bad landing when I need him to. He can even drag a wing like it's broken."

"So, there was never any chance of Eirjiri or Bailon actually damaging Soir?" Cymin asked.

"I'd like to see them try," Mazilane replied. "Soir has survived curses, a shipwreck, electrocution, and being shot by Lui Dane himself. Twice. He always comes through."

Cymin studied Mazilane's face as the man admired the beautifully maintained camera. Despite his dismissal of the idea, Cymin perceived that Mazilane truly was deeply attached to Soir. Whether Mazilane would thank him for it or not, Cymin decided to treat the ancillary as respectfully as he could when he operated it.

The trolley soon slowed at the Palace Complex, and Mazilane jumped off ahead of a troop of tourists. Cymin followed quickly on his heels. They walked several blocks east and met up with Yinni and Hiral outside the service entry to the Coronation Amphitheater.

Then, catching the sharp scent of citrus and spellcraft, Cymin froze in his tracks. But an instant later he recovered, remembering the orange oil solvents he'd personally delivered to Hiral only the day before. That sweet, tart tangerine perfume didn't creep from some bomber but instead wafted from the refurbished camera that Yinni carefully balanced on her shoulder. Cymin relaxed and hurried to join them and find their places in the amphitheater.

The structure was relatively small, only five stories, and it was encircled by a massively tall and very plain security screen that blocked all street views of the grand carvings and enormous spells that adorned the amphitheater's granite outer wall and watchtowers.

Sightseers regularly walked past, studying their tour maps with puzzled and disappointed expressions.

Once Cymin and the others were allowed through the service doors and into the actual amphitheater, all the understated subtlety evaporated.

The five stories of gilded audience seating curved around the polished ebony stage like ornate crescent moons. The stage itself was a pool of polished darkness, like a huge iris staring up into the sky.

Originally, the ebony planks of the stage would have flashed gold with concentric rings of inlaid spells. At different times, mage-kings, their progeny, concubines and even bodyguards would have stood within the circle of those spells and bound their lives to the oaths they swore there. Now, the spells and gold were all long gone, having been dug out and melted down. Though Cymin thought he caught a breath of a clinging, smoky spell residue drifting off the polished ebony planks.

Then his eyes fell on a tin of burnt-bone wood polish and a stained rag sitting on the far side of the stage. Cymin smiled at his own flight of imagination.

Where the back of the stage met the amphitheater wall, there rose a two-story domed sanctuary. Its arched doorway stood open with only black velvet drapes obscuring the view. Cymin guessed the dressing rooms and all of the backstage area lay back there, though it was also rumored that a secret tunnel leading all the way into the Royal Palace was hidden somewhere in the sanctuary as well. Peering between the velvet curtains now, Cymin only spotted a NS marshal standing amidst several stacks of bags and boxes. Then a young woman darted past the marshal to snatch up the floor polish Cymin had noticed earlier. She disappeared back behind the drapes an instant later.

As Cymin and the rest of their camera crew tromped up the wide staircase leading to the heights of the amphitheater, he eyed the rows and rows of gilded seats he passed. All of them sported clawed feet, deer-like legs and wings that arched up to provide backrests, but some also flaunted intricate, curling tails, while still others were decorated with sprays of carved flowers.

Far below, a group of middle-aged politicians and businessmen dressed in beige and blue suits were being escorted to their seats by an attendant in quasi-historic dress. Cymin couldn't help but think that the modern men looked a little absurd in such flamboyant and whimsical chairs. Though he imagined that the Waethir with their archaic clothes and hair would likely seem right at home.

At last he, Mazilane, Hiral and Yinni all found their way up onto the raised overlook that ringed the entire amphitheater. This was where royal guards would once have kept watch, armed with raining-sorrows bows and quicksilver lances. Now some two dozen NS officers watched over the gathering and the grounds outside with rifles in hand.

"Try not to film any of them if you can help it," Mazilane instructed, and then he shot Cymin a hard look. "And if there's trouble, don't rush into the middle of it. Just stay where you are and let NS handle it."

"Yes sir," Hiral responded. Yinni and Cymin both nodded.

"Alright, then." Mazilane flipped open his cigarette case, selected a cigarette and tucked it in the corner of his mouth. "I'm going to have a smoke and chat up the security boys to make certain none of them take a pot shot at us if the proceedings below get too dull."

Mazilane strolled away, blowing clouds of cigarette smoke into the afternoon air. Watching him walk the entire perimeter of the amphitheater,

Cymin wondered if Mazilane was secretly surveying their surroundings for signs of the Piiroc bomber. Though earlier, he'd dismissed the bomber as a threat to the Waethir's candidates with seeming certainty, so maybe Mazilane was simply bored.

In his absence, Cymin, Yinni and Hiral all warmed up by circulating streams of fei'lux through their bodies before passing the tempered energy into the cameras and setting them aloft. Yinni gave Cymin a questioning look, and he knew without exchanging a word that she worried that he wouldn't be able to manage the magecraft without spell filaments. He also knew she wouldn't want to say as much for fear of costing Cymin his position on the crew. To reassure her, Cymin rolled a tempered stream of fei'lux between his hands like he was juggling and then shot her a grin.

"You're such a show-off," Yinni muttered, but her surprise and relief were obvious. Then she added, "I'm so proud of you."

Below them, the tiered seating steadily began to fill with audience members and students from the Five Schools. The faint sound of a few dozen people chatting grew into waves of noise and laughter as more and more bodies filled the glittering seats. Cymin didn't notice when the Waethir arrived, but at one point, Eirjiri peeked out from behind the velvet curtains of the sanctuary to beam across the crowd at Saum. Then she ducked backstage, and Cymin's attention refocused on the tether on his wrist and Soir's swooping flight.

Mazilane returned soon after that, and under his guidance Cymin and Yinni took turns capturing panoramic shots of the amphitheater and city skyline as well as candid exchanges between various young mages from the Five Schools. They mostly focused on the students whom Una Bayan had decided were the most likely to be chosen.

Hiral dutifully focused on filming the speakers at center stage.

Eirjiri skipped from behind the black curtain and flipped her gold hair back over her shoulder. Then without much preamble besides stating her name and title, she called her students out from the audience one at a time.

Cymin had known since they'd had lunch together at the Palace Complex that Eirjiri had decided on Saum, so there wasn't any surprise there—just happiness. He applauded loudly when Saum scampered up onto the stage and beamed at the surrounding audience. She made a small show of swinging her ancillary hammer from her back and saluting her fellow Ryde Academy students. The girls in yellow cheered and yelled Saum's sobriquet:"The Hammer". Paeth's clear voice rang out like she was singing, and even Ovelah managed a few quavering shouts. Eirjiri and Saum exchanged a quick hug.

Eirjiri's second student was a muscular, bearded swordsman named Jeshri. He wore his red Orae jacket open and the shirt beneath only buttoned to his sternum. His classmates hooted and called him "The Wall."

Cymin recalled Una Bayan remarking that the young man had drunkenly attempted to entertain everyone at Benevolence Hall by stripping. Cymin himself recognized the bearded swordsman from his visit to the Royal Armory. Jeshri had been the Orae student who'd expressed his disbelief in the secret weakness of the Hundred Deaths Armor with a resounding shout of "Fuck me . . . no way!"

Now the robust young man loped up the stage steps and clapped Saum on the back like the two of them were already teammates who were destined to be great friends.

Saum's expression turned a little giddy as she gazed up at his brawny exposed chest.

At the same time, Jeshiri introduced his absurdly oversized ancillary sword, Jo, to Eijiri as though it were a third student to be trained. Eijiri greeted the sword warmly, then drew her students to the far end of the stage.

Bailon came next. Her vivid red lipstick contrasted nicely with her pale archaic clothing. Cymin suspected that she had also discovered Chyrenese rouge and eyeliner, but she wore them subtly enough that he couldn't be certain. Either way, she looked eye-catching and self-assured as she swept her gaze over the crowd and drew her selection out just long enough to make it feel exciting. Then, at last, she called out the two birds, as Una Bayan had described them.

They both heralded from the eccentric Chohe Institute but only wore flashes of violet in acknowledgment of their school's color. Kimrin, with his ruffled brown hair, downturned nose and round gold spectacles, did really resemble an owl—that is, if an owl were to dress in rich silk brocade and exquisitely tooled leather boots that rose nearly to his hips. The fine-boned girl, Quin, wore a dress and matching shoes adorned with a rainbow of satin ribbons. They swirled and fluttered around her as she zipped onto the stage all but vibrating with an excited energy. Una Bayan's comparison of the young woman to a hummingbird did seem quite apt. Her long black hair boasted a violet rinse that caught the light with a sheen of iridescent feathers.

"Two birds for Sky Deity," Yinni whispered to Cymin.

"And not dull little chickens, either. Look at the plumage on them," he whispered back.

Yinni smiled and a soft chuckle escaped Hiral as well.

When Arnaith summoned Paeth and Ovelah from the gathered crowd, Cymin briefly turned the camera onto Yinni, capturing her delighted cheers for them. Hiral angled his camera to swoop over the stage to record Paeth's lovely smile. The afternoon light lent her a rosy glow, while Ovelah next to her appeared a little washed out but still very happy. Arnaith graciously accepted the humble ancillary tool kit that Paeth presented to her as a teacher's gift, and then she escorted the two girls over to join the other Waethir and their students. The twins stood on either side of her like perfect reflections.

When Cymin angled Soir down to film them, Paeth seemed to notice and looked up to offer him a shy little wave. Cymin waved back. Then Yinni nudged him and he refocused on Vessreid's long, elegant form as the Waethir swept through the velvet drapes to announce his selection.

Vessreid also chose a pair of female students, Ife and Zevlyn. They were the scythe-wielding fighters Cymin remembered dominating many of the pairs competitions in the previous year's Spring Exhibition. They came from the pedantic Guishuun College and wore cream-colored unisex uniforms. With their neat black ponytails, squared shoulders and glinting hand-scythes, they presented an ideal image of young revolutionary girls. Ife was the taller of the two and had two red moles above her right eyebrow. Zevlyn's dimpled chin was her most distinguishing feature. Their expressions and manners struck Cymin as very precise and a little forbidding, much like the Lux Temple librarians who regularly hushed him when he snickered too loudly at the absurd texts in their keeping.

"Vessreid is too nice to be saddled with those two snots," Yinni whispered.

"He's good-hearted but . . . " Cymin sourly recalled Vessreid's refusal to bribe a single official, despite the fact that doing so would have released Yinni from her tuteli obligations and allowed her to become Vessreid's student. If it hadn't been for Vessreid's pride, Yinni would have been on the stage right now. "He seems like he can be a little high-handed himself—"

"He's not!" Yinni protested.

Cymin glanced to her and was startled to see that she looked quite serious.

How did she develop such a strong attachment to Vessreid after just one walk in a garden?

Then Cymin remembered that Yinni hadn't been there for the earlier conversation, so she didn't know that Vessreid had chosen his principles over assisting her. All she knew was that the Waethir had argued for the right to select tuteli as his students—Yinni in particular—so he supposed Yinni's defense of him was natural.

"You're right. I'm just being an ass," Cymin said.

"He's the prettiest of the Waethir, if nothing else," Mazilane put in. Yinni spun on Mazilane, looking like she might deliver him a dressing down. Fortunately, Laithondi strode forward to announce his selections at that moment, and Yinni's attention returned to the stage below.

Cymin too stared down at the stage. He didn't know if it was just a chance gust or a whisper of fei'lux, but he felt the air tremble around him, and at the same time Laithondi's long white hair swirled like a banner catching a breeze.

Laithondi paused, gazing across the gathered audience. He glanced up to where Cymin stood with Yinni, Mazilane and Hiral, and for just an instant, Cymin imagined that Laithondi had sought him out in particular. A flutter of excitement rushed through Cymin's chest. Then Laithondi dropped his gaze to the seats occupied by mages from the Five Schools.

"Xaon of Orae Academy." Laithondi's angular face remained expressionless as a deity mask as he spoke the name.

Thunderous applause and whoops erupted from the Orae crowd.

A tall, scarlet-haired swordsman with clean features rose from the audience and swaggered up the steps onto the stage. Behind him, the Orae boys chanted "Bloo-dy Blade, Bloo-dy Blade."

Even Jeshri joined, shouting and grinning from where he stood beside Saum.

Between Xaon's long sword and thick sweep of bright red hair, Cymin could see how he'd gotten the moniker. When Hiral's camera swept past him, Xaon smiled and gave the lens a roguish wink.

Definitely not shy. Cymin silently concurred with Mazilane's earlier assessment.

Once Xaon came to stand at Laithondi's side, Laithondi narrowed his gaze at the boisterous Orae students. They went silent at once.

"Nyle of Boshyin School," Laithondi called into the quiet.

Cymin sighed. He'd expected as much but still found it vexing that Laithondi had selected Nyle. He didn't think too much about why that was. He mostly concentrated on maneuvering the camera to try and capture Nyle's haughty expression at an unflattering angle.

It was remarkably difficult.

Between his slender, graceful figure, handsome features and reserved poise, there was very little to find physically unappealing about Nyle. His long black hair hung down his back in braids so glossy they looked like they'd been carved from obsidian. His eyes were dark and his lashes thicker than even Una Bayan's. Even the stark black of his school robes seemed to only highlight the clear quality of his porcelain complexion.

The applause of the Boshyin students and teachers sounded tastefully reserved, as if Nyle's selection had been a given. Even Mazilane joined in, giving a short, polite clap of such consistency with the rest of the alumni that Cymin wondered if Boshyin students all learned it in some kind of etiquette class.

As Laithodi and his students took their place alongside the rest of the Waethir, Cymin slowly swept the camera past them all. He couldn't help but think that the Waethir all looked like they'd chosen an heir and a spare. Wasn't that how ancient nobility had done it?

But they were all so happy that Cymin couldn't really summon the pettiness to feel jealous. He smiled back at the group, basking in their elation and feeling happy for them.

Even Nyle.

"Orphans preferred, it would seem." The faint pandan scent of Mazilane's tobacco drifted along with his words.

"What do you mean?" Yinni asked.

Cymin listened but kept his eyes on his tether and Soir's flight path, so as not to disturb the Waethir or their chosen students.

"Didn't you look through the biographies with Hiral?" Mazilane asked.

"I glanced at them." Yinni shrugged. They'd both been too busy preparing to leave the temple to read through the entire biographies of recent graduates that Mazilane had collected.

Good answer, as it's not actually a lie. East Deity applauds your discretion.

"Zevlyn, Ife, Jeshri and Xaon all lost their parents fourteen years ago when the Municipal Courthouse and Trade Towers in Yanyeo collapsed in a landslide. It was during the Haelon Spring Flood." Hiral edged nearer to Yinni and spoke quietly as if whispering the answer to a quiz to her. He then glanced to Mazilane. "But the rest of them have family, I believe."

"Well, I know that Paeth and Ovelah live with their stepfather and his second wife. I've been to their house once," Yinni replied. "And Saum's grandparents are her guardians, but she's not orphaned. Her parents are serving in Piiroc as diplomats."

"Diplomats? That's what she told you?" Mazilane asked. Cymin glanced back in time to see Mazilane's amused expression. "Well, who am I to disagree?"

"What do you mean?" Yinni asked. But Mazilane didn't answer her. Instead he leaned forward and tapped Cymin's shoulder.

"Pull the camera back for a wider pan of the scene. Hiral will get the close-ups when Una Bayan comes forward to give her speech." Then he turned back to Yinni and handed a small redwood box to her. "Try to follow her with the refraction light. Keep the shadows off her face. Last night's travel negotiations left her with a hellacious hangover, but it won't do for her to look haggard in front of this crowd."

Yinni immediately took the small device, and with the slightest flex of her left hand, she drew a stream of fei'lux out of the air and channeled it easily into the box. Shafts of subtle golden light shot out just as Una Bayan rose from her seat at the front of the audience and ascended the steps leading to the small stage. Yinni tracked her perfectly, adding radiance to the actress's already striking presence. Unlike the practically silent Waethir or the stiff officials who had previously spoken, Una Bayan charmed the audience with a few gentle jokes and then briefly described her documentary project and encouraged the wealthy onlookers to make donations at specially marked tables near the exits.

Cymin captured the reactions of audience members—some interested, others absent or bored, but Mazilane's earlier remark lingered in his mind. He glanced again to where the ten mages stood in pairs beside the Waethir. His gaze caught on Nyle's arrogant expression.

"What about the rest of them?" Cymin asked.

"Hmm?" Mazilane's attention seemed focused on a distant shadow far across the city. Maybe a camera filming events at the Spring Fair?

"Kimrin and Quin?" Cymin prompted, not wanting to be caught out asking about Nyle. "Are they orphans too?"

"Might as well be. Both come from sprawling reactionary families that pass children around like library books. The parents are always busy having affairs or squandering their fortunes on drugs and fashion. So the kids circulate between cousins, aunts and uncles—all of whom are always under investigation for anarchist involvements, sedition or the manufacture of pornography. Even though the two are very distant cousins, they actually spent most of their childhoods together being shipped from one relative to another. I'm told that it's a common practice among people with noble backgrounds, be they Chyrenese or Piiroc," Mazilane stated.

"They're Piiroc?" Cymin asked.

Mazilane shook his head.

Hiral surprised Cymin by answering. "Their ancestors were. Their families own property and businesses in Yanyeo and all across Haelon Province on the border. But they lost a lot of that during the flood." He seemed entirely focused on his camerawork, even as he added, "Quin and Kimrin were sent to the capital while the older members of their families cleaned up and recovered what they could of their estates."

Cymin hadn't thought about it too much before, but now he realized that so very many lives had been impacted by the Haelon Flood. He and Yinni were just two among tens of thousands. Still, wasn't it odd that so many of the mages the Waethir chose had also been affected by the floods?

"What about Nyle?" Cymin gave up resisting the question.

He glanced again to where Nyle stood beside Laithondi. As far as their builds, features and coloring went, the two had nothing in common but their stances—the way they held their heads high and squared their shoulders before the stares of onlookers did seem very similar.

"A boy after my own background, actually," Mazilane stated. "A Boshyin scholarship student from a family with so many offspring that they can't keep track of them all, much less feed them. He's number eleven of seventeen. His eldest sister took custody of him and his younger siblings after their mother was institutionalized. He was ten when he won his scholarship to attend Boshyin and moved to the capital. One of the Boshyin cooks took him in as a boarder. He's lived with her since."

"Really? I would never have guessed," Cymin remarked. He and Yinni exchanged a glance of mutual surprise before both turning their attention back to Nyle.

Cymin studied the rigid young man and attempted to reconsider some of his previous assumptions. Was it possible that Nyle sported the archaic-style robes favored by reactionaries not because he came from the lineage of mage-kings but because his clothes were actually quite old—perhaps even handed down from more than one generation? Did he maintain an air of austerity because he looked down on the gaudy colors and ornaments so beloved to the middling classes of up-and-coming workers, or was it possible that Nyle was actually too poor himself to afford such things? The only jewelry he displayed was the gold champion's ring that he'd won a few days before.

A feeling very like guilt crept over Cymin.

He looked to the space in the audience from which Nyle had originally been called to the stage. A very modest-looking elderly woman sat next to Nyle's empty seat. Her face was ruddy and weathered from the dry heat of industrial ovens, but her features were still quite distinct and very unlike Nyle's. Still, she gazed at the young man with a mixture of pride and grief. It was an expression Cymin knew well and understood innately. Over the years, he'd seen any number of impoverished parents and grandparents watch the tuteli parade past them with the same expression. She was proud of what Nyle had accomplished but also heartbroken that he'd be leaving.

She held a kerchief to her eyes, wiping her tears before they could fall. Cymin had to look away from her face. That was when he noticed the travel bag waiting in Nyle's empty seat and the small trunk at the old woman's feet. Odd that Nyle would have packed and brought his belongings to this event. Out of curiosity, Cymin angled Soir to peer backstage between the black curtains and noted that several other travel trunks were stacked to the side and being watched over by attendants from the Five Schools.

Had he and Yinni missed the news of a change in the Waethir's travel plans? Several train schedules had been altered recently due to northern storms. Cymin tapped Mazilane on the elbow to get his attention, then whispered, "The Waethir and their chosen students aren't supposed to leave tonight, are they?"

"There are still two days," Mazilane replied. "Why?"

"Nothing." Cymin shrugged and returned his attention to guiding the camera through a buffeting crosswind. "It just looks like they all packed up to sneak off in the dead of the night."

"You make it sound like they're eloping," Yinni commented. "They're probably just staying together in the same hotel to make sure they all make it to the train station. That little Quin girl looks like the type to flit off at the last moment if someone doesn't keep after her."

Hiral gave a quiet laugh, while Mazilane frowned down at the Waethir. Cymin found a rising breeze and let the camera soar up to capture a panoramic sweep of the surrounding city drenched in sunset hues. On the display of the tether, he could just make out the fine red line made by the walls surrounding Lux Temple.

The Waethir's ceremony closed with a few speeches from dignitaries and ministry officials about building an alliance between their nations, a display of chrysanthemum fireworks and a brassy version of the Chyrenese national anthem. As far as representation of Saigrath went, only the Waethir were present, and none of them seemed at all inclined to share long speeches or perform a national song—if they even had one.

Most of the people attending departed via glossy vehicles drawn by teams of tall, long-necked carriage birds. Cymin and Yinni returned the filmmaking ancillaries to Mazilane and Hiral and then raced on foot back to Lux Temple to take part in a far more modest ceremony in the temple's sedate Common Hall.

There, tuteli gathered beneath the aged columns without fanfare or cameras. Common oil lamps lent a golden luster to the polished wood floor and incense-perfumed arrangements of paper flowers.

Cymin, Yinni and the ten tuteli adepts who were soon departing for the Storm Towers all assisted Master Tam and Master Shuun to welcome and bless the dozen new children Grand Master Ryn had brought into Lux Temple at the end of this year's Spring Exhibition.

Seeing their freshly shorn heads and meeting their uncertain gazes, Cymin felt a bittersweet nostalgia. When one little girl insisted on splitting her tiny prayer cake with her younger sister, Cymin exchanged a smile with Yinni. He slipped an additional cake to the girls before solemnly continuing along the line, distributing the sweets. Then he chanted prayers along with the rest of the tuteli adepts while the masters blessed the children and handed them their first clay-brown robes and the coarse wooden spheres that they would learn to carve into their first string of prayer beads.

In past years, Cymin had found the ceremony a little tedious. It contained no fireworks or displays of vibrant spells. No battles took place, nor did it boast any artistic performances. The entire initiation ceremony amounted to little more than one generation of tuteli handing a few meager gifts to a group of hungry, scared novices and then sharing a meal. But now that he was a departing tuteli pressing a small, sweet prayer cake into each child's trembling hand, he remembered how scared he'd been when he'd first arrived—and then how sweet that first cake had tasted, how relieved he'd been to sleep on a soft bed and wear clean clothes.

He glanced to Master Tam and Master Shuun who'd trained him and then to Grand Master Ryn who'd chosen him and Yinni from so many children who had been offered that year. He felt suddenly very moved. For fourteen of the eighteen years of his life, they'd nourished, taught and sheltered him. They'd made Lux Temple a safe home. But now he was grown and had to depart to make room for these children who needed the same care.

Previously, he'd often wondered why so many of the departing tuteli adepts appeared teary-eyed. Wiping at his own eyes, now he realized that he'd been wrong when he'd thought that they were just afraid of the futures they faced beyond the temple walls. He'd even clicked his tongue at some of their tear-streaked faces, thinking, "It's not as though you can't come back, what's there to cry about?"

But now he understood that they had been moved by the knowledge that the shelter and care they now surrendered would provide for these new children. From now on, he and Yinni, like the adepts before them, would venture into the world as adults, and the work they did—the money and fame they earned—wouldn't just be for themselves but for this next generation of tuteli.

If he ever did return to the temple, it couldn't be as a dependent seeking sanctuary but as a guardian providing protection.

And then it occurred to him that even elder tuteli like Master Tam, Master Shuun and Grand Master Ryn had all once been hungry, hopeless and abandoned just like him and Yinni and these children standing before him now. At some point, each of them for their own reasons had chosen to return to the temple and devote their lives to the well-being of other tuteli.

They became the families that they themselves had lost.

"We have to be strong from now on." Yinni's voice trembled, but her expression remained resolute.

Cymin sniffed and nodded. "We'll make them proud."

They recited evening prayers together and dined on a small feast of blue lentils, stuffed peppers and flatbread. Master Shuun indulged each of the departing adepts in cups of his "medicinal" palm wine while novices, adepts and masters reminisced about sweet, foolish and funny events of the past year.

Evening bells sounded out and ancillary lanterns illuminated the dark grounds of the gardens. At last, they bid one another goodnight.

Cymin strolled back to his dormitory, humming to himself and pondering how different his life might become in just a matter of two days.

In his room, he discovered five red bills and a note written in Master Tam's unmistakable style wishing him a happy eighteenth birthday. At the foot of the bed sat a new pair of shoes. The first pair of shoes Cymin could remember ever owning.

He stared at the shoes for a long time, then picked them up and traced the thick leather tops, the hard soles and stiff laces. They looked expensive and modern, unlike anything that belonged in Lux Temple. Instinctively he knew that they would be uncomfortable at first, and yet he would need them to make his way in the larger, secular world.

At last, he extinguished his bedside light and fell asleep.

Five hours later, after Mazilane shook him awake, his consideration of the shoes was far less symbolic. He simply jammed them into his travel pack and snatched up his secular money. After hardly five minutes of packing the rest of his belongings, he chased after Mazilane, Hiral and Yinni, intent on catching the Waethir as they slyly boarded a northern freight train waiting at the dockside station.

CHAPTER 15

By the time the four of them reached the rail yard, the freight engine roared ahead, clouds of steam streaming from the smokestack. Train cars hurtled after it in an odd assortment. Steel boxcars painted with the national postal seal and wood-paneled cars loaded with dry goods and ancillary supplies weren't out of the ordinary. Even the flatbed of shining sigil-inscribed stones wasn't too unusual. However, the three sleeping cars and sleek passenger coaches at the back weren't the common freight sent to repair and resupply the northern towns and Storm Towers.

They pulled away with the rest of the train cars just as Cymin charged onto the platform.

"It's too late," Mazilane shouted.

"Fuck that!" Cymin sprinted through the gush of hot steam, frustration lending him a surge of strength. He wouldn't just give up.

I won't let you go. I won't let you go.

The refrain hammered through Cymin's thoughts with a furious intensity as his feet pounded the railway platform. He focused on the narrow gangway that coupled the last two passenger coaches together. He surged ahead, legs pumping like pistons.

He hurled his travel pack onto the gangway. His heart hammered and steam poured over him. He vaulted onto the gangway and steadied himself with a hand against the door of one of the passenger coaches.

"Cy!" Yinni's voice rang out. He spun around just in time to catch her pack. Then she landed beside him on the gangway. Together they reached out to Hiral, who pelted alongside the train, red-faced and sweat-soaked. They each seized one of Hiral's outstretched hands and hauled him, his camera and tripod onboard. A moment later, Mazilane leapt up as well. He soared far higher than Cymin expected, nearly overshooting the narrow shaking gangway. Cymin grasped Mazilane to steady him. His body slammed against Cymin's chest like a sandbag filled with bolts.

Cymin staggered and suppressed a gasp of pain as an assortment of hard, metal edges gouged into him through Mazilane's neat blue coat.

Mazilane brushed off Cymin's grasp immediately.

"I'm getting too fucking old for this shit," Mazilane muttered. Then he turned to Hiral. "Didn't you say you liked to start mornings with a little exercise?"

Hiral, still bent over panting and gasping from the exertion, gave a weak laugh and nodded. To his credit, he'd lugged a camera supply case and a heavy pack with him when he'd sprinted after Cymin and Yinni.

The train flew out from beneath the shadows of the depot roof. Mazilane turned his attention to the tether on his wrist, adjusting a trajectory. Cymin looked up to see Mazilane's camera, Soir, swoop over them. It circled the rail yard twice, then glided through a plume of steam to settle on Mazilane's shoulder.

He'd been filming the whole time, capturing their daring, unorthodox and probably illegal method of embarkation.

Yinni smiled at the camera, then dropped down beside Hiral, who crouched down, still flushed.

"I haven't sprinted that hard since school," Hiral muttered. He wiped his sweat-soaked face with the back of his sleeve.

"You did great!" Yinni patted his back. "Just don't throw up."

At the same time, Cymin thrust his hand out to Hiral in a victory gesture. Though an instant later, he brought both hands up, waving aside a burst of steam that gushed from the engine.

Hiral laughed and nodded, then straightened to his feet. He nearly toppled as the train accelerated down a steep hill and the gangway began to rattle and shake beneath them. Yinni steadied him.

Industrial views of the dockside shipyards and warehouses whipped past on a chill wind. The streets appeared bleak and abandoned in the pre-dawn gloom, the only sound the roar of the train engine and the relentless clatter of its wheels. As the tracks turned, the wheels shrieked, steel shearing against steel, and a piercing noise seemed to echo for miles through the quiet.

"Let's get inside." Yinni's voice quavered with the vibrations of the gangway. She leaned against the door of the nearest passenger coach and waved at someone on the other side of the thick portal window.

The door swung open, and Eirjiri beckoned the four of them forward. She looked delighted to see them and moved aside quickly to usher them in from the cold rushing wind.

Once inside, they walked between two towering brass luggage racks crammed with travel trunks, carpet bags, hat boxes and numerous ancillary weapon boxes. Stepping past them, Cymin took in the lounge car and its occupants. There were fourteen tables in all, each flanked by two long high-backed benches—seven on the left and seven on the right. At a glance, Cymin guessed that each table could have easily accommodated four people.

Only three of the brass spell-lamps shone, but their light was enough to display the richness of the interior. Mother-of-pearl inlay adorned the high-backed seats as well as the fixed tables standing between them. Indigo silk covered the ceiling and walls. Matching silk decorated the circular shades that obscured the large portal windows. Gold shade pull cords with fat tassels swayed with the train's motions. The highly polished wood of the aisle running between the rows of seats reflected the diffused light with the warm glow of a brass mirror.

The Waethir had claimed three tables nearest the door. Another three entire tables and seats directly behind them appeared to be stacked with still more luggage—including a locked book cabinet, heaps of velvet and leather and numerous file boxes. The ten mages from the Five Schools occupied the seats further back in the coach. They looked to have paired up according to which of the Waethir they would be training with, though Bailon's two flamboyantly dressed students, Quin and Kimrin, appeared to have left their seats and crossed the aisle to play cards with the twins, Paeth and Ovelah.

Paeth paused in the midst of dealing to beam at Cymin. Ovelah seemed more tentative about his arrival, while Quin and Kimrin peered back at him over their shoulders with candid curiosity.

An owl and a hummingbird, Una Bayan had called them. Though, taking in their vivid clothes and assortments of glittering accessories, Cymin wondered if birds of paradise might not have been an equally apt comparison.

Particularly impressive was the fact that they'd donned their ensembles—curled their hair and even applied touches of makeup—at this horrifically early hour.

In the style arena, East Deity must bow down to you two.

Behind them, Ife and Zevlyn—both dressed in the same slack cream Guishuun uniforms they'd worn yesterday—looked up from amidst stacks of workbooks and old textbooks. The two considered Cymin with faintly disapproving expressions, as if they were considering summoning a conductor to check his ticket.

Cymin glanced away quickly and noticed that Saum and Jeshri occupied the seats directly opposite on the left side of the aisle. Saum slept with a fur-lined coat draped over her and her oversized ancillary hammer cradled in her arms like a favorite pillow. Across the table from her, shirt open and head drooping to his expansive, hairy chest, Jeshri dozed into his black beard.

Xaon and Nyle occupied the seats behind Ife and Zevlyn. Nyle—Porcelain Prince that he was—appeared composed as he briefly lifted his dark gaze from his sketchbook to observe Cymin's entrance. Then he returned to drawing. A far cry from Nyle's refined figure, Xaon splayed across his bench, sleeping with his head dangling into the aisle. A gray blanket draped over half his face and his bright red hair spilled down in an unkempt mass. One of his boots rested on the ledge of the portal window.

"You managed to keep up after all. Good for you!" Bailon spoke up, and Cymin's attention snapped back to the Waethir directly in front of him.

They lounged with their heavy coats tossed across their benches and languid expressions on their faces, as if they'd long anticipated Cymin, Yinni, Mazilane and Hiral's unconventional boarding. From the mountain pattern embroidered on the coat in the seat opposite Bailon, Cymin guessed that Eirjiri had been sitting across the table from her. A set of dice lay there, as well as a stack of gold ingots and gemstones.

Vessreid and Arnaith sat across the aisle from them with maps and a disassembled radio spread out between them. Laithondi occupied the table directly behind Bailon and Eirjiri. He stretched his long legs out to claim both the bench where he sat and the one on the other side. A black hard leather case rested on the table in front of him. Cymin recognized it as the magical pall that held the scepter. Its dull appearance gave away nothing of the murderous curses that guarded the interior or the treasure inside it.

Cymin lifted his eyes from the pall to meet Laithondi's gaze. Earlier, when they were racing to the train depot, Mazilane had informed them that NS security arranged for the Waethir to secretly depart two days early, after several sabotage attempts had been discovered on northern passenger trains. Cymin recalled that Arnaith had summoned Laithondi to discuss their travel plans four days ago. That had been before the mage candidates were formally announced. So, they'd obviously had enough time and more than one opportunity to inform him and Yinni of the change of plans, if they'd wanted to make sure they made it onto this train.

But they hadn't.

Cymin shot Laithondi a long, aggrieved glare.

If Laithondi didn't want to teach him, then that was his right. However, actually leaving him and Yinni behind was another matter. This documentary film was now their work—and not just their own livelihoods but a means of repaying the debts that Lux Temple had taken on for their sake. If the Waethir were a hundred miles away, what were they supposed to do? How were they going to earn enough money to lift a little of the burden from the masters who'd raised them?

Would it have been so hard for Laithondi, or any of the other Waethir, to inform them that they were leaving early? The faintest trace of a wry smile played on Laithondi's lips, as if he were laughing at Cymin's thoughts. Annoyance surged through Cymin, but he restrained himself from walking over and smacking Laithondi. That would have been too rude and too familiar, by far. He contented himself with sending the Waethir a tight, triumphant smile.

Sneak out in the middle of the night. East Deity will still find you!

"I told you they would catch on and follow us." Eirjiri held out her hand, and Bailon tossed her two gold coins. Eirjiri wiggled her fingers in Laithondi's direction, but he shook his head.

"They didn't catch *us*; they caught the train." The fact that Laithondi seemed a little amused vexed Cymin all the more.

"What a cheap technicality." Eirjiri dropped down into the empty seat across the table from Bailon, pulled her coat around herself and closed her eyes.

"How *did* you know to follow us this morning?" Laithondi addressed this question to Mazilane, who stood behind Cymin.

"Our young jackal, Cymin, noticed that your students had already packed their luggage last night." Mazilane shifted his travel pack and withdrew his Bluecloud cigarette case from his coat. He turned the silver case between his fingers. "Later, Una Bayan sent me word that her father and Lui Dane were frantically making arrangements for a special freight to leave the dockside depot at four this morning. The two things added up to a secret early departure."

"Entirely too early," Eirjiri mumbled without opening her eyes.

"Well, at least Una Bayan won't have to worry about the documentary opening with a lackluster start." Yinni rubbed her face.

"Very true. It was fascinating to observe each of you bounding onto the train just now." Arnaith gave them all a faint smile, then leaned forward and began reassembling the radio in front of her.

"Worrying as well," Vessreid said from the opposite side of the table from Arnaith. "In the future, you should value yourselves more and not take such risks." Vessreid looked at Yinni in particular. Then he moved his coat aside and patted the empty place on the bench next to him. "Come sit and rest a little. You look exhausted."

"Thank you. I was up most of the night researching . . . things." Yinni dropped down beside Vessreid.

Cymin wondered if he should give Yinni a chance to chat with, and perhaps even charm, Vessreid or crowd in with them. Or maybe try to sit next to Arnaith? Though she didn't look exactly inviting, with all those screwdrivers, wire snips and pliers laid out around her. And in any case, it wasn't as if anything inappropriate was likely to happen with so many other people around.

Still, Cymin cast Yinni a questioning glance—if she needed him to stay beside her, he'd do so, even if that meant plopping himself down onto Vessreid's lap. Fortunately, Yinni just gave him an easy nod and then relaxed into the back of the bench.

"But where's Una Bayan?" Bailon asked.

"Shockingly, she didn't want to risk her life jumping a train before sunrise," Mazilane replied. "Once she's finalized all our fees and permits, she plans to bring our supplies along with her private train cars. She'll meet us in Yanyeo in ten days."

"Excellent. I would have been sorry if we didn't get to see her again." Bailon appeared genuine. Cymin warmed to her for that.

Vessreid nodded and then retrieved a silver cookie tin from beneath his coat and slid it toward Yinni.

"These were sent by your Prime Minister's office. They're supposed to be good for the constitution and stave off travel fatigue. Do have some." Vessreid looked to Cymin, Hiral and Mazilane. "All of you."

Yinni opened the tin but didn't take anything for herself; instead, she held it out, offering first choice to Cymin, Hiral and Mazilane.

Cymin eyed the golden almond tarts inside with extreme avarice. Each one brimmed with jewel-like glazed cherries and threads of candied ginger. They sat in individual nests of pink and blue laced paper. They looked expensive, and Cymin wasn't certain how many he could snatch up without embarrassing Yinni and Lux Temple. The tin was already half empty. Cymin surreptitiously noted the empty pastel papers on several of the mages' tables. On average, they appeared to have taken three per person, though five empty paper wrappers lay near Jeshri's elbow.

"Thank you." Cymin accepted two, as did Yinni and Hiral.

Mazilane declined and then excused himself to smoke. Turning his cigarette case through his fingers, he stole back past the luggage racks and out onto the gangway.

Cymin and Hiral headed in the opposite direction, working their way down the aisle towards the empty places farther back in the coach.

Cymin exchanged quick smiles as he passed Paeth and Ovelah. Kimrin and Quin said nothing but watched them from behind their playing cards with curious expressions. Paeth looked like she might stand up, but Ovelah nudged her, and she seemed to realize that it was her turn to draw a card from the deck.

Cymin moved on.

Zevlyn and Ife whispered something between themselves as he and Hiral passed, but Cymin couldn't make out their words over the juddering rumble of the train wheels. Ife scribbled phonetic script into one of the notebooks in front of her. Zevlyn pushed a textbook towards her. Cymin wondered what type of people did schoolwork even after they'd graduated.

Then the train swayed, taking a sharp turn. Cymin braced himself, gripping the back of the seat where Saum slept. Across the table from her, Jeshri briefly roused, offered Cymin a dazed nod of acknowledgement, wiped the corner of his mouth and then returned to dozing. Saum continued to snooze with her hammer and a contented smile on her face.

Cymin moved on quietly. He'd intended to take the spot directly behind Jeshri and Saum. But now he realized that both the benches were already occupied by Jeshri and Xaon's huge ancillary swords. Across the aisle from the weapons were Nyle and Xaon. But both tables beyond them appeared to actually be empty. Cymin moved ahead.

As he went, he noticed Xaon twitching slightly beneath his blanket, his booted foot kicking the window weakly. Cymin smiled at Xaon, reminded of the time he'd seen one of the stray dogs who slept in the temple quivering and flicking its feet while it dreamed of chasing down some rat or rabbit.

Not so much the Bloody Blade just now as he is a Sleepy Swordsman.

Nyle, on the other hand, frowned at Xaon's twitchy motions. He spared Cymin and Hiral a silent, imperious glance as they passed by. Then he returned to drawing in his thick black sketchbook. An open tin of stubby, chipped colored pencils rested by his empty right hand. Cymin glimpsed curves that might have been indigo waves, but he didn't stop to gawk at Nyle's drawing or the notes written on the opposite page. He already felt guilty for all the assumptions he'd previously made about Nyle. He didn't want to add snooping to his list of wrongs.

At last, he dropped down at the empty table on the left side of the aisle and settled his travel pack on the floor at his feet, where he could easily reach it. Hiral took the table on the right, directly across from Cymin and behind Nyle. He lifted the silk window shade and fixed his camera lens on the view streaming past the portal window. Cymin, too, raised a blind and gazed out the portal.

Outside, warehouses steadily gave way to blocks of factories. Massive bridge girders flashed by as they roared across the first of the city's five Grand River bridges. The lights of fishing boats below flashed through the gloom and reflected across the water like dancing fireflies.

Cymin heard Jeshri yawn and couldn't resist the urge himself. The train wasn't quiet, but its steady rhythm and the dim lights began to wear away Cymin's wakefulness. Across from him, Hiral sighed, capped his camera and ate the two tarts he'd chosen. Then he stretched out, resting his head on the table and closed his eyes to nap.

Cymin glanced back and saw that Yinni had already drifted off to sleep. Vessreid slid a small pillow behind her head. Yinni clutched it to her cheek without opening her eyes and settled back to dozing. As Vessreid watched over Yinni with a gentle expression, Cymin stole a glance at where Laithondi slouched, frowning out his portal window.

His expression gave Cymin the impression of someone planning to pick a fight with the night itself. What was there to glare at on the empty streets at this hour? A few sleep-deprived night watchmen, waiting for the morning bells, and dumpling sellers, setting up their carts to catch the first shifts of commuters on their way to work? Maybe a vagrant or a couple of feral cats?

Whatever occupied his thoughts, it clearly had nothing to do with Cymin. Laithondi didn't spare him a glance, and after staring at the man's sharp profile for a bit, Cymin began to feel absurd. He turned his own attention to the narrow polished table in front of him and his own belongings. He picked up one of the two precious tarts and slowly nibbled around the edges, trying to make the sweet, rich flavors last as long as possible.

The cherries and almonds tasted so good. Vessreid truly was generous for sharing them with everyone. Cymin took another bite, savoring the sweet tang of the cherries and the toasted warmth of the almonds.

Though, hadn't Master Shuun once said that both contained traces of poison? Yes, Cymin recalled now, cyanide. Apricots and peaches too—in their pits. Cymin sighed and nibbled the last of the tart.

How can poison be so appealing? Cymin nearly succumbed to the urge to stare at Laithondi again but caught himself.

Instead, he lifted the book of Minroa Haeyi's letters from his travel sack. Just as he opened the book, a shadow fell over him. He glanced up and felt stupidly disappointed that it wasn't Laithondi who stood in the aisle studying him. Instead, Ife and Zevlyn peered at him. Their long black ponytails swayed as the train wove through the city. Zevlyn placed her hand on Cymin's table. She was the shorter of the two, with a cleft chin, thin brows and soft eyes. Ife stood behind Zevlyn, eyeing Cymin from over her friend's shoulder. She sported two red moles above her right eyebrow and a mouth that pitched down into an innate expression of skepticism. Both women's expressions were oddly speculative.

"You're called Cymin, right?" Zevlyn asked. "I remember you from the Spring Expo last year. You and . . . "

"Yinni," Ife provided for her quickly, and Zevlyn nodded.

"Right. Yinni. You two were like a matched pair. East and West Deities." Zevlyn shot a meaningful glance to where Yinni slept next to Vessreid. "Why aren't you together now?"

"If that's not too personal," Ife put in, though her tone was perfunctory, as if she were required to add those words by law.

"I think Vessreid wanted to talk with her, once she's rested," Cymin responded. He had no idea why it mattered to these two. Or what they might be up to, approaching him like this.

"So, you're still *together*?" Zevlyn leaned down close enough for Cymin to smell her basil flower perfume.

"Together?" Cymin moved slightly back from her.

"They're not *together*, Zevlyn. They're brother and sister!" Paeth shouted from her table. At this announcement, Ovelah quietly snickered from behind her cards, while Kimrin and Quin gasped simultaneously, their mouths set in matching O's. They, too, seemed to have thought Yinni and Cymin were in some kind of romantic relationship.

Every mage who was still awake, even Nyle, turned to gawk at Cymin. Though, unlike the others, Nyle quickly averted his gaze.

"But you and Yinni *did* leave the temple together?" Zevlyn asked.

"Aren't tuteli debtors required to serve in the Storm Towers?" Ife fired off the second question before Cymin could respond to Zevlyn's query. He found their curiosity a little annoying but decided that since they'd be traveling together for days on end in the confines of a train, he'd be polite.

"We were both hired by Una Bayan as part of her documentary crew," Cymin addressed Zevlyn, then shifted his gaze to Ife. "As long as neither Lux Temple nor National Security objects, tuteli adepts can accept any legal work to repay our temple debts. Storm Tower conscription is a default if we can't secure employment that pays more than the towers."

"Oh, I didn't know that." To his surprise, Ife's expression softened with genuine interest. "That's just the kind of detail I needed to know. Thank you."

"You're welcome," Cymin responded automatically. Though he had to wonder why Ife needed to know about tuteli employment and conscription. Did she have an impoverished relative who was considering sending a child to the temple?

"Everyone always assumed there was something between you and Adept Yinni because you were both so pretty and well matched," Zevlyn stated. "I was sure it was confirmed at the exhibition this year, when you were so exhausted after casting those Thousand Blessings spell arrays, and Adept Yinni raced to you and supported you."

"She was clearly your rock when you were your weakest." Ife glanced in Yinni's direction with an admiring expression. "You're very lucky."

Out of the corner of his eye, Cymin noticed Paeth scowl, but Kimrin seemed rather engaged. Quin and Ovelah, too.

"It would have been so romantic if you weren't siblings." Zevlyn's expression took on an oddly dreamy quality. "A lot of us from the Five Schools thought the two of you were swept up in a secret love affair. You know, like in the radio dramas. A tuteli couple, dodging conscription and fleeing the temple together, driven to desperation to find a safe place to raise their lovechild."

When did a lovechild show up?

Cymin stared at the two Guishuun College girls, stunned in equal measure by the wildness of their assumptions and the opulence of their imaginations. Was this what came of spending too much time immersed in dull textbooks and dissertations? Even ignoring the absurdity of him and Yinni eloping, how stupid would they have to be to desert Lux Temple and then document their grand escape as part of a film? The more Cymin thought about the entire proposition, the more hilarious it became for him.

At last, he laughed.

"Well, I'm sorry to have disappointed you," Cymin said quickly.

"It's fine. Not everything can be a radio drama." Zevlyn sighed and flipped her ponytail back over her shoulder. "There's nothing wrong with being boring and normal, really. Most of us are."

Kimrin, Quin, Paeth and Ovelah seemed to concur that Cymin's real life lacked appealing drama, and they returned to playing their card game.

"I'm actually a little relieved that you two weren't having a forbidden affair," Ife said. "It would have been a shame for Adept Yinni to wreck her life for that sort of thing."

"Also, we won't have to turn you in when NS comes after you! So, that's good too." Zevlyn dropped into the seat across the table from Cymin. "Anyway, what are you reading?"

Ife slid into the seat beside Zevlyn and looked at the book on Cymin's table as well.

"A . . . book?" Cymin replied. Why were they sitting with him suddenly? Hadn't he just proved how boring he was?

"You're funny." Zevlyn poked at the vermilion slipcover. "Are you hiding the cover because it's obscene?"

"No." Cymin hoped that he didn't sound too guilty and quickly added, "It's old and beaten up. I don't want it to fall apart."

Zevlyn arched her brows, her expression disbelieving. She gave Ife a knowing nudge with her elbow.

"Would it be against the rules for you to read erotica? I mean, as a tuteli?" Ife asked. She laced her fingers together on the table in front of her and regarded him with a direct, calm gaze. "Instructors never bother to teach us much about regulations in Lux Temple. But I'm quite curious."

Cymin wasn't certain if these two were attempting to intimidate him, get to know him or—Heavens forbid—flirt with him. Zevlyn eyed him with a slightly provocative gaze, while Ife seemed more inquisitive.

"We're free to read anything we want," Cymin informed her. "I mean, anything that isn't nationally banned."

Strictly speaking, tuteli weren't even barred from enjoying sex, liquor or costly meats. What they could not do—under threat of confinement to a labor camp—was burden the temple or the state with further debts incurred by gambling, indulgence or procreation. But as far as the general populace was concerned, modern tuteli were expected to publicly behave just as their ancient predecessors did: living as celibate ascetics dedicated to the magecraft bestowed upon humanity by the deities.

"So then, what are you reading?" Zevlyn peered at the book.

"A collection of letters describing Saigrath 200 years ago." Cymin opened the book to a random page to prove his point. Minroa was describing the wild creatures of Saigrath, beginning with bandimanders, which he loathed. Cymin skimmed ahead and then panicked as his eyes fell on the words at the bottom of the page.

I was sick to death of fucking when I arrived, and for the longest time I felt quite glad to be left alone. Now though, it's been nearly four years. Longing has become a hunger gnawing on my eager bones, and I am beyond restless these summer nights. Most maddening of all is how well Ondi has filled out and grown up beside me. Limbs that were gawky as a hatchling's now ripple with limber, lithe muscles. His chest is broad, his ass taut and his loins heavy as daikon.

Even the way he's grown steadily more and more pale—his hair is nearly white now and his skin the color of milk—no longer disturbs me. It makes him a rarity, even in the Heights.

He is beyond eye-catching and yet so frustratingly pure. He's hardly a year younger than me—a blooded man who has battled armies and monstrous beasts. The horrific Chuupran that arise here after fei'lux storms would make Piiroc and Chyrenese warriors shit themselves, I promise you; yet Ondi readily engages them. When I promised him that I would join him in combat against them, he merely smiled at me like a dream-eyed child and hugged me as if he didn't understand the hard heat of my—

Cymin snapped the book shut, hoping that neither Ife nor Zevlyn had skimmed down as far as he had.

"It's still too dark in here to read," Cymin stated.

"I like the description of the bandimander creature, but who uses the term 'bedighted' anymore?" Ife gave Cymin a puzzled look. "Is this the sort of thing you tuteli often read? I mean, out of date and secondhand?"

"If you consider ancient texts full of rare spells out of date and secondhand, then yes," Cymin said. "Otherwise, no."

"Oh, she didn't mean any offense. Ife is writing a novel, and one of the main characters is supposed to come from Lux Temple," Zevlyn said, by way of clarification. "I'm helping her with her research. That's why we're asking so many questions."

"I want to get the details right," Ife went on. "But there's nearly nothing written about the daily lives of tuteli. For example, what are your mealtimes like? What are your dormitory arrangements? Are you divided up by age or sex or skill levels? I don't just want to make things up, but you wouldn't believe how hard it is to learn any of this information."

"Oh." Cymin truly hadn't considered anything like that. He wondered at once what sort of book she might be writing. The idea was actually exciting. He'd never encountered a novel featuring a tuteli protagonist, though there were several that depicted them as villains or, more often, sad victims of various crimes. "If you really want to know about life in Lux Temple, we accept volunteers for short-term training and—"

Suddenly Xaon let loose a wild howl. All three of them startled and stared at him. Xaon's arms swung out, and he kicked against the window in a panic. He struck the table at least twice as he jolted upright. Then he sat, panting. His red hair stuck out at wild angles and his eyes were wide with shock.

"Are you all right?" Ife bolted to her feet and started towards Xaon. Zevlyn, too, stood, while an exclamation of "Whooo?" escaped Kimrin.

"Fuck! Fuck," Xaon gasped. His hands clutched at his chest. "Ugh ... fuck *me*."

Nyle had pulled his sketchbook and tin of pencils clear of Xaon's flailing limbs, but his expression remained impassive, as if this was how he expected everyone to wake up.

"Holy Heavens!" Quin peeped.

At the same time, Saum blearily demanded, "Who screaming ... *why* screaming?"

"It's that fucking dream again," Xaon scrubbed at his face with both hands, then looked to Ife and Zevlyn. "I'm fine. Sorry to startle you."

Just then, their train veered into another sharp turn. Ife and Zevlyn both stumbled forward, and Xaon reached out, attempting to catch them. Ife instantly blocked his hand with a swift blow while Zevlyn flailed out, latching onto his head with one hand and gripping Ife's ponytail with the other. All three of them tumbled to the floor. Then as the train straightened, they quickly disentangled themselves. Xaon recoiled into his seat with a confused expression and a vivid scratch running across his cheek.

"Thanks so much for your concern on his behalf," Nyle addressed Ife and Zevlyn.

Both women looked embarrassed.

"We should get back to our seats," Ife stated. The two of them hurried away at once.

"You've got an amazing left hook!" Xaon called after Ife. Then he craned his head back towards Jeshri. "Is it just me, or have the dreams been getting more and more intense?"

"Not sure. I wasn't dreaming yet," Jeshri replied. "Just now, were you in the Red Marsh or the White Chamber?"

"Neither. The gates. The fucking Black Gates . . ." Xaon pressed his hand to his chest, looking ill. "Right when arrows hit me."

Cymin gazed back as well, but his attention shifted farther away to where the Waethir sat. First, he noticed that Mazilane had returned from smoking and now stood near Bailon. Then he realized that all of them were studying Jeshri and Xaon. But where Mazilane appeared fascinated and Yinni looked concerned, the Waethir wore expressions of varying degrees of expectation. Eirjiri's eyes sparkled with excitement, while Laithondi's carried a trace of dread.

Belatedly, the content of Xaon and Jeshri's exchange sank in for him.

They'd dreamed of the same places: the Red Marsh, the White Chamber and the Black Gates. The Black Gates . . .

Unconsciously, Cymin pressed his hand to his chest. A memory sparked up, sizzling and snapping at his nerves. The Black Gates, where deities stood guard and mortals in seething Hundred Deaths Armor swarmed the walls like ants laying claim to a carcass . . . Cymin shuddered, and both the images and his dread dissipated to a vague uneasiness.

"Oh fuck . . ." Jeshri swore with a tone of such sympathy that Cymin found it a little amusing. Leave it to Orae Academy students to be able to express anger, happiness, compassion and regard all with the same obscenity. Jeshri went on, "I've been lucky. I haven't dreamed about the gates in a couple weeks."

"Wait, wait. What gates are you two talking about?" Paeth had turned to lean over the back of her bench. One of the cards clenched in her hand fell, but she didn't seem to notice. Instead, she turned her whole attention to Xaon.

"The Black Gates that defend the only pass to the Heights." Xaon massaged his chest and then leaned back in his seat as if utterly exhausted. Strands of sweat-soaked red hair clung to his brow like trails of dry blood.

"They're part of this series of fucking insane dreams that Xaon and I both have," Jeshri explained. "We discovered it thirteen years ago when we first came to the capital and boarded together. But we don't know why it happens."

"If you live together in the same place, it's not that unusual to dream of the same spaces," Zevlyn commented. Though there was something oddly tense about her expression. She stole a glance to Ife, who shot a curious glance between Xaon and Jeshri.

"But none of them take place at the boarding school. Not even close," Jeshri stretched, giving everyone a clear view of his bare chest. "And the shit we go through . . . fuuuuuuuuck . . ."

"You wouldn't understand," Xaon murmured. He stared at the ceiling of the train with a harrowed expression. "It's so real. It must have been our past lives."

"Fucking past lives." Jeshri nodded.

"The White Chamber . . ." Saum whispered. A red impression from her hammer marked one of her round cheeks. Sitting directly across from Jeshri, she looked dazed as she stared into the depths of his chest hair.

"I, eh, we . . . I mean . . . the red one, could it be the same . . . ?" Ovelah's words faded out as she cast a meaningful glance to her twin. Paeth looked torn but then sighed.

"You mentioned a red marsh. Is it a floodland with countless little red creatures drifting on the water like lotus flowers, but the leaves are actually translucent fins, and they have long tentacles hanging beneath them?" Paeth asked, as if that was a perfectly regular thing to be dreaming about.

Jeshri and Xaon both stared at her wide-eyed, while Saum, Quin and Kimrin gaped. Cymin marveled as well. He'd dreamed a scene very like that once. Back when he'd first entered Lux Temple. At least, he thought he had . . . though as he tried to recall it now, the memory seemed to fade to nothing.

"Oh fuck!" Jeshri murmured in wonder.

"Shit . . . yes, that's the Red Marsh." Xaon nodded, face clearly transmitting his astonishment. Nyle retained his unperturbed air. He merely glanced around at the others, taking in their reactions, and then continued drawing in his sketchbook.

"And the . . . the whi . . . the whi . . . white—" Ovelah gave up and just tugged at Paeth's sleeve.

Before Paeth could speak for her, Kimrin cleared his throat and asked, "Would there happen to be a pearly altar made of bones, gold and silverwork in the White Chamber?"

Cymin immediately remembered his own dreams of the huge altar filled with carved bone ancillaries and silverwork machinery. And, from the looks of shocked recognition on the faces of the other mages, Cymin realized that he wasn't the only one. Even Zevlyn and Ife seemed to recognize Kimrin's description. Yinni, too, appeared stunned. She met Cymin's gaze. She stood and seemed ready to join him when the train jolted. Vessreid steadied her, and she sat back down beside him. "Have we *all* dreamed of this same place?" Yinni called out.

"Wait!" Jeshri gaped back at Yinni. "Even you tuteli have been there?"

Even you tuteli? East Deity is not amused.

"Of course." Cymin responded dryly. "We're too poor to afford our own dreams, so we have to tag along in yours."

"Fuck me! You can do that?" Jeshri stared at him in wonder, then a look of worry crossed his face, and he flushed. "Even *those* kinds of dreams?"

"He's just teasing you." Paeth rolled her eyes.

"Oh." Jeshri nodded but still cast Cymin a sidelong look of worry.

Cymin winked at him in response.

"Stop confusing matters, Cy," Yinni chided. She rose to her feet again and this time made her way as far as the table occupied by Ife and Zevlyn before she was forced to sit again. She didn't look too happy about sharing Ife and Zevlyn's table, but the two of them seemed delighted to have her.

Yinni looked to the other Five Schools mages. "It sounds like we have all dreamed of a huge white chamber with an altar made of bones, gold and silver. Am I correct?"

Calls of "I have," "Me too" and "Yes" sounded from all throughout the train. Belatedly, Saum seemed to rouse from her daze and called out, "I have too! I have too!"

Nyle only gave a slight nod, as if none of this was particularly surprising or interesting to him. When he did briefly lift his head from his sketchbook, he didn't seek the attention of any of his fellow Chyrenese mages but only stole a glance to Laithondi.

Laithondi offered him a subtle nod in response.

Cymin found the intimacy of their exchange irritating, but neither of them seemed to notice or care about his scowl.

Paeth spoke up. "When we were little, Ovelah and I thought we had the same dreams because we were twins, but then we met Yinni two years ago and found out that she'd had the dreams too—ever since she was six years old."

"I was eight when I had my first dreams of the White Chamber." Kimrin took off his spectacles to wipe the lens. "But I haven't ever dreamed of any battle at a gate."

"I haven't been to the Red Marsh," Quin chirped. "But I have seen the White Chamber. Has anyone else been to the ocean when there's a brilliant blue aurora filling the sky and a bone-white island in the distance?"

"Oh, yes! I dream of the island all the time," Ife responded. She stole a shy glance to Yinni, but Yinni didn't look at her, despite the fact that they shared a bench.

"Me too," Saum said. "I don't remember a blue aurora, though. Just mist and clouds of gold sandbees circling me in rings. So many sandbees . . . "

"The auroras aren't constant," Nyle spoke up at last. "They're caused by storms of fei'lux and are easiest to see at night. They often trigger murmurations, mass spawning and mass blooms among sandbees, driftweeds, barroworms, jellyfish—mostly species that are symbiotic with fei'thallus."

Cymin remembered the pulsing sensation of the jellyfish fluttering in his hands and felt as if his heart was trembling with the same excited, agitated rhythm.

Xaon leaned across the table to study Nyle's sketchbook. His curious expression turned to shock, then wonder, and he looked up at Nyle.

"Whoa! You've drawn it! That's the beach during the fei'lux storm. When we returned the jellyfish." Xaon stared at Nyle. "You were there, too?"

"Yes, obviously." Nyle gestured at his drawing.

Cymin and all the other mages on the train moved forward a little, staring at Nyle's sketchbook. Cymin even started to stand up to take a closer look, and he wasn't alone. But before any of them could do more than shift in their seats, Nyle flipped the sketchbook closed and placed his hand over the battered black cover as if guarding it from them.

"Damn. I wanted to see," Saum muttered.

"It probably wasn't all that good, anyway," Kimrin consoled. "It would only dash your dreams to learn that *the* Porcelain Prince doesn't know what color sand is and that he's filled half his sketchbook with sloppy, lopsided tits."

"Or worse, crooked dicks!" Quin burst into laughter. Kimrin grinned at her. Quiet snickers escaped several of the other mages, though, to Cymin's surprise, Xaon and Ife weren't among them.

In response, Nyle merely lifted his chin as if the comments and derision were beneath acknowledgement.

An awkward quiet filled the train car.

Then Paeth cleared her throat and asked, "So, does anyone else remember the beach?"

Cymin opened his mouth but somehow choked on the admission that he, too, had experienced that intimate evening running through cold ocean spray beneath a luminous blue sky. All at once, he understood Nyle's sudden decision to hide the picture and whatever notes he'd made. That place and the memories associated with it were far too personal. He didn't think he could endure all those fragile emotions inspiring another round of mockery.

"Isn't the larger question why we all dream about the same place? And what that means?" Ife asked. "Is it a real location? Or a dream world we all share?"

"If I've guessed correctly," Nyle responded, "then the place is real. Or at least, it was a long time ago. It's Saigrath. The fact that we all dream of it—perhaps even remember pieces of it from a past life—is the reason that the Waethir chose to instruct us."

"Correct." The response came from Vessreid.

As all of them turned to look at him, Cymin noticed Hiral's subtle movements for the first time. He kept his head down, resting on his crossed hands as if sleeping. His lowered lashes hid the thin crack of his open eyes. Only his thumb and forefinger moved as he slowly turned a dial of the camera tether on his wrist. His camera's lens rotated quietly. He was filming. No doubt he'd been filming this entire time, Cymin realized.

You're a sly one, aren't you? Maybe you should work for NS instead of me. Could we swap?

"Each of you carries the trace of a deity. That's why you've been selected to study in Saigrath." Vessreid stood. His long silver braids swayed around him, but that seemed to be his only concession to the jolts and jittering of the train. He strode to where Yinni sat with Zevlyn and Ife and rested his hand on the back of their bench. "You possess the potential to become truly great."

"Even—" Jeshri began.

"If you ask, 'Even the tuteli?' I will pop you in the nose," Cymin cut him off.

Jeshri gaped at him, then whispered, "Seriously, Cymin, can you read my mind?"

"He's just f—fu—fu . . ." Ovelah stammered.

"Fooling with you," Paeth finished for her. Though from Ovelah's expression, Cymin guessed that she'd wanted to use a different word.

"So," Mazilane cleared his throat, rather obtrusively drawing attention to himself. Then he addressed Vessreid as he strode forward. "You didn't argue long and loud with all those ministers for the sake of every random Chyrenese tuteli. You'd already singled Yinni out as having this deity trace. And you wanted her specifically?"

"The two aren't mutually exclusive. But yes, my priority was to free Tuteli Yinni, so that she could realize her full potential." Vessreid gave Yinni a friendly smile.

"A good thing we didn't miss the train, then," Mazilane commented. He dropped his pack into the seat across from Hiral and then settled down himself.

"Let's take that as a test." Vessreid shot Laithondi a quick glance but then returned his attention to Mazilane. "It proved that the Heavens employed all of you to ensure she could join us."

"Sure, let's say that's what happened." Mazilane shrugged. He shot Hiral and Cymin a wry smile. "Don't tell Una Bayan that we're moonlighting for the Heavens."

"I imagine that Una Bayan provides better pay." The joke came from Bailon. She and Eirjiri both turned and leaned over the back of the bench to observe.

"Or at least time off!" Eirjiri added. "The Heavens have no concept of vacations, that's for certain."

"But, but, but . . ." Ovelah gripped Paeth's arm. "What exactly does . . ."

"Yes. What exactly *is* a trace of a deity?" Paeth asked. She looked between Vessreid and Bailon. "How did we get them?"

"Wh—wh—why the dreams?" Ovelah added in an urgent whisper.

"It's complicated, but . . ." Bailon paused. She glanced to Laithondi. He scowled and lowered his head so that the early morning gloom hid his features. Cymin found the exchange strange.

But then Arnaith turned and leaned over the back of her seat. She held long needle-nosed pliers in one hand and a gold wire in the other.

"Just think of them as blessings blown across the sea from Saigrath." Arnaith went on, twisting the gold wire between her fingers and the pliers. "They fell to each of you along with the rains of your Haelon Spring Flood."

"They were part of the flood?" Xaon looked stricken, and he wasn't alone. Cymin felt horrified himself. He knew that most of the other mages on board the train had lost their homes or members of their families to the flood. All their lives had been disrupted by that relentless inundation. No matter what gift they might have brought, none of them could feel anything about the deluge but horror.

"No, your blessings weren't the cause of the flood. Just spells that got caught up in the wind along with seeds and leaves." Bailon waved her hand as if the suggestion was an annoying fly to be shooed away. "Saigrath is the homeland of deities, awash in countless blessings. They constantly drift from our borders, like dandelion seeds floating on the breeze. Normally, they dissipate or fall into the sea before reaching another nation. Few, if any, ever cross the Great Chasm Sea. But I suspect that fourteen years ago, the storm that eventually flooded Haelon passed over Saigrath and swept up a larger number of deity blessings. It carried them all the way across the chasm and into Chyre."

"Each of those blessings carried a trace of the original deity that created it. Not just their skills but their character as well," Eirjiri spoke up as if she couldn't hold back any longer. "For example, within me, Earth Deity's blessing isn't just a dry litany of information. It's memories and aspirations. A sense of excitement and optimism. The certainty that I will endure and prevail even if I must struggle for a thousand years. I know that I have crossed the Red Marsh and the Mist Moors to raise the mountains of the Black Gate. Even if I die in this form, I cannot be defeated. Eirjiri will continue on."

As she made that final pronouncement, Cymin noted how her gaze settled on Saum and then Jeshri. An almost fervent quality appeared in her smile. Then Cymin stole a glance to Yinni, observing Vessreid's protective presence beside her.

"Those impressions from old memories are what you've each seen in your dreams," Arnaith put in. "They will be different for each deity and may even differ between incarnations of the same deity, depending on how complete the blessing is and how well it flourished within a given person."

Cymin frowned. If he'd received a blessing, was it somehow lacking? Was that why Laithondi rejected him? He recalled his own dream of the jellyfish. Had that dream come from a deity's blessing or merely been inspired by the passages he read in Minroa's letters? He glanced to Xaon and Nyle, who seemed to have also dreamed of that night. They'd been selected by Laithondi and so had certainly received a complete deity's blessing. But Laithondi had rejected him . . . twice.

And yet he had dreamed of that altar of bones. He'd torn the scepter from it, while mages invaded the heights . . .

Cymin closed his eyes, attempting to remember more of the chaotic dream, but he only dredged up his feeling of despair, verging upon panic.

He sighed in frustration and gave up attempting to summon the memory. Instead, he massaged his temple and then consoled himself with a bite from his remaining almond tart.

"So, does that make us deities in Saigrath?" Saum suddenly asked. At the suggestion, Kimrin, Zevlyn, Xaon and Paeth all looked excited. Cymin held rather fewer illusions about playing the role of a deity. Yinni shook her head slightly, and the two of them exchanged an ironic glance.

Laithondi and Vessreid both frowned, but Eirjiri laughed outright.

"Not really, no." Bailon seemed indulgent. "As I said, these sorts of blessings abound in Saigrath. Nearly everyone and everything has been touched by some blessing. Yours have given you potential, but they alone won't make deities of you."

"Oh." Saum frowned and deflated back into her seat like a dumpling deprived of its filling. Across from her, Jeshri sighed as if relieved.

"Think about it. It would be so much responsibility," he whispered to Saum. "It's better to have free time."

"Agreed," Quin chirped from across the aisle, and Ovelah nodded.

"Other than gifting you all with early insights into manipulating fei'lux, the blessings merely qualify you to train as Waethir," Vessreid stated. "Think of them as . . . hmm . . . tickets. They simply allowed us to recognize that you have a right to board this train."

"They would have slightly enhanced your natural sympathy with fei'lux. But just a little." Arnaith lifted up her forefinger and thumb as if holding a pinch of salt.

"But . . . how did you all recognize that we were the ones with the blessings?" Ife asked.

Nyle glanced up from his sketchbook as if searching for the answer as well.

"Fuck! Is it the dreams?" Jeshri looked suddenly stricken. "Can you see us in those dreams?"

Jeshri, you look so guilty that now we're all suspicious of what you've been getting up to in your sleep. Cymin hid his smirk with a last bite of his tart.

"Of course it's not the dreams. How would that even work?" Paeth shot Jeshri a disbelieving glance. "They knew because of how we manipulated fei'lux and because we could recognize certain objects when they interviewed us after the Spring Exhibition."

Cymin glanced to Laithondi. He'd said almost nothing throughout this entire conversation. Now he returned Cymin's gaze for a moment before shifting his attention to the brickwork buildings and railway station platforms flickering past the portal windows. Cymin dropped his hand into his bag but resisted the urge to dig out the celestial pearl that Laithondi had given him.

"That's right," Eirjiri stated.

Saum popped back upright and grinned at Eirjiri. "I wondered why you asked if I liked the brooch on your coat."

"The obsidian and diamond brooch? You recognized it too?" Jeshri beamed at Saum and then Eirjiri. She lifted up her leather coat and displayed the glinting brooch affixed to the lapel.

"All the treasures of the Earth—" Eirjiri began, and Saum and Jeshri joined her, "—belong to Eirjiri!" Then all three laughed.

Cheerful in the face of uncertainty, they truly are three of a kind.

"So, you Waethir have the same dreams that we do?" Ife asked. "And those dreams are actually fragmented memories from the past deities lives? In essence, they are our past lives—"

"Yes, but no!" Eirjiri responded.

"She means that you mustn't focus too much on the memories." Bailon shook her head. "Those times are gone and done. Never to come again. You've been given the opportunity to free yourselves from the past. Remember the skills. But forget all the rest."

"But—" Xaon began to protest, only to be cut off by Laithondi.

"You learned to read as a child but needn't cling to the identity of a child to continue reading. This is just the same." Laithondi spoke with the firm tone of an instructor who brooked no argument. Disappointment showed on all the mages' faces, but none of them offered any retort. Laithondi continued, "You must let the past go and push forward to a greater future." Then he cocked his head to the side and narrowed his gaze. All at once, fei'lux shot through the air. White sparks burst up from Hiral's camera. The cameraman jumped into the aisle to avoid being struck.

"This matter is private and should be kept that way." Laithondi pinned Hiral, then Mazilane with a firm gaze before sweeping an icy glower over the rest of the train car. "As for the rest of you, I advise that you leave the past behind from this point on and save your strength to face the challenges that lay ahead of us."

Then he settled back into his seat, glowering out the portal window as the first streaks of the rising sun lit his hard profile.

CHAPTER 16

Half an hour later, morning sun lit the outskirts of the city and their steaming engine punched through the translucent perimeter of the fei'lux shields. Streams of silver and gold light danced across the train cars, and faint impressions of disrupted sigils flickered over the portal windows before they dissipated. A ticklish buzz swept over Cymin along with a faint odor, like a dry kettle left too long on the fire. Cymin sneezed. He noticed that the other mages in the train car responded as well.

Most shivered, though Xaon wrinkled his nose and sneezed as Cymin had.

Quin giggled, and Nyle tensed as if attempting to suppress any response.

Saum jolted upright, twitching like a spider was running up her back. Her coat fell from her shoulders. Jeshri caught it, handed it back to her and then stiffened as he too felt the agitated fei'lux. His face twitched, and an enormous belch erupted from him. He and Saum both burst into laughter.

Across the aisle from Cymin, Hiral muttered under his breath as he replaced the blown fuse in his camera, pausing only occasionally to shoot aggrieved looks at Laithondi. Seated opposite Hiral, Mazilane furrowed his brow at the deformed, scorched fuse. Then he angled his own camera at the portal window, capturing the flashing sigils.

Of the Waethir, only Eirjiri seemed to pay any attention to their passage through the city's fei'lux shield. She beamed at the displays of flickering sigils.

"They're so delicate and tiny here." Eirjiri pointed to the portal window. Bailon roused herself to look. She smiled and nodded then returned to napping. Vessreid and Arnaith also slept through it. Laithondi, on the other hand, glowered out his window with none of Eirjiri's delight. He lifted his hand, pressing the tips of two fingers against the window glass and shook his head.

Cymin echoed this motion, though the cause of his dismay was Laithondi himself.

Has even the fei'lux offended you today? Or are you just grumpy from lack of sleep? Did you miss breakfast? Is that why you're behaving so childishly and being needlessly bossy?

If the ancient Waethir had been as overbearing in their pronouncements as modern Laithondi, then Cymin could see why so many mage-kings resented and defied their dictates—even when the laws themselves were humane and wise rulings. No one liked to feel overruled and browbeaten.

And it wasn't as if that approach had worked here either. Laithondi could declare the past a matter to best be forgotten and short out Hiral's camera in a fountain of sparks, but it only resulted in the Five Schools mages furtively whispering among themselves and growing all the more fascinated with sharing the memories that had haunted their dreams for the past fourteen years.

Jeshri and Saum leaned so close that their foreheads nearly touched while whispering back and forth. They barely managed to keep their voices down as they discussed what they could recall of the Ivory Island as well as immense stoneworks that they remembered raising from the black sea surrounding it. Quin darted over to join them for a time and then zipped back to Kimrin, Paeth and Ovelah to report what Saum and Jeshri had shared. Zevlyn and Ife leaned over the seatbacks behind Paeth and Ovelah. They listened and added comments as well. Yinni had seemed reticent to converse at first, but after Paeth beckoned her to come and sit beside her, Yinni too joined in, recalling details from her dreams. Ife and Zevlyn provided the names and locations of several medicinal herbs for her. Yinni thanked them, but with a fixed smile that made Cymin certain that she suspected them of trying to embarrass her. Fortunately, there were so many other topics brought up that the conversation moved on right away.

Listening to them all, it became clear to Cymin that they'd fought in many, many battles together in their past lives, but two stood out as particularly intense: the defense of the Black Gates and a later stand during a terrible storm when invaders breached the Heights.

Cymin could picture everything that they mentioned, despite the fact that none of them recalled every single place and occurrence in each other's dreams. The oddity of that made him uneasy and a little suspicious that he wasn't actually remembering any of it but rather unconsciously imagining scenes based on their words, the same way he could picture so many events from Minroa Haeyi's letters.

Cymin strained to hear more and test his imaginings against actual descriptions. Paeth translated Ovelah's murmurs as she spoke of a vast city blanketed in snow as well as the Waethir's mountain citadel above it—the Heights. But from the onion-domed towers, to the stained glass atriums where tuteli trained, Minroa's letters had mentioned each locale already, so Cymin couldn't be certain that he didn't know them from the book and not his own dreams.

Cymin shifted his attention to Quin's petulant face as she heaved a sigh.

"I don't like thinking about the battle at the Heights." Quin twisted a lock of her violet-washed hair around one thin finger after another until she'd almost woven her hand closed. "I get a gross feeling every time I dream about it."

"Same, Quiny, same." Beside her, Kimrin grimaced, then gently pulled her hair free from her hand and pinned the lock back up into one of her gold combs. "I'm pretty certain we burned to death that day."

"Ewww," Quin responded. "That's so disgusting."

"Very." Kimrin adjusted the delicately tooled leather cuff of his jacket with a pained expression. "Can't even leave an attractive corpse when you go like that, can you?"

"Oh, but if it's any consolation," Saum said as she leaned across the aisle, "Jeshri and I are pretty certain we went up in flames then too."

"For some fucking reason we were trying to channel a fuck-load of wild fei'lux," Jeshri muttered. "It just wouldn't stop pouring in through some fucking doors . . . or gates . . . or . . . fuck if I know."

"The hall—hallo—hall . . . " Ovelah stuttered and tugged Paeth's arm, but her twin was in the midst of an intense, whispered discussion with Ife, Zevlyn and Yinni. All four bowed their heads close, leaving Ovelah to trail off into silence.

"For the longest time, all I could remember was the feeling of that knife blade sinking into my body again and again. Then I'd wake up screaming." Zevlyn's face drained of color as she spoke. "But last night, I stayed in the dream longer. This time I saw who broke into the White Chamber to steal the scepter and murdered me—us—"

"It was Vessreid who was killed," Yinni corrected. She glanced over her shoulder to where Vessreid and Arnaith napped. "He probably remembers it more vividly than any of us."

"You think he already knows who the killer was, then?" Ife asked.

Yinni nodded, and Zevlyn looked a little crestfallen.

"I was thinking that I could get Nyle to draw a sketch from what I remember, but if Vessreid already . . ."

"If you feel like you must ask him about it, please be tactful," Yinni said. "He's a sensitive soul, and I think his nightmares are probably much worse than ours."

"We don't need to upset him because there's only one possible culprit," Ife stated firmly. "Minroa Haeyi masterminded the invasion, stole the scepter and killed both Vessreid and Ondi."

Cymin had to stop himself from spinning around in his seat at the mention of Minroa. He'd only leafed through the man's letters, but somehow, he felt deeply connected to him. Revulsion and outrage filled him in a feverish rush just at the suggestion of Minroa killing Ondi.

"Because who else could have done it?" Ife went on. "He was the only one with opportunity, means and motive. So much motive! He and his brother colluded previously. I think it's obvious that they worked together again and engineered the invasion as—"

"No, it wasn't him," Paeth broke in, but then she looked a little at a loss. "I—I mean . . . Minroa wouldn't kill Ondi. He just wouldn't have. And we don't know who worked with Xondir or why they did it."

Cymin felt oddly thankful to her for her defense of Minroa. Though at the same time, a feeling somewhere between dread and guilt seemed to ripple through his chest. His fingertips tingled as the stinging sensation of ripping the scepter from its altar played through his hands. He remembered the smell of blood and the still-warm corpse laying at his feet.

"Then who do you think did?" Ife's voice remained hushed, but her frustration carried clearly. "Because *someone* stole the scepter, butchered Vessreid and utterly destroyed Ondi that day."

"I know," Paeth responded softly. "But I've been thinking about it for a while, and I just don't feel right letting Minroa take all the blame. In the end, he wasn't there to defend himself. Or explain why—"

"He wasn't there because he left with the scepter after betraying us all," Ife pointed out. "It seems pretty cut and dried."

Yinni nodded but then patted Paeth's shoulder when she noticed how forlorn the other girl looked.

"We should just ask Vessreid," Zevlyn suggested.

"But maybe not right away," Yinni put in. "The Waethir did just tell us not to brood on the past. And besides that, it has to be a painful subject for him."

"Le—le—let it go," Ovelah at last broke into the conversation, clutching Paeth's arm. "Blame Minroa . . . he . . ."

Cymin strained to catch the rest of her furtive whispers, but they were drowned out when Xaon's voice rose in an exasperated groan.

"For fuck's sake, Nyle, just let me see it." Xaon had spent every minute since they'd left the city squabbling with Nyle and trying to get a chance to look through Nyle's sketchbook.

"No," Nyle reiterated his denial for the hundredth time. "It's private."

"Is it, though?" Xaon argued. "If we share the same past life, aren't we basically the same person? Or at least . . . I don't know . . . brothers? What's there to hide from me?"

"I already have nine brothers who I don't share my journal with." Nyle didn't even look up at Xaon. "You can be one more."

"You let Laithondi look through it yesterday," Xaon protested.

"But you aren't Laithondi," Nyle said.

"In a way, I am, though. Right?" Xaon responded gamely.

"And in many more important ways, you aren't," Nyle replied. "So, my answer is still no."

"Come on."

"No."

"But—"

"No. No, and also no," Nyle stated firmly. Xaon looked like he was about to protest further when Nyle added, "Ask and you shall receive an eternity of no. Now and forever—no."

"Fine. Have it your way." Xaon heaved a dramatic sigh. "Enjoy playing on a team of one, then."

Xaon stood, picked up his patched green blanket and tromped to Cymin's side. "Mind if I sit with you?"

Cymin was a little surprised to have been singled out, but it wasn't as if he was using the other three spaces at his table.

"Feel free," Cymin replied. He was actually relieved to escape the speculation concerning Minroa. He felt absurd for having allowed it to disturb him so deeply in the first place. And he was rather curious about the other mages' dreams and past identities—particularly those of Laithondi's students, though he felt uncertain of his right to ask. He wasn't confident that he possessed any trace of any deity. The other students had been vetted by the Waethir. Even Yinni had been selected by Vessreid. He had said as much. But none of the Waethir had acknowledged Cymin.

Xaon dropped down in the seat opposite him. The pronounced angles of his jaw and chin reminded Cymin a little of Laithondi, but Xaon's eyes were far more narrow and mischievous. This close, Cymin also noted the freckles that splashed across his nose and cheeks as well as the faint line of an old scar running across his throat. A powerful smell of cedar, sweat and wool wafted from his blanket.

Cymin shifted his legs, making room for Xaon's lanky splayed limbs. He guessed that Xaon didn't regularly share cramped quarters with people as long-legged and large-footed as himself. But, recalling that Xaon and Jeshri had boarded together for more than a decade, Cymin reconsidered. Maybe Xaon and Jeshri had sprawled over each other for so long that Xaon just didn't have much sense of personal space anymore.

Xaon scowled over his shoulder at Nyle's profile with such a petulant expression that Cymin almost laughed. Nyle shot Xaon a cold glare, then resumed drawing in his sketchbook. The two of them were a perfect bickering couple; Master Tam and Master Shuun often feigned the same kind of indifference when they argued.

"He's the asshole. Not me," Xaon muttered. "What's the point of drawing a bunch of pictures that no one else gets to see? There's no way he and I are related."

"Definitely not," Cymin confirmed.

Xaon appeared a little dispirited by his ready agreement. He kicked the floorboards and sighed.

"So, what about you?" Xaon asked a moment later. Then he lowered his voice to a whisper, "You're one of us too, right?"

"I don't know," Cymin replied. "Maybe."

"You've had the dreams?"

"I think I have, but . . ." Cymin trailed off.

"You have. I can feel it here, and here too." Xaon thumped his chest and tapped the tip of his own nose. "Come on, tell me what you've dreamed about. I'll bet you a blue bill that I'll recognize the same things."

"I don't have a blue bill to wager," Cymin replied. He was reluctant to share his dreams. Most faded from his memory too quickly for him to be certain of what happened in them. Those he could recall at all were either far too intimate or too confusing to put into words. Of all his muddled, messy dreams, the two scenes he recalled most vividly were also those he least wanted to confess to.

In the first, he tore a scepter from its altar in the White Chamber. In the second, he plummeted from the Heavens bloody and wrecked, with a dead man cradled in his arms and "I won't let go" repeating through his head.

If he truly had been responsible for those things—even in another life—he didn't think he wanted to know. Never mind telling anyone else.

"Fine. I'll let the money slide, this time," Xaon responded with an easy smile. "Come on. I know you're one of us."

"How?" Cymin couldn't help but wonder because no one else seemed so sure.

"I was right there on the exhibition grounds, maybe ten feet from you. I sensed that weird tangerine-scented spell sizzle up from the ground, just like you did. Then, boom! You launched into the sky on an explosion of blessings. Later, I realized that it had been a bomb that you absorbed." Xaon gestured to the fresh scars where the melted spell filaments had been excised from Cymin's hands and forearms. "But before any of that, I recognized that you were a bloodhound, like me."

"A what?" Cymin had been preparing himself to make up some lie about the bomb—if only for the benefit of Mazilane, sitting across the aisle from them. But Xaon randomly bringing up hunting dogs threw him off.

"A bloodhound." Xaon tapped the tip of his nose again. "Laithondi mastered hunting chuuraun and tracking mage assassins by the scents they left in the fei'lux. I got that from him. And so did you. Am I right?"

Cymin darted a glance back to where Laithondi sat glowering at the passing scenery. When he shifted, Cymin looked away, returning his attention to Xaon.

"I'm right," Xaon stated with a smug smile. "I knew it."

"That was just a spell residue," Cymin replied. "Most mages can sense them if they practice."

"But have you practiced? Because I haven't." Xaon looked at ease admitting as much. "The skill just unfolded inside me after a schoolmaster mentioned that it was possible. I dozed off in his class and woke up able to trace a love-spell back to the girl who cast it on Jeshri even though she was four miles away."

The mention of a love-spell distracted Cymin. He didn't think he'd ever encountered one, and he couldn't help but be a little curious.

"What did it smell like?" Cymin had to ask.

"Popcorn. Fresh, buttered popcorn." Xaon smiled wistfully. "I was so hungry by the time I found the girl, that halfway through chewing her out for oppressing Jeshri's free will, I started in on how she ought to have made buttered popcorn or at least put on a pot of rice-tea if she was going to cause so much trouble. I probably seemed crazy, but it convinced her to break her spell and swear never to do it again. Eventually, I got a bag of cinema popcorn off Jeshri. So it worked out."

Cymin laughed and Xaon grinned.

"Come on," Xaon cajoled. "Tell me what you've dreamed of. I'll buy you some popcorn, first chance I get."

"Fine, but there's not much to say. I've seen the White Chamber . . . that's about all." Cymin didn't really want to talk about the body he remembered clutching in his arms or the scepter that he'd wrenched from the altar. The emotions surrounding those dreams were too raw and wretched. He tried to focus back on other dreams—the earliest ones of his childhood. Lots of misty woodlands and spiraling towers, but those were just vague settings. Hazy, distant silhouettes of shaggy mountains rising up on countless root-like legs and wading out into the sea—but that might have just been a childhood fantasy.

What he wanted was something specific. Then he remembered.

"I had a nightmare about being in a battle," Cymin said. "The first day, there were countless soldiers in Hundred Deaths Armor mounted on huge black carriage birds. They looked like a dark, gleaming river pouring through a narrow mountain pass. And I plunged down from the clouds into their midst." Cymin frowned. As a child, he'd been terrified upon waking from those nightmares with the obscene screams and curses still ringing in his ears. He'd always awakened shaking with pain and fury and with the smell of bloody, burning bodies choking his lungs. But now he felt oddly divorced from those responses. It was so strange to consider them, not as his own outlandish, private dreams, but as someone else's displaced memories.

I wish to be more than a costly mirror, suited only to reflect another man's dreams and designs.

Minroa had written that in one of his letters. It seemed rather apt at the moment. Though that protest had been against serving as a cat's paw for his father's political stratagems in Saigrath. Cymin came back to the moment, recollecting that he was halfway through describing one of his old dreams. He refocused on Xaon, who sat calmly waiting for him to continue.

"Go on," Xaon prompted.

"And then . . . I strike the battleground like a bolt of lightning. My body feels like fei'lux is exploding from me, ripping the people and animals all around me apart. The ground at my feet sears to glass, and the fallen bodies burn as I charge through their formations to seize their mage-king." Cymin frowned at the flutter of anger that the recollection brought on.

In the dream, he'd been shot through with arrows and seething with rage that these petty, ignorant creatures dared to rise up against him. At the same time, he felt a subtle edge of guilt. He'd sworn to protect them—so why did they have to rebel? Why did they force him to hurt them?

"Yes. That's exactly what happens after I've been shot at the gates," Xaon agreed. "Those fucking arrows. Right in the chest. They pissed you off, right? Ugh. I always wake up so frustrated."

Cymin nodded.

Only it isn't actually you or me who's frustrated. Turns out, it's a long-dead Waethir. A ghost living inside of us . . . or maybe just you? How pathetic am I, if I'm imagining it all and subconsciously hoping that some phantom chose to haunt me?

Cymin and Xaon both sat in silence while the train engine sang out in a shrill whistle. Outside the portal window, another freight train whipped past in the opposite direction on adjacent tracks. Then it was gone, leaving the serene view of countless newly planted rice paddies spread out like miles of green lily pads.

Xaon leaned closer to Cymin, nudging his leg.

"Alright. So it's exactly like I thought. You and me, we're the same," Xaon whispered. "We have to have been Laithondi in our past lives. East Deity, right?"

"I'm not certain—"

"Seriously?" Xaon's red brows rose dramatically. "I've seen you manifest the Thousand Blessings of the Black Staff. And the way you fight . . . if you weren't East Deity in your past life, then nobody was. It's the same for me—since I was six years old, I've felt a force blazing inside me. Fiery red like the sun, you know?" Then Xaon raised his voice slightly and added, "If anyone's identity should be in question, it's Nyle's."

Nyle frowned but didn't look up from his sketchbook.

"I don't think—" Cymin began.

"I know, I know. I'm just fucking with him because he's so snotty." Xaon cut Cymin off with a wave of his hand. "Nyle passed the Waethir's test right away. Laithondi even picked him before me, so Nyle is definitely one of us. He just pisses me off. So fucking secretive and cold. Asshole."

Cymin couldn't argue that Nyle wasn't secretive or cold, nor that his aloof manner wasn't irritating. At the same time, all of this was a bit much to absorb. Not everyone could take this sort of revelation as well as Xaon seemed to. Nyle might just need time to think it through. Cymin certainly did. Right now, he wasn't at all sure about how he felt about this alleged new identity.

He hadn't even come to terms with serving as a spy for Lui Dane, and now he had to contend with the possibility of being host to the memories of a dead Waethir. Did that make him a Wraith?

"Alright, so here's the sticky question." Xaon lowered his voice and hunched down. His left leg bounced with nervous energy. "Do you remember anything about . . . you know?"

Cymin waited while Xaon stared at him with an expectant expression.

"You *know*. . ." Xaon repeated.

"No," Cymin said.

"You don't?" Xaon scowled. "Not at all?"

"No, I mean don't know what you're talking about." Cymin felt a little like they'd descended into a comedic routine.

Xaon's face flushed nearly as red as his hair.

"You know . . ." Xaon whispered. "Fucking. Like going at it crazy hard all night long. Waking up soaked in sweat and . . . you know . . ."

Cymin blinked at Xaon. He felt a flush slowly heating his face and all at once understood why Nyle might not want to discuss these things with Xaon.

"I'm not trying to be strange or disgusting. I'm asking seriously," Xaon whispered. He shot Nyle another sidelong glare. "It's just I've had a *lot* of those dreams. Jeshri did too, and for a while we thought they were connected, but it turns out that Jeshri's are . . . you know . . . standard stuff. With a girl and . . . you know, just normal." Xaon appeared at a loss for any better terms or description.

"It's not abnormal to dream about *being* with a man," Cymin assured Xaon. "It simply reflects the nature that the Heavens imparted to you. It may not be common, but neither are jewels." Master Shuun had once reassured Cymin in nearly the same way.

Xaon frowned and was quiet for a moment.

"So . . . is that a yes or a no?" Xaon asked at last.

Cymin opened his mouth to answer, but before he could speak, Nyle slammed his sketchbook closed with a resounding bang. Cymin jolted at the sudden noise, and as he looked to Nyle, he noticed that not only was Hiral once again filming, but Ife, Zevlyn, Paeth, Kimrin and Quin were all gaping in his direction, wearing fascinated expressions. Ovelah's head was bowed down to stare at the floor, but her ears blazed red. Yinni cupped her face in her hands, looking mortified.

Seeing her, Cymin came back to his senses completely. He was a tuteli adept; the last thing he ought to be *filmed* doing was recounting sexual adventures from his dreams. Cymin was certain that if he craned his head back just a little further, he'd catch Jeshri and Saum observing. He prayed that the topic hadn't captured the Waethir's attention as well.

Nyle set his sketchbook aside and stepped into the aisle. His long black braids swayed with the rocking motion of the train. He strode to the side of Cymin's seat, and a faint perfume—like fragrant sumac—seemed to drift off his pale skin. His attention remained focused on Xaon.

"Even if the answer is yes in a past life, it's still a private matter in this one," Nyle stated. "Bailon and Laithondi were both very clear about that. The past is over and done with. We shouldn't focus on it."

Xaon scowled back at Nyle.

"But what about *him*?" Xaon countered. "You're truly willing to just forget about Min?"

Min? Cymin's mind immediately jumped to Minroa.

He couldn't associate that name with anyone else, particularly not after hearing it spoken with such yearning. The intensity of longing in Xaon's tone was only matched by the seething anger that had permeated Vessreid's voice earlier at the Palace Complex.

"Yes. Forget about him. That's what it means to leave the past behind. Let him go." A pained expression flickered across Nyle's delicate features. Xaon continued to glare at him.

"I won't!" Xaon crossed his muscular arms across his broad chest. "I don't believe that he simply betrayed me—us. There has to have been more to it."

"There doesn't, actually," Nyle replied. "But even if there was, what would it matter now? It's literally hundreds of years too late to change anything. He's long, long dead and best just forgotten."

"You know as well as I do that he couldn't have been lost in time like other mortals. I didn't plunge to the depths of the Sea of Eternity just to lose him," Xaon spoke in a whisper. "The pearl—"

"Fine," Nyle cut him off quickly, though Cymin was rather curious. What had he been about to say about a pearl? Could it have been another of the Waethir's celestial pearls? What had been inside that one?

"Even if you're right," Nyle went on. "There's still no going back. No way to change anything. You ought to let him go."

"Never. I'm going to keep looking for him," Xaon stated, then he jabbed a finger at Cymin. "The same goes for Cymin. He burned Min's sigil into the Heavens for everyone to see. You think he's going to just give up and forget about Min because you say so?"

"And what are you two going to do when you find him?" Nyle demanded. "Murder him? Try and rekindle that absurd romance? Everything that happened between you took place in an entirely different life. What's the point of wasting this new start searching for him or writing a twenty-foot sigil of his name—"

"But I didn't!" Cymin cut Nyle off before the misunderstanding could go any further. "I didn't write anyone else's name. I wrote my own name."

Both Xaon and Nyle stared at Cymin with disbelieving expressions.

"Honestly. Min is short for Cy-*Min*," Cymin explained. "I write it everywhere."

The two of them appeared completely at a loss, both studying Cymin as if he had transformed into someone utterly strange and alien to them.

"But you do remember him, don't you? You must remember—" Xaon's voice was soft and oddly hurt. "That night when he stole castoffs of tuteli armor so that he could join me in battle. He was more scared for me than he was for himself. I—we—knew that we would always protect him then. We lay together beneath the full moon and swore our love to each other . . . I—we couldn't bear to lose him." Xaon's voice again dropped to a low whisper. "We risked everything to share the Sea of Eternity with him. Give him our immortality. Remember?"

"I—" Cymin scowled. Xaon's words evoked vivid images. His hands trembling as he stripped away filthy, bloody armor and revealed the beautiful young man who'd followed him, unbidden, to fight monsters in the mountains. Moonlight, glowing over the same young man's supple naked body and the lustrous pearl gripped in his hand. But Cymin didn't know that he could claim any of that as a memory so much as his rampant imagination and mad predilection toward fantasy.

East Deity's imagination does outstrip his memory sometimes.

"You don't even remember returning jellyfish to the Black Sea?" Nyle asked with an arched brow.

"I—" Cymin didn't know what to say. He *had* dreamed of that, but only after he'd read about it in Minroa's letters. Suddenly, he felt very uncertain. What if his dreams weren't the same as the other mages'? What if his arose from impressions of writings he'd encountered in Lux Temple and things he'd overheard Yinni mention? Like his memory of the celestial pearl—what if his inclusion here was a mere coincidence?

Say no, and I'm a liar. Say yes, and I'm an imposter.

"As fascinating as your conversation is," Mazilane suddenly spoke from across the aisle, making Nyle and Xaon both startle like nervous cats. Mazilane's lips curled in sardonic amusement. "I feel like I might lose another camera if you all continue this discussion directly beside me."

Nyle and Xaon frowned in confusion, but Cymin immediately looked down the aisle to see Laithondi striding towards them. Mazilane turned away from them and very obviously angled his camera out the window to film the green terraces of young rice plants and water ferns.

Laithondi's shadow fell across Cymin as his hand rested on the back of Cymin's bench seat.

"This sort of mess is exactly why we were hesitant to tell you all everything from the start," Laithondi stated. "And why I *strongly* advise that you don't focus on those remnants of the past that you've inherited. They are meant to help you access the skills and physical memories of your previous experiences, not to alter your current characters or fates. They should be lessons to learn from but no more than fantastic stories to you now. The past is over." Laithondi lifted his hand and lightly touched the bones hanging from his neck. "Dead. Let it go."

"But I've been looking for him since I was six years old, and I will not ever stop. That's part of who I am, isn't it?" Xaon protested.

"Clearly, it's not as much a part of who you are as defying a direct order is," Nyle muttered.

"Or as much as nitpicking is for you," Xaon returned.

"I'm not the one arguing against Laithondi's instructions right in front of him." Nyle jabbed the corner of his sketchbook into Xaon's chest.

"Both of you—" Laithondi's low voice sounded like a clap of thunder, and both Xaon and Nyle went silent, staring at him like they expected him to cane them. Laithondi seemed exasperated but spoke more gently as he went on. "Go back to your seats and try to rest up." Laithondi indicated their vacated table with a bob of his head. "In three hours, we should reach a water station. While the engineers refill the steam tanks, you'll all have your first real lessons."

Xaon and Nyle's mutual irritation turned to excitement at the mention of a lesson. Xaon looked like he wanted to ask a question, but Nyle nudged him.

"I just want to say one last thing to Cymin," Xaon stated.

Nyle scowled then turned and retreated to his seat, where he packed his sketchbook and pencils away.

Xaon collected his blanket and rose to his feet.

"I thought about it. It's actually better if you don't remember him." Xaon smiled. "This way you won't get hurt when *I* find him, right?"

Emotionally or physically hurt? Because East Deity could knock you and Nyle on your asses in a Spring Exhibition bout. Have no doubt of that. However, Cymin didn't say anything of the kind aloud.

He simply nodded. It wasn't as if he wanted to argue with Xaon, particularly over something as impossible as meeting Minroa Haeyi.

Xaon looked relieved then returned to his vacated bench to nap. Across the table from Xaon, Nyle stretched his arms and hands, going through the warm-ups advised by mage-instructors but rarely practiced by any but the most fastidious of students.

Laithondi watched him for a moment. Then he swung into the place Xaon had vacated opposite Cymin.

Cymin studied him, feeling oddly conflicted. On one hand, having Laithondi's attention and company sent flutters of excitement rippling through him. But it also made Laithondi's air of indifference all the more annoying.

You won't even look at me sometimes, but you can't seem to let me alone either. What are you thinking?

Finally, Laithondi said, "I have a request to ask of you."

"Oh?" Cymin asked.

"I'd like you to assist Xaon to circulate fei'lux—the way I demonstrated to you previously," Laithondi said. "You're a good match for him, training-wise, and I think that I'll have my hands full with Nyle."

Jealousy flared through him at the mention of Nyle, and Cymin took a moment to suppress it. It would be too petty to resent Nyle for being outstanding. Even so, Cymin couldn't help but feel aggrieved. He looked away from Laithondi's sharp gaze, taking in Mazilane and Hiral across the aisle.

"I'm Mazilane's assistant, so I have to ask him if he'll need me for anything before I can agree," Cymin responded.

At the mention of his name, Mazilane turned to them. He regarded Cymin with an amused expression. They were so close that Cymin knew he must have overheard the entire exchange, but Mazilane still feigned ignorance rather believably, and even appeared to take some kind of pleasure in mulling over the question of lending Cymin out to Laithondi.

"Hmm, I was planning to send you to fetch a tin of spare fuses while we're stopped at the next station." Mazilane tapped his chin. "I'd hate to be caught unprepared if either of the cameras were to blow out again."

Laithondi frowned at Mazilane, while Hiral bowed his head to hide a smug smile.

Mazilane toyed with a lens cap as if unaware of Laithondi's intense displeased glower. None of them spoke, and the silence began to feel a little too tense for Cymin's liking. It was one thing to tease Laithondi, but actually angering him seemed dangerous. Cymin knew too little about him to be certain of how easily or deeply he could be offended.

"Actually, I packed several spare tins of fuses. We should be fine," Hiral spoke up. Cymin shot him a thankful glance. Mazilane stretched in his seat and kicked Hiral's shin.

"Good," Laithondi said briskly. "Then Cymin will follow me and my students to practice."

"Xaon is a sword mage, but I don't have an ancillary to match his. Should I improvise someth—" Cymin began, but Laithondi cut him off by drawing his own sword and placing it on the table in front of Cymin. In shape and size, it resembled a common long-saber, with its single-edge gracefully curved blade and simple loop of a grip and handguard. It was certainly much smaller than either Xaon's massive cutlass or Jeshri's huge broadsword. But the intensity and abundance of sigils suffusing its body lent the sword a stunning gold radiance. The blade didn't seem like it had been forged from steel but rather manifested through countless folded spells and blazing fei'lux.

"The Sun-Piercing Blade, Yuelaith," Laithondi stated as he stood. He removed the sheath from his belt and set it in the empty seat. Cymin looked between Laithondi's cool expression and the shining blade, feeling stunned. He didn't need to touch the hilt to sense the residual power that centuries of use had imparted to it.

"This is—" Cymin didn't have words powerful enough to sum up the honor of being trusted to wield such a masterwork of ancillary craft. "Thank you."

Cymin held his hand over the hilt, reveling in the sensation of highly refined fei'lux radiating from it and playing across his palm like flickering sunbeams. The flesh of his hand glowed pink as the swordlight backlit the long shadows of his finger bones. Sigils all along the blade shimmered and flashed as Cymin ran his hand over them. He said, "I promise I'll be very careful with it. And get it back to you as soon as we're done."

"You're doing me a favor. It's the least I can do." Laithondi toyed with something on his wrist, his expression almost self-conscious. "Keep it for now. Xaon will probably need to practice with you more than once to master the circulation of fei'lux."

Laithondi turned as if to leave but then paused and looked back at Cymin. He reached into his vest pocket and drew out a thin, leaf-wrapped packet and set it on the table as well. The tang of birch and bergamot didn't quite disguise the scent of kelp, herbs and fish that drifted from the packet.

"Dried sailfin, sour grass and glassweed," Laithondi said. "Eat, then get some rest."

Then he strode back to his place with the other Waethir.

Cymin carefully sheathed the sword. Then he peeled away the desiccated leaves that protected the food Laithondi had left him. A strong scent rose from the exposed layer of shiny black kelp—pungent but not exactly unpleasant. Between the interwoven kelp he glimpsed strips of dark red dried meat and tiny green berries. The entire thing didn't look particularly appetizing—certainly not compared to the pretty tarts Vessreid had handed out earlier, but Cymin still took a nibble. The kelp was crisp and fragrant as smoked tea leaves, while the green berries popped in his mouth, spilling a lemony freshness across the salty strips of dried fish. Cymin chewed thoughtfully and then took another bite and then a third. To his surprise, he found that he quite liked the taste and was disappointed when it was gone.

He stole a look back to Laithondi but found that the other man had returned to staring out the window at the early-morning landscape, paying him no attention at all.

Laithondi's appearance and admonition to forget the past had thrown a pall over the excitement of the Five Schools mages, who all more or less sunk into pensive, contemplative silence.

Deprived of further opportunities to converse, or even eavesdrop, Cymin retrieved his book from his pack. After turning through a few pages, Cymin found an entry that he'd previously skimmed over while searching for descriptions of the land and living conditions. At the time, it hadn't seemed particularly notable. Now he fixated on the words Minroa had written.

Eirjiri died seven days ago.

Cymin couldn't help but glance at the Eirjiri who rode with them now and then at Jeshri and Saum. Did they remember their deaths as vividly as he and Xaon remembered being pierced through with arrows at the Black Gate? He hoped not.

Then he returned to his reading.

I wept for her and kept proper vigil. She was one of the few Waethir, other than Ondi, who readily accepted me here in the Heights. Without her here, I fear that when next Ondi is dispatched to battle chuuraun, I'll go cold and hungry.

If ever Ondi fails to return, your poor brother will likely starve to death. Vessreid will see to that. As much as he loves and covets Ondi, he resents me in equal measure.

Coward that I am, I cried a little for myself as well as dear old Eirjiri, who shared her hearth, bread and jokes with me.

Strangely, the Waethir do not mourn the deaths of their own at all. Even the mortal tuteli and Eirjiri's closest companions hardly displayed any sorrow. Bailon mocked my vigil, telling me that I looked very ugly when I cried.

Of course, Vessreid was particularly fierce, admonishing me for disrupting the flocks of birds with all my wailing and weeping. He struck me across the face so hard that it split my lip, and I nearly fell from the balcony. Then he ordered me dragged down into the caverns to shut me up.

Someday, I will repay him in kind, I swear it. But not yet.

Twelve days later, when Ondi returned from battling another chuuraun, he found me down there and brought me back out. He reassured me that Waethir do not ever truly die. Not even if their divine bodies are destroyed. They merely shed their flesh the way dragonflies molt. After seven days, their memories and minds are summoned back from where they've been imprinted upon flights of honeybees, schools of jellyfish, flocks of starlings, ancient trees and even seams of buried gold.

Then this evening he took me to the vast moss gardens and introduced me to a toddler whom all the Waethir, their attendants and companions treat as Eirjiri, returned to this world. Despite her tender age and poor coordination, she claimed to remember me. And after playing with her for an hour, I could almost believe that she is the same soul I knew before. Almost.

Afterwards, Ondi said that mortal lives are like clouds and flowers—beautiful and delicate and ephemeral—but the deities are mountains and seas. Eternal.

Of course, I teased him that what he really meant was that they were stodgy, set in their ways and hopelessly behind the times. He laughed, because he is magnanimous. Then, quite shyly, he gifted me with the string of prayer beads that he carved and blessed himself. In the future, I can use the sigils in them to escape or enter any door in the Heights. I was touched by his trust. In his place, I would have been far more wary.

But I don't think that he or any of them recognize the danger of their isolated, intractable ways. We, on the other hand, are always striving, innovating and struggling to tear down those old gods that oppress us.

I'm trying to put my thoughts—my argument with him—into a poem, but I'm too tired to complete it tonight. So I close this letter with a half-assed scribbling.

Bright, ephemeral creatures,
Our lives come and go, seeming harmless.
Passing like clouds and flowers,
While you remain steadfast as cliffs
And calm as mountain lakes.
Your placid waters reflect our frenzied colors,
But your depths remain ever unmoved.
Our generations spread like ripples,
Rising and falling.
Growing with the ambition of waves,
Gnawing stone to dust.
We come and go so quickly.
Like mayflies dying before you in our millions.
And though you remain indomitable as cliffs,
Isolated as mountain lakes,
Our bodies accrue below your placid waters
Like slow poison.

Not much of anything, is it? Still, I send it to you along with my love.

Your brother, Minroa.

Chapter 17

In the drifting haze of his dream, Cymin could recall how the ruin of Saigrath unfolded with a clarity he never possessed in his waking hours. He could see it being acted out as if it were a moving picture he'd watched a dozen times and knew by heart.

Yet, in this moment, none of it had yet come to fruition. The future still felt hopeful, filled with mystery and unexplored possibilities. Very like the entry to the pearlescent spiral staircase that stood before Laithondi and Minroa now.

Five years living in Saigrath had toned Minroa's once-slender body, adding hard muscle to his elegant height. Gold flecks of night-vision spells flickered beneath the shadows of long dark lashes, and his black hair hung loose. He looked young and handsome but also uncharacteristically tense.

A singed string of pitted and cracked prayer beads drooped around his right wrist. Minroa worried the few remaining beads between his fingers. More than half of them had already been crushed to dust by curses lurking in this exact staircase.

Two days before, Minroa had used the blessings in the prayer beads to pick apart the spells that hid the entry to the Pearly Staircase. They worked so perfectly that he hadn't hesitated to race ahead, attempting to reach the summit.

The instant he had crossed the threshold of the alcove, seven steps appeared before him. They curved up in such a tight spiral that he could only see the corner of the seventh step. A thin crack marred the riser of that last step, making it look as if someone had scratched a jagged grin into its pale surface. Heedless of how little he knew of this place, he raced up, taking the steps two at a time. After half an hour, he slowed but still pushed onward. After an hour, he stopped and faced the fact that it couldn't possibly be mere chance that every seventh step displayed that same wicked smile of a crack. He turned around, only to discover that the same cycle of seven steps continued to repeat. He was trapped in an endless helix. Both ahead of him and behind were only the narrow arch of gleaming white walls and those same seven steps.

Exhausted and frustrated, he lashed out, hurling a fury of Piiroc, Chyrenese and Saigrathic spells at the pearly walls. Miraculously, a doorway appeared. He raced through, hoping for his freedom.

Instead, ice-strewn seawater enveloped him, crushing the air from his lungs and plunging him down. Black waves gripped him and yanked him deeper. He used every sigil he could summon to fight. However, the curses dragging him down into the frigid depths were as powerful as they were merciless. Minroa's strength steadily drained away. He sank, and his consciousness waned as the air in his lungs staled. His ribs began to crack under the weight of an ocean.

Then the blessings strung through Ondi's prayer beads had flared to life around him. Luminous gold spells unfurled around him, driving back the frigid black pressure. Minroa fought to the surface, but not before nearly every one of Ondi's prayer beads shattered apart while protecting him from dark, drowning curses. With the few remaining blessings, Minroa fought through the crashing waves and dragged himself ashore to the Red Marsh. At that time, he had feared that the Waethir were now aware of his attempt to trespass in their secret sanctum, but in the winter wilderness of Saigrath, he had nowhere to go but back to them.

In the two days since then, neither Vessreid nor Arnaith had accused him of trespassing. Eirjiri had even beckoned him to join her and Bailon for songs and games of dice. But when Ondi returned from hunting chuuraun, he'd hardly greeted Minroa before leading him back to this same staircase.

Now, Minroa studied Ondi intently, and his thoughts seemed very clear to Cymin. He feared that Ondi had been designated to punish him. Perhaps to mete out a beating or maybe to lead him into the dim staircase and strangle him to death—or drive him back through that door into the drowning waters.

Minroa had fought for his life in close quarters before. At least now he was a grown adult. His fingers brushed the hilt of his hunting knife, but then he stilled, simply resting his gaze on Ondi.

It had been Ondi—his blessings—that had saved Minroa's life on these very stairs two days ago. And over the last five years, Ondi had battled alongside Minroa, defeating monstrous chuuraun and enduring numerous injuries defending him. So many injuries that the sovereign fei'thallus, which leached the living color from Ondi's body each time it healed him, had turned his skin and hair nearly as pale as their pearly surroundings.

Soft iridescent light glowed up from the stairs, and Ondi, too, seemed luminous. Yet for all his physical transformation, his character had never altered. He was up-front, loyal and direct, never the sort to lure anyone into an ambush.

Ondi looked back over his shoulder, returning Minroa's gaze with such open friendship. It was obvious to Cymin that, in that moment, Minroa fought down the terror lingering from his childhood and dared to trust Ondi. He let his hand fall from the sheath hanging at his hip. Once again he gripped the battered prayer beads. He followed Ondi through the entry as if passing through the fires of his private heavenly trial.

"What are you staring at so hard?" Ondi smiled as he spoke.

"What do you think I'm staring at, Ondi? Obviously, I'm admiring my surroundings. So very . . . handsome," Minroa replied—his gaze lingered as he relished Ondi's striking features and enjoyed the affection that allowed him to address Laithondi, the East Deity, as "Ondi" just as the Waethir did. He very lightly ran a finger down the curve of Ondi's back. He wasn't a boy anymore—neither of them was. He withdrew his hand before his touch could grow too distracting.

"Isn't the Pearl Staircase off-limits to a scoundrel such as myself?" Minroa asked. "Are you certain you want to let me in?"

Ondi frowned.

Cymin knew that Ondi considered himself upright and honest, so violating the statutes of the Heights didn't sit easily with him. But at the same time, he'd come to know Minroa well enough to understand that he would not give up his search. Nearly drowning and suffering from exposure afterwards wouldn't deter him for long. But if he was caught trespassing into the sanctum, Arnaith wouldn't hesitate to kill him. She'd only failed to notice Minroa's earlier trespass because Ondi's prayer beads had disguised Minroa's presence. Now the blessings were nearly all destroyed. Minroa's next violation could cost him his life.

"I trust you," Ondi told him. "And I also think that once you've seen the White Chamber, you'll understand why we keep certain things hidden."

"Well, some things do need hiding," Minroa replied. "Though, I truly hope this isn't something like the lockbox my great-aunt secreted away in an attic. It took me weeks to break in, only to discover that the thing was filled with nothing but taxidermied newts and toads in the most unfortunate poses."

"Truly?"

"I wish it weren't." Minroa paused to mimic the sigils that Ondi drew and then took the next step following his ascent. "So, if it's just stuffed toads up there, you can tell me, and we can turn around."

"It's not stuffed toads." Ondi laughed. He continued teaching Minroa how to unlock the spells guarding the stairs, carefully demonstrating the succession of Waethir sigils required to successfully cross over each step. It required only five sigils, but their placement was exacting and aligned along a different plane on every step.

Now and then, when Minroa asked him to repeat his demonstration, Ondi turned back and, taking Minroa's hand in his own, gently moved his fingers to the exact spot to place each sigil. More often than not, Minroa offered some gentle flirtation.

Ondi flushed, but his gaze always remained on the sigils and the flow of fei'lux through them. He'd studied Minroa's features so extensively over the past five years that he didn't need to look to know the man's full mouth was quirking in a sly smile while looking out from underneath his thick eyelashes—playfully teasing, but never reducing himself to the pleading gaze that too many mortals cast upon Waethir. Even taken as a hostage, starved and half-frozen, Minroa had never begged.

Ondi admired that about him just as much as he admired the sculpted strength of his body and the striking beauty of his features. He was undeniably proud. Justifiably so, as he possessed immense innate talent for magecraft as well as a smoldering drive to control his own fate. He was unlike anyone Ondi knew—reckless, irreverent and indomitable.

"Do you use this same exact combination of sigils to access the stairs every time you go to the White Chamber?" Minroa asked. "Or does it change?"

"The combination changes every day," Ondi responded. "Over a span of 210 years."

Minroa stopped where he stood, looking briefly stunned.

"A different combination of five sigils, each positioned somewhere within a 380-degree sphere for over 300 steps. Every day? And it doesn't repeat over a span of 210 years? That's . . . I can't even calculate." Minroa shook his head. "No. It would take me years." And one misstep would either trap him in an endless loop of steps or deliver him into the crushing depths of the frigid sea.

No matter what marvel was hidden up in the White Chamber, if Minroa died on the stairs, then it would be useless to him.

Cymin could sense his disappointment. But there was also a kind of relief in Minroa's expression. People often claimed that Minroa had been born with boundless ambition for power, but the truth was that he'd already endured years of deprivation and pain. Now, even the blazing rage within him had burned down to a single ember in a bed of ashes. And if nothing else, his desperate childhood had taught him enough pragmatism to recognize a battle that he could not win.

His gaze fell to the bruises and scrapes that still marred his hands after his struggle to survive his previous attempt to traverse this staircase. A wry smile flashed across his full lips. To anyone who didn't know him well, he might have appeared merely amused. Ondi, however, had been his constant companion through the past five years. He recognized both the self-derision and fleeting despair behind that smile.

Even in his dream, Cymin tensed. This was the moment when everything could still have been saved. Right now, Minroa teetered on the verge of abandoning his ambition for both power and vengeance.

"It's not actually that difficult," Ondi assured him. "If you know the trick to it."

No! Shut up, you fool! Just let him give up. Cymin silently raged, but the figures in his dream went on, utterly unaware of his ranting.

"Isn't it?" Minroa asked, and Cymin could almost feel the determination returning to him. "It certainly seems beyond my grasp."

"It's really just a matter of knowing the Saigrath calendar and the Promenade of a Thousand Blessings. Our calendar follows the course of the five Hallow Gates, so those are the five sigils that must be manifested on each step. And their positions are those every tuteli practices when they learn the Thousand Blessings," Ondi informed him, and then he indicated the stair at his feet. "Every step of this staircase represents the positions of the five gates, which is just a date. When you enter, the first step is always today's date and, as you ascend, you track the five gates through their orbits and alignments. At the end of the year, you will have reached the White Chamber."

"Wait. What do you mean, 'track the positions of the Hallow Gates'? Aren't they always here in Saigrath? They move?" Minroa asked.

Cymin, too, felt a little startled by the revelation, though this was his own dream and he'd experienced it thousands of times. Yet somehow, the knowledge within it always seemed to abandon him upon waking.

"Yes and no," Ondi replied, then he laughed at his own lack of clarity. "Technically, the five Hallow *Gateways* are always here in Saigrath—on the Ivory Island, to be exact. Think of them like five cracks punched through the hull of a ship. Torrents of fei'lux constantly flood through them from a raging ocean of fei'lux. Left on their own, those five ruptures would quickly inundate and overwhelm our whole world in blazing fei'lux. But luckily, most of the time, the fei'lux is deflected and blocked by the orbits of five celestial bodies. *Those* are what we Waethir are actually referring to when we talk about the gates. Not the passageways, but the objects that literally close them off. Gates. Does that make sense?"

"Yes. But wait . . . what? Five celestial bodies?" Minroa rarely betrayed genuine astonishment, but now he couldn't hide his shock.

"Five satellites—like the planets and moons in our sky—but these move unseen through the celestial sea of fei'lux. They safeguard our world." Ondi nodded. "Most years, they all align, deflecting just enough fei'lux to ensure that the streams pouring through Saigrath are strong enough to nourish the rest of the world but not so fierce that life is scoured away."

Minroa considered this in silence, as did Cymin.

In a way, it made sense that the gates would refer to the objects that closed an entry and not the entry itself. At the same time, it was at odds with the pretty illustrations and modern conjecture that he was familiar with.

"So then . . . the movements you track to access the stairs . . . they're those five celestial bodies in the sea of fei'lux?" Minroa asked.

"Exactly. They move through the same Heavenly realm that blazes with fei'lux. We can't see them with our eyes. But we can sense them through the fei'lux." Ondi closed his eyes and lifted his hands as he spoke, striking the tuteli pose of *attending the Heavens*. "Each gate alters the quantity and quality of fei'lux that passes through its sphere. Streams that are swift and billowing as the wind have come past Bailon's gate—the Sky Gate. Those that are cold and compacted into fluid masses have arrived from Arnaith's—the Sea Gate. Eirjiri's Earth Gate produces a sparking, metallic quality. Fei'lux influenced by Vessreid's Moon Gate is crisp, while Laithondi's Sun Gate produces fei'lux with a tempered warm quality."

As he spoke, Ondi shifted and turned his hands as if plucking separate streams of fei'lux from the air. A subtle breeze whirled around him and brushed over Minroa like a caress.

"Tempered and warm? You make it sound like a mulled wine," Minroa teased. "Might you be a little biased toward the qualities of the gate you're named for?"

"Maybe a little, but it's also true. The Sun Gate strips away the most ferocious, killing aspects of fei'lux," Ondi replied. "The year before you arrived in Saigrath, do you remember that the spring fei'lux storms were particularly ferocious? Even when the weather seemed mild, the fei'lux would sometimes shock and sear your skin?"

Minroa had spent much of his fourteenth year imprisoned, but even deep in the king's dungeon, he'd felt the harsh sting of fei'lux storms. His sister, Diron, had rocked him in her arms, trying to ease the pain of his blistered fingers, while their older brother, Xondir, insisted that the Heavens themselves had turned bleak and bitter over the injustice of their mother's execution.

"Yes, I remember it," he told Ondi.

"It was because that was the fifteenth year in the orbit of the Sun Gate—Laithondi's gate. Every fifteen years, its orbit doesn't synchronize perfectly, and a gap opens in its protection of our world. Throughout the year, the gap grows, and much more harsh fei'lux floods us in greater and greater amounts. In early spring, the Sun Gate falls so far out of alignment that it eventually leaves our world completely exposed to raw celestial fei'lux for twelve hours."

"I see. So when you Waethir talk about the gates opening, you mean that their orbits have left Saigrath exposed." Minroa's sharp brows rose with a sudden realization. "That's the key to the Pearl Staircase? The positions of the gates on each day of the year . . . leading to when they open?"

"You are so quick." Ondi smiled in delight. "Yes, that's it exactly. At certain points in their orbits, each of the gates leaves our world exposed. At those times, the Waethir enter the White Chamber and defend our world in the place of our gates."

"When the Sun Gate opens, *you* take its place?" Minroa asked.

Ondi nodded but then looked a little embarrassed.

"I haven't done so in this body. Not yet. The Sun Gate orbits on a fifteen-year cycle. The year before you arrived in Saigrath, the Laithondi before me gave his life. I've inherited his skills and wisdom. To an extent, I even recall the blaze of fei'lux searing through me, but it's distant—more like something remembered from a dream. So I can't truly claim to have faced my destiny, yet. But I will."

Minroa stared at him and parted his lips as if to offer some objection or jest but then said nothing.

Ondi gazed at the pearly step before him and then lifted his hand and drew the sun sigil. "This is the position of the Sun Gate—my gate. Right now, it's hidden behind the lion constellation, keeping us all safe. But in nine years and ten days, it will fall back. That's when I will stand in the White Chamber to defend creation." He didn't look back, but Cymin knew he was thinking that it would be Minroa whom he would be defending, and he felt a surge of determination to endure, no matter what.

East Deity is so melodramatic, Cymin thought. *Or perhaps he's too romantic.*

Ondi seemed to find himself a little ridiculous as well. He shook his head and then drew a second sigil. Then a third, fourth and fifth, positioning each exactly as he spoke. "Vessreid's Moon Gate opens every thirty years. Eirjiri's Earth Gate is every thirty-fifth year. Bailon's Sky Gate opens every forty-two years, and Arnaith's Sea Gate every seventy years. All five gates stand open for a single day every 210 years."

"And all five of you take the place of your gates then?" Minroa asked.

Ondi nodded.

"Each step we cross on the stairs represents a day closer to our destinies." Ondi stared at the steps curling up ahead of him.

"So, this entire thing is a spell, charting the Hallow Gates' exact positions across 210 years." Minroa stared at the shining sigils intently and for so long that his eyes grew glassy, and the faintest of quavers sounded in his voice. "And you only have . . . nine years left."

"Nine years and ten days." Ondi nodded again.

Minroa turned his face away, brushing something from his cheek. Both of them were quiet, contemplating their own thoughts in the soft glow of iridescent light. Streams of fei'lux whirled between them like spring breezes, warm but rippling with stormy potential. Minroa kicked at the tread of the step he stood on.

"And you claimed the key to this staircase was simple." Minroa shook his head, his expression a mask of practiced equanimity. "To navigate it, you've memorized 365 positions of five separate orbital paths as they change across 210 years. That's . . . that's over 300,000 coordinates! All just to race up to your fucking doom."

"Are you worried for me?" Ondi asked. "Or angry about the staircase?"

"A little of both, honestly," Minroa snapped. "It doesn't seem fair for everything to be so difficult or to come at such a cost."

"To me, the cost seems small considering the power and honor I've been entrusted with. The lives I can protect—"

"Are you trying to tell me that it's worth your life?" Minroa demanded. "That's what you're telling me, isn't it? You won't survive this?"

Ondi paused for only a moment, but Minroa's face drained of color and his hands began to shake.

"I might live," Ondi quickly assured him. "Eirjiri did. She was seventy-four when you first met her. She lived another twenty-four years after she held the Earth Gate."

"And how common is that?" Minroa asked.

Ondi sighed.

"Rare. Particularly for the Sun Gate. But even if I must sacrifice this body, my memories will live on in the next tuteli who becomes Laithondi." Ondi smiled at Minroa. "I *will* remember you—"

"So, I'll be a twenty–nine-year-old man, stuck with some pre-adolescent version of you going through all the awkward phases of puberty? Or will you be a five-year-old like Eirjiri is?" Minroa scowled at him.

"If I lose this body, I promise that I'll try my best to choose a winsome, well-endowed tuteli of appropriate maturity to keep you company. How about that?" Ondi grinned.

Minroa sighed and then said, "Fine. But don't go too far. I still want to be the more attractive of the two of us."

"You're such a dick," Ondi laughed, and Minroa smiled.

A moment later, Ondi turned his attention back to the steps at his feet.

"As for the matter of navigating the stairs, I think you're making it needlessly hard for yourself. Right now, you're approaching it as if you'd learn a dance by working out every shift in angle of every bone in your body. No one could remember that. But if you simply relax and feel the flow of fei'lux surrounding you, the positions of the gates will begin to become obvious."

Ondi paused, closing his eyes, and then he struck a posture deeply familiar to Cymin. "Then you simply follow the positions of the Thousand Blessings and dance."

"It's not a dance anyone's ever taught me. Nor are they likely to, are they?" Minroa's expression betrayed an instant of vexation, but then he met Ondi's gaze and smiled. "Not to mention that there are far too many stairs to climb, much less dance all the way up. Three hundred and sixty-five steps every time you want to go up here—it's no wonder your legs are so very toned."

Ondi flushed but then shrugged.

At the same time, Cymin wanted desperately to reach out and clap a hand over Ondi's mouth.

He's impressed with your legs, so maybe just shut your mouth and don't give up every secret you've ever known! You've already told him too much. Let him give up on the Pearl Stairs and look somewhere else!

But Ondi had no desire to be guarded from Minroa, nor any awareness of how a few sentences could utterly alter his entire future.

"Actually, the entryway is a countdown. There are only a full 365 steps in the years when none of the gates leave Saigrath exposed. As the date of a gate opening draws closer, so does the access to the White Chamber. If any of the gates were opening today, I would only need to place the five sigils of today's date at the entry, and I could step directly into the White Chamber."

"Really?" Minroa's brows rose. "So, nine years from now?"

"Nine years and ten days from now, there will only be a single step to cross." Ondi nodded. "See, I told you it was actually quite simple."

"And this year?"

"This year, we can enjoy each other's company for all 365 steps." Ondi laughed.

"Lead on, then."

They slogged up the pearlescent stairs, bathed in the soft glow that emanated from the walls and steps themselves. At last, they rounded a corner and reached a white archway completely filled by a black sphere. The surrounding light refracted across the sphere, lending it the dark iridescence of a scarab's shell. Five gold circles arranged in a pentagon shape adorned its center.

Ondi drew the sigils of the Five Deities in the air and then pressed one into each of the gold circles. As he pulled his hand away, cascades of hundreds of other sigils lit up from deep within the sphere, like distant lights glowing up through dark waters. The light of those hundreds of tiny sigils grew and intensified steadily, turning the sphere milky white, then transparent.

In seconds, it disappeared completely, leaving only a fine veil of delicate fei'thallus threads drifting down from the archway like mist.

"Come." Ondi took Minroa's hand and drew him through. Clear threads of fei'thallus brushed over them and fluttered aside but didn't hinder their passage.

They strode into a bright five-walled chamber with a high arched ceiling. Round floor-to-ceiling windows loomed up at each of the room's five corners. A deity's sigil marked the top of each of the window frames in shining gold script. At the base of each window a gold circle stretched across the white floor like a reflection. And in the center of the chamber stood a towering altar. Most of the structure appeared to be made of silverwork, gold wires and ivory bones. Cascades of white threads, like those they'd just passed through, poured down from the pearly ceiling to swathe the altar in translucent veils. Breezes blew through the open windows, and the gossamer veils swirled around the altar. Pale silhouettes like those of darting fish, birds in flight and fluttering moth wings rippled across their surfaces like passing shadows.

Outside the windows, swifts chased a swarm of gold sandbees through clouds of drifting mist. The view beyond the White Chamber didn't appear to overlook the mountain stronghold of the Heights where they'd entered the staircase, though they did still command such a great elevation that the land below appeared to roll out beneath them like a map. Mounds of gold and green luxfungi formed spiraling hills like giant snail shells all across a crescent of ivory land. Here and there, small lakes formed in the gullies of the luxfungi mounds. Others supported both common and exotic varieties of trees, brush and wildflowers, creating a startlingly diverse woodland. Beneath the trees, strange, wild creatures moved. Cymin peered after a fleeting form that he was nearly certain had been a three-eyed deer.

But Minroa's attention moved beyond the woodlands and the mythic creatures in them to the crashing waves, where a white pebbled beach gave way to a vast dark sea.

"We've crossed the Black Sea and reached the Ivory Island in only 365 steps," Minroa said.

Ondi nodded.

"The array of spells guarding this place truly is . . . incredible," Minroa whispered. Ondi heard only the wonder in his voice, but Cymin recognized assessment as well. No doubt Minroa was trying to work out whether it would be more difficult to master the celestial orbits that accessed the staircase or overcome the murderous spells that defended the Black Sea.

While Minroa calculated, Ondi strolled along the perimeter of the altar. He glanced up as a flight of sandbees rushed through the window, followed by two swifts. The bees circled the apex of the chamber and then fled out a different window with the swifts still in pursuit.

Only a single bright gold sandbee remained, and it alighted on Ondi's thumb.

"A newly fledged queen," Ondi called to Minroa as he smiled down at the tiny insect. "Her abdomen hasn't faded to white yet. She must have just completed her nuptial flight." Ondi knelt down and rested his hand on the floor.

"The other bees in the swarm would have been her suitors. They were quite brave, leading the birds away, don't you think?"

"Maybe. Or maybe your little queen used them to distract the birds from herself." Minroa strode to Ondi's side. He spared the bee on Ondi's hand a fleeting glance. "Rulers naturally expect sacrifice from their consorts."

"So cynical," Ondi replied. He imitated the flattering tone of a Chyrenese diplomat as he returned his gaze to the bee resting on his hand. "Don't listen to him, Your Majesty. Your companions were brave and valiant, and your children will remember them when they, too, take to the skies."

A derisive snort escaped Minroa; however, the focus of his attention wasn't on Ondi or the little queen but on the altar before them. His gaze roved over the millions and millions of tiny sigils etched into every surface as well as the ghostly shadows fluttering through the gently undulating veils of fei'thallus that surrounded them. He ran a finger over the abalone-like surface of the wall nearest him. Threads finer than spider silk caught beneath his nail.

"Go on." Ondi blew softly on the bee. She clung to his thumb for a second longer, then flitted to one of the five large gold circles that adorned the floor. An instant later, pale white filaments arose from the floor and curled around her body. Then they drew her down below the surface.

Minroa stared at the spot where the bee had been, and then he looked at the walls and ceiling surrounding him.

"This entire chamber is formed from fei'thallus, isn't it?" Minroa asked.

"Yes. You realized it so much faster than I did when I was first brought here." Ondi stood again. "The White Chamber is a treasure in itself—a nexus where countless fei'thallus have amassed the lives and souls of everything they've touched."

Ondi paused and pointed to the place inside the gold circle where the bee had disappeared. As he did, a tiny ripple appeared on the surface of the floor, and all at once the queen bee burst free. Her head and thorax still gleamed bright gold, but her abdomen had faded to a pale cream. She flew in a circle once and then darted out one of the windows.

"She and her descendants will carry the spores of new fei'thallus out into the world." Ondi smiled after her. "And in return, the fei'thallus here retains the essence of her mind and body. From the taste of salt on her antennae to the barbs on the tip of her stinger. She will live forever in the Sea of Eternity."

"Sea of Eternity. This is the Sea of Eternity?" Minroa frowned at the floor as iridescent light shimmered across the golden circles like sunlight. "The depths that gave rise to *all* of creation? The entirety of the world and all life in it arose from those five little circles?"

Ondi nodded. "Did you imagine it differently?"

"Well, larger for a start," Minroa admitted.

"The true extent of matters can be deceptive at a glance," Ondi replied. "We did just cross thirty miles of mountain and ocean by climbing a single staircase."

"We did." Minroa's expression turned thoughtful, and his gaze again sought out the altar. "If you're not just having a joke at my expense and this really is the Sea of Eternity, then the Fei'suul Scepter that governs it and can grant immortality must be here as well."

Ondi shrugged.

Minroa's eyes narrowed, taking in the details of the altar as a breeze shifted the veils of fei'thallus aside. Mechanical ancillaries, not too dissimilar to those of Chyrenese mages, appeared to fuse with the carved bones and resonant chimes employed by Piirocs. Their arrangement mirrored that of an astronomical compass, individual ancillaries moving slowly in circles as if each was tracing the motions of a different distant star. At the center of it all stood an intricately carved bone, inlaid with silver and gold. The base was held in place by a circle of silver clasps. A latticework of carved sigils lent the shaft the deceptively delicate look of lace. However, the warm light radiating from its depths cast faint shadows of a multitude of more carved bones and spells moving inside it. At the very top, a finial assembled from hundreds of petal-thin slices of bone spread open like a lotus blossom. Pale mist rolled from the petals, swirling and changing shape like windswept clouds as it drifted into the surrounding veils of fei'thallus.

"Piiroc bards have a story about a mage who stole the Fei'suul Scepter to destroy the world and rebuilt a new one to his liking inside a celestial pearl," Minroa murmured.

"How does it end?" Ondi asked.

"Sadly," Minroa replied. "Piirocs excel in tragedy."

Both of them were quiet, lost in their own thoughts.

A pair of swallows flew into the chamber, plucked fei'thallus threads from the walls and then soared away. Cymin wondered if they would use the threads to line their nest or feed their chicks. Either way, the fine threads would grow and suffuse each life they touched with energy absorbed from fei'lux.

Ondi watched the birds disappear into the distant trees while Minroa continued to study the altar. No doubt he was working out the best way to excise the scepter from the rest of the altar. At the same time, his expression betrayed a flicker of something like pain, or perhaps it was frustration.

"The year before you arrived, I and four of my fellow tuteli knelt down on this floor inside the gold rings, just like that little bee," Ondi suddenly told him. "I wasn't the most outstanding of the five of us, but the Fei'suul Scepter still chose me to take into the depths of the Sea of Eternity. I sank so far down that I could nearly reach out and touch one of the tiny buds of a celestial pearl growing up from the Sea of Eternity. I don't remember much else, but when I arose seven days later, the wisdom of East Deity blazed inside me, as did an immense sense of purpose. We Waethir exist to defend this world, and in return for our service, the scepter ensures that we are always reborn. If the Fei'suul Scepter is stolen from us, then where will this world find the next Waethir to defend it?" Ondi asked.

Minroa frowned down at his hands. Ondi stepped closer to him and bowed his head to catch Minroa's attention.

"I don't know what you've been told about the scepter or the power it can grant you, but taking it from the White Chamber will only cause endless tragedy," Ondi said. "But if you let it go, I promise you that I will teach you all I know about spells and magecraft. I will share everything I can—"

"My father is the one who's obsessed with it. Believes that it will make him an immortal god. He conquered Piiroc on the meager basis of a dozen ancient ballads and tore down half the sacred necropolises searching for the scepter and the Sea of Eternity," Minroa snapped. "Now he's promised to give my sister and my brother to me—if I can deliver the scepter to him."

"*Give* your sister and brother to you?" Ondi looked taken aback. "They're people, not properties."

"Are you joking?" Minroa demanded. "To Chyrenese mage-kings and Piiroc apotheoses, everything and everyone is a piece of property. And we all have a price. If I want to ensure that my sister isn't handed over to jackals and warlords, and that my brother isn't worked to death in the army, then I have to deliver the scepter to my father."

Ondi stared at Minroa, and Minroa bowed his head, hiding his face behind a cascade of long black hair.

"I . . . I could try to intervene on behalf of your siblings," Ondi suggested. "I could go to Chyre—"

"And do what?" Minroa raised his head, displaying red-rimmed eyes and a full mouth distorted by anger. "Make it painfully clear that my siblings can be used as pawns to manipulate the Waethir? You'd only demonstrate to him that the deity Laithondi can be played like a love-struck schoolboy!"

Ondi stared at Minroa in stunned silence.

"Are you imagining that simply sweeping in, making a proclamation and then dashing back to Saigrath will actually change anything? The minute you leave, everything goes back to the way it was," Minroa snapped. "You Waethir are so fucking naïve."

"I could bring them back to Saigrath with me. Your sister and your brother. I could demand them from your father and arrange their passage to Saigrath."

Another bitter laugh escaped Minroa.

"Bring them? Bring them to this frigid cultureless wasteland to bow and scrape to the likes of Vessreid? Do you actually think they'd thank me for that? If the cold didn't kill them, they'd probably slit their own throats after a month here."

Ondi stood, silent.

"If you truly wanted to give them freedom—to give *me* freedom—then you'd just kill my fucking monster of a father," Minroa muttered.

"I can't harm a mortal without cause," Ondi spoke softly, his expression full of apology.

"And what would give you cause?" Minroa demanded.

"He'd have to openly attack me or threaten Saigrath," Ondi replied. "Otherwise, we Waethir are sworn to protect mortal lives."

Another bitter laugh escaped Minroa. "So you would kill me if I tried to steal the scepter, but you'll let him live, though he's destroyed countless lives, because you're sworn not to harm mortals. What a joke. What a fucking joke."

The two men stood in silence. In the woodlands far below, a herd of three-eyed deer startled and fled deeper into the trees, leaving a single doe shuddering beneath the dark mass of a panther. The veils of fei'thallus rustled, and the radiant scepter continued to cast the dappled shadows of spells across the altar.

"I wouldn't kill you," Ondi said at last.

"No?" Derision rang through Minroa's tone, but when he met Ondi's gaze, the mockery fell from his expression. "You really wouldn't?"

Ondi held his gaze and shook his head.

"But why?" Minroa asked in disbelief. "I'm a liar and a whore. I'm petty, and I cheat. I'm not better than my fucking father, just less powerful."

"To me, you're none of those things," Ondi told him. "I think you're incredibly brave and clever. Outspoken and daring . . . and beautiful."

"Beautiful," Minroa all but spat the word. "I'm a tawdry prize for my father to pass around. I have no say, no ability to protect the people I care for. Nothing. Even risking my life, I can't grasp the smallest fucking shred of power."

Minroa bowed his face into his hands. Ondi stood, looking helpless. Then he reached out and gently embraced Minroa. In response, Minroa wrapped his arms around him and laid his face against Ondi's shoulder. He wept in almost complete silence, and Ondi held him.

At last, Minroa regained his composure and drew away from Ondi's embrace. He wiped his tear-streaked face self-consciously.

"I shouldn't have lashed out at you like that earlier. I'm sorry. Your home isn't a cultureless wasteland. I was just so frustrated." The apology seemed to drain all the spirit from Minroa's voice. "I appreciate your offer, and I know you mean the best by it. But Saigrath isn't a place where my family would thrive. Or even survive, if Vessreid had his way. As much as he dislikes me, he'd despise my siblings even more. I want better for them, you know?"

"I understand," Ondi said. "I just don't know how else to help you."

"Would it make any sense to you if I told you that I don't actually want help?" Minroa crouched down to the floor and ran his hands over the iridescent surface. "What I truly want is power. The power to change things for myself."

Then he looked up at Ondi.

"I want the power to free the people I love. To save them," he spoke almost too softly to be heard. "Nine years isn't nearly enough."

"It's what fate has given us," Ondi replied.

"Fuck fate." Minroa glowered at the scepter, shining on the altar. "I'll tear it down and forge our futures from the ruins, if I have to. I swear I will."

Hearing the resolve in Minroa's voice, Cymin knew that he would accomplish exactly what he promised. Though Cymin did wonder if he truly ever understood the cost of keeping his oath.

"Don't . . . " Cymin mumbled. In the depths of his dream, neither Ondi nor Minroa heard him.

But in the waking world, the weight of a hand fell on his shoulder. Someone shook Cymin gently. Blearily, he cracked his eyes open to see that the train had stopped and now stood almost empty. Laithondi alone lingered in the aisle beside Cymin's seat. As he drew his hand back from Cymin's shoulder, the crude tuteli prayer beads wound around his wrist caught Cymin's attention. Cymin had carved the beads and gifted the entire string to Laithondi, so their appearances shouldn't have surprised him. But at this moment, the clumsy cuts and humble wooden surfaces seemed out of place. For some reason, he'd expected perfectly etched spheres of ivory and gold to entwine Laithondi's wrist.

When Cymin looked up at him, Laithondi smiled at him with startling warmth. Then he seemed to catch himself, and at once his expression turned stern.

"Time to leave your dreams and rejoin the living world," Laithondi said. "Linger too long and you'll miss breakfast." Then he turned and strode to the exit.

The sight of Laithondi's retreating back was oddly familiar, but with his dream already fading from his memory, Cymin didn't know why. But with breakfast at stake, he didn't think on it too long. He bounced up from his seat and raced after Laithondi.

Ahead of him was somewhere he'd never been—with all the promises of new sights, sounds, sensations and flavors. Even more enticing were the wild sparks of fei'lux filling the air and the new realm of magecraft to learn from the Waethir. He couldn't wait.

Chapter 18

Growing up in the capital, Cymin had imagined all the rural villages scattered across the nation as largely the same: packed dirt streets winding around rows of noisy workshops, a few small stores and dozens and dozens of simple wooden houses where large families spilled out onto the porches to gossip, flirt and bicker with their neighbors. The blue post office building, a public mill, sweltering community ovens and the market green occupied the center of town. Ancient stone walls, with their etchings of archaic and worn-down spells, upheld ancient boundaries and provided erratic shelter from fei'lux storms. If any modern utilities existed, such as streetlights or public radio, they came thanks to the newly built steel turbines for National Communication towers which served NS patrol troops and the railway stations.

All that proved to be largely true, but what he hadn't appreciated until he spent seven days traveling through the countryside was the uniqueness and diversity of every community he visited.

Leaving behind the tropical lowlands of the south and chuffing up into the cooler hills, they had rested at a train station canteen where Cymin received a fragrant, creamy drink unlike any tea he'd ever tasted before. In a different town, he encountered station workers singing twanging jaunty tunes and painting white warning signs on the dark shells of the hulking, two-ton tortoises that sometimes napped on the warm train tracks.

At another station, down in a deep valley ravine, the women managing the ticket office and the depot canteen all wore their black tresses up in serpentine coils of vivid red yarn. The married men working in the train yard hid their hair—or lack of it—beneath intricately embroidered orange cloths. Farther west, passengers lounging in the park-like rest area beside the station conversed with such strong accents that at first Cymin thought they were imitating the birds nesting in the surrounding trees.

A long time ago, Master Shuun had told him that all Chyre's provinces had originally been distinct kingdoms which Xondir Haeyi battered into a single nation. But until now, he hadn't truly grasped how unique each kingdom's culture and population must have been.

As Cymin wondered what new scents and colors of magecraft he might encounter in these distant places, the prospect of each new encounter thrilled him all the more.

At dawn on the eighth day, they pulled into a mist-shrouded station on a forested hillside. Cymin launched himself from the train even before it had come to a complete stop. Wild fei'lux and lush spell residues tingled across his skin as he broke through the translucent barrier of spells protecting the train's ancillary engine.

Or maybe the sensation came from the fine aerosols floating from the surrounding forest of flowering sassafras trees. The cinnamon-lemon fragrance of the yellow blossoms filled his lungs and lent an exotic air to the otherwise mundane buildings and platforms. Squinting through the haze of steam and mist, Cymin felt certain he would need directions from a local resident if he wanted to locate anything here or in the nearby town.

(Previous outings had taught him that when it came to these remote locations, the tidy maps supplied by the National Tourism Board were either decades out of date or works of pure fantasy.)

Cymin peered around the wooden platform and across the weather-beaten stone walls of the railway station. A masculine figure reclined on a bench near the station doors, while out in the train yard members of the station crew in striped yellow overalls shouted to one another as they hurried to greet the newly arrived train.

Then Cymin noted the rectangular silhouette of an unfamiliar shrine at the far end of the platform. He moved closer to it, unable to work out which of the Five Deities it was dedicated to. The rock crystal obelisk stood about five feet in height and almost swirled with the multitude of translucent butterfly wings carved across its surface. None of the sigils marking it looked at all familiar to Cymin. He guessed that the shrine—like that two-ton tortoise—was lingering evidence of some older kingdom's now-obscure religion.

He thought he might ask one of the members of the train station staff about the shrine's meaning. But they seemed too occupied with racing out through the damp pre-dawn morning toward the other passenger cars for him to waste their time asking about a random shrine.

Whereas the young man idling on the bench wore a soldier's dull blue uniform and his left arm hung in a sling. Something about the combination made Cymin suspect that he was only passing through and probably unfamiliar with both the town and the shrine.

But even without knowing the identity of the deity it served, Cymin guessed from the placement of the shrine that it must be lucky for travelers. The way the rising sun glowed through its crystal facets looked warm and cheery; pairs of gray glassy wings steadily turned gold and red as they caught the light. So Cymin bowed in the direction of the shrine and offered the little butterflies a blessing hand sign.

"You're really going to start today hailing emissaries of death?" Laithondi's voice cut through the quiet like a searchlight slicing through fog.

The station workers down on the tracks and up on the platform jolted. Cymin looked up to the train's roof along with them. Laithondi strode over the top of the dark engine, his towering pale figure parting clouds of steam like a phantasm summoned from the shadows. Several men gave startled shouts, while the soldier dived from the bench to dart behind the cover of the station door. A grizzled old engineer trembled like his knees were about to give out as he gaped up at Laithondi and whispered, "Wraith."

Cymin, however, had already grown accustomed to Laithondi's bizarre practice of riding atop the train throughout the night keeping guard.

He simply waved to Laithondi and received a nod in response.

Then Laithondi leapt from the train's roof. His white hair and gray robes billowed around his lean figure. Fei'lux ringed him in halos bright enough to cast rainbows through the surrounding steam and morning mist. He alighted on the platform as if weightless and looked at Cymin as if completely unaware of the train staff staring at them in shock.

"It's said that souls of travelers who died in distant lands cling to the wings of ember butterflies to search out their lost homes. So unless you're looking for a lost loved one, it's unlucky to attract their attention." Laithondi glanced in the direction of the shrine, then bowed his head, speaking softly next to Cymin's cheek. "Who knows what kind of spectral scoundrel might take to haunting you?"

Something from one of those capricious, defective dreams that Cymin never clearly recalled stirred, and for an instant Cymin almost heard a soft voice ask, " . . . *a scoundrel such as myself?*"

Then the memory was gone. Cymin didn't waste energy attempting to track it down. Instead, he focused on Laithondi's teasing smile.

"My humble thanks for your concern," Cymin replied. "The inconsistent attention of a *second feckless* Wraith might truly send me around the bend, so your warning comes just in time."

"Feckless." Laithondi snorted as if the description of him couldn't have been more absurd. Then he glanced again to the shrine. With the sun at last cresting the hills, it began to glow like molten glass.

"Ember butterflies were originally sacred to Piiroc's Flame Sect," Laithondi said. "I wonder what the Chyrenese people here make of them."

"Master Tam once showed me an old memorial scroll listing sailors lost at sea, and there were red butterfly wings painted beside each name. So maybe the meaning is the same." Cymin lifted his hands in the gesture of blessing and recited the short prayer that Master Tam had read to him from the scroll. "Though my body is lost, my soul will ever search a way home to you."

The symbol made so much more sense now. Cymin couldn't help but smile at Laithondi for enlightening him, even if mockery had been the Wraith's original intent.

Laithondi gazed back at him with an expectant expression. Cymin had no idea why, but he couldn't seem to look away. A moment passed as they both stood there, eyes locked. Cymin began to feel distinctly uncomfortable, while Laithondi appeared to grow more and more anxious.

Was he waiting for Cymin to tell him something more? Or maybe give him something? But what could Laithondi possibly want from him? It wasn't as if Cymin had something of his that he ought to have returned.

Except he did, didn't he? The obvious struck Cymin, and he felt like an idiot. He'd spent the last seven days with Yuelaith, Laithondi's personal ancillary, hanging from his belt. Cymin's hand dropped to the sheathed sword. His fingers curled around the hilt reflexively, and a warm hum—almost a purr—played over his palm. He'd grown so comfortable wielding the sword that he'd actually forgotten that it didn't belong to him.

"Speaking of things going home, it's probably high time I return Yuelaith . . . " Cymin trailed off, not wanting to return the sword and feeling frustrated at himself for childishly coveting something merely lent to him.

But of course Laithondi would want his own exquisite sword back.

At the very least, he would need it to begin personally teaching Xaon. All this last week he'd focused on training Nyle.

Other than a few vague instructions and encouragements, Laithondi had left Xaon's continued study of magecraft to Cymin. Exchanging sword blows, spells and fei'lux with the red-haired swordsman, Cymin had grown to respect and like Xaon's honest, determined character. So, though it pained Cymin to lose Yuelaith, he felt happy for Xaon.

"Thank you for lending—" Cymin cut himself off short. In the time he'd managed to steel himself to return Yuelaith, Laithondi had apparently changed his mind.

Now he turned on his heel and strode away to the gangway steps at the back of the third train car where the other Waethir were disembarking.

Still gripping Yuelaith, Cymin scowled at Laithondi's back.

"Feckless," Cymin muttered.

Then he spied Yinni, Hiral and Mazilane exiting the first train car with the cameras, and he recalled his original reason for rushing off the train. When they'd chased the Waethir down the previous week, they'd left so many supplies behind that they were now out of resonance crystals and worryingly low on replacement transmission wires and antimony oil. So he'd hoped to get directions to a local chemist's shop or industrial apothecary where they could resupply.

Since the train engineers and conductors had made themselves scarce right after Laithondi set foot on the platform, Cymin hurried into the homely station. Inside, the tang of sassafras gave way to the hot metallic scent of tin tea kettles bubbling away in the adjoining canteen. A plump elderly woman already sat in the ticket booth, despite the early hour and absence of passengers waiting to board. She greeted Cymin with a wide, welcoming smile, but unfortunately her lilting, musical dialect left him uncertain if she'd given him directions to an apothecary, the public washroom or the next town. Worse, the woman seemed so genial and kind that Cymin felt incredibly awkward for failing to understand her and couldn't bring himself to ask her to clarify.

Just then, the young soldier who'd bolted inside the station earlier approached him. He introduced himself as Falhep. He was a ranger in a border patrol unit and appeared a little sheepish about his earlier flight from Laithondi, but he was happy to help Cymin.

"I'm still a little jumpy, I guess," Falhep admitted with a nod to his sling. The man wasn't any sort of mage, but he was affable and injured, so Cymin didn't think less of him for his retreat in the face of Laithondi's dramatic entrance.

As it turned out, Falhep had been recovering in town after smugglers ambushed his unit, so he knew the way to both an apothecary and the smithy that supplied transmission wires for the communication towers. When Hiral and Mazilane entered the station with their cameras, the soldier even volunteered to personally escort them the quarter mile to the apothecary.

Mazilane declined with a shake of his head and scanned the rundown station with an expression of dissatisfaction. He looked pale and irritable this morning. Cymin guessed that he hadn't slept well.

Hiral, however, remained as genial and easygoing as ever. He accepted Falhep's offer and seemed quite glad for the company and conversation. Even before they'd exited the station, Hiral had gotten the young soldier to tell him when he was rejoining his unit and where they were patrolling. Cymin watched the two of them retreat, chatting away like long-lost friends.

Mazilane, too, observed them. He pushed a lock of black hair back from his face, and his amber eyes narrowed on Falhep's back. A sneer curved his elegant features, and Cymin felt fei'lux shudder beneath the folds of Mazilane's long coat as if some old spell were slowly rousing. But then Mazilane shook his head and looked away. The fei'lux dispersed in an instant.

Cymin guessed that the train's portal windows had given him a clear view of Falhep's flight from Laithondi. Mazilane wasn't the type to overlook a momentary weakness, though Cymin felt it only made finding courage later more powerful. And Falhep seemed like he deserved a little compassion. After all, he was returning to duty even after surviving a violent attack.

"A sling is certainly an easy prop for winning sympathy and confidences," Mazilane muttered. "Let's hope Hiral still has anything left in his wallet when he gets back to us."

"Do you always have to be so cynical about everyone?" Cymin demanded. At the same time, he felt flustered to realize that—*if* Falhep was a con man—he'd been taken in along with Hiral.

"It's funny that you think this is me being cynical, little jackal." Mazilane withdrew his cigarette case from a deep pocket of his blue coat and turned it through his fingers. The early morning light made the pale scar running down his throat look particularly stark.

Cymin craned his head back towards the rail yard doors, searching for Yinni and wondering what had delayed her.

"If you're looking for your sister, Vessreid wanted her to practice with Ife and Zevlyn," Mazilane answered before Cymin could inquire. "Laithondi asked me to send you along to practice with Xaon as soon as I'm done with you."

"When do you think that will be?" Cymin tried not to sound too excited, but the fact was that he enjoyed magecraft, and Xaon made for an excellent—if challenging—partner to practice with. "I mean, when you're done with me."

"Let's hope we never actually find that out, hmm?" Mazilane offered him a wolfish grin but then shook his head. "For now, go on and stick close to the other students. I can handle filming our scenic little setting on my own. Though keep on guard. There's something odd here."

Cymin waited as Mazilane turned the cigarette case over in his hands again and scowled back in the direction of the train.

"What is it?" Cymin asked in a low voice.

"Has something about the fei'lux felt off to you lately?" Mazilane asked.

"It's been really erratic and rough. I figured that was down to us practicing without the benefit of a city's shield," Cymin replied.

Outside shielded towns and cities, natural fei'lux surged and ebbed in wildly unpredictable voltages and directions. It could drift gently on a breeze, or sear clouds apart in bursts more vivid and violent than lightning storms. In the ground, it sometimes hummed along seams of conductive minerals but also erratically burst up in geysers. Or it might just fade away completely, like dew evaporated by morning sun. The variation made for astoundingly colorful sunrises and sunsets and lent iridescent haloes to the stars and moon.

But it was hellish for working magecraft. Especially for those accustomed to manipulating the sedate streams of fei'lux that had already been tempered by passing through city shields. These last few days in particular, the turbulence of northern storms made the fei'lux currents ferocious, unpredictable, and above all else, unreliable. At times they inundated the atmosphere like surging waves, blasting spells apart in riots of sparks and flames. Then, without warning, the fei'lux disappeared completely, leaving Cymin and his fellow mages grasping after nothing as their practice spells collapsed all around them.

"Not just that," Mazilane replied. He flipped his cigarette case again.

"It has been sort of jittery and . . . " Cymin searched for a word to describe the agitated, unpredictable quality that he'd noticed recently. "Erratic. But that's supposed to be down to storms rolling in from the north. The weather reports—"

"No, that's not what I mean." Mazilane looked annoyed but not with Cymin. "I thought I noticed something like a spell signal in the midst of the fei'lux waves and surges. Like a secret code hidden in radio static. A pattern masked as chaos."

Cymin wished he was so attuned to spell patterns that he could discern anything like that. All he'd noticed had been the shocks and scalds that splashed over him and the other mages when the fei'lux turned wild. He shook his head, and Mazilane sighed. For an instant, he looked uncharacteristically nervous. The camera on his shoulder seemed to lean into him as if offering the cold comfort of its metallic body.

"It's probably just being in this province again. The storms and the rain started like this last time," Mazilane said. "Then the floods . . . "

He glanced to Cymin but didn't go on. Cymin gazed back at him, unsure of how to respond. Until just now he hadn't realized that Mazilane was also a survivor of the Haelon Flood. No wonder the storms made him restless. If Cymin could have remembered anything about that time in his life, he might have felt more confident offering some commiseration—though maybe not to someone as sarcastic as Mazilane.

After staring at Cymin with a dazed sort of expression, Mazilane's attention flickered to Soir. He shook his head and then strode off to smoke outside.

Cymin frowned at Mazilane's retreating back and wondered if there was something about his face this morning that made men trail off while looking at him and then beat a quick retreat. First Laithondi, then Mazilane. He studied his reflection in the glass of the ticket booth as surreptitiously as he could. He didn't find a horrifying new mole in the shape of a curse, nor an unbearable trail of snot, just his usual countenance. His thick bristle of black hair had grown out a bit, and he looked a little tired, but nothing unusual.

He hurried out to the rest area, and after having a look at the Five Schools' mages, Cymin decided that he actually looked pretty good by comparison. Jeshri, Saum, Kimrin and Quin all flopped across wooden benches beneath the redolent sassafras trees. Jeshri's rumpled robes looked slept-in and hung open to expose the thick musculature of his abdomen. He ran his fingers through his black beard like he was attempting to shake it awake. Next to him, Saum wore her yellow school coat over a set of pajamas printed with cartoon monkeys. She yawned and listlessly prodded Jeshri's muscular leg with the toe of her yellow slipper. Despite her tiny stature, she easily claimed most of the space on the bench.

Kimrin and Quin appeared even more fatigued, albeit better dressed than the other two. They'd obviously roused themselves at least an hour earlier than Cymin to dress in their magnificent layered ensembles and style their hair to match. A violet chiffon gown enveloped Quin's spindly body. Perfectly curled gold ribbons coiled within each of her dozens of violet-dyed ringlets. The gold feathers threaded through Kimrin's brown locks matched the intricate cut-outs decorating his velvet waistcoat and his thigh-high leather boots. Sadly, the vivacity of their clothing only emphasized the deep shadows beneath their eyes.

Like the rest of the Waethir's students, they'd experienced a profound increase in vivid dreams about their previous lives. Very few of the past seven nights had proved restful. Now Quin and Kimrin drooped in their splendor like peonies wilting amidst their fallen petals. Quin listlessly sucked on a sugar drop candy, while Kimrin yawned and leafed through a stack of yellowed postcards.

Cymin supposed he was lucky to have few if any dreams—almost none that he could remember. What weariness he felt, he put down to waking early and practicing hard.

A little way across the clover lawn, Cymin caught sight of Ife and Zevlyn. They'd worn the same beige school uniforms the past five days, and their black ponytails appeared a little stringy. An aroma somewhere between aged basil and musky catnip had grown up around them over the week. Privately, Cymin amused himself by replacing Guishuun College's motto of *Wisdom Before Battle* with *Wisdom Before Baths.*

Though in all fairness, even after seven days, the two women couldn't approach the sour pong of one of Jeshri's socks.

The two red moles over Ife's right eyebrow seemed to stand out as particularly bright this morning, or maybe her complexion was a bit sallow. Despite the week of travel and work, their expressions were lively and thoughtful. Both of them watched Yinni trace the circle of a shield-line through the lawn with her toe. Zevlyn cupped a bruised hand over her mouth, hiding her dimpled chin, while Ife stared at Yinni like an eager novice studying a great master.

Yinni moved calmly and gracefully as if utterly unconcerned by worldly matters, though Cymin guessed from the way that she consistently avoided meeting Ife's and Zevlyn's gazes that she was highly conscious of them observing her and at pains not to make a single error, despite the early hour.

Cymin started towards her, but then Paeth called out to him. Three days ago, she'd gotten caught in the middle of a spell during a fei'lux surge and taken a bad fall onto her right wrist. The bandage and sling she now wore helped to further differentiate her from Ovelah, who trailed behind her. Otherwise, the twins wore matching flower-print dresses that Quin had declared to be "dreadfully middle-class" and kept their long curling brown hair loosely clipped back with flower combs.

"If you aren't busy, I was hoping you could help us—or me, actually—with my shield-lines. The tuteli method seems superior," Paeth called to him as she started across the lawn. "And there's something else I was hoping to talk about. One of my dreams—"

She was cut off as Ovelah gave a sudden shrill cry of distress from behind her. Paeth spun around, and Cymin hurried towards the twins. But a moment later, his concern dispersed. It turned out that a little firethorn bush, planted on the perimeter of the rest area, had caught the hem of her flower-print dress. It became more tangled on the shrub's long thorns the more frantically Ovelah attempted to wrench it free. Just then, a branch of bright evergreen leaves and wicked thorns broke off from the shrub, further entangling Ovelah's skirt. For one worrying moment, Cymin feared that Ovelah's panicked thrashing might snag her hair in the thorns as well.

"It's fine. It's fine." Paeth caught her sister. "Hold still, and I'll have you out in no time. Nothing to worry about."

Ovelah stilled at once and put her hands over her face. Paeth knelt down and, whipping out a pair of sewing scissors from her coat, began to cut the branch free.

At the same time, Cymin could see Ovelah's ears flushing bright red with embarrassment. He realized that the kindest thing he could do now was pretend he hadn't noticed anything and make himself scarce. Fortunately, the commotion had roused Xaon from where he sprawled on the clover beneath a sassafras tree. His bright red hair jutted up around his face like a disheveled bird's nest as he waved Cymin over. When Cymin drew near, he noticed Nyle seated cross-legged on the other side of the tree from Xaon. He appeared to be sketching, but when Cymin tried to steal a casual glimpse, Nyle calmly closed his sketchbook.

"Is Ovelah all right?" Xaon asked. He peered across the green at the twins.

"She's fine," Cymin assured him. "A firethorn bush snagged her dress. They're really sharp and can be pretty startling this early in the morning."

Xaon appeared puzzled by the assertion that a two-foot shrub could prove to be a startling combatant to a sober adult, but he didn't argue. Instead, he nodded to where the Waethir were approaching them from across the train yard.

Cymin, too, forgot about the mishap as he took in the Waethir. Their expressions struck Cymin as both serious and preoccupied by a larger concern than their drowsy students.

"Looks like I woke up just in time." Xaon's hand went to his cutlass, though he didn't grip the hilt but instead ran his thumb over the small brass charm hanging from the pommel. It was shaped like a phoenix and apparently contained an heirloom guardian spell of some kind. It wasn't very active, except on the one occasion that Cymin had come close to injuring Xaon; then it spat a plume of sparks out at Cymin's face.

Xaon stretched and stood. He was only an inch or so shorter than Cymin, and his hair made up for that as he swept it back from his face. "Nap time's up, everyone! On your feet! Look lively for our good masters!"

In response to Xaon's shout, the other students roused themselves. Nyle silently unfolded and rose to his feet. Stuffing his pencil into the pocket of his black coat, he withdrew a simple ancillary brush and removed the steel cap protecting the spell-etched copper hairs of its tip. Jeshri swept his massive broadsword up from beneath the bench. Saum opened her coat, revealing her ancillary hammer. Kimrin and Quin both fluttered open folding fans. Kimrin's had been cast from silver, while Quin's appeared to be carved from ivory, but both glittered with gold sigils as delicate as spell filaments.

Ife and Zevlyn wore their hand-scythes on their belts. The sheathed weapons swung at their hips as they jogged over. Yinni walked behind them, but she seemed preoccupied, tempering waves of fei'lux into a sweet, almost minty halo. She only nodded to Cymin when he greeted her with a broad wave.

Ovelah completely forgot her earlier distress and hurried with Paeth to snatch up their oversized ancillary compasses from the bench seat where Yinni had deposited the emergency medical kit. Then the twins joined the rest of them in the middle of the clearing. As all the students gathered, Cymin edged to the side of the group. He wasn't actually one of them, after all. But before he got more than two steps away, a hand caught his elbow. Cymin looked back and was surprised to see that Nyle had stopped him.

"I know it's embarrassing to have to stand alongside this bunch, but if you go off on your own, Laithondi will just call you back," Nyle stated. He cast a sidelong glance to where Xaon now bobbed and swayed, dodging Jeshri's playful boxing maneuvers. "And Xaon needs all the help he can get. So stay."

A week earlier, Cymin might have assured Nyle that he wasn't embarrassed to be grouped with him and the other students, or he would have wondered what Nyle had against Xaon. But after seven days on a cramped train, practicing spells, tempering fei'lux, filming, dining, conversing, shitting, farting, grumbling, gossiping and sleeping with the other mages, he'd gained a better understanding of all of them. He recognized that Nyle often hid good intentions beneath his aloof reproaches—as if he couldn't stand for anyone to know he could be kind. Other times, his cutting quips were merely provocations for attention—particularly when aimed at Xaon. Not all that different from Jeshri's various feigned jabs at other students' heads or Zevlyn's outbursts of cheeky personal questions.

"You're kind to worry for him so much. He'd be touched if he realized," Cymin teased. He was amused to notice a flush briefly color Nyle's face and turn his ears bright red.

Nyle looked away quickly and managed a terse reply. "The two of you let other people push you around and distract you too much. Someone has to keep you on track."

Cymin smiled at Nyle, feeling surprised that he'd been grouped in with Xaon. "I'll stay, then."

The next moment, the Waethir swept before them. The last wisps of fading mist clung to the hems of their clothes, and the scents of oddly cold spell residues wafted from them. Or maybe that was just the perfume of the surrounding sassafras forest. Cymin couldn't be certain.

He didn't waste his time trying to interpret the fixed, calm expressions Laithondi and Arnaith wore. The entire train yard would have to burst into flames before either of them openly expressed fear. Instead he peered to Eirjiri and then Bailon, noting that neither of them was teasing the other. Then he glanced to Vessreid. Of all the Waethir, he was the most gentle and sensitive but also the most prone to attacks of anxiety. (It was a trait he shared with a number of tuteli who'd survived shocking violence, and Cymin always felt a little concerned for him because of that.)

But just now, Vessreid appeared more exasperated rather than agitated as he explained that yet another storm appeared to be on the rise. And since the last leg of their journey to Yanyeo would take them directly north through steep mountain passes, Laithondi and Bailon were going to visit the communications tower in town and check the forecasts and fei'lux reports from Yanyeo. In the meantime, Arnaith and Eirjiri had made an appointment with the local engineers to discuss the fei'lux capacities of the narrow-gauge tracks laid down on the mountain routes. If the fei'lux inundations proved to be serious, then they all might have to stay in town a few days. At the very least, they'd remain at the station while mechanics swapped their train's bogies out for the axles and chassis suited to narrow tracks. So most likely they'd breakfast here—maybe even stay on for lunch.

Jeshri, Saum, Ife, Quin and Xaon cheered at the mention of breakfast, while a look of open avarice briefly flickered over Nyle's lean face. Quin started towards the station canteen. But Kimrin caught her sleeve with a look to Arnaith's disapproving expression.

"You are promising and powerful mages in the midst of mortals who have no power over the fei'lux threatening them." She flipped the silver loops of her hair over her shoulders and pinned each of the students in turn with a glower. "This is not the time to demand they serve up all their food for you or to invade what little shelter they have."

Quin looked like she might object to Arnaith's unique interpretation of the act of buying breakfast in the station canteen, but then she seemed to notice Bailon shake her head in warning. Quin closed her mouth.

"In Saigrath, storms a thousand times more powerful than this will rage down from the Hallow Gates, and you *must* be prepared to face them." Arnaith rested her hand meaningfully against her abdomen, where the mythic ignis gland was supposed to reside. "So use this storm as an opportunity to practice tempering turbulent fei'lux. Build your tolerance and endurance. And if it becomes necessary, be prepared to defend the mortals who cannot defend themselves."

"Yes, ma'am!" Paeth and Ovelah responded automatically.

Cymin sighed but accepted Arnaith's decree at once. Being a tuteli meant repaying the Heavens for the gift of magecraft by protecting others in much the same way as it required him to compensate the state for the food, shelter and education that had sustained him. Yinni, too, appeared resigned.

Xaon groaned and Nyle's shoulders slumped, while Saum and Jeshri just cast one another commiserating smiles. Quin, however, wasn't nearly so unassuming. She kicked the ground and stamped her feet so hard that the flashing metallic tassels on her shoes startled half a dozen rabbits from beneath the surrounding underbrush.

Arnaith was unmoved by the tantrum, but Bailon hurried over. A handful of furtively delivered sugar drops settled Quin almost at once. When Bailon turned away, Quin smiled with smug delight and handed a candy to Kimrin.

After that, the entire group of Chyrenese mages, Cymin included, refocused themselves and got to work. Linking hands, they formed a ring and drew streams of fei'lux whipping down from the sky and jolting across the hillside. Steadily, Cymin and the other students captured eddies of crackling fei'lux and circulated them around the circle, passing them counter-clockwise from left hand to right.

As always, curious insects were enticed by this. At first, a few lightning flies flitted around them, flashing like tiny sparklers. Then as the mist cleared and the sun warmed the open grounds, bees and butterflies appeared. Cymin hardly noticed them anymore. Instead, he focused on the jittery fei'lux that Quin fed into the circle and the crackling charges Xaon dragged in. They snapped at Cymin's nerves as he circulated them through his body, again and again, until at last he could pass a single uniform charge from his right hand to Nyle's left.

See this, Laithondi? Even without spell filaments, or mystical dreams, East Deity can keep up with your chosen students.

Cymin's smug assurance didn't last long, though. Soon, the constant flood of stinging, burning fei'lux began to wear him down, and the fingers of his left hand began to shake in Xaon's intense grip.

"Xaon," Laithondi spoke from behind them. "Slow down and calm the current before passing it on."

"Yes, sir," Xaon responded, and at once, the snarling surge of fei'lux scalding through Cymin's hand slowed.

"You don't need to prove your abilities to anyone but yourself. Be patient, trust in your instincts. The skills are already within you, waiting to be reclaimed." Laithondi lifted his voice, addressing all the students, but to Cymin, it almost felt as if the assurance was for him alone. "You've achieved this and much more already, and you will master it again."

Over the last week, Laithondi had repeated assurances like these to him and Xaon. But as far as direct instruction went, he offered them almost nothing. Maybe he was more detailed when he taught Nyle alone. But either way, the reminder helped Cymin to slow down and nudge Xaon when he got too excited and sloppy. By the end of the warm-up, Cymin felt far more comfortable.

As normal, once they'd circulated fei'lux to a state where none of them could sense the slightest flaw, they released it. Then they split into groups for individual instruction from the Waethir. Today, Laithondi simply gave Nyle a confident nod—the kind Cymin recalled Master Tam offering Grand Master Ryn when she'd first taken up her post. Then Laithondi offhandedly assigned Cymin and Xaon the challenge of manifesting an Invocation of Silence together.

"Make sure your ancillary swords absorb the feedback at a stable rate once the spell takes form." Laithondi started to turn to join Bailon as she strode away. Over his shoulder he added, "Stay alert and you'll be fine."

Cymin nodded, and Xaon saluted Laithondi's back.

Then Cymin laid down a shield-line around them to protect the people and the grounds surrounding them. He wasn't all that confident in his own ability to perfectly control fei'lux under these conditions, much less his ability to synchronize with Xaon to construct something as elaborate as an Invocation of Silence.

A few moments later, Eirjiri and Arnaith departed too. Vessreid remained to watch over them all.

For nearly three hours after that, Cymin and Xaon stood ten feet apart, swords lifted and ablaze with fei'lux as they activated one sigil after another within their blades. In theory, their task was far easier than the bouts of combat they'd previously engaged in. They weren't dodging razor edges or thrusting the weightless luminous blades at each other while also directing fei'lux to manifest battle spells. Instead, they only had to focus both their swords on a single spell, and perfectly balance the flow of fei'lux so that the two ancillaries worked in harmony.

But with the fei'lux behaving so erratically, many of the streams he and Xaon channeled into their sword ancillaries startled half a dozen other spells awake, disrupting the fragile manifestations of the Invocation of Silence and igniting geysers of flame up the blades. Remnants of scorched sigils and incinerated insects spattered Cymin and Xaon like rain showers.

They weren't the only ones struggling. All across the grounds, other mages swore and bolted back from erratic, explosive miscast spells. Even Nyle—poised as he appeared to be with his long ancillary paintbrush—had cast a spell that badly charred the brush's copper tip and steel ferrule. After that, he withdrew to a bench to repair the thing.

"This is just stupid," Quin announced. "I'm too hungry to concentrate, and it's only making me frustrated to keep failing like this!" She snapped her fan shut and then brushed a pair of lantern flies off the sleeve of her gown.

"Agreed." Kimrin, too, closed his fan. He withdrew a kerchief from his vest and walked to where Ife and Zevlyn stood amidst scorched lawn and an uprooted firethorn bush. Kimrin handed the kerchief to Ife. She wiped a trail of dark blood from her nose and mouth, while Zevlyn dropped down beside her on the lawn, looking guilty.

When Vessreid didn't object to any of them stopping, his silence became a tacit permission. Soon after, Paeth and Ovelah abandoned the shield spell that had already knocked them both off their feet a few times and volunteered to fetch refreshments and food from the canteen for everyone to enjoy.

"Thank you! My treat at the next stop," Saum shouted, though she and Jeshri continued to circle, exchanging shocking blows against one another's shields. Farther off, Yinni completed her own assignment but continued circulating fei'lux as she quietly set about building the wind spell that Quin and Kimrin had given up on.

Cymin shot Xaon a questioning glance. Officially, he was only here to help Xaon train, so if Xaon wanted to stop, Cymin wouldn't argue. Though quitting before they manifested the invocation even once grated against Cymin's pride.

And just drawing in a deep breath of the spell residues floating around the two of them, he was certain that they were on the verge of a breakthrough there. Once or twice more, and they'd likely have it.

"We're close," Xaon said. He tapped the tip of his nose. "I can sense it. You?"

"Absolutely." Cymin grinned at him and lifted his sword.

East Deity salutes you. Let's show them what we can do.

Overhead, a film camera swept through the trees and circled the park.

Cymin and Xaon began again. This time, they circulated the fei'lux between them a little longer, tempering it until it flowed as smoothly as quicksilver. Then they channeled the supple fei'lux into their swords, synchronizing their motions. The blades lit with sigils, and the first glassy strings of the Invocation of Silence began to manifest between them.

As they pulled down more and more fei'lux, the loop of transparent strings grew into a tower. A refreshing quiet pervaded the space between them as the invocation absorbed the sound waves rippling through the air. As it did so, the spell returned the energy of the vibrations to the swords. With each cycle, Cymin and Xaon moved further apart, growing the invocation's size and strength, as well as the power it fed back to the swords. Steadily, the Invocation of Silence arose to a twenty-foot column of watery glinting threads and perfectly still air.

In ages past, such invocations were embedded in armor worn by royal assassins and even laid over entire armies waiting in ambush to ensure the absolute silence of their movements. But in the modern world, weaker versions of the invocation served to dampen the clamor of industrial machinery near apartment blocks and public schools. Lux Temple maintained several Invocations of Silence to preserve the serenity of the grounds in the middle of a bustling city. Cymin thought that they smelled like geraniums and enjoyed maintaining them. So, normally, he felt quite comfortable manifesting one, even on a larger scale.

Today, however, the rate of fei'lux they needed to feed into the spell didn't leave enough time to properly temper it all. Those uneven charges lent the invocation a disturbing intensity. White arcs spit and spattered between him and Xaon like boiling oil hitting ice water. Sigils along Xaon's cutlass released a spray of gold flames.

"Shit! Fuck! Sorry!" Xaon shouted, though his voice hardly carried around the invocation. Cymin gritted his teeth and swore under his breath in response. The burnt bodies of flies and bees caught between them fell like smoldering rain.

"How the fuck do we always attract so many more bugs than everybody else?" Xaon shook his head, trying to dislodge the remnants of a butterfly wing from his red hair.

Cymin coughed but maintained his focus on the turbulent streams of fei'lux inundating their spell. Something smelled off. That fresh, clean quality of the spell was turning too crisp, too cold—becoming sterile, the silence of suffocation, rather than respite.

He noted that the Invocation of Silence wasn't only absorbing the energy of sound waves and feeding them back into his and Xaon's raised swords. The surges of fei'lux were causing it to drain much more. The air between him and Xaon grew cold, and needles of frost limed the clover. The watery quality of the spell itself became more solid. Icy—almost glass-like. At the same time, Xaon's sword began to glow and emit a thin piercing whistle, like a tea kettle about to boil over. In Cymin's grip, Yuelaith threw off wild flares of light as it absorbed more and more kinetic energy from their surroundings.

Cymin turned his left hand, signaling to Xaon to join him in slowly dissipating the Invocation of Silence. Xaon nodded, but as he too closed his left hand, a huge, bristling mass of fei'lux surged over them. It arced to Xaon's sword like lightning finding a lightning rod and jumped past his fingers, striking the charm hanging from the hilt.

Xaon's expression was horrified, and he shouted something to Cymin, but the Invocation of Silence devoured his voice, leaving Cymin with only the sight of Xaon's panicked expression and straining muscles as he struggled to suppress the spell unfurling from his sword charm.

A huge scarlet phoenix—wrought from flames and molten sigils—erupted from the charm, shrieking into the air only feet from Cymin's face.

Cymin hurled a stream of fei'lux up, blocking the phoenix's blazing talons and burning wings as it swooped down at him. The heat still singed his hair and dried the water in his eyes. The phoenix wheeled and dived for him again. Unbidden, an array of frigid blue sigils appeared in Cymin's mind, and a tingling sensation rushed through the core of his body. He swung Yuelaith up, immediately manifesting a shield of thousands of razor-thin ice crystals that whirled around him like saw blades. Cymin thrust the spell and sword into the phoenix's chest. The fiery bird burst apart in a geyser of severed gold sigils. Cymin leapt back, dodging the blazing spell-debris.

At the same time, Xaon reached out with his left arm, reeling the gold sparking remnants of the phoenix spell back to him until it coalesced once again as a tiny brass charm in his hand.

Cymin squeezed his eyes closed. Afterimages of the phoenix burned beneath his eyelids, the skin of his hands felt scorched and a deep hum churned through his belly. But strangest of all was the delicate fragrance that washed over him. Sweet and citric, like lemon oil or tangerine peel. For a sick moment, he was reminded of the weird sensations that had swarmed him when the bomb exploded during the Spring Exhibition. In addition to the citrus perfume, the stench of singed hair hung over his face, rousing the memory of spell filaments burning through his skin. Cymin's stomach flipped as he fought down his reflexive fear.

Think of something else. Anything else.

Then the tiny sword charm in Xaon's hand captured his attention. He stared at it and, slowly, amazement overwhelmed his agitation. The lush complexity of the arrays of spells hidden inside that tiny brass charm were astounding. That phoenix it released hadn't seemed rote or mechanical in its attack. Instead, it had wheeled, struck and dived like something genuinely . . . alive. He had no other way to describe it.

"Was that a wae?" Cymin asked Xaon. "A real wae?"

"Uhm . . . maybe? She's called Lazhu. Grandad claimed that back in Piiroc, a thousand generations ago, she was a genuine wae, but . . . Grandad was crazy. So I never thought . . . " Xaon's expression turned surprisingly sheepish as he returned the charm to his sword hilt. "She's never burst out like that before . . . sorry."

"Not your fault." Cymin shook his head, still feeling stunned by the revelation. A wae . . . he'd just encountered a genuine wae—a mythic array of guardian spells that could challenge a living creature in complexity and loyalty. Magecraft so powerful, intricate and mysterious that no modern mage-scholars had been able to recreate one. All this time, a wonder of the mythic ages had just been dangling from Xaon's sword hilt like a tacky souvenir.

Cymin eyed the charm again. If it was of Piiroc origin, then did that explain why its spell residue seemed so much like that of the Piiroc bomb—and those tacky little lighters that had startled Cymin in the Palace Complex as well? Cymin wanted to examine the wae more closely, but it seemed intent on returning to that dormant state after its short outburst. Cymin could only detect the faintest of spells humming through it now, and even those quickly quieted.

"Are you hurt—" Xaon began, but there was no time for him to complete the question.

Distracted by the phoenix wae, they'd neglected the Invocation of Silence looming between them. Now the huge, glassy tower lost its balance and crashed down, releasing an explosion of violent wind and booming thunder. The force hurled the two of them in opposite directions. Xaon howled as he tumbled backwards, somersaulting through a bed of violet lilies. Cymin slammed into the trunk of a sassafras tree, sending a cloud of scarlet swallowtail butterflies scattering from the tree's yellow blossoms. He sank down to the ground, while Xaon lay dazed and cursing on his back.

Xaon's cutlass flickered with misshapen sigils, then dulled to steel gray. The sword in Cymin's hand buzzed as the same sigils partly lit and then faded out. Grasshoppers bounded away, and bees darted off. The insects originally drawn to their exchanges of fei'lux dispersed like a crowd of disappointed spectators.

Chapter 19

"Shit! Sorry!" Xaon scrambled to his knees but couldn't quite manage to stand yet. "I—Cy? Are you all right?"

"Eyebrows a little crisp, otherwise I'm fine." Cymin assessed Xaon in return. Over the last seven days, he'd learned that Xaon often hid his own injuries while fretting absurdly over inflicting the slightest unintentional scratch on a partner.

"What about you?" Cymin asked. "Your hand?"

"Uhm…good?" Xaon withdrew his blistered left hand into the sleeve of his coat. Cymin sighed and started to rise to go check for himself.

But an instant later, he flattened to the ground as Saum—caught by a different inundation of fei'lux—came hurtling past him, shrieking like a kid on a merry-go-round. Jeshri tumbled over the lawn along with her but lower to the ground. He scrabbled for anything to slow his flight, but only grasped one of Saum's flailing legs and then caught a boot to the side of his head. Then the spell propelling them fizzled. Jeshri dropped to the ground, and Saum toppled down on top of him.

"Are you hurt?" Saum scrambled off of Jeshri's back.

"I'm just fucked. So, so fucked . . . " Jeshri spat out a mouthful of clover and wiped leaves from his beard. Then he laughed as he caught sight of Saum's concerned expression. "I can't believe how fucking bad I am at this now. I haven't fucked up this much since I was six."

"You and me both." Xaon staggered over to join them and Cymin near the stand of sweet-scented sassafras trees.

"Same here." Saum sighed and scrubbed at the grass-stained knees of her pajamas. "But it's not you—or me. It's the fei'lux that's causing the problems, right? Because we're not inside a city shield."

"True, but according to the Waethir, we won't ever be inside a shield in Saigrath." Jeshri shook his head. "How the fuck are we going to manage it?"

"The same way the Waethir must have first learned to," Cymin told him. "We've just got to keep practicing, and we'll get used to it."

After all, he'd already managed to mostly adapt to working without spell filaments. They just needed time and practice, Cymin expected.

A breeze washed the lemon scent of the leaves over them. Cymin noticed Nyle rise from the bench that he'd claimed earlier while repairing his ancillary. He quietly put the paintbrush in its case and drifted nearer to Xaon. A trace of concern fluttered through Nyle's aloof expression, but he looked away when he noticed Cymin watching him.

"At least we're pretty much all struggling. I think I'd feel worse if it was just me." Saum glanced across the rest area to where Kimrin and Quin slumped beside Ife and Zevlyn on a separate bench, several yards from Nyle. Their ancillary weapons had already been packed up: sickles sheathed, fans closed and set aside with Paeth and Ovelah's compasses in their leather cases.

Quin flopped a twiggy arm across Zevlyn's shoulder and groaned—whether from hunger or an injury, Cymin wasn't certain. Zevlyn patted Quin's head, then shot Ife another apologetic look. Ife smiled at her but then flinched. She quickly stuffed Kimrin's kerchief back into a nostril before more blood dribbled out her nose.

Kimrin himself lounged next to Quin, listlessly flipping through his postcards again. But the beginning of a black eye already showed beneath his round gold glasses. He sighed at the postcards in his hand, seemingly too spent to keep peering at them through his swollen eye. Then he returned the cards to the pocket of his velvet coat.

"What is keeping breakfast?" Kimrin demanded.

"Yes, it's been forever, and I'm so desperately hungry! Kim-kim, I'm about to die!" Quin announced. "Right now, I'd even trade my shoes for a steam bun."

"Quinny darling, no!" Kimrin roused himself to strike a melodramatic pose and take Quin's tiny hand in his own. "Never even think such a thing! Better to starve as an icon of style than to live the dull existence of a barefoot pauper! Chin up, Quinny, chin up!"

Barefoot pauper that he was, Cymin couldn't help but frown. Across the lawn, Yinni rolled her eyes.

"I'm sure he didn't mean that how it sounded," Saum whispered quickly. "He's just being funny and . . ."

"Stupid?" Nyle suggested.

Saum startled at Nyle's sudden intrusion. Cymin had noticed him approaching earlier, but even so he was impressed by how stealthily Nyle had joined them.

"No, more ignorant, I think." Jeshri rolled his shoulders, his expression thoughtful. "Kimrin's family and mine socialize in Yanyeo. Quin's too. They aren't bad. Just sometimes a person knows fuck-all about something but they also don't *know* that they know fuck-all. Like before

I met Xaon I knew *fuck-all* about real pleasure-houses and gambling halls. I just thought they were all good fun and games. But then Xaon told me all about the pimps, extortion, blackmail, knee-capping, drug addicts . . . oh, and the sex diseases. Ugh. Shocked the fuck out of me."

Cymin glanced sidelong to Xaon. He wasn't alone. Nyle and Saum also squinted between Xaon and Jeshri.

"Weren't you two seven when you started boarding together?" Saum asked. "How were you visiting pleasure-houses and gambling halls at that age?"

Xaon frowned, but Jeshri laughed.

"Oh fuck no! Not the real things. I mean in books and on the radio!" Jeshri explained. "Adventure stories and such."

"Oh." Saum nodded, then looked to Xaon. "I bet Ife would be interested. For her novel, you know. She's got a big fight set in a gambling hall, but I don't think she's ever been inside one."

"Maybe." Xaon shrugged. "If she asks, I'll tell her, I guess."

At the mention of Ife and her ongoing novel, all of their attention turned to her. Even with Kimrin's kerchief stuffed in her nose, she'd already dug her thick green notebook from her school bag and propped it on her knees. She wrote at a furious rate and with an intensely focused expression. As she did this, Zevlyn, Quin and Kimrin all stole glances at the lines of script flooding the pages.

The contents of Ife's ongoing novel had become a source of great conversation and even a few readings on the train throughout the last week. Just now, Kimrin appeared rapt, and Quin looked both excited and scandalized.

"Come on, let's go see what we can read over her shoulder. I hope it's racy." Saum rose and started towards the others. Jeshri and Xaon followed. Cymin was only a step behind them, and when he peeked over his shoulder, he noticed Nyle trailing along as well.

"Your flight through the air was amazing!" Zevlyn called out to Saum and Jeshri, then she looked to Xaon and Cymin. "And that invocation. I can't believe you managed to manifest it as well as you did with the fei'lux going so wild. Three days ago, none of us would have dared to cast a tiny illumination spell with conditions this unstable. Then you two blow apart all expectations with that invocation."

We nearly blew a lot more than that apart.

But seeing the proud way Xaon lifted his head in response to the praise, Cymin kept the thought to himself. He supposed that they hadn't done all that badly, really.

"We're getting better as we grow bolder," Quin stated. She kicked her feet, and a riot of tassels danced around her toes. "Just like my shoes!"

"I was thinking the same. I mean, about us all improving." Saum brushed a clump of dirt off of Jeshri's back.

"We couldn't possibly have gotten worse, could we?" Xaon responded.

"You all might have. But some people never missed a beat no matter what." Ife, at last, looked up from her notebook and gestured to where Yinni stood opposite Vessreid.

Yinni's hands moved swiftly as she chased small, fluctuating streams of fei'lux and circulated them around herself. Vessreid observed her with a placid expression and folded hands. He said nothing, nor did he intercede.

With her left hand, Yinni drew thin stream after stream of fei'lux in a clockwise circle around her body. At the same time, she manifested a fine thread of tempered fei'lux into razor-bright sigils with her right hand. Holding the sharp spell into the wild streams circling her, Yinni sheared away the jittery edges of the fei'lux and smoothed their surfaces, as if she were peeling the skin from a carrot.

"What is it she's doing?" Kimrin adjusted his glasses on the bridge of his nose as he squinted at Yinni.

"She's manipulating a minor wind spell to create a whirlpool around herself and corral wild fei'lux into organized streams. Then she lets their momentum drive them through a minor blade spell to refine them further," Ife explained. "By the time she draws the fei'lux into her spell filaments, it'll be nearly as tempered as if it had already gone through a city shield."

Cymin smiled, studying the way Yinni meticulously directed the small currents of fei'lux to maintain the whirlwind fluttering around her, truly creating order within chaos.

Hadn't Mazilane mentioned something about that? Even at the time, Cymin hadn't understood Mazilane's description. But he felt certain that, in his place, Yinni would have grasped it at once. She probably would have had an insight into the matter as well.

Ife pulled the kerchief from her nose and hid it away in her schoolbag.

"You're a hero in real life as well as in my novel!" Ife shouted at Yinni. At the same time, Zevlyn roused herself to hoot Yinni's name and applaud.

Yinni scowled but didn't look at either of them.

Cymin knew that Yinni believed the two of them were poking fun at her, but now that he'd observed them all together, he'd come to the conclusion that Ife and Zevlyn's admiration was truly sincere. Maybe too much so, since Yinni only grew more uncomfortable and then suspicious the more Zevlyn and Ife cheered, gushed and complimented her. No matter what Cymin told her, she couldn't seem to accept their unbridled veneration. The miscommunication had become almost farcical, and it went in both directions. On more than one occasion, Cymin had overheard Ife describe Yinni's irritated glowers as, "So dignified."

The whirlwind intensified around Yinni, and her expression grew quite "dignified."

"She's just like a mythic frost princess," Ife murmured.

"My thought exactly," Zevlyn agreed. Then she stole a gleeful sidelong glance to Nyle. "Who could possibly match her, other than someone just as reserved and beautiful?"

Cymin scowled at the suggestion. To his surprise, Kimrin shot him a look of commiseration, as if he too found the idea of matchmaking Yinni and Nyle distasteful. Then Kimrin leaned forward to catch Zevlyn's attention.

"Zev, I doubt such an outstanding woman is in need of an aloof introvert to two-time her." Kimrin squared his shoulders. "Wouldn't a fling with a charming, cheery man make for a more joyous adventure of erotic awakening? Someone happy to buy her nice things and teach her how to properly pluck her eyebrows."

"Weren't you just chatting Paeth up yesterday?" Zevlyn responded.

"She's hopeless," Quin stated. She darted a glance towards Cymin, maybe worrying—rightly—that Cymin wouldn't like her talking about Paeth behind her back. Then she went on anyway. "The poor thing's ridiculously obsessed. Though how she hasn't noticed what a doomed undertaking it is, I've no idea."

Quin cast Kimrin a sympathetic look, and he made a brief display of wiping a nonexistent tear from his cheek. Then he laughed.

"Honestly, *I* have a better chance of landing that catch than Paeth does. Poor thing." Kimrin shrugged and returned his gaze to Yinni. "But seriously. What's not to find attractive about a man who can pay her debts and set her up in a quaint little garret for weekend flings?"

"I'm sure it could be fun, but you do make it sound a little . . . transactional, don't you think?" Zevlyn considered Kimrin, then her gaze shifted to Jeshri's broad bare chest. "Maybe she's waiting for something more passionate. Someone who ruins her common sense and sweeps her off her feet."

"Oh Zev, I understand the attraction completely." Quin patted Zevlyn's shoulder. "But in the long run, you'll be happier just getting a dog. Easier to house train, and people will actually think it's smart when it learns to speak."

Saum and Xaon both looked offended, but Jeshri just laughed and shook his head at Quin's comment.

"Four years back, on holiday, our grandparents tried to betroth me and Quin," Jeshri explained. "So we pretended to be all for it and then both spent the rest of the holiday acting too stupid and batshit mental for the other's family to stand."

"Oh." Saum seemed to reassess Quin. Cymin did as well.

"That's actually rather clever of the two of you," Saum said.

"Yeah, it was all Quin's planning. Quick as she is cracked." Jeshri grinned at Quin. Then he dropped his voice into a tone of profound stupidity, proclaiming, "Fuckin' love you, Ditzy-bird!"

In an instant, both Kimrin and Quin's postures altered entirely. Kimrin looked like he'd been splashed with hot vomit. Quin, on the other hand, beamed lewdly at Jeshri's chest and began to rock maniacally. Her chiffon gown quivered around her spindly body like a jellyfish attempting to digest a fishhook.

"Oh, my biggest, bestest Hump-doggy!" Quin kicked her feet into the air. "I can't wait to have all your puppies! A whole litter!"

"Ditzy-bird, you make my ears stand up," Jeshri stated.

"You make my nose wet," Quin responded.

Jeshri covered his laugh by barking.

Quin yipped in reply.

The two of them continued their canine call and response with growing fervor and volume.

Cymin stared on, feeling awed but also embarrassed to be standing with them as they barked, yipped, whined, panted and whimpered at each other. Several workers in the rail yard shot them confused looks. A young woman passing by turned around and walked away.

Like Cymin, Saum stared wide-eyed, while Nyle turned away as if he couldn't endure the sight of them. Zevlyn, Ife and Xaon seemed resigned, but Kimrin clearly was not.

"No! No, no, no," Kimrin shouted over an exchange of barks and howls. "The two of you swore there'd be no more doggy-duos if I supported you! Stop this instant, or I will have your engagement announced in every publication in Yanyeo. Just try getting out of a wedding after that."

Jeshri and Quin abandoned their outlandish behavior immediately.

"Thank the Heavens," Nyle muttered under his breath.

They all stood in a dazed sort of silence for a moment. Cymin noted that Vessreid simply shook his head at them, while Yinni continued practicing her magecraft with a far too fixed expression of calm.

"What were we talking about before all this?" Kimrin asked Zevlyn.

"The heroine of Ife's book," Zevlyn supplied.

"Yes, right." Kimrin smoothed the gold feathers woven through his brown locks and then looked to Ife. "Give me a rough idea of the plot, and I'll run it by my uncle once we reach Yanyeo. He's been on the hunt for a heroine-led serial to publish in his adventure periodical. So long as the girl has some kick and a little mystery to her, he'll love it."

Ife turned her pen through her fingers, still gazing at Yinni. "She's definitely a princess, but one hidden away in rags and hardship."

"Then who am I?" Paeth demanded. During Jeshri and Quin's antics, she and Ovelah had trundled out from the station canteen. Between them, they brought three large trays piled with towering steam baskets and tin tea kettles. Ovelah hefted two of the large trays while Paeth balanced the third with her left arm.

"A goddess of kindness who has heard my prayers and brought manna and refreshments?" Ife replied, but then she tapped her notebook with her pen. "Actually, I'm using you as the inspiration for the mysterious, kindhearted owner of a traveler's pavilion who shelters my fleeing tuteli heroine. I could give you a secret lover, if you'd like."

"Make him strikingly handsome and madly in love with me, and I'll accept the supporting role." Paeth laughed and then set her tray down on an empty bench. "Your heroine's burden of rags and hardship seems a bit overrated, in any case."

"Ife, wouldn't it be fun if you could work *all* of us into your book?" Quin asked.

"I guess I could try," Ife responded. "But I can't promise all happy endings. There do have to be some villains, after all."

"Oh, what about Xaon and me?" Jeshri asked, and he hefted his sheathed broadsword over his shoulder. "Fucking wicked pirates, am I right?"

"No, you're more likely to end up love interests," Ife supplied.

Xaon and Jeshri scowled, and both Ife and Zevlyn burst into laughter.

"Not for each other—or my heroine. She's far too elegant for the likes of Orae Academy's 'Bloody Blade.' Or Jeshri 'The Wall.'" Ife snickered. "Maybe you'll end up with the villain of the novel."

"Definitely," Zevlyn agreed. Then she waved her fingers in greeting to Cymin. "Forbidden passions and hopeless obsession."

Quin and Kimrin both appeared quite excited by the prospect, and Paeth seemed amused, while Ovelah just looked uncertain of the entire conversation. Or perhaps she just wanted people to eat while the buns she'd gone to all the trouble of carting over to them were still hot.

For his part, Cymin didn't take any of it too seriously. He'd gotten used to the wild flights of fantasy and gossip that Zevlyn, Kimrin and Quin enjoyed. He certainly found the conversation easier to accommodate than their luggage. Kimrin and Quin in particular had each brought an absurd amount of clothing. A full third of the sleeping carriages seemed to have been taken over by the pair's collections of hats and shoes alone.

Xaon regarded the group of them with an expression of exasperated confusion.

"What are they on about with forbidden passion?" he whispered to Cymin. "Which one of us is the villain of the novel?"

"Not you or Jeshri, since you've been cast to fall in love with the villain," Cymin answered.

"It would be shitty to make Paeth or Ovelah villains after they bought us all breakfast," Xaon remarked. "It would be better if it were just me. It's not like I'd care."

"It's just a story, so I suppose I wouldn't mind either." Cymin nodded absently. His attention had already shifted to the trays of covered dishes. Ovelah lifted the lids, and clouds of fragrant steam rolled off the heaps of pillowy buns. Some were marked with pink spots, others with little gold speckles, and altogether they must have numbered more than fifty.

Cymin's stomach gurgled, and his jaw dropped slightly.

Paeth and Ovelah must have spent at least two blue bills on all of this. The two of them were so kind, it shamed him that he never managed more than a feeling of distant friendliness when he thought of them.

He really ought to find a way to repay their generosity.

As he was pondering that, he noticed Nyle silently sidle up beside Xaon and tug at his left elbow. Xaon resisted briefly but then allowed Nyle to see his blistered, scalded hand. Cymin opened his mouth to offer a cooling spell, but Nyle already lifted his brush and flicked a tiny healing spell over Xaon's freckled wrist. Gold sigils spread across his skin like a balm. The red streaks covering the back of Xaon's hand faded.

"Thanks," Xaon murmured.

Nyle only inclined his head in response, his long black hair hiding his expression. Then he lifted his chin and turned his indifferent gaze to Cymin.

"What about you?" Nyle asked

"I'm fine," Cymin assured him. "Were you hurt at all?"

Nyle shook his head as if he couldn't possibly be injured and looked away to where Yinni was, at last, dispersing her spell. Xaon scowled at the back of Nyle's head, and Cymin suppressed a sigh.

Nyle's behavior—both his acts of care and his feigned air of disinterest—really did resemble Laithondi's actions sometimes—certainly more than his or Xaon's did.

"Enough talk. Let's eat," Xaon stated. He elbowed Jeshri, and the two of them swooped over to the trays of steamed buns, though Quin still beat them to the steaming dishes. She snatched up two buns for herself and another two for Kimrin. Saum, Ife and Zevlyn all followed suit.

While the others helped themselves to buns and tea, Cymin held back, as was proper for a tuteli. Across the lawn, Yinni too stood aside, bowing her head and steepling her long fingers as if in deep contemplation.

Cymin's stomach grumbled, and he didn't think he could pull off Yinni's pretense of prayer. Instead, he sat down on the clover lawn and tried to think of something other than his gnawing hunger. Contemplating Laithondi always distracted him, though today it was his prolonged absence that gripped Cymin's attention.

Shouldn't he have returned by now?

Cymin studied the hazy outline of radio antennae that bristled from the distant communication tower. That injured soldier, Falhep, had said the tower wasn't much more than a mile away, but it had been hours now. How long could it take just to check a weather report? And why would it require Laithondi and Bailon both?

Vessreid, too, appeared to have grown anxious, but he hid it well, smiling in response to Zevlyn and Ife's invitation to join them for their late breakfast.

"Perhaps a little later. I want to have a brief stroll first," Vessreid told them. Then he looked to Yinni in particular. "You did very well today. Please go and eat. Enjoy your meal and a good rest."

Given permission, Yinni moved quickly to the bench and snatched a bun for herself.

Vessreid observed her with a kind smile, then turned and strode away in the direction of the communication tower.

The gray shadow cast by a film camera glided silently after him.

Cymin stole a glance back to the train where Mazilane stood on the gangway, smoking. Cymin didn't think Hiral had returned from the apothecary yet, so he guessed that it was Mazilane's camera, Soir, that tracked Vessreid. Cymin recalled Mazilane's earlier agitation about spell patterns hidden beneath the chaos of the recent fei'lux storms.

Something's really off about all of this. But none of them want us to worry.

Cymin ran his hand over Yuelaith's hilt and felt the buzz of restless spells churning through the sword. As he traced the sword hilt, the spells seemed to settle, and some of Cymin's own uneasiness relented.

"Do you like mushroom or duck better?" Paeth asked.

It took Cymin a moment to look up from his sword and realize that Paeth had addressed him. She held out two pale steamed buns with her left hand. Pale green leaf-papers cupped the bases of the fluffy white buns, and yellow turmeric patterns freckled the tops.

"Oh sorry, I was lost in thought. Either is good by me." Cymin accepted one of the warm buns and automatically offered Paeth a gesture of blessing as he added, "My thanks, kind benefactor."

"No trouble. We're all basically classmates now, aren't we? So, there's no need to be so formal." Paeth settled down to his left. Normally, he would have reserved the spot for Yinni, but just now Quin had cornered her with excited questions about whether she might be interested in taking work as a clothing model.

Quin had been designing a number of gowns that she felt would perfectly suit someone of Yinni's stature and stately bearing. Yinni listened to Quin's descriptions of golden cloaks inspired by ancient Piiroc queens with an indulgent smile. But the longer Quin chattered away, the more hunted her expression grew. Ovelah stood meekly to the side, watching Yinni and clutching two buns without taking a bite from either.

As Quin chatted on and on, Yinni shot Cymin an entreating glance. But he wasn't about to get up and try to distract Quin for her. He'd already made that mistake once and nearly ended up squeezed to death by the steel stays of an outlandish corset while Quin affixed bright candy wrappers to his head and explained that the entire ensemble symbolized the way society treated wealthy girls as fetish objects and disposable commodities.

"Is yours mushroom or duck?" Paeth asked.

"Oh." Cymin realized that he'd been ignoring her again and felt like a complete ass for it. He smiled and took a quick bite from the bun Paeth had given him, then briefly froze, flummoxed by both the bun's flavor and texture. It was nothing like any dish served in Lux Temple. "It's not mushroom," he decided. "Or duck, I don't think."

"You probably got one of the pork and black bean paste! The canteen gave us three for free because we bought so much." Paeth leaned a little closer, looking at the bun in his hand. A soft curl of her long hair brushed over his arm. "Those are my favorite, actually. Do you like it?"

Did he? He wasn't sure, but he had no intention of complaining about any food someone else spent their money on and gave to him for free. Cymin nodded and took another bite of the pungent and intense filling.

Paeth beamed at him, and he set his mind to liking the bun. Shortly after that, Xaon settled down on his right with an armload of steaming white buns. He tossed one into Cymin's lap and then thrust two buns out to Nyle.

"What's in them?" Nyle asked.

"What do you care? It's food," Xaon replied.

"Most are peppersnake and mushroom or duck and leek, but Cymin and I are having pork and black bean," Paeth supplied. Then, for no reason Cymin could understand, she gazed at him, as if their shared bun filling held some special significance.

Nyle's brow arched, but he made no comment.

"Just take a bite and enjoy the discovery," Xaon said. "It's not like it'll be in your mouth long enough for you to taste it anyway, is it?"

Nyle accepted the buns and then crammed one after the other into his mouth. He hardly seemed to chew them before he reached out and snatched another two from Xaon and jammed them into his maw as well.

"Porcelain Prince . . . " Xaon shook his head, handing two more buns to Nyle. "Python Prince is more like it."

Paeth stared at Nyle, slack-jawed, and Cymin bowed his head to hide his smirk. Nyle habitually devoured his food as if he was terrified it would be stolen from him at any moment. He also tended to keep to himself, particularly when he ate, so very few people had actually witnessed him cram an entire meal down his throat in mere seconds. But having served in Benevolence Hall, Cymin had seen him disappear an entire bowl of fat ribbon noodles in two grotesquely massive mouthfuls that would choke a regular person.

Xaon's lack of surprise showed he'd also witnessed this worrying spectacle before.

But Saum, Paeth and Jeshri all gaped at Nyle. In response, he hunched defensively over his food, shoveling a fifth and sixth steamed bun into his mouth even more quickly.

"Fuck!" Jeshri's voice rang with admiration. "Fucking amazing! How many grapes can you get in your mouth in one go? My best is fifty-four."

"Eighty-eight," Nyle replied coolly.

"Told you he's a fucking python," Xaon asserted as if that were an accolade. Then he frowned down at the three buns remaining in his lap and quickly bit into one of them. "These are mine."

Saum and Paeth exchanged confused glances. Both having attended the all-girl boarding school of Ryde Academy, they'd probably imagined the male students at other schools would be pursuing greater achievements and goals than discovering the maximum volume of their mouths. Paeth glanced to Cymin with a questioning expression.

"Never had enough grapes to find out," Cymin informed her.

Xaon and Jeshri both laughed, while Nyle simply nodded as if he'd expected as much.

"I wonder how many I could get in my mouth," Saum pondered. Jeshri appeared intrigued by the prospect and suggested that if anyone had a bag of marbles, they could make an estimate.

Paeth objected on grounds of the choking hazard involved but then began to ponder aloud about other, more scientific methods of determining "absolute oral capacity,"—a phrase that elicited a sudden bark of laughter from Jeshri as well as suppressed snickers from Quin and Kimrin.

Cymin chewed over another mouthful of his bun, making it last, while listening to Paeth naïvely continue her ruminations.

Absently, he considered the long plumes of storm clouds gathering over the forested hills to the north. They were moving fast and steadily darkening from silver to leaden gray. Could that be the approaching storm that Laithondi had gone to investigate? Cymin thought he saw a flash of scarlet flicker through the gray masses and frowned as a very faint but familiar sensation tingled up his fingertips and toes.

Cymin stole a glance at the other mages to see if any of them felt the same disturbance. Saum and Paeth lay back on the grass, while Nyle and Jeshri eyed the last bun in Xaon's lap. Xaon snatched it up and finished it off with a smug expression. A little distance from them, the rest of the mages ate and chatted as well. But none of them, not even Yinni, took any notice of the distant storm. Cymin looked to Mazilane, only to see him greet Hiral. The two of them ducked into the canteen, probably to secure their own meals and repack the crate of supplies Hiral carried in his arms.

Cymin sighed and decided that he was making too much of nothing. He'd done the same thing at the Palace Complex when he'd thought he sensed another bomb, and he'd let himself nearly fall apart.

The raised hairs along his arms and the little shiver wriggling down his spine were likely just chills. After all, they'd traveled nearly 2,000 miles, leaving the balmy lowlands he was accustomed to far behind. Here in the wooded foothills, the frost-laden winds sheared down from snowy mountain peaks, and the rivers were frigid with ice melt.

Cymin frowned down at his bare tanned feet.

East Deity really ought to overcome his fear of blistered heels and start wearing the shoes that Master Tam gave him.

"You should ask Cymin." Kimrin's comment caught Cymin's attention, though it came from far away and was addressed to Ife.

Whereas Quin adored candy and cutting-edge fashion, Kimrin lived for gossip of every kind. He and Zevlyn shared that trait. But just now, he addressed Ife. "If he's a version of Laithondi, then he might have a clearer memory of what happened after Minroa murdered Vessreid for the scepter. I'm betting that he was the one who gave Xondir the keys to the Heights. Then Minroa offed him and brought the scepter to his brother in Chyre. So the real question is whether he or Xondir used it to make themselves into deities."

Ife frowned and scribbled something in her notebook.

"Of course, that's assuming Minroa wasn't a deity already," Kimrin went on. "Laithondi indulged him, and Paeth mentioned that she'd noticed signs in her most recent dreams—like Minroa's complexion growing more pale towards the end and—"

"I'm just taking down notes right now and trying to avoid too much speculation," Ife cut him short. "It's tricky to piece it together into a coherent timeline. And my novel takes precedence over untangling the events of our past lives."

"But the novel is just fiction, darling. The dreams are actual history. Our previous lives," Kimrin argued. "Don't you want to know what happened to Laithondi's remains? Did he actually chase Minroa and the scepter all the way to Chyre? Did the two of them die in a bloody lover's battle? Is that why there's no record of Minroa or Xondir or anyone else ever using the scepter? Aren't you curious?"

"Sure I am. But I'm not stupid. The Waethir obviously don't want us looking into this. Particularly not Laithondi." Ife lowered her voice and leaned closer to Kimrin. "And Laithondi is very protective of Cymin. Haven't you noticed?"

"He is?" Kimrin looked in Cymin's direction. Cymin was just as disbelieving of the claim, and it clearly showed in his face. So, when he met Kimrin's gaze, it became abundantly obvious that he'd been eavesdropping. Caught out, Cymin glanced away quickly, and the remainder of the conversation between Ife and Kimrin passed in whispers.

Cymin frowned, thinking about the scepter and that piece of a dream that he could remember. He'd wrenched it from the altar while a battle had raged through the city below him, invaders battering down walls and shattering gates that had stood for thousands of years. Cymin remembered a terrible pain in his chest and the certainty that he must keep the scepter from falling into enemy hands, even if it meant destroying the altar. He remembered a body lying prone as he wrenched the scepter free.

Could that have been Vessreid, dying at his feet? Ife, Zevlyn and Yinni, who all shared Vessreid's past life, had mentioned dreams of Minroa murdering them to steal the scepter.

So why were his own dreams haunted by the certainty of wrenching the scepter from the altar. Had he stolen it? Would Laithondi have done such a thing? Or did the hazy memories haunting Cymin's dreams belong to someone else entirely?

Cymin was gripped with a certainty that he truly did not want to learn the answer to those questions. Bailon and Laithondi were right; the past was better left alone.

With a growing uneasiness, he finished off his bun. To his right, Xaon leaned back on his elbows, looking drowsy while Nyle bowed his head to hide his sly expression as he sketched Xaon's profile. Neither of them seemed to suffer from the ambivalence that Cymin did. A few feet away, Jeshri and Saum also lounged, appearing at peace with themselves and their past identities.

"I dreamed of you last night." Paeth looked up at him from the grass with her long hair strewn out around her pretty face like glossy ribbons. She wore a slight but expectant smile.

"Me? As in, Tuteli Cymin?" Cymin felt strange having to ask, but he wanted to be certain. "Or do you mean—"

"Not Laithondi." Paeth frowned. "But the dream was from our past, so he couldn't have been you, either, obviously. But . . . he looked so much like you, and his voice, too. It's just so strange."

"Maybe the dream-memories aren't quite complete? You couldn't recall what the person actually looked like, so your imagination just filled in a familiar face, like mine," Cymin suggested. "Dreams can still be strange. Even when they're memories."

Cymin himself had once dreamed of a Lux Temple where the entire tuteli populace were just Master Tam's stray cats with their heads shaved.

"True. But I first dreamed of *him* a long time before you and I ever met. That's why I was so shocked the first time Yinni introduced us." Paeth stared at him meaningfully, then sighed and closed her eyes. "When I was still little, I dreamed of *him* all the time. Ovelah almost never did. I thought that meant there was something special. Maybe a portent of my future. But now that I know that everything in my dreams happened 200 years ago, it just seems . . . I don't know. Sort of ridiculous."

Cymin considered his own worry about who he might have been—if he'd actually been anyone—and what he might have done as that other person. Did it actually matter?

Here and now, he was Cymin. He hadn't killed anyone, stolen the scepter or betrayed his friends' trust—not yet, at least—and he didn't intend to.

Cymin smiled at Paeth as she opened her eyes.

"Thank you," Cymin told her.

"You're welcome," Paeth responded automatically, then a pink flush spread across her cheeks. "What for, though?"

"Just being yourself and reminding me of who I am," Cymin replied. "I'm glad that we're the people we are now."

"Oh." Paeth smiled back at him.

Cymin relaxed and gazed up at the yellow flowers in the surrounding sassafras trees. The individual blossoms were small and unassuming. However, the waves of perfume wafting from them was so potent and rich that Cymin's mind filled with vivid flashes of gold flames and scarlet lightning. He closed his eyes, imagining the complex arrays of spells that would release such a fragrant spell residue.

Something fast, powerful and blazing, like Xaon's phoenix wae. But far more immense—vast enough to sweep over an entire forest. The luminous outlines of sigils began to appear before him. Something like the faintest melody sounded from far away as Cymin's consciousness skimmed along the edge of a dream.

"Do you believe in love at first sight?" Paeth's voice broke into Cymin's drifting thoughts.

His eyes flashed open and took in Paeth's curious expression. But his mind had been so far away that it took him a while to even register her question. Then he immediately thought of that sly, inviting portrait of Minroa Haeyi, and then, absurdly, he recalled the first time he'd seen Laithondi. He wasn't in love with either of them, so he didn't know why they came to mind.

"Absolutely," Saum spoke up, though her gaze focused on the sky overhead. "I can't tell you how many times I've fallen in love at first sight. That actor who played the revolutionary poet in *Great Freedom*. Oh, I dreamed about him for weeks afterwards."

"I'm not certain that's love," Nyle remarked, "so much as infatuation."

"Same thing," Jeshri responded. "I'm with Saum on this."

The two of them bumped fists.

Paeth's delicate expression turned to exasperation.

"Ife," Paeth called out. "When you write me into your novel, make sure to surround me with jokers and clowns."

Cymin laughed, though next to him Xaon appeared deep in thought.

"I wonder what he looks like now," Xaon said quietly, then he sighed and closed his eyes. "I don't know if it would even matter . . . if I could just find him again."

Nyle glared at Xaon's melancholy face. Cymin wasn't certain which of them he agreed with more. Those past memories were riveting and undeniably powerful, but they also arose from a long-lost age. Clinging to them would be like reviving the misdeeds of the ancient dead.

He picked up his very last steamed bun—the one Xaon had given him—and bit into it. The delightful flavors of peppersnake and mushrooms filled his mouth. Cymin finished it off quickly despite his desire to make it last, then rose to fetch a pot of tea to share.

As he stood, a shiver went up his back along with the ache of stiff muscles and new bruises. He hadn't realized how hard he'd struck that tree earlier. His robe probably looked a mess from all the bark and burnt insects. As he started for the tray of tea kettles, the shiver running up his spine grew into a hot, humming sensation, and a pungent tangerine scent filled his lungs. For an instant, he feared he'd suffered nerve damage or gotten a concussion without noticing. Then he realized the strange sensations were all flooding him from an outside source.

Cymin spun and saw that dark storm clouds had enveloped the northern skyline, and now they heaved over mountaintops and forest like a surging flood.

Those faint sparks of red light he'd noted earlier had grown larger now. They flickered down like spidery legs of lighting, grasping entire hillsides and engulfing them in flames. A gust of wind briefly broke the clouds apart. Cymin glimpsed countless miles of forest engulfed in radiant gold fires, and he realized that the fast-approaching clouds weren't black with rain but smoke.

And this wasn't a natural wildfire blazing towards them.

It was a gigantic array of fire spells—one he'd thought he was merely imagining when he'd breathed in its spell residues along with the perfume of the sassafras trees. Exactly as he'd pictured them, the spell's gold flames and scarlet lightning moved fast with a blazing drive that was as vibrant as Xaon's phoenix wae. It even shared the same sort of buzzing texture and citrus scent. But this spell was far more immense—and destructive. Very much like the Piiroc bomb that had ignited beneath him the week before.

Same scent, same buzz, same . . . everything.

Cymin's entire body stiffened with horror as he made the connection. This spell and the bomb didn't merely resemble each other. They were one and the same thing, like two blossoms growing from a single tree. It was just that Cymin had stopped the bomb before it could fully manifest, clipping it in the bud.

What he stared out at now was the complete fire spell the Piiroc bomb would have become if it had bloomed into its full glory, powerful as a deity and ravenous as a demon.

Intent upon hunting, its lightning tongues flickered across the hillsides. Thousands of long fingers of flames groped through trees, feeling their way along the narrow line of train tracks leading towards the station.

"Everyone!" Cymin pointed to the black clouds "We need to—"

"Everyone up! Now!" Vessreid's shout drowned out Cymin's words. Cymin spun towards the train station and Vessreid.

He, Eirjiri and Arnaith sprinted for the park clearing. Hiral hurried behind them with two pharmacy crates gripped under one arm and a fearful expression on his face.

"All of you come!" Arnaith called to the student mages. "We're changing trains and leaving."

"But we just—" Zevlyn began to protest, then she took in the black clouds climbing into the sky and the pillars of red lightning groping and searching through the hills. Trees and boulders ignited as scarlet lightning tore them open. Flames and cinders lay in their wake.

"Now!" Vessreid roared. Urgency stripped all traces of patience and gentleness from his demeanor.

"Grab what you can carry from the old train and follow us to the new train!" Eirjiri shouted as she bounded past. "Quick, quick, quick!"

Their meals, tea and conversations were forgotten. All of them raced after the Waethir, though Yinni dropped back to carry one of Hiral's crates, and Cymin sprinted alongside them.

"Where's Mazilane?" Cymin shouted to Hiral.

"He's coming," Hiral assured him. "Don't wait for him. Come on!"

"I'm right behind you," Cymin called back, but he only ran a few more steps before again pausing to search for Bailon and Laithondi. His hand sought his sword hilt as he scanned the train yard and station platform.

This morning, Yuelaith had easily scattered Xaon's guardian phoenix—and the phoenix definitely shared characteristics with the Piiroc bomb and this huge spell. Yuelaith might also be able to counter the fiery array coming after them. Laithondi could definitely use it now. Cymin cursed himself for hanging onto the weapon this morning when Laithondi had clearly wanted him to return it.

Where were Laithondi and Bailon? A terrible fear clenched Cymin's chest as he watched dark clouds engulf the distant communications tower.

He had to get to them.

A hand gripped his shoulder from behind, turning him back towards the train yard. Cymin spun, half-expecting Laithondi, only to see Mazilane scowl at him.

The rising storm wind whipped through his long blue coat and set his dark hair swirling around his face. Compared to how uneasy he'd been this morning when their surroundings had seemed peaceful, Mazilane now appeared bright-eyed and lively—almost in his element. He gazed at the smoldering sky like a prizefighter at last facing a worthy challenger, and Cymin wondered suddenly if he'd been anticipating all these flames and chaos all morning. His gaze dropped to Cymin, and the edge of eagerness drained from his face.

"What are you standing around for? Get to cover!" Mazilane snapped at him.

"But Laithondi and Bailon—"

"There's no point in waiting for them." Mazilane tightened his grip on Cymin's arm as he pulled him across the gravel toward the tracks and their train car.

"We can't leave them," Cymin protested.

In response, Mazilane lifted his free arm, showing Cymin his camera tether. Wisps of black smoke floated past the scene displayed in the glass face. Two pale figures leapt and twirled as if weightless in the black clouds. Bailon soared, and winds all around her hurled back the smoke and pushed forest fires down into the desolate charred soil to die out.

Laithondi dived into the scarlet lightning bolts, blocking them from striking the ground with his own body. Flames engulfed him as he ripped the fiery spells apart with his hands. Steam rose off his clothes, and broken sigils fell all around him. His entire body smoldered as he hurled into one torrent of flames after another.

Mazilane said, "We're not leaving them. They're fighting so we can escape. So escape, damn it!"

Cymin looked up to the distant clouds. For the first time, he picked out two specks of pale light shining against the walls of black smoke like tiny stars. Then the clouds engulfed them completely, and Mazilane yanked Cymin to the train car.

CHAPTER 20

Chaos reigned inside the train as the other mages scrambled to snatch up what they could of their belongings. Cymin edged around them, attempting to make it to his travel pack. He ducked as Ife and Zevlyn cast aside a flurry of blouses and cotton slacks. They frantically cleared space in their suitcases for the trunk-loads of books they'd originally brought. He couldn't believe Ife and Zevlyn were so intent on saving books at a time like this.

You won't be able to read any of them if you burn to death, you know. Cymin shook his head, then ducked as a boot winged past his face.

Ife didn't look up as she tossed aside her other boot and then threw away her heavy coat. Cymin realized that she was searching frantically through a bulky trunk.

"Forget it," Zevlyn urged her. "Let's just go."

"It's the only thing my mom left me," Ife replied without lifting her head from the trunk. "You go ahead. I'll catch up, I promise."

Zevlyn looked uncertain but then shouldered her book bag and gripped her suitcase. She edged into the aisle, passed Cymin and then rushed away.

Ife continued to search until she at last found the water stained, moldering volume and hurriedly secured it in her book bag. Then she too bolted for the exit.

A few feet away, Jeshri pulled an extra coat over the one he already wore, abandoned his suitcase altogether and then strapped his four massive weapon cases across his chest and back. Between those and Jo's sheath, which hung from his belt, Jeshri took on the appearance of a human windmill. He scooted sideways down the aisle like a tugboat.

"Fuck, it's tight in here. Sorry." He shouldered into Cymin and bumped into Xaon. Mazilane sidestepped him but was still nearly knocked in the head by the corner of a weapon case.

"Right behind you. Excuse me! Coming through." Saum carried her hammer across her back and a bulging suitcase with a dozen glossy magazines piled atop it in her arms. She ducked and dodged along in Jeshri's wake.

Quin hopped over the backs of the seats and zipped across tabletops, passing them all, though not before pressing three vibrantly painted shoeboxes to Xaon's chest as if she were handing her children to a firefighter. Then she turned and dashed back to gather more shoeboxes as well as her collection of ancillary fans and three tiny gilded suitcases. At last, she spun around and raced for the exit. Cymin made way for her and ended up with one of her gold valises slung over his arm.

"Thank you," Quin called back to him as she shot out of the train car.

Conditioned to defer to others, it took Cymin some time to reach the row of seats he'd occupied earlier. But at last, he snatched up his travel pack and swung it onto his back. It felt heavier than he'd expected and weirdly stiff—or maybe his back was just tender from when he'd slammed into a tree. Now wasn't the time to open it up and have a rummage through, in any case.

However, when he turned to leave, he found two of Kimrin's bright orange hatboxes pressed into his arms.

"Thank you so much for your assistance, Tuteli Cymin!" Kimrin shouted as he dodged between Xaon, Mazilane and Nyle, then disappeared after Quin.

Really?

Cymin was sorely tempted to toss the hats and valise aside, only he wasn't completely certain there wasn't something actually important in them. He stole a glance to Xaon, who seemed to consider Quin's shoeboxes in much the same manner.

"If you two strong youths wouldn't mind, there's a player piano in the back that I rather like the look of. How about we trot over and pick that up as well?" Mazilane smiled as he swung his own travel pack over his shoulder. He gripped a machine case in his other hand.

"This is no time for jests. Pack up and go." Vessreid stood at the door of the passenger coach. He frowned when Xaon stilled beside his belongings, but he said nothing more. Instead, Vessreid turned his attention to the view outside the gangway. Gray smoke wafted over him, and the incense-like smell of blazing sassafras trees pervaded the air.

Cymin stole a quick glance at the scene playing in Mazilane's tether, but all he could distinguish were rolling masses of flames and smoke.

"What the fuck is that spell fire? Why is it after us?" Xaon muttered as he attempted to grasp his own luggage while balancing Quin's shoe boxes in his arms. He seemed to be searching for something. Cymin scowled and hoped he found it quickly, since he currently blocked the aisle.

"It's an extensive array of spells," Nyle answered. "The shapes of the sigils look more Piiroc than Chyrenese. They're complex and archaic enough to have come from the early days of mage-kings. But something about it feels very . . . familiar to me. I think we've encountered part of it before."

Nyle shifted his patched travel pack on his back, then he glanced to Cymin. "You recognized it too, didn't you?"

"I—" Cymin's throat caught on the smoky air, and for an instant, all he sensed were agonized memories of his flesh burning as the Piiroc bomb seared through his body. Cold sweat drenched his back and his heart raced.

No! Calm down, East Deity! That's not happening again. You're going to escape this time. You're going to be fine.

Cymin coughed to cover his moment of panic. He wiped his clammy palms against Kimrin's hatboxes, then shifted them, freeing his right hand to grip Yuelaith's hilt. He stroked the sigil Min against his sword hilt. His anxiety receded enough for him to speak.

"Actually, the spell most like it that I've encountered recently was Xaon's sword charm." Cymin focused on following Nyle's lead and concentrating on the structures of the spells attacking them rather than the horror of the attack itself. "His family's guardian wae—"

"Lazhu," Xaon supplied the wae's name without looking up. "I can't imagine her doing anything like this. She's too sleepy, for one thing, but also . . . not horrible."

"I don't mean it's her, exactly," Cymin clarified. "But an array of spells that's complex and channels fei'lux in the same way she does. It could be another guardian array. Another genuine wae that was roused somehow."

"Or a corrupted guardian array—a sharwae?" Nyle absently drew the two sigils in the air with his finger: *Shar* for corruption and *Wae* for guardian. "But those are things from storybooks."

"So are Wraiths and mages inheriting ancient past lives," Cymin stated. "But here we are."

Nyle frowned, and Cymin wasn't certain if that was in response to his comment or Xaon's protracted survey of his belongings.

Cymin released his sword hilt. Then he picked up a small suitcase for Xaon—hoping that would speed him up and clear the way out of the aisle. If he hadn't been raised as a tuteli, he might have shoved Xaon aside, but as it was, his training, dignity and humility didn't allow for it. But the temptation grew along with the feeling of a smoky heat wrapping around him. He startled as timbers outside the train splintered apart in flames with thunderous bangs.

Nyle studied the scene outside the portal window. His expression remained aloof, but Cymin could see his eyes widening in fear.

"I remember reading somewhere that the spells in a wae can only be corrupted by their true masters. Though I'd guess that an outsider could circumvent their security barriers if they were clever enough . . . " Nyle shifted his attention back to Xaon, and his cool expression broke into outright anger. "Why are you still holding onto these damn things?" He grabbed Quin's shoe boxes from Xaon and flung the boxes aside, sending satin slippers festooned with ribbons flying. "Can we go now?"

"I just need one thing," Xaon said.

Cymin tried to smile at him but only managed a grimace. Sweat beaded his arms, and Kimrin's large hatboxes kept wobbling and tipping over. Or maybe Cymin's hands were shaking too much to keep them still. Cymin cleared his throat.

The smoke seeping into the train car seemed thicker and warmer than ever. Cymin's throat and nose began to burn. His chest ached, and he really wanted out of the train car. But Xaon was still blocking his way, still searching for something among his belongings.

Nyle narrowed his gaze at the hatboxes in Cymin's arms. He snatched them away and hurled them over his shoulder into the empty seat across the aisle. Then he threw Quin's valise away as well.

"If Kimrin complains, just tell him that I did it. He already dislikes me," Nyle said.

Fine by me, but can we just get out of here?

Cymin gritted his teeth and forced himself to remain composed. He tried to draw in a slow, calming breath, only to choke on the smoky air.

"Go already, you ass!" Nyle shoved Xaon's shoulder hard. "You're blocking Cymin's way out!"

"Oh, fuck! Sorry, Cy—ah, here it is!" Xaon, at last, plucked a silver-framed postcard from a pouch in his open suitcase, then stepped aside to allow Cymin and Mazilane to pass by. Cymin raced for the door with Mazilane on his heels. Behind them, Nyle hauled Xaon along.

"I had to find his picture," Xaon protested to Nyle.

Cymin stole a glance back and realized that the framed color postcard Xaon clutched depicted the same provocative portrait of Minroa Haeyi that graced the cover of Cymin's book.

"Truly a treasure worth risking your life for," Nyle said. "No wonder Ife is writing you into her novel as a love-sick obsessive."

"Everyone out now!" Vessreid hefted a suitcase Zevlyn had entrusted to him. The leather groaned and the latches squealed, but the luggage held together. Then, as a group, they all sprinted across the smoky train yard.

Quin, Kimrin and Eirjiri arrived first, bounding into the gray train car that waited for them on a narrow track fifty feet across the train yard. Saum and Jeshri followed at some distance, hunched under the weight of their belongings. Yinni and Hiral ran right behind them. One of Saum's magazines caught the wind and took flight, and Jeshri turned to chase it, but Saum bumped him back.

"Last summer's issue. Let it go." Saum glanced to the northern sky, and her expression turned horrified. "Let's just get out of here."

As the group of them boarded the new passenger coach, Arnaith intercepted two fearful-looking engineers on their way to drive the locomotive.

"Do not endanger yourselves, mortals," Arnaith told them. "Shelter behind your village walls with your loved ones. We will lead the sharwae into the mountains and dispatch it far from you."

Cymin paused for just an instant. So the Waethir recognized that they were being attacked by a sharwae. He and Nyle had been right.

But have the Waethir known since the bombing, or have they only realized that it was a sharwae today?

Arnaith beckoned, and Paeth and Ovelah pelted to her side, both carrying their complex ancillary compasses. Cymin thought the one in Ovelah's arms looked particularly intricate. Already, it lit with blue- and green-hued sigils, which turned like constellations and cast cool colors over her and across Arnaith's silvery hair and clothes.

"We can drive the engine! We covered it in our mechanics classes!" Paeth assured the engineers. Ovelah nodded.

Just glimpsing the engineers' faces, Cymin could tell that the two old men were torn between the desire to escape and hesitance to abandon their train to the care of two random young women and their foreign companion.

Arnaith didn't wait for their response. She bounded into the air as if she were weightless and landed lightly on the roof of the train engine. With a sweep of her arms, she brought hundreds of blue sigils to life and then slammed them down into the train's steel body. Plumes of steam erupted from the smokestack, forming haloes around her. Rainbows danced through the water vapor as Arnaith herself threw off beams of light and shaped the steam into interlocking sigils. With a wave of her right hand, she swathed the train in misty blue spells. With her left hand, she beckoned Paeth and Ovelah.

"This machine will carry you as its masters now," Arnaith announced.

"We'll take good care of it, don't worry," Paeth assured the engineers.

The men briefly stood, looking stunned, but then a wave of pungent sassafras smoke rolled over them. To Cymin's relief, they both turned and made their escape while Paeth and Ovelah raced to climb inside the train engine's cab. Arnaith remained perched atop the engine near the steam dome, like a figurehead at the prow of a ship.

Then the red glow suffusing the hazy skyline flared, and a scorching wind roared over the train yard. The gravel beneath Cymin's bare feet flared like embers reigniting in a hearth. He hopped from foot to foot and struggled to suppress his memories of a raging explosion unfurling inside him. Another gust of wind engulfed him in a wall of hot smoke, obscuring the entire train yard. He couldn't imagine what Bailon and Laithondi must be enduring as they battled the fiery spell up close. Cymin covered his mouth and nose with his hand. Tears filled his irritated eyes as he tried to see through the murky air stinging them.

He had to get out of here, but he couldn't see a thing. And it was growing more and more difficult to breathe.

Before panic could seize him, Cymin remembered how Yinni had manipulated the wind earlier during practice. He flexed his left hand and caught a thin ribbon of fei'lux. Then he sent it sweeping through the air around him. At the same moment, he became aware of other breezes washing through the smoke. Mazilane's camera, Soir, swooped past him, clearing the air with its long wings.

Cymin's surroundings became startlingly clear.

He looked back over his shoulder and realized that the entire park where they'd eaten was crawling with weird fires. Masses of red flame encircled the tree Cymin had leaned against, like searing hands clutching at the bark.

Or, Cymin thought, watching the flames split into more and more legs and creep down the trunk, they were like giant spiders, skittering through the woods and leaping through the trees. Each time a spider's burning limb touched a spot Cymin and the other mages had occupied, it lit up with the golden coiled sigil of *Uuhir*—hunt—and a dozen more fiery arachnids burst from it like embers. Those sprouted legs and grew large as they consumed their surroundings, and then they raced onward, ravenously searching. In the space of a single breath, the one blazing spell proliferated into hundreds.

Flames engulfed the entire rest area and began to burn through the canteen.

Cymin's heart hammered in horror at the thought of what those things would do to him if they found him. There were already hundreds of them.

With a surge of energy, Cymin bounded onto the new train car's gangway. As he passed through the shield that Arnaith had cast over the train, a veil of tiny blue sigils swam before his eyes, and he felt a hum quiver across his exposed skin. Then he landed on the gangway and relieving, cool, clean air washed over him.

Cymin pulled the door to the passenger coach open. The interior was austere and a little grimy. A narrow aisle divided the twenty-four wooden bench seats into two rows. The stained benches looked wide enough to accommodate three people, though their straight backs and tight confines didn't offer much in the way of comfort or legroom. Cymin guessed the coach normally delivered new troops to distant patrol stations. Here and there, initials had been scratched into the metal faces of the reinforced portal windows. A faded blue NS seal decorated the far wall, and all around it burnished patches of metal revealed where graffiti had been sanded away.

Still, at this moment, the place provided welcome refuge.

From within, Eirjiri offered him a relieved smile. Smoke streaked her gray clothes, but her skin and golden hair remained untouched. She beckoned him in, but he stepped back. Out of habit, he moved aside and held the door, making way for anyone else behind him. Only after Mazilane leapt onboard with his camera did Cymin enter and haul the heavy door closed.

He leaned back against the wall of the train. His sweat-soaked robe clung to his back like a damp rag, and tremors shuddered through his thighs.

"That's everyone," Eirjiri announced.

"I'll inform Arnaith," Vessreid replied. Like Eirjiri, his pale skin and silver braids remained free of soot and ash, while the hems and cuffs of his clothes appeared dark from smoke. He raised his hand and flicked his first two fingers across his thumb. A green sigil flared up from his long fingers and flashed through the ceiling of the passenger coach.

Instantly, the train shot forward like a loosed arrow. Its momentum threw Cymin back. He staggered and caught his balance, gripping the bench seats on either side of him. The floor of the train shook, and a sharp screech arose from the train wheels as they ground against the tracks. Then the train tore past the tight turn in the track and quieted as it sped ahead.

The raging fires outside the portal windows gave way to hillsides of deep green forest.

Cymin straightened.

"Cy, come sit with us," Xaon called from a bench in the middle of the train. He leaned against a portal window and waved Cymin forward.

Smoke grayed strands of his red hair and darkened the fine creases in his face, making him seem to have suddenly aged a decade or more. But his smile was still broad and boyish.

Nyle already occupied the space beside Xaon. To Cymin's surprise, he didn't protest, but instead shifted closer to Xaon, making room on the end of the bench for Cymin.

Yinni also looked up at the call of Cymin's name. They exchanged brief smiles, both reassured that the other was safe, then Yinni returned her attention to helping Hiral secure his camera cases and supplies.

Cymin hurried ahead to the bench Nyle and Xaon shared. Xaon shifted, resettling his ancillary cutlass, which Nyle nudged back with his foot. Nyle had clearly already cleaned the smoke and soot from his own face, but now he shoved a gray kerchief into Xaon's hand.

"Wipe your face," Nyle said. Then, glancing to Cymin, he remarked, "You kept surprisingly clean."

"Soir—Mazilane's camera—cleared an opening through the smoke. I kept close to it." Cymin dropped down next to Nyle, then shifted his legs into the aisle, so as not to crowd the other two too much. He wasn't certain why they wanted him taking up space on their bench, but somehow solidarity felt more important to him than legroom.

The other Five Schools' mages also kept close together, sitting in pairs. Jeshri and Saum occupied the bench just behind him, while Yinni and Hiral seated themselves three rows back across the aisle. Ife and Zevlyn had settled themselves and their loads of books across the aisle from Yinni.

Only Mazilane claimed a bench for himself alone.

Two rows ahead, Kimrin and Quin both turned back. They studied Cymin and then Xaon with concerned countenances. Cymin smiled at them. They didn't return his relieved expression. Then it occurred to him why. He'd completely forgotten about the luggage they'd foisted onto him and Xaon. Cymin frowned down at his travel pack and wondered how best to break the news about their now-abandoned hats and shoes.

Nyle beat him to it.

"The hats were last year's style. And the slippers made your feet look like mops." Nyle's tone was offhanded, but the way he lifted his hand and pretended to study his grand champion's ring clearly was not. Only two weeks ago, he'd defeated both Kimrin and Quin in battle, and the gold ring was a clear reminder of that fact. Then Nyle offered the two of them a faint smile. "I did you both the kindness of freeing you of them. No need to thank me."

"Thank you?" Kimrin scowled at Nyle. The soot speckling his velvet coat and the gold feathers in his hair made him look all the more like an affronted owl.

"It was my pleasure; you're welcome. They were ugly and out of date. One or the other would have been bearable, but both makes it seem like you've given up on yourself," Nyle stated. "Not at all the impression you want to make when we disembark in Yanyeo, I think."

Kimrin furrowed his brows but said nothing more. Quin slapped the back of her seat. Her violet dress shuddered and billowed around her. Even the gold ribbons coiled in her dark ringlets seemed to tremble with emotion.

"We're not going to forget about this, Nyle. You owe us both at least *five* blue bills. And an apology." Quin glared at Nyle, then crossed her arms over her thin chest.

Nyle gazed back at her with cool disdain. Quin turned back to Kimrin.

"They didn't give me mop-feet," Quin muttered. Kimrin patted her hand.

"They were splendid," he told her. "I'll buy you three more pairs when we get home to Yanyeo."

Xaon leaned over to Nyle and asked in a whisper, "Would it kill you to apologize? Or at least make some excuse?"

"Yes, because I'm not sorry, and I owe them nothing." Nyle flipped one of his long black braids over his shoulder. "Their style is hideous. And anyway, you and Cymin aren't their pack animals."

Hearing that from Nyle, Cymin felt absurdly touched. Xaon appeared somewhat moved as well.

"Oh . . . well, thanks for looking out for us, then." Xaon bumped Nyle's shoulder with his own. It was the same gesture he shared with Jeshri and Cymin.

A very slight but undeniably smug smile curled the corners of Nyle's lips. He leaned back in his seat with his hands neatly folded, while Xaon flopped beside him. Cymin wanted to share their relief and rest within the spell array that Arnaith created around them.

However, an anxiety continued to gnaw at him. Laithondi and Bailon were still out there, battling those ravenous conflagrations. Unconsciously, he gripped the hilt of Laithondi's sword. A comforting hum rumbled against his palm, and faint gold sigils arose to ring Cymin's fingers. Yuelaith was so responsive, so reassuring, Cymin couldn't help but think that Laithondi would miss the sword in battle.

Worse, he might need the ice spells inside the sword to defeat the fiery sharwae pursuing them. Cymin peered past Xaon to the forest outside the portal. Was there a way to return Yuelaith to Laithondi that didn't involve walking into a forest fire?

Glancing between Vessreid and Eirjiri, he noticed tension in their faces as they both paced the aisle, staring out the portal windows.

“When will Laithondi and Bailon join us?” Cymin asked.

“They'll rejoin us once we've drawn the sharwae attack far from the mortals' village. Then we'll attempt to pin it down and break the sigils at its heart,” Vessreid replied.

“The summit of the next hill should be far enough.” Eirjiri nodded and started to offer Cymin a reassuring smile, but her expression turned worried as her gaze dropped to his hand and the sword hanging from Cymin's belt.

“You still have Yuelaith!” Eirjiri exclaimed, staring down at the gold sigils dancing up from the hilt of the sheathed sword. Xaon and Nyle both stared at it as well. As did everyone else aboard the train. Cymin was too concerned for Laithondi and Bailon to feel self-conscious.

“Yes. I was worried about that as well.” Cymin rose to his feet. “Do you think Laithondi needs it? Is there a way we can get it to him? I read once about a spell that—”

“If he left it with Cymin, then he knew he could handle the sharwae without it.” Vessreid didn't respond to Cymin's question but instead addressed Eirjiri. She, however, appeared far from reassured. She eyed Cymin closely.

“Did he say anything to you before he left today? Any instructions?” Eirjiri asked.

“Nothing out of the ordinary.” Cymin struggled to recall anything notable that Laithondi had mentioned before he strolled away with the other Waethir. Their discussion of wandering spirits and ember wing butterflies didn't seem relevant to anything. “He told me to let my instincts guide me and that the memories are within me. But that's what—”

Eirjiri gripped his arm so hard that Cymin cut himself off.

“And *did* Yuelaith wake a memory within you?” Eirjiri's normally lighthearted demeanor turned intent. Her pale gold eyes seemed to blaze as she stared into his face.

“Yes.” Cymin nodded, remembering the sudden inspiration that had blossomed through him in response to the fiery guardian that had escaped Xaon's sword charm. “An array of freezing blades that dispelled Xaon's phoenix wae.”

Eirjiri glanced to Xaon, and he held up the small brassy charm. Studying it closely, Cymin noted that the ancient phoenix's design looked distinctly Piiroc and also a little sulky. He was almost certain that one of its tiny eyes briefly cracked open to pin him with a glare before squeezing closed again.

“Lazhu is too old to be much more than a lucky charm. She mostly sleeps,” Xaon said. “But this morning, she manifested by mistake when that freak surge of fei'lux struck us."

"Not entirely by mistake, I don't think." Eirjiri tucked a loose lock of gold hair back behind her ear as she continued to study the brass charm. "Someone wanted to rouse and corrupt a guardian array from the old times. Yours woke, along with the one hunting us now. They likely share a common essence."

"I thought that they might be related to each other." Cymin felt urgency rising within him the more he considered the connections. "The sharwae that's hunting us unfurled in the same way as Xaon's phoenix. And . . . actually, it was the same for the explosion at the Spring Exhibition too. I think they must share a core fire spell design—one that Yuelaith can counter—and that's why I thought Laithondi might need his sword to dispel it."

"You sensed all that from just holding the sword." Eirjiri looked from Cymin to Vessreid. "I told you. He *has* to be one of us."

Cymin glimpsed Saum and Jeshri both grinning at him. Farther back, Ife and Zevlyn looked more concerned than happy about Eirjiri's pronouncement.

"He's not. Laith said as much himself," Vessreid responded firmly and with an expression that made Cymin suspect that this was far from the first time they'd had this argument. "Cymin is an extremely gifted tuteli mage, but he is not a deity."

"Then how did he recognize royal Piiroc guardians or remember Yuelaith's arrays to dispel them?" Eirjiri demanded.

Vessreid scowled but didn't have an immediate response.

Eirjiri shifted her attention back to Cymin as if seizing on a prize. "This is important, Cymin. Early on, when Laithondi showed you an object from the past, did you recognize it?"

"I . . . I did, but not really." Cymin went on quickly. "He showed me a celestial pearl with a seam of gold running along one side like a bolt of lightning. I remembered it from somewhere and guessed how to open it. But that was just luck. I'd seen it in some old book, I think. I only recalled it at all because I'd really liked the picture—"

"Hold up! That's the celestial pearl I forged for Minroa Haeyi," Xaon murmured. "I mean, when we were Laithondi. We made it as a lover's gift for Minroa Haeyi. You remember?" he asked Nyle.

"Yes." Nyle appeared pained by the recollection. Or perhaps disgusted. "He could be reckless, and the Waethir were often hard on him. He was often injured. The pearl secreted a balm to soothe his injuries and nurture fei'thallus."

"So you did pass the test." Eirjiri squeezed Cymin's arm again but much more gently this time. "You *are* one of us, after all."

"No, I don't think I did pass, though. I just remembered a picture and an obscure poem and guessed," Cymin protested. "After that, Laithondi gave me the celestial pearl as a consolation."

"He *gave* it to you?" Vessreid demanded suddenly. His eyes narrowed. "He gave it to *you*!"

His normally gentle countenance twisted with alarm. Cymin recalled Vessreid flashing that same furious expression and demanding to know why he'd written the sigil Min in the sky. It had seemed as if Vessreid suspected him of some connection to Minroa Haeyi then. Now, his gaze grew more and more accusatory the longer he considered Cymin. In seconds, it bordered on threatening. Fei'lux surged around him, and he took a step towards Cymin.

Yinni shot up from her seat, but Hiral reached out and caught her hand, his expression worried. Ife and Zevlyn, too, appeared alarmed.

Cymin met Vessreid's enraged stare.

What is wrong with you? Do you realize how paranoid and crazed you're acting right now?

Then he remembered Kimrin and Ife discussing the fact that Minroa Haeyi had murdered Vessreid in their past lives. Hissing green sigils flickered between Vessreid's hands. The air between his fingers grew sour and seething.

Out of the corner of his eye, Cymin noticed Mazilane rise and pull his cigarette case out of his coat pocket. But it was Nyle, directly beside Cymin, who spoke out.

"No!" Nyle objected. "He didn't gift the pearl to Cymin. Laithondi just left it with him because Cymin was badly injured at the time. He told us so the night before we departed. You remember, don't you?" He nudged Xaon.

"Ah . . . yes." Xaon nodded. "Yes, that's what he said."

Cymin suspected Nyle was lying—Xaon certainly was; that was obvious from his bewildered expression. But Cymin was grateful for their defense of him.

Vessreid eyed the two of them with disdain.

To Cymin's surprise, Nyle straightened in his seat and stared directly back at Vessreid as if challenging him. Nyle even picked up one of his ancillary brushes without looking away from Vessreid. Xaon appeared distinctly nervous but also curled his hand around the hilt of his cutlass.

The train shook and screeched as it swung around another sharp curve, wheels grinding against the rails. They all rocked and tottered as it surged up a steep incline. Outside the portal windows, hundreds of fiery arachnids—some the size of greyhounds—suddenly bounded up, racing alongside them. Flames licked the windows, burning and prying at the portal seals. But somehow the view outside seemed less dangerous to Cymin than the tension playing through Vessreid's flexed hands right now.

From between Vessreid's fingers, half-formed sigils whispered murder.

"What's so important about this celestial pearl? I don't understand," Saum interjected. "What does it have to do with Cymin using Laithondi's sword?"

"It's because Minroa stole the Fei'suul Scepter," Kimrin responded. "There's a chance that he used it to preserve his memories amongst those of the true deities. So, he could have been reborn with them—with us—as well."

"And if that's the case, then he could be among us right now," Quin chirped, and she looked a little excited by the prospect.

Cymin glared at her, and Quin shrugged.

"I'm not accusing you, Cy," Quin stated. She narrowed her gaze at Nyle. "As I recall, Minroa was much more arrogant and insolent than you are. But there is someone—"

"Nyle would be too obvious, Quinny. Minroa would hide his character better than that," Kimrin broke in, and he pointed to Cymin. "My money is on Cymin. I mean, look at him. That skilled, handsome and humble? No, that's a little too good to be true. And I know for a fact that his family backgroun—"

"This isn't a joke," Zevlyn cut him off. She looked almost as alarmed as Vessreid, but her expression was more fearful than furious. "Minroa Haeyi was an abomination. He cannot be allowed to live again. Especially not as a Waethir."

Beside her, Ife also appeared uneasy but far more skeptical. She glanced from Nyle to Xaon and Cymin before turning her attention to where Yinni still stood with Hiral gripping her hand.

"But why are half of you looking daggers at Cymin suddenly?" Saum objected. "*He* hasn't done anything wrong. Even if he carries some of Minroa Haeyi's memories from the past—not saying that he does—but that doesn't mean he *is* Minroa, does it? I'm not Eirjiri. We share a distant past and some memories, but I'm my own person. I've lived my own life and made all kinds of different choices."

"Fuck, that's right!" Jeshri agreed. "Saum and I have a bunch of Eirjiri's memories, but we're not the same person. I mean, we do have a lot in common, but we're clearly different people. For one thing, she's like a foot shorter than me, and has bigger . . . " He trailed off, cupping his hands over his chest.

"Brain," Ife muttered. "She has a much more robust brain than you."

"I don't remember much about the scepter," Saum picked up as if Jeshri and Ife hadn't spoken. She looked to Eirjiri. "But becoming a deity wasn't as simple as just grabbing the thing. There was much more involved, right?"

Eirjiri nodded, but her gaze never left Vessreid. Cymin was almost certain he could see faint sigils of some spell hidden between her cupped hands, glowing up through her fingernails.

"True, but remember, Minroa possessed a natural genius for magecraft." Kimrin's attention remained focused on Cymin. "He mastered spells in minutes and memorized sigils in his sleep. By the end, he could emulate and counter nearly all of our battle arrays. He'd mastered Laithondi's to perfection, and that would have included control of the scepter."

Cymin found it strange that so many of them seemed to know so very much more about Minroa Haeyi than he did, even as they accused him of being an incarnation of the man.

"Cymin is not Minroa!" Xaon snapped. "I'd know if he was."

"Would you, though?" Zevlyn asked. "Minroa was a sly liar. He fooled all of us more than once."

"He probably deceived you the most of all of us," Ife added. "Your judgment definitely can't be trusted where he's concerned."

Xaon scowled and looked to Nyle, obviously hoping he'd offer some rebuttal, but Nyle remained tensed, watching Vessreid and gripping his ancillary as if readying for battle.

For his part, Cymin had no idea how everything had gotten so appallingly out of hand. Wasn't it bad enough that they were being hunted by a massive blazing array of gigantic spiders? Did they have to go for each other's throats right now too? And why? Laithondi had merely given away a celestial pearl.

If everyone around him reacted like this to the pearl, then maybe Laithondi was sick to death of carrying it around with him. He'd probably felt relieved to unburden himself of the thing and discard a relic of his tragic romance. Certainly there was no reason for such a small confusion to cause this much strife.

"Look, I can return the pearl right now. Any of you can have it." Cymin grabbed his travel pack from the floor and started to open it.

"No. No need." Eirjiri shook her head.

It was just as well that she stopped him because Cymin was too stunned by what he glimpsed in his pack to keep digging through it.

If people were suspicious and angry over him having a celestial pearl, then he had no idea what they would do if they discovered that Laithondi had apparently stowed the bone-white Fei'suul Scepter in

Cymin's travel pack earlier today. The very same scepter that Minroa Haeyi had apparently stolen ages ago.

What are you trying to do to me here, Laithondi? Are you going to stash a bloody knife and a dead body with me next?

Cymin just managed to lift his gaze from the pack and somewhat naturally buckle the flap closed. He swung the pack up over his shoulder. As he did so, he noted that Mazilane and Hiral's cameras were both recording the scene. Mazilane opened his cigarette case and briefly met Cymin's gaze with a sardonic smile.

"Cymin is not Minroa Haeyi. Not even a phantom of him." Yinni pulled free of Hiral, and despite the shaking of the train, she strode to Vessreid's side and gently but very firmly placed her hand over his, blocking his murderous spell with her own flesh.

"He remembers things about the deities and Saigrath because I've told him stories from my memories since he was four years old," Yinni explained. "He knows about the pearl because I told him about it. I promise you, Vess. He's my brother, not your enemy. Not *our* enemy. You saw him risk his life for you and countless strangers at the Spring Exhibition. Does that sound anything like Minroa?"

Cymin wasn't sure if it was her touch or her words that reached Vessreid, but at last he released the fei'lux he'd been refining to a knife-edge between his hands. He sighed, and the snarling tension appeared to drain away, leaving him looking shaken.

Thank you, thank you, thank you, Yinni!

"Indeed . . . Minroa Haeyi would never have imperiled his life as Cymin did when we first met. He wouldn't have held the door or waited for the rest of us before ensuring his own safety." Vessreid sounded like he was reassuring himself but only just believed his own words.

"Cymin didn't know what the celestial pearl was when he accepted it. He had no way of understanding its importance," Yinni pointed out. "And what else could he have done under the circumstances? There's nothing in that—or anything else—to connect him with Minroa Haeyi at all."

"Yes. Yes, you're right," Vessreid said. "Thank you for speaking up, Yinni. I wasn't thinking clearly."

Sapped of his fury, Vessreid appeared exhausted and unnerved—as if he'd just woken to find himself in unknown surroundings. He looked at Cymin with a sad, uncertain expression. "Cymin, I—I apologize for my baseless accusation."

Cymin nodded, but he still felt truly uneasy about how quickly Vessreid had snapped to accusing him, and how fast others had been to join in. Quin jumping in to try and accuse Nyle as well was certainly not reassuring.

"Wonderful! Apology offered. Apology accepted. Everyone all friends again—hooray!" Eirjiri called out with forced glee. She stepped forward and gripped Cymin by the arm and pulled him from his seat. "Now, you come with me so we can return Laithondi's sword and get Bailon down from all that smoke. Quick, quick, quick!"

She whipped him out of the passenger coach and onto the gangway before anyone else could utter another word. Then she slammed the door closed behind them.

The train raced up a narrow track cut into the precarious edge of a forested mountainside. Swift winds buffeted them from all sides, and flurries of smoldering branches swept past. Overhead, black streams of smoke curled down from a murky red sky. Countless blazing spiders poured from the smoke. They struck Arnaith's translucent blue shield like hail hammering a windowpane. They stabbed at the small blue sigils shimmering in the shield, burning them, even as the sigils ate away at the spiders' limbs.

In the distance, a huge scarlet bolt crackled through the clouds of smoke, and the entire hill shook with the thunder that followed it. Cymin momentarily glimpsed the white lights in the sky that were Bailon and Laithondi encircled in rings of protective sigils. Behind them, a furious red sphere shone like a small sun. Then the smoke swallowed them again.

Cymin gripped the handrail of the gangway, fighting to remain calm.

"Just for future warning," Eirjiri shouted over the roar of the train engine, "avoid anything to do with Minroa Haeyi if you're anywhere near Vessreid. He's had to endure Minroa murdering him too many times. It's turned him a little—" She gave a strangely twisted grimace, as if that summed up Vessreid's feelings. Perhaps it did. "He can't be rational about Minroa."

Cymin nodded and thought that Vessreid wasn't the only one who'd responded poorly—though perhaps Zevlyn sharing many of Vessreid's memories put her in the same position as him. However, Kimrin and Quin appeared to just be spiting him and Nyle over their lost accessories.

"Bailon has a grudge against him as well," Eirjiri commented. Then she added, "Obviously, you know how Laithondi feels."

"I do?" He most certainly did not.

Eirjiri rolled her eyes. "He returned the pearl to you, so . . . "

"No, he didn't. Because I'm not—"

"Sure, sure." Eirjiri cut him off. "This is a new lifetime, and you were brought up right this time, so you won't make the same mistakes. No need to tell me, just keep doing what's right, and I'll keep supporting you both."

Cymin pressed his mouth shut on the numerous arguments he might have offered. Now was not the time.

"How do we get to Laithondi?" Cymin's fingers brushed the hilt of the sword sheathed at his hip.

Eirjiri pointed to the five iron rungs running up the side of the train car. "Climb up to the roof of this machine. You first. I'll signal Bailon and follow you."

Cymin abandoned any further conversation and leapt onto the rungs.

As he climbed, he felt the air grow hotter as the buffer of Arnaith's shield thinned. When he crawled onto the rattling rooftop of the train, he couldn't rise higher than his knees and remain protected. Even crawling along on his belly, hot winds buffeted him, and clusters of spiders rushed over the shield's transparent surface, chasing him.

Up ahead of them, he made out Arnaith's slender form. She still crouched atop the steam engine, blue sigils pouring from her like massive ocean waves. Their swells drowned and washed away swaths of fiery spiders. But seconds later, more of the blazing spells rushed over the train.

More and more of them gathered over Cymin with each passing moment. Some hurled themselves against Arnaith's shield with such force that they burst apart, spilling out steaming strings of red and gold sigils like entrails. Wisps of blue smoke rose from the shield where the exposed sigils bled out. Hordes of other spiders skittered over the remains, chewing and burning the shield directly over Cymin.

He stared up at the orb-bellies all gleaming with the gold Uuhir sigil and watched the red legs scrape as scarlet mandibles tore into the shield. He felt so horrified by how life-like and desperate the spells seemed that he had to remind himself that these were all just part of an immense array, not living creatures but some mage's creation. Not all that different from the chirping spells in the Lucky Cricket.

Except they want to burn me alive. And there are millions of them, swarming inches above my face. But otherwise, not different at all.

Eirjiri slithered up onto the roof but didn't draw nearly so many spiders to her.

"They are really attracted to you," Eirjiri shouted over the wind and engine. She grinned. "Are you wearing a special cologne?"

Cymin grimaced.

He'd barely gotten used to drawing clouds of bees, butterflies and grasshoppers when he tempered fei'lux. Laithondi had mentioned that it was a common occurrence for mages who manipulated fei'lux without spell filaments. But this was entirely revolting. If any creature had to be madly attracted to streams of fei'lux unmarked by filament technology, did it have to be huge flaming arachnids?

A particularly large spider skittered directly over Cymin's face, offering him a close view of the searing red plasma that made up the orb of its body. Small flames flicked out towards Cymin like snake tongues, tasting his presence. At the same time, the gold sigils inside it grew and divided rapidly. The spherical body and its long jointed legs steadily deformed as the sigils pushed up from it like polyps. Then a dozen of them burst from the original body, each swathed in its own orb of flames. They swarmed around Cymin like hungry spiderlings while the larger spell slammed into Arnaith's shield, splattering apart.

Cymin felt the intense heat of the exposed sigils as they burned. The spiderlings surged forth, digging and burning at the weakened shield above Cymin. The orbs of their bodies swelled with more and more sigils.

Cymin crawled nearer Eirjiri. The spiders followed him.

He reconsidered his earlier comparison to bees and butterflies, because these things blazing inches from his face merely resembled spiders, but they weren't actually arachnids of any sort; they were smaller spells belonging to a vast array—more like tiny cogs relentlessly driven by a greater machine. So their fixation on him wasn't likely to be for the same reason. No, these spells were hunting something—that was the sigil that had been placed at the center of their beings. But why would they hunt him?

The answer came to Cymin as he once again shifted. He wasn't anything special, but he was carrying something quite remarkable: the scepter.

Experimentally, Cymin rolled slightly to his side, shifting his pack and the scepter inside it. The spiders trailed his pack. His entire body stiffened with terror, and then a rush of adrenaline flooded him with the need to act at once—run, fight, escape—do something! He wanted to just hurl his pack off the train and get free that way, but he stopped himself. Lifting his right hand quickly to his brow, he imagined securing East Deity's mask over his own frightened features.

East Deity would not crumble into cowardice, nor would he forsake that which was entrusted to his care. The scepter meant too much to too many people—it had even saved his life once. He couldn't throw it away any more than he could have discarded the celestial pearl Laithondi had given him. Though both caused him a great deal of trouble.

If I live through this, I'm going to have a serious conversation with Laithondi about dumping all his dangerous crap on me.

Cymin exhaled a slow, calm breath and crawled forward, leaving all thought of the orgy of flaming arachnid spells behind him.

"What do we do now?" Cymin asked Eirjiri.

Eirjiri raised her gold brows, considering him with an amused expression.

"Suddenly so calm and ready for action," she commented. "Finally got sick of acting like a meek tuteli?"

"Meek as ever, thank you very much. I just want to hurry things along before I piss myself from terror," Cymin replied, and Eirjiri laughed.

"First we get comfortable and wait for Bailon. I've already signaled. She's on her way to us." Eirjiri spread her hands out against the metal of the train roof, and Arnaith's blue sigils swirled and coiled around her hands. She lifted her arms over her head, raising the shield, and then sat upright. Cymin edged nearer to her.

"And once she's here?" Cymin asked.

"She'll get you and Yuelaith to Laithondi. Laithondi will dispel or destroy the sharwae. It'll be like the old days, hmm?"

"I honestly don't remember the old days," Cymin shouted over the roar of the engine.

"Just as well." Eirjiri smiled at him. "If you did, you'd probably jump off the train right now."

Then she waved up at the sky as the shadow of a long figure broke through the smoke and descended towards them. Soot streaked Bailon's pale hair, and her long coat was singed and smoldering in places. She glowered at the spidery spells swarming over the top of the train. With a sweep of her arms, Bailon released a powerful gust that ripped the flaming spiders to pieces and hurled them aside. The spells that weren't blown clear of her path, she crushed beneath her boots when she dropped to the roof of the train. Flames and sigils burst and split apart beneath her heels.

Arnaith's shield rose as if lifted by the wind to cover her. Eirjiri bounced up to her feet and hurried to Bailon's side despite the raging wind and shaky footing. She hugged Bailon while Cymin straightened and steadied himself and began to walk down the rattling, wind-buffeted train car roof.

As he drew near, he heard Eirjiri explaining Laithondi having left his sword with Cymin and the need to deliver it to him. Up close, he could see the grime of smoke pitting Bailon's pores and deepening the wrinkles beneath her eyes to dark lines. She looked exhausted and twenty years older.

"Cymin discovered a spell that should dissipate this sharwae," Eirjiri said.

"Really?" Bailon looked surprised but also relieved. Her already-deep voice sounded raspy from smoke. "Yuelaith has been so unreliable lately, I was worried. It's about time it stopped throwing fits."

"Should I hand over the sword to you?" Cymin reached to his belt, fingers already catching the leather tongs that secured the sword's sheath.

"No, no." Bailon held up her hand and shot the sword a hostile glance. "Yuelaith is a bitch of an ancillary. It won't abide most deities touching it, much less wielding it. If the thing is playing nice with you, then you'd best keep handling it."

Cymin hadn't found Laithondi's ancillary particularly moody, but he wasn't going to argue. He simply took a deep breath and steeled himself for what had to come next.

"Ever walked on the wind before?" Bailon asked.

"I've only read of it being done in books," Cymin answered.

"Well, you may be taking a literal crash course now," Bailon responded dryly. She reached out and placed both her hands on Cymin's shoulders. He felt fei'lux surge past the nape of his neck. Blue sigils—not too different from Arnaith's—flared to life and floated over his chest and around to his back. A subtle scent, like the perfume of plum blossoms on a winter wind, filled his lungs.

"Ready?" Bailon asked.

"No—"

Bailon lifted her hands away, and Cymin was swept up into the sky.

CHAPTER 21

For the second time since he'd met the Waethir, Cymin was blown into the sky in an explosive, uncontrolled flight. The sheer velocity rammed his shout of alarm back into his throat. His legs fluttered like the tail of a kite caught in a cyclone. He hurtled up past towering trees and rocky mountain slopes. In seconds, the train and its narrow track shrank to miniatures beneath him, and a vast red sky enveloped him.

Beneath him, thousands of raging red spells leapt up from the top of the train in pursuit. Hundreds of them collided with the voracious arachnid spells raining down. From the corner of his eye, Cymin thought he glimpsed the dark wings of two cameras dodging through the explosions, but he couldn't spare them any further attention. Smoke, sigils and flames burst around him like bombs, buffeting him with hot air and streams of sizzling fei'lux.

Bailon's crash course is no fucking joke.

Cymin flinched and jolted, but the wind-walking spells that Bailon had placed on him continued to heedlessly drive him upward into the masses of flaming arachnid spells. He wracked his memory for anything he'd read or heard about walking on the wind. Anything at all to offer him a chance at controlling his flight. Fractured, panicked thoughts scattered through his mind.

He ducked as a spider whizzed past. Flickering legs scorched the shoulder of his robe and scalded his ear. Cymin hissed in pain.

Then, suddenly, like the recall of a dream, or the physical memory of balancing on a bicycle, knowledge suffused him. The image of the blue sigils that Bailon had ringed all around his chest flashed before him as if being drawn by an instructor. He heard children's voices singing a playful poem as they danced at the edge of a precipice.

Walking on the wind, dancing in air
Fall to ascend. Jump if you dare.

In that instant, he knew the wind-walking spell started like a firework, blasting into the air on a massive charge of fei'lux. As it ascended, it absorbed kinetic energy from the air resistance, becoming stronger and stronger until it no longer required a mage to feed it fei'lux. Cymin's body hurtling through the air amplified each of the spells Bailon had placed on him, in the same way that violent booms and crashes of noise fed an Invocation of Silence.

So, the force of gravity pulling me down will actually keep me aloft? Clever, but then how do I descend?

Again, the knowledge of how to modulate the spell came to him like muscle memory. He shifted his weight, adding a small rush of energy to the spells on his right and veered in that direction. Another shift, and he dodged two wriggling spiders on his left. With a kick, he punched through a cloud of black smoke. A dozen large spider spells swept towards him. Instinctively, Cymin spun and leapt to the side. The same motions he'd practiced and performed as East Deity in countless parades now carried him through the air. The wind felt like a sprung theater floor bouncing beneath his bare feet. A motion of his left hand let him veer easily between another two spiders' outstretched flaming legs.

Ha! I'm great at this!

His self-congratulatory mood was shattered an instant later when a third arachnid spell plunged down straight at his face. With a frantic motion of his right hand, he sketched one of the Thousand Blessings. Fei'lux surged up his left hand and flooded the sigils he traced with his right. Huge petals of shining sigils unfurled around him, overlapping and expanding until they formed a radiant shield. One searing spider after another slammed into the shield, spattering apart in gushes of flame and fizzling sigils.

The multiple impacts jarred through Cymin's right arm and shoulder. But the blessing-shield held despite the haste of its summoning. Within its small sanctuary, the air cleared and cooled. Cymin gasped in a breath and calmed himself, imagining that he wore his deity mask and retained the Black Staff that had allowed him to command all of the Thousand Blessings just as he had in countless performances. Years of training lent him a conditioned assurance.

He spun in three circles, and his ascent slowed enough for him to angle his body towards the huge masses of black smoke and red light surging up the mountainside in pursuit of the train. That would be where the sharwae lurked and where Laithondi was still battling alone.

In a bound, Cymin pierced the haze of smoke and drifting embers. At last, he saw the full form of the sharwae, and he felt a shock of awe and terror.

Previously, he'd read descriptions of guardian wae and seen their images in carvings, statues and even his favorite braziers. They were luminous beings, said to be as sentient as creatures of flesh and blood but created entirely from spells. According to banned texts, they assumed the shapes of mythic beasts because the Piiroc Apotheoses—not Chyrenese mages—originally created them in the images of their lost Carnal Gods.

Feeling the heat rolling off the three immense winged salamanders that filled the sky before him, Cymin could believe that they might well have arisen from gods. Their radiant bodies were composed of countless layers of intricately linked gold sigils, and they stretched out as long as oceangoing sailboats. Scarlet flame spells arched from their backs, forming huge wings. The sharwae nearest Cymin shifted, and he glimpsed its face. Small black eyes glinted in the sharwae's massive head, and its mouth stretched back in a long curve, lending its huge maw the illusion of a benevolent smile.

Cymin had found the expression endearing when he'd seen it carved into a brazier in Benevolence Hall, but the sheer scale of the creature made the reality of it terrifying.

The sharwae flicked its tail, and a scorching wind buffeted Cymin.

The sharwae nearest Cymin and another that looked like its twin both swam through the air, circling a third identical sharwae. The third sharwae coiled around a small pale light. Arachnid spells burst from the flaming wings of the two spiraling salamanders, and red bands of Uuhir floated over all their heads like crowns of corruption.

The third sharwae salamander curled inward around a sphere of white light, its huge mouth gaping wide to expose millions of needle-like teeth. Within the sphere, Laithondi turned, twisted and spun, throwing sigil after sigil into the black well of the salamander's open mouth. He invoked torrents of spells at such speed that he looked almost like a bolt of lighting dancing at the center of an array. A slow radiance, like a growing fire, lit the back of the salamander's throat but didn't slow the descent of its jaws. Any moment, the salamander would swallow Laithondi and his spells whole, Cymin realized.

"Laithondi!" Cymin charged forward, desperate to deliver the sword in time. "I brought Yuelaith for you!"

"Go back!" Laithondi shouted. Cymin couldn't see his expression, but he sounded furious. He threw his arms wide, and white sigils washed over the central salamander's head like delicate hoarfrost, only to melt away in an instant.

"You're welcome!" Cymin shouted in return. He dodged between streams of blazing spiders and gripped the hilt of the sword. He had to get closer to Laithondi to pass it to him.

Then one of the two circling salamanders dived down on Cymin. The Uuhir hunting sigils crowning its head blazed to life, and a flood of arachnid spells burst from its splayed red wings.

Cymin didn't think; he tore Yuelaith from its sheath and threw every ounce of fei'lux he could draw into the blade. His shield evaporated, and even Bailon's wind-walking sigils shuddered. Cymin's mind filled with that array of millions of circular saw blades, each as frigid and beautiful as a snowflake yet merciless as an avalanche. The array erupted from Yuelaith in a violent flurry. It sheared through the fiery spiders as if passing through mist and ripped open the salamander's torso. Gold sigils spewed like blood, and tattered verses of spells spilled out into the wind. The wounded sharwae appeared oddly serene—and Cymin realized why. In seconds, gold filaments burst up from the sigils edging the salamander's gaping wound. They caught gusts of fei'lux and spun together, weaving the mortal injury closed. The huge salamander angled its giant head slightly, taking in Cymin.

Its benign smile parted, exposing a vast chasm of vicious teeth.

At the same time, Cymin felt a pulse throb against his back. Something in his pack whirred, and a weird tingle shot through Cymin's entire body.

The scepter! The Fei'suul Scepter in my pack!

An electric sensation coursed through his muscles, and hairs all across his body stood on end. Countless invisible threads seemed to burst up from him, arcing through streams of fei'lux and catching every spell, sigil and array near him. The power and purpose of them all surged into Cymin. He heard Laithondi shout a warning to him, but he couldn't register the words as sensations and images flooded him.

In his hand, Yuelaith no longer appeared as a simple sword; instead, its metallic body seemed to drop away like a loose robe falling aside to expose the bare body beneath. Cymin stared down at a multitude of spells, their intricacy easily rivaling the most beautiful illuminated book he'd ever seen in complexity and nuance.

A feeling very like provocative vanity emanated from the ancillary as it revealed its multitude of interlocking sigils, each connected to the next by a tapestry of filaments and light. The spell of frigid blades—which had seemed so ruthlessly cruel—now flashed and fluttered before Cymin as if offering him a coquettish wink. Then it settled demurely among the other spells that made up the sword's essence.

Was it possible that the ancillary blade of East Deity was something of a flirt?

Before the strangeness of that sank in, the presence of the two salamander sharwae approaching him flooded Cymin's awareness.

First, the tattered, broken remains of the salamander he'd injured swept over him like a song stuttering apart on a fragmented radio signal. Images and sensations flickered before him. He saw a vast chamber of raised sarcophagi. Lamplight reflected off gilded walls adorned with sacred Piiroc guardian wae—phoenixes, dragons, sea serpents, winged snakes and three-headed salamanders. The air rippled with a single note from a jewel-studded funereal chime, only to be silenced by a woman's quick hand.

A tiny group of furtive worshippers followed her, their heads bowed and their faces shadowed beneath gray mourning veils. They filed past quickly, eager to escape unseen. Only one boy lingered to gaze up at the winged salamander occupying the gilded wall beside him. Despite his youth, cochineal crimson already stained the boy's eyelids and lips, marking him as a courtesan to the Haeyi mage-king. Vibrant silk flowers and delicate gold chains decorated his long black hair, but very little else clothed his thin body.

"Do you remember me?" The youth smiled as he touched the relief carving. From within the salamander's consciousness, Cymin recognized the dark-eyed boy. This was Minroa Haeyi, joining his mother, sister and brother in their secret annual worship of their defeated Piiroc ancestors and Carnal Gods. Most worshippers had already made their offerings and fled. Minroa's mother strode past him, followed by two men. But Minroa remained, carefully drawing the smallest flame of fei'lux into his hand. He caressed the guardian again, his delicate fingertips stroking over the secret sigils that could rouse the guardian from its rest.

A young girl—perhaps two years older than Minroa and dressed in even less—caught his hand before he touched the final sigil, admonishing him in a whisper. With a fast, nervous gesture, Minroa returned the guardian to its light doze. He fled, holding his sister's hand.

Torpor enfolded the guardian and Cymin. Years passed. Minroa's presence fluttered through the guardian's awareness, but only briefly. He was older and brought a strange, white-haired man with him. Together, they made offerings of golden spells and influxes of fei'lux to the guardian. Minroa's song at last woke it, and it enfolded the two of them, carrying them down to the sacred cavern shining with radiant spells. There the two of them swore eternal faith and made desperate, passionate love under the eyes of the Carnal Gods.

The tomb fell silent for a long, long time. The guardian slept again. Great storms of fei'lux raged over the land. The guardian's slumber turned anxious, its dreams filled with nightmarish apparitions. Men in snarling, poison armor came to dig out the bones and hearts of its companions. And then those too passed away.

Not even Minroa visited the tomb anymore. There was nothing. Ages passed, stones wore down and passageways collapsed. Seedlings grew into trees, and those gave rise to forests. The guardian's sleep deepened as the arrays of spells that made up its purpose and lent it consciousness lost their strength. It forgot its own existence, just as the world outside forgot the sacred altars and tombs of the ancient necropolis.

Then, with a crash of rain and lightning, a faint stream of fei'lux entered the buried chamber, and the guardian roused ever so slightly. A feeling like joy lit up inside it as it seemed to sense Minroa race past like a gust of wind, as if he were again that little boy fleeing out into the night. Behind him, the flooded chambers of the tomb echoed with the plaintive wail of a dying toddler.

Through the guardian's dim senses, Cymin gazed coldly down at himself as a toddler—a scrawny, hollow-eyed creature, choking on floodwaters and clinging to the warmth of a luminous white scepter. Fei'lux arced and whirled around him.

Cymin flinched from the sight, feeling lost in time and his own body. He blinked, hoping to clear his vision, but fei'lux still streamed around him. He seemed to float on waves of feverish dizziness.

Where am I now? Not still a baby in a flooded crypt. Not a lonely guardian locked away in a tomb either. But . . . where am I? When is this?

I was on a train, wasn't I? And then I was in the sky looking for Laithondi . . .

Cymin wrenched himself free from the salamander sharwae's memories to take in his surroundings. He still hung in a smoky sky above a tiny train track on a wooded mountainside. Soot covered his scorched robes, and he gripped Yuelaith in his right hand. White arcs of fei'lux flashed from his body, and his head felt as if it were on fire.

The salamander sharwae that had attacked him was gone. The sigils and spells that once created the giant guardian dissolved into a shimmering veil of white filaments and fei'lux. Then even that was whipped away from Cymin to be devoured into the scepter whirring at his back.

A second salamander loomed over him with its red wings spread wide, and just past it, Cymin glimpsed the third salamander coiled around Laithondi.

Laithondi still stared at Cymin with a harrowed expression. Only an instant of time could have passed since the scepter whirred to life—despite it feeling like he'd experienced years within the salamander sharwae's memories.

"Cymin, don't use the scepter!" Laithondi's shout penetrated Cymin's consciousness this time. But even so, the warning came too late.

Every fiber of Cymin's body resonated with the hum of the scepter. Fei'lux shot through him, and the vast array of spells that made up the second guardian were instantly laid bare before him. Its consciousness played through Cymin's mind. This time, he felt the Uuhir hunting sigil that had corrupted the guardian wae. He expected to be overwhelmed with fire and fury but instead found tapestries of gold spells rippling around him, as soft and fine as the bright scales of butterfly wings.

And again, he recognized Minroa Haeyi's touch, waking him in the desolate ruin of a long-since plundered tomb. All around him lay the desecrated resting places of his fellow guardians—their bones stolen, the sigils of their sarcophagi chipped apart by thieves and the fei'lux drained from them by time. Only he remained, alone among the ruins.

But Minroa had not forgotten him. He caressed him and praised him, spoke to him and sang for him, all while feeding him rich streams of fei'lux. After years abandoned to a half-life of hapless starvation, his power and purpose returned to him.

Minroa gave him life again.

He felt such gratitude—such immense love and so much desire to protect Minroa; nothing could matter to him more. Adoration throbbed through him like the pulse of a living heart.

When Minroa called to him, his entire being filled with radiant joy. When Minroa wept against him, he wanted only to comfort him. And when Minroa crowned him with the Uuhir Corruption—infesting him with burning, relentless arachnid spells—he endured the agony and revulsion. When the spiders fed on him, he surrendered his sigils and fei'lux to them, because Minroa asked it of him.

I would gladly die for him.

"No. Don't be so selfless. You deserve better." Cymin came back to himself in that moment. Then a terrible realization struck him. "It's not even Minroa who you're serving—who you are suffering for. He's been dead for centuries. It's some modern imposter who's just using you to get the scepter."

Outrage sparked Cymin's need for action. Before he could consider how he knew what he was doing, Cymin reached out into the dense tapestries of the guardian's spells with his left hand. At his back, the scepter purred like an excited cat. Cymin stripped away the ugly red infestations of Uuhir sigils as if he were picking worms out from the flesh of a peach. He hurled them aside, and the scepter devoured them.

In the open wounds where they had taken root, Cymin quickly drew new sigils and set them alight with streams of fei'lux.

"You were betrayed." Cymin's own chest ached with pain and anger, as if he too had loved with all his being, only to be deceived. "Go, take vengeance for both of us. Find the one who wanted to corrupt you. Lay him low!"

Beneath his fingers, fei'lux seared into the string of spells, making his words into commands. Then Cymin drew his hand back and stroked the secret sigils that reawakened the guardian. Its small black eyes flickered with light, and its hot breath blew over Cymin like steam. The contact felt deeply familiar—as if they'd had this same interaction before.

But that wasn't possible.

Cymin stared intently at the guardian wae. He felt as if he were seeing it not just as it appeared now, but overlaid by impressions of it from ages past. The superimposed, hazy images flickering through his mind filled him with a dizzy confusion but also a sense of deep fondness.

The guardian wae nodded to him. Then, with a flash of its wings, the huge salamander knifed away from him and swung up on a current of hot wind. It searched for a trace of the mage who had corrupted it. Rays of afternoon sun flashed off its body, piercing the clouds of drifting smoke. Then it dived down.

At the same time, Cymin reclaimed more of his own senses. His head ached like it was going to split open, and his eyes stung with drops of his own sweat. He looked up to see Laithondi staring at him from the grip of the third salamander. The crown of corrupting sigils that had floated over its head had burned out and now scattered like smoke.

"Cymin, don't use the scepter!" Laithondi called out that same warning yet again, with the same expression and tone. And somehow, the very same cloud drifted behind him.

Cymin stared at the little puff of cloud in a daze. How had it drifted by three times in a row?

Then Cymin realized that this wasn't the third time Laithondi had shouted to him, but the first time. Somehow, the scepter was stretching a single second on and on, while Cymin used it to deal with the sharwae.

Amazing, Cymin thought, and he wiped at the sweat dripping down his face. He felt like he was burning up. It was so exhausting. So confusing. He felt suddenly very dizzy—almost nauseated.

Laithondi broke away from the last salamander wae; it remained drifting in place with its huge mouth hanging open as if it had fallen asleep. Laithondi gestured, and fei'lux blazed around him. The delicate white sigils traced all across the sharwae's body glinted and then glowed like frost caught in sunlight. Then the entire creature diffused into the pale vapor of clouds. Laithondi bounded to Cymin and yanked the pack off his back. All at once, Cymin's sweat-soaked body felt icy cold.

"Idiot! It could have devoured you—me, everything—without the altar," Laithondi snapped.

How was I supposed to know that? And who is the idiot for hiding it in my pack without telling me anything?

"No need to thank me for coming to your rescue," Cymin shot back, but he lost his concentration as the blue sigils holding him aloft fluttered, making him sway like a drunk. Cymin righted himself, but Bailon's spells felt heavy. The one at the center of his chest flickered, then faded to gray.

Cymin faltered forward, and Laithondi reached out, steadying him.

"It's almost drained all the wind-walking spells. We need to descend." Laithondi sounded exhausted. This close, Cymin realized the dark marks he'd thought were soot caking Laithondi's right hand were drying blood. Red welts marked his throat and cheek, and his left arm shook noticeably as he gripped Cymin's pack.

"Are you all right?" Cymin asked.

But Laithondi didn't respond. Instead, he scowled down at the guardian that Cymin had sent away.

"What did you do to it?" Laithondi asked.

Cymin, too, peered after the guardian and then frowned. Why was it diving along the train tracks?

"I sent it back after whoever unleashed it on us." Cymin wanted to sound pleased with himself, but his voice came out rough and uncertain. He swayed as a wind-walking spell at his back waned and then revived.

Cymin didn't know why, but the air seemed to have grown even more murky, almost as if his vision were failing. Cymin squinted after the golden salamander. Maybe it, too, was having difficulty seeing its surroundings? Was that why it followed the train tracks? Cymin could barely make out the shining guardian as it closed in on the train.

Then a terrible thought occurred to him—could the one who corrupted the guardian be on their train? But how was that possible?

"It can't break through Arnaith's shield, can it?" Cymin demanded.

"It was empowered by the scepter, and Arnaith isn't as . . ." Laithondi's expression was calm, but his tone was grim. "It might."

Yinni was in that train.

He had to stop the guardian wae!

Cymin bounded forward to intercept it. He swept through clouds of gray smoke and kicked hard, demanding more speed from the wind-walking spells.

"Cymin, no!" Laithondi shouted.

"I have to—" Cymin's reply was jarred from his throat, and he abruptly dropped a dozen yards and then jerked to the side like a marionette being dragged on only one string. Three more of his wind-walking spells died out. He flailed, then swung his arms out and spun to recapture his center. He had nearly reclaimed his balance when, an instant later, the last wind-walking spell dissipated.

Cymin plummeted towards the mountainside, helpless to do anything but fall as the guardian at last reached the train. It slammed into the passenger coaches. As its blazing body impacted Arnaith's shields, both shredded apart in an explosion of gold sigils and blue light. Steel screamed and the entire train heaved violently. Then the engine toppled down the cliff face.

THE ADVENTURE CONTINUES WITH

PRICE OF A THOUSAND BLESSINGS

VOLUME TWO.

Glossary of Places and Terms

Amei—Capital city of the modern Chyre Republic.

Ancillary—Anything that houses one or more spells and is capable of conducting fei'lux. Ancillaries can range from complex heirlooms containing millions of discrete spells—such as swords, staves and crowns—to a simple broom handle with a few sigils carved into it. Mages manifest the spells within their ancillaries by carefully directing streams of fei'lux into them.

Apotheoses of Piiroc—Five families who were said to have tamed and controlled the Carnal Gods. They are each associated with an element: Fire, Ice, Water, Wind, Earth. The lands bordering northern Chyre are protected by the Fire Apotheoses, members of the Royal Laosha family.

Avisdomi—Carriage bird riders who served the mage-kings. Avisdomi cavalries are largely ceremonial in the modern age.

Bandimanders—Creatures native to Saigrath. Five-to ten-foot-long blue-gray worms that hunt through frigid water and beneath sheets of ice. (Also the Waethir nickname for National Security Marshals and NS personnel in general.)

Black Gates—A set of gigantic gates that guard the only pass leading from the Mist Moors to the Heights in Saigrath.

Bluecloud cigarettes—Popular brand of Chyrenese cigarette. Associated with the original revolutionaries who often hid secret messages beneath the pandan-scented wrapping papers.

Carnal Gods—Piiroc pantheon of twenty-five immense, divine creatures embodying the elements of creation: Fire, Ice, Water, Wind, Earth. Legend claims that five ancestors of the Holy Royal families sacrificed their lives to the Carnal Gods. In return, the Carnal Gods became the guardians of the Piiroc people, protecting the world from inundations of fei'lux. Later, an alliance of mage-kings and deities struck down the Carnal Gods, reducing them to the Divinity Bones and wae. Many Piirocs believe that the Carnal Gods will arise again from the Divinity Bones. Chyrenese legends surrounding the

Carnal Gods paint them as oppressive monsters that devoured entire villages and crushed any who opposed the Piiroc theocracy. Their defeat allowed numerous territories to break away from Piiroc rule and saw the Waethir take control of the Hallow Gates. For the majority of Piirocs, however, the Carnal Gods represent a reverence and respect for nature.

Celestial pearls—Luminous spheres said to contain magical wonders—even entire worlds—in myths. They are formed deep within the Sea of Eternity. Those that have been brought back from its depths are not much larger than a plum; however, it is said that far deeper in the Sea of Eternity there grow far more immense Celestial Pearls.

Chuuraun—Hybrid creatures born during intense fei'lux surges. Overstimulated fei'thallus in one or more creatures fuse together with discarded or broken spells. Chuuraun are not always dangerous—many are merely simple plants that take on an odd characteristic from a spell, such as glowing or producing musical notes. When chuuraun do become dangerous, however, they can prove almost impossible to kill because their overabundance of fei'thallus constantly heals them and often spreads to other beings. Chuuraun is written with the sigils Chuu + Raun, literally "madness creature."

Chyre—Once a small nation ruled by mage-kings, Chyre rose to power after invading several other adjacent nations, including the Haelon territory of Piiroc. Later, under the rule of Xondir Haeyi, Chyre expanded to dominate half the continent. In 1819, the People's Revolution overthrew the rule of mage-kings and established a republic. The modern government consists of a Prime Minister and cabinet of powerful ministers. The seven national ministries of Chyre are Culture and Arts, Health and Medicine, Information and Education, Law and Justice, Security and Defense, Transportation and Communication, and Treasury and Trade.

Dajiryn Islands—Numerous small islands north of Yanyeo. The five largest islands were invaded and taken over by Xondir Haeyi to serve as bases for his Storm Towers.

Ember Knife—Criminal organization centered in Yanyeo. Xondir Haeyi's second in command, Tsike, is said to have founded the organization. Their symbol is a sea serpent entwined with a phoenix—the personal emblems of Tsike and Xondier Haeyi. Because of their involvement in the People's Revolution, the group is sometimes viewed romantically as "freedom fighters." Recently, leaders in the group have made overtures at legitimate business. Their most famous establishment is the Pavilion of Twin Fates.

Fei'lux—Fierce, magical energy that pours through the Hallow Gates. Untempered, it can burn away organic and inorganic matter. Even when tempered, surges of fei'lux can injure or kill living organisms. It also permeates matter, altering the characteristics of the air, water and earth it suffuses.

Fei'suul Scepter—Ancillary source of sovereign fei'thallus and the universal nexus where all information collected by any and all fei'thallus is stored. When linked to the Sea of Eternity, the scepter ensures that a deity's skill and life experience is imparted to the next generation without destroying the latter's individual personality. When housed within the White Chamber during an inundation of fei'lux, the scepter receives enough power—tempered by one or more deities—to direct the Sea of Eternity to rebuild entire environments destroyed by the fei'lux surges.

Fei'thallus—Hyper-symbiotic microscopic organisms that form relationships with most other organisms they encounter. Fei'thallus can absorb and process fei'lux into metabolic energy, which they share with their hosts. In return, their hosts shelter and spread fei'thallus. While there are thousands of varieties of native fei'thallus (all able to share energy and information), those that prompt their hosts to develop ignis glands are highly useful for magecraft. Of them, sovereign fei'thallus, native to Saigrath, is the rarest and most capable of absorbing and conducting fei'lux.

Five Guardian Deities—Mythic figures worshiped by Lux Temple and invoked by the tuteli. The deities are:

Arnaith (sea)
Bailon (sky)
Eirjiri (earth)
Laithondi (day/sun/east)
Vessreid (night/moon/west)

Five Mage Schools—The only secular institutions where magecraft can be legally taught in Chyre. Known commonly as "The Five Schools" they are: Boshyin School, Chohe Institute, Guishuun College, Orae Academy, Ryde Academy.

Boshyin School—Established by Xondir Haeyi as the first secular mage school and also the first school to admit both male and female students. Boshyin was considered revolutionary when it first opened; now, it;s thought of as an elite school for reactionaries and secret royalists. Nevertheless, many graduates go on to hold positions of high office in the modern government. The school offers three scholarship positions. To qualify for a scholarship, a student must continue to rank in the top ten students nationally every quarter for their entire academic career. Founded: 1712. School color: black. Motto: "Command With Courage."

Chohe Institute—An experimental co-ed institute for the study and exploration of mage-craft. Student mages often come from more wealthy backgrounds (like those of Boshyin) but are considered less ambitious and usually enter the arts. Founded: 1760. School color: purple. Motto: "Forever Free."

Guishuun College—A co-ed school that focuses on social science and history of mage-craft, established directly after the People's Revolution as a secular mage school. Founded: 1819. School color: cream. Motto: "Wisdom Before Battle."

Orae Academy—A male-only boarding school specializing in combat mage-craft. Established after the revolution as a means for members of the revolutionary militia to better their stations in society—and a way to improve discipline among mage-soldiers. Founded: 1822. School color: red. Motto: "Excellence In Action."

Ryde Academy—A female-only boarding school focusing on the engineering, design and creation of mage-craft ancillaries. Most recently founded of all the schools. Ryde strives to nurture the skills of female mages and to promote greater gender equity. Founded: 1900. School color: yellow. Motto: "Achievement Empowered."

Great Chasm Sea—Extremely dangerous stretch of ocean far north of Chyre and Piiroc. Ships entering the Great Chasm Sea often encounter deep mists that confuse their compasses and hide the stars. Some sailors claim to have seen the edge of the world there, where the ocean's waters pour down like a giant waterfall into an endless misty haze. Saigrath lays across the sea but is extremely difficult to reach without a blessing of safe passage from the Waethir.

Haelon Necropolis / Laosha Tombs—Originally part of the Piiroc nation, this underground city and holy place remained hidden after Mage-King Omn Haeyo conquered Haelon in his quest for immortality. The necropolis was later captured by his son, Xondier Haeyi, but its exact location was lost to history.

Haelon Province—Northern province of Chyre, where the Storm Towers were raised. Haelon lies on the Pirroc border and originally belonged to the Piiroc nation. It was home to the Flame Apotheosis and the holy necropolis that she safeguarded. Later, Haelon was captured by Chyrenese Mage-King Omn Haeyi; his son, Xondir Haeyi, completed the conquest in 1706. Haelon has remained a Chyrenese province since then. The capital city is Yanyeo, which is also the province's center of trade.

Hallow Gates—Believed by the Chyrenese and Piirocs to be mythological doors to the realm of creation, from which all life came. The Carnal Gods were said to feed from them. After the Carnal Gods were destroyed, the Five Deities were said to protect the Hallow Gates. The Waethir in Saigrath have a very different understanding of the Hallow Gates, which they guard. In Waethir belief, they are five heavenly bodies that orbit between a breach in the realm of pure fei'lux and the world of Niilha. They and their magnetospheres block and diffuse the pure fei'lux that would otherwise flood Niilha. They move in and out of alignment with each other and the world of Niilha, leaving a period of 12 hours every 210 years when there is no obstruction in the breach between Niilha and the pure fei'lux. At this time, if nothing else tempers the flood of fei'ux, Niilha is in danger of being wiped out. Hallow Gates opening intervals:

Sea—Every 70 years
Sky—Every 42 years
Earth—Every 35 years
Moon—Every 30 years
Sun—Every 15 years
All five gates open at once every 210 years.

Heights—Mountainous home of the Five Deities and their chosen tuteli. The Heights overlook Joryn, Saigrath's largest city, and boast orchards and gardens that bloom throughout the harsh winter as well as hot springs.

Ignis gland— Located about an inch below the navel. The organ is believed to be a matter of superstition and poor education in Chyre. Old lore mentions ignis glands as being associated with the equally mythic fei'thallus. Stories describe the organ as housing extraordinary power, allowing mages to easily manifest and build complex spells. Some even claim that ancient mages were capable of powering and sheltering huge arrays of spells within the ignis itself. According to the Waethir, the ignis gland develops in children and young adults after they are exposed to—or inoculated with—large quantities of fei'thallus over a period of seven days. The organ shelters large colonies of the fei'thallus, which in turn easily process fei'lux. The host mage can then endure far greater loads of fei'lux. These mages may also be capable of exchanging information and energy between their own fei'thallus and those in other organisms and the surrounding environment.

Ishyi Bridge—A bridge in the city of Amei, the capital of Chyre.

Ivory Island—Physical location of the Hallow Gates and the White Chamber.

Joryn—Saigrath's largest city. Situated below the Heights and behind the protection of the Black Gates.

Lux Temple—The home of the tuteli. Its members follow the mandates of the Five Deities: protect the mortal world, safeguard ancient wisdom, advance magecraft and uphold justice. Lux Temples exist all across the world and have adapted to different political policies. In Chyre, Lux Temple is supported by the state, and in return, the tuteli are required to serve in the Storm Towers to repay the debts owed to the nation. The temple also hosts philosophical debates, provides blessings and puts on performances based on the myths and teachings of the Five Deities. The tuteli assist secular mages in improving and assessing their magecraft through challenges. The most famous of these is the annual Spring Exhibition.

Magecraft—Practices by which mages manifest spells. The forms magecraft takes often vary by nation. These are:

> **Chyre**—Ancillary and direct. Chyrenese mages most commonly use ancillaries to manifest spells. To do so, mages draw down fei'lux from the atmosphere with the assistance of implanted spell filaments. They then circulate the raw fei'lux through their bodies, tempering it into an even stream of power. Then they guide that power into an ancillary, which already contains the spell they wish to manifest.

Direct manifestation of a spell requires a mage to both attract and temper a perfect stream of fei'lux while also speaking or drawing the sigils of the spell. This method is rarely used because it's more dangerous, difficult to master and exhausting.

Piiroc—In addition to limited ancillaries, mages in Piiroc use song, (or sound vibrations of any kind) to temper surrounding fei'lux and form a spell. Commonly, they then release that spell into a biological medium such as blood, plant tissue or bone. That biological matrix then houses, sustains and manifests the spell.

Saigrath—The magecraft of Saigrath is a great mystery. In lore, the Wraiths in particular are described as manifesting huge numbers of complex spells directly, but modern mage-scholars believe that this is hyperbole.

Mist Moors—Mossy, grassy hills in Saigrath.

Money: In Chyre, coins are associated with the age of mage-kings and no longer used. Paper bills are the modern currency. They are designed to be torn in half and thus represent two denominations each. For example, a complete red bill represents 2 credits, while half a red bill is 1 credit. The colors and values of the bills are as follows:

Red:2/1
Yellow:10/5
Green:50/25
Blue:200/100
Purple:1000/500

Niilha—The world in which this story takes place.

Pearl Staircase—A magical spiral staircase that leads to the White Chamber.

Piiroc—A country to the west of Chyre. Originally ruled by a coalition of five Apotheoses, each associated with an element and several Carnal Gods. Piiroc has developed into a constitutional monarchy. However, a new uprising of religious extremists has caused strife with their demands for a return to theocratic rule of the Holy Apotheoses—the Fire Apotheoses, in particular.

Prayer beads—Strings of forty-two beads each carved with a spell sigil.

Used to teach novice mages and help them focus on the intent of each sigil. Older strings have many more beads, since numerous sigils have been outlawed by the modern government. (Haeyi in particular.)

Prithzue river—River that feeds from Eomarn Bay to the Delta of Yanyeo.

Red Marsh—A giant neuston colony, dominated by scarlet cnidarians which resemble red water lilies. The red marsh stretches across most of the coastline of Saigrath, growing and receding with environmental conditions.

Sai—People of Saigrath.

Saigrath—A nearly mythic land in the far north beyond the Great Chasm Sea. The native people call themselves Sai. Saigrath is the home of the Waethir—sometimes called "Wraiths" by the Piiroc and Chyrenese—as well as the Hallow Gates.

Sea of Eternity—Nexus of fei'thallus which absorbs and retains the memories of all living things and their environments. An entry to the Sea of Eternity exists in the White Chamber, but the Sea of Eternity descends far below the chamber. The Fei'suul Scepter was created to direct and control the Sea of Eternity.

Sharwae—Guardian spell array that has been altered and corrupted to a different, usually harmful purpose. Written with the sigils Shar + Wae meaning "corrupt" + "guardian."

Spell filaments—Sets of long gold threads etched with spells that assist in attracting and manipulating fei'lux. Spell filaments are surgically grafted to the hands and arms of young mages. The left set of filaments draws down fei'lux while the set for the right hand releases it. Any modern Chyrenese mage hoping to secure good employment will have purchased spell filaments and undergone grafting surgery.

Storm Towers—Five giant ancillary structures constructed by Mage-King Xondir Haeyi. The Storm Towers shield Chyre as well as the rest of the continent by capturing eruptions of fei'lux that threaten to scour away both land and life. The Storm Towers then temper these inundations into calmer streams, which are then released as a steady supply of energy, which powers Chyre's cities. The Storm Towers are manned and maintained by conscripted tuteli.

Tempest House—Sanctuaries maintained by Lux Temple. The largest and most famous Tempest House is in Yanyeo. It not only boasts a temple complex but also a medical facility where injured tuteli are nursed during and after their conscriptions in the Storm Towers. Yanyeo's Tempest House regularly attracts crowds of tourists, and its guesthouse is a highly prized vacation spot.

Thousand Blessings to the Sea of Eternity—A lost scroll left by the Five Deities that details how to write and arrange all the spells that make up the Thousand Blessings of Creation to create different spell arrays. The protective Veil of a Thousand Blessings is one of those arrays of spells stored in the Black Staves kept by Lux Temple.

Tuteli—Members of Lux Temple who are taken in as children and raised according to the mandates of the Five Deities. Most tuteli come from disadvantaged backgrounds, many being either orphaned or sold to Lux Temple by their impoverished relatives. All tuteli are required to possess natural talents for manipulating fei'lux, since they are expected to serve as opponents for the secular mages of the Five Schools and represent the Five Deities during sacred festivals and ceremonies.

Because Lux Temple must secure national loans to pay for their upbringing, training and education, tuteli are also expected to repay those loans through conscription to the Storm Towers. The tuteli of Lux Temple wear clay-brown robes, shave their heads and go barefoot. Despite their humble presentation, the tuteli of Lux Temple safeguard and regularly use some of the oldest magical treasures of Chyre's history.

During the Age of Mage-Kings, tuteli were expected to remain celibate, humble and impoverished. Modern tuteli have more rights but are still expected to uphold the traditional image of their order. Ranks of tuteli are Novice, Adept, Master, Grand Master.

Uumthal—A Waethir medicine / poison that kills fei'thallus. Used in moderation, it can keep a body from being completely overwhelmed by overactive fei'thallus. Uumthal can kill chuuraun and is also deadly to the Waethir.

Varyo Storm Tower—Largest of the five towers that protect the continent from inundations of fei'lux that surge from the Hallow Gates. Varyo overlooks the port of Yanyeo.

Wae—Legendary guardian spells of immense power dating back to the fall of the Carnal Gods. The network of spells that made up a wae are said to have been so complex and powerful that the resulting guardian took on the qualities of a living creature. No modern mages have successfully created one. However, many old mage families claim to possess the remnants of a wae in various talismans and charms.

Waethir / Wraiths—The five defenders of the Hallow Gates in the northlands of Saigrath. They are named for the Five Deities and are selected from Saigrath's native tuteli. In the Heights, the Sea of Eternity performs the final selection, choosing a candidate to gift with the previous deity's experiences as well as an inoculation of sovereign fei'thallus which links them directly to the Fei'suul Scepter. This allows them to commune with the scepter and the Sea of Eternity. (Waethir is written with the sigils Wae + Thir, meaning "guardian spell" and "deity.")

White Chamber—A giant pearly "shell" that houses the Sea of Eternity and the Fei'suul Scepter. It can be reached through the Pearl Staircase in the Heights but actually occupies the Ivory Island where the Hallow Gates align.

Yanyeo—Built up from mudflats into a bustling canal city. Yanyeo is famous for its many floating markets, music halls and gambling dens. It is the largest city in Haelon Province. It is the center of government and trade and is also the base of operations for the Storm Towers and the tuteli that serve in them. Throughout its history, it has always been a haven for heretics, revolutionaries, artists, eccentrics and dissidents. Originally a Piiroc holy city, it was home to Diron, Minroa and Xondir Haeyi. Yanyeo's historians also claim it was the birthplace of the People's Revolution.

Characters

Arnaith—One of five Waethir who have come to Chyre from Saigrath. Arnaith is named after the Sea Deity of the Five Guardian Deities. Despite her silver hair, she appears to be in her mid-twenties. She is curious, science-minded and fascinated with Chyrenese ancillaries, but very reserved in the company of strangers.

Bailon—One of the five Waethir from Saigrath. Named for the Sky Deity. The tallest of the Waethir women, Bailon possesses strong features, white hair and a great interest in drama and fashion. She loves art, gossiping, and drinking, as well as playful flirtations.

Cymin—Naturally talented tuteli adept, chosen to represent East Deity for Lux Temple. He lost most of his family in the Great Haelon Flood when he was four. His surviving family member is his fellow tuteli and sister, Yinni. His birth name: Chirii.

Diron Haeyi (Laosha)—Historic figure. Middle sibling between Xondir Haeyi and Minroa Haeyi. Diron's father gave her to Piiroc nobles as an alliance gift. She seized the opportunity to claim her own title and eventually became the Flame Apotheosis. She ruled in the northern Piiroc Fire Temple with great hope that she and Xondir would forge an alliance and end persecution of Piirocs in Chyre. Instead, Xondir broke the existing truce and seized Northern Piiroc lands to build his Storm Towers. Diron never forgave him and spent the rest of her life battling his armies.

Eirjiri—One of the five Waethir from Saigrath. Eirjiri shares her name with the Earth Deity. Her hair is golden, and she appears to be about fifteen years old. She's optimistic, enthusiastic and open to anything new, but she is also extremely loyal to her old friends.

Falhep—Border patrol soldier, recovering from injuries.

Hiral—Second cameraman on Una Bayan's team.

Ife—Mage adept graduate from Guishuun College. In mage exhibition competitions, Ife competed in the Pairs Division using ancillary scythes. Zevlyn is her partner and fellow graduate. Ife wears her black hair in a high ponytail and has two red moles above her right eyebrow and lips that pitch down into an innate expression of skepticism. She's a would-be novelist and ardent researcher.

Ilhani— Sea Serpent Wae.

Jeshri—An outgoing Orae Academy graduate. Jeshri is muscular, sports a thick black beard and wields a sword Ancillary called Jo. He swears enthusiastically and has earned the nickname "The Wall" for his performances in mage exhibition battles. Jeshri originally hails from a wealthy family in Yanyeo but was sent to Amei as a boy for his education. He had boarded with his classmate, Xaon, since they were both children.

Jolon Dane—Lui Dane's grandson and the Development Director of the Armory Division of NS. Jolon Dane is a master mage, having graduated from Boshyin School alongside Una Bayan and Mazilane.

Kais— Saum's Grandmother and a retired Ryde Academy instructor. She taught Paeth and Ovelah and was close with Paeth in particular.She and her husband live in Yanyeo.

Kimrin—Adept mage from Chohe Institute. Kimrin uses and collects ancillary fans. He wears round gold glasses and likes to add gold adornments to his brown hair. He descends from two old aristocratic families in Yanyeo. His uncle, Wanlo, owns several newspapers and publishing houses. His aunt is a socialite and high fashion designer. Kimrin loves gossip, hats and shoes and has a keen eye for quality, be it in lovely people or high-end leather work.

Laithondi—One of the five Waethir from Saigrath. Laithondi is named for East Deity, (Guardian of the Day). He's exceptionally tall, white-haired and appears to be in his twenties. He is first to take action in a crisis but can be taciturn in social environments.

Lazhu—Phoenix guardian spell (wae) enclosed in a sword charm belonging to Xaon's family.

Lui Dane—The gaunt, seventy-something Minister of National Security and Defense. Lui Dane was one of the first mages to undergo surgery for modern spell filaments.

Mazilane—Una Bayan's classmate and cameraman, but secretly also an agent for NS in the Armory Division. Mazilane possesses outstanding mage skills and is particularly adept with mechanical ancillaries. He attended Boshyin as a scholarship student. He is very attached to his ancillary camera, Soir.

Minroa Haeyi (Laosha)—Historical figure. Member of the Haelon royal family. Minroa was sent to the Waethir of Saigrath as part of a diplomatic party at the age of fifteen, though his mage-king father also tasked him with spy work. Eventually Minroa and his brother Xondir tricked their father into attacking the Waethir. Minroa's lover, Ondi, killed Minroa's father in battle and then crowned Xondir Haeyi as the new mage-king of Chyre, at Minroa's request. Little beyond that is known of his history except that he returned to Saigrath after his brother's coronation.

Nyle—Highly skilled mage adept. Nyle won a Boshyin scholarship as well as a Lux Temple champion ring. He is the eleventh of seventeen children from an impoverished family. After winning his scholarship, he was sent to board with one of the Boshyin school cooks. He wears his long black hair in old-fashioned braids and dresses in an unadorned, conservative style. His delicate appearance has earned him the nickname "Porcelain Prince" in mage exhibition competitions.

Omn Haeyi—Historical figure. Ancient mage-king and father of Xondir, Diron and Minroa. Omn conquered parts of Piiroc in an attempt to find the secrets to eternal life. Later, he moved his attention and ambition to Saigrath. He was killed in an attempt to invade the Waethir's stronghold.

Ovelah—Mage adept from Ryde Academy. Ovelah and her more outspoken twin, Paeth, fight in the Pairs Division. Ovelah is skilled at building ancillaries but suffers from a speech impediment, and so she often relies on her sister to convey her ideas to outsiders. Both girls have long curly brown hair and hazel eyes.

Paeth—Mage adept from Ryde Academy. Ovelah's twin and partner in the Pairs Division of mage exhibition competitions. Paeth uses a compass ancillary. Like Ovelah, she has long curly brown hair and hazel eyes. Being kind and sociable, Paeth has befriended both Saum and Yinni.

Quin—Mage adept from Chohe Institute, Quin is distantly related to Kimrin and was at one time nearly engaged to Jeshri. Like them, she hails from Yanyeo's fallen aristocrats. Incredibly fast and tiny with purple-rinsed hair, she is readily likened to a hummingbird. She loves design and is creating her own collection of artistic gowns and accessories. She adores shoes, hats and Kimrin. She uses an ancillary fan in mage battles.

Ramei—A fit commander of NS Security border patrol. In his mid-forties.

Rokea—A wae in the form of three golden winged salamanders. Faithful, Fearless, and Friendly are the three aspects. Rokea is extremely attached to Minroa.

Ryn, Grand Master—Current battle leader of Lux Temple. In her late forties.

Saum—Mage adept from Ryde Academy. Saum wields an ancillary hammer and has won a Lux Temple champion ring. She's short, sturdy and wears her black hair in a short bob, emulating the actress Una Bayan. She has a gleeful, outgoing personality and has readily befriended Paeth, Ovelah and Yinni. She loves moving pictures and film stars. Her nickname is 'The Hammer.'

Soa—Saum's grandfather. Retired Orea Academy teacher. Soa is a trained mage-physician. During the Haelon Flood, he served as a volunteer director for the refugee camp.

Soir—Mazilane's highly complex ancillary camera.

Shuun, Master— Tuteli instructor and physician. In his seventies. Shuun took vows and joined Lux Temple after meeting and treating Master Tam in Yanyeo. They have been partners for forty-five years. Shuun enjoys brewing and offering scathing criticism as hobbies, though he and Master Tam are attached to Cymin and Yinni.

Tam, Master—Sixty-eight-year-old tuteli instructor at Lux Temple. Master Tam is strict but generous to his students. In his time, he was an outstanding fighter at Spring Exhibitions. However, injuries resulting from his service in a Storm Tower have greatly reduced his ability to temper fei'lux. He adores Shunn and the many cats that have taken to living on the temple grounds. He is extremely proud of Yinni and Cymin, though Cymin's pranks often frustrate him.

Tsike—Historical figure. Second in command under Xondir Haeyi during northern expeditions and building of the Storm Towers. Given Xondir's personal wae, Lazhu, and ordered to remain in Yanyeo to protect the secrets of the Storm Towers. His family eventually became the Ember Knife crime family who rule the underworld of Yanyeo.

Una Bayan—Famous film star, mage adept from Boshyin School and an aspiring director of documentary film. Una Bayan is the daughter of the Minister of Transportation and also an outspoken opponent of many NS policies. She schooled with Jolon Dane and Mazilane.

Vessreid—One of the five Waethir from Saigrath. Vessreid shares his name with West Deity, Guardian of the Night. His hair is silver-gray, but he appears to be in his twenties. His features are gentle, and he's largely soft-spoken. He's benevolent and protective of those less powerful than himself and can become volatile on their behalf. He loves gardening and is fond of persimmons.

Wanlo—Kimrin's Uncle, publishing magnate.

Wilal—Hiral's mother, trained medic and mage.

Xaon—Mage adept and Orea Academy graduate. Xaon is called "the Blood Blade" in part because of his vivid red hair, honed body and his ferocious sword ancillary. He has boarded with Jeshri since childhood, and despite coming from very different backgrounds, they are fast friends. His two personal treasures are a phoenix-stamped sword charm and a postcard featuring a portrait of Minroa Haeyi.

Xondir Haeyi (Laosha)—Historical figure. Minroa's full brother. Chyre's greatest and most infamous mage-king, Xondir conquered and united a multitude of the different kingdoms into one vast nation. He designed and oversaw the construction of the Storm Towers and instituted the Spring Exhibitions. Later in his life, he was said to succumb to paranoia, refusing to take off his Hundred Deaths armor and requiring numerous young mages be sacrificed to him.

Yinni—Naturally talented mage and tuteli adept. Yinni is Cymin's older sister by two years. She has the honor of representing West Deity for Lux Temple. Her birth name was Yaral. She is friends with Paeth, Ovelah and Saum.

Zevlyn— Mage adept and Guishuun College graduate. Zevlyn is Ife's partner in the Pairs Division of mage exhibitions. She uses ancillary scythes. Her features are naturally a little somber and her chin dimpled. She loves books and research.

History Timeline

1670: In exchange for a truce, the Piiroc Flame Apotheosis is forced to cede much of her land in Haelon and give her youngest daughter, Irin Loasha, to the Chyrenese mage-king, Omn Haeyi.

1677: Xondir born to Irin Laosha

1679: Diron born to Irin Laosha

1681 Minroa born to Irin Laosha

1693: Xondir, Diron and Minroa are imprisoned after their mother is accused of plotting an assassination against the Chyrenese mage-king. They remain in prison for three years.

1695: In Saigrath, a thirteen-year-old tuteli is chosen by the Sea of Eternity as the new incarnation of Laithondi, East Deity.

1696: Minrao Haeyi—age fifteen—is at last freed from prison and sent to Saigrath. On the surface, he is to assist the Chyrenese ambassador, but his true purpose is to be a spy for his father and discover the Waethir's secret to eternal life. Diron is sent to Pirroc as a gift to the mage-king's new Piiroc ally. Xondir is placed in the army and sent to the southeast border of Piiroc lands.

1699: Eirjiri dies of old age. New toddler Eirjiri is awoken from the tuteli at the Heights.

1700: Laithondi takes Minroa to the White Chamber.

1703: Diron wins the battle to become the Piiroc Flame Apotheosis. She begins to secure her rule over the north of Piiroc and reaches out to her brothers, hoping to form stronger alliances.

1704: Inspired by Diron, Minroa and Xondir lure their father into invading Saigrath. They then inform the Waethir of their father's plans and assist the Waethir in laying a trap at the Black Gates. There, Minroa and the Waethir wipe out the mage-king's army. Ondi personally kills the mage-king. Minroa refuses the crown when it's offered to him. Instead, he appoints Xondir to be the next mage-king of Chyre.

1704: Xondir begins to decriminalize the practice of Piiroc religion. Minroa writes extensively to Diron about Saigrath and the Waethir, preparing for the day when all three nations will be allied and open their borders.

1705: Attempted coup against Xondir by Chyrenese nobles begins in the fall. They oppose him for enforcing the Waethir's equality commandments and his attempts to decriminalize Piiroc religious rites. But there is also unrest over new taxes, which go to construct the Storm Towers. Xondir wipes out the rebels and executes their entire extended families. The executions lead Vessreid to publicly chastise and punish him. Xondir is infuriated.

1706: Xondir invades Haelon and begins the war against Diron.

1708: Xondir wins total control of Haelon and the necropolis, but the war continues and Xondir's second in command, Tsike, takes charge of the fighting while Xondir focuses on designing the spells for the storm towers and conquering the Dajiryn Islands where they will be built.

1709: Construction of the Storm Towers begins in secret. Throughout the fall and winter, the Waethir are seen less and less.

1710: The first of the year, the Waethir are completely absent from the "mortal realm". They will not appear again for centuries. In the spring, a fierce fei'lux storm surges across the lands.Late summer: Xondir Haeyi retreats from Yanyeo to the capital Amei in the south.

1711: Xondir is rumored to be ill and begins to withdraw from the public.

1712: Xondir founds Boshyin Academy, focusing on ancillary and spell advances. They begin work at once on the first spell filaments as well as new classes of Hundred Deaths armor. He also increases the number of tuteli and young mages to be tithed to him personally.

1722: Storm Towers are completed. Tuteli are required to serve the towers. The first Spring Exhibition takes place, allowing Xondir to choose the best mages to serve his court and his towers.

1745: Xondir Haeyi passes rule to his heir—distant nephew—and is never seen again.

1760: Chohe Institute established

1819: Revolution won. Mage-king assassinated.

1819: Guishuun College established

1822: Orae Academy established

1899: Yaral born

1901: Chirii born

1900: Ryde Academy established

1905: Fei'lux storms set off the Great Haelon Flood which devastates the province.

1905: Orphans, Yaral and Chirii are placed in a refugee camp for those displaced by the flood. Their names are changed to Yinni and Cymin. They are selected by Grand Master Ryn and taken to live in Lux Temple.

1919: Waethir arrive in the Chyre capital for the Spring Exhibition.

Sigils

Aith—suppress / calm
Arn—sea
Bhun—brown
Bia—wind
Bosh—knowledge / wisdom (classic works)
Byul—south
Cha—one
Cho—black
Chuu—madness
Chuuraun—(compound sigil: chuu + raun)
Cy—abundant
Dagni—honey
Daji—white
Daoh—sleep
Dir—joy
Eir—iron
Eom—east
Fei—power / force of creation. That which imbues life into the inanimate.
Fuu—West
Ghan—sew or stitch together
Ghon—return / reunite / reunion
Grath—home
Gui—the future
Haeyi—enlighten / epiphany
Hi—violet
Hiral—comet (but also the wandering eye of a Halibut in Piiroc slang)
Huu—fury
Ife—moon
Ilha—unquenchable / voracious
Ish—green
Jeshri—laughter
Jiri—command
Jo—unyielding
Kae—salamander
Ke—blue
Kes—watchful
Kim—quick
Kue—death / die

Laith—advance / charge forward
Lon—stride across / stand on
Lux—shining
Lyn—flower
Min—spring rain
Moh—health
Nath—gold
Nau—yellow
Ni—treasure
Nol—gray / silver
Nyle—sedge / long grass
Oadu—north
On—flame
Ondi—sun
Prith—converge in union / harmony
Quin—clear/ pure/ innocent
Raun—creature
Reid—grasp / hold
Ro—three/ Third
Roa—summer fire
Ryn—rotect / shield
Sai—mist
Shar—poison or corruption
Sharwae—(compound sigil Shar + Wae = poison + guardian) Guardian array that has been altered to a different / harmful purpose
Shua—to seek or find
Shuun—truth
Suul—cultivate / encourage
Tam—cut apart / behead
Thir—deities / supernatural beings and creatures
Tsai—snow (winter)
Tsi—ice / sleet
Uuhir—hunt or stalk prey
Uuli—submission (sigil used in Piiroc to enslave / bond violent criminals who would otherwise be executed)
Uum—rot / decay
Uusae—kill / murder
Var—first / beginning / primary
Vess—night

Wae—guardian. Unified arrays of spells so complex that they have taken on consciousness.
Win—song
Xaon—red/ scarlet, but can also mean blood
Xon—heart
Yan—lotus
Yeo—fortress
Yin—exalted
Yo—tower
Yue—to pierce
Zev—stars
Zue—freshwater / drinking water

Acknowledgements

This book wouldn't exist if it hadn't been for the advice, insight and encouragement of Nicole, Astrid and Jinny. I'm so grateful to you all for courageously reading the first, very rough drafts of *Price of a Thousand Blessings.*

I also owe a tremendous debt to everyone who supported this book on Patreon.

At a time when I was very uncertain of the value of my work, you made me love this project and look forward to posting the chapters each week. Thank you!

A, Abby Lagrow, Alan Williams, Aleash, Amy Cordova, Andrea Canada, Anne-Julia Voillat-Sauer, Antonella, Arden, Atarni A, aurorawest, Austin Shirley, Beige, Caroline G, Christine Danse, Colette, David, elrhiarhodan, EW, fuckyeaharthuriana, Hikuyama, Hollye Barrett, I, Jennifer, Jennifer Brett, Jessi Johnson, Jinny, joancotilla, Judith Utz, K, Karla Smith, Katie, Lazu, Llama Bean, Lynne McCullough, Lyveria, M.F., Mackenzie Cowan, Maris Fairchild, Matty, Meg, Megan Hannel, MV, nautilus, Nieves Sánchez Castillo, Op16No1, PC, Raye, Renee Cardineau, RJK, Sharon, Sheila Hooper, Silbrith, sirloin, SJ, Tracy Timmons-Gray, Zan.

About the Author

Ginn Hale is a multi-award-winning author of fantasy and science fiction. She lives in the Pacific Northwest with her wife of over thirty years and their indulged cat. There, she spends the cloudy days and rainy evenings drinking coffee and writing books featuring LGBTQ+ characters.

Her most recent publications include the Cadeleonian Series: *Lord of the White Hell, Champion of the Scarlet Wolf* and *Master of Restless Shadows*.

She can be reached on Patreon as well as through her website www.ginnhale.com. Her Instagram account, however, is largely a collection of botanical photos . . . so, be warned.

Other publications from Ginn Hale

Novels

Wicked Gentlemen
Lord of the White Hell Book One
Lord of the White Hell Book Two
Champion of the Scarlet Wolf Book One
Champion of the Scarlet Wolf Book Two
Master of Restless Shadows Book One
Master of Restless Shadows Book Two
The Shattered Gates
The Holy Road
His Sacred Bones

Novellas

Feral Machines—Tangle (Anthology)
Touching Sparks—Hell Cop (Anthology)
Such Heights— Hell Cop Two (Anthology)
Things Unseen and Deadly—Irregulars (Anthology)
Swift and the Black Dog—Charmed and Dangerous (Anthology)
The Long Past—The Long Past and Other Stories (Anthology)
Get Lucky—The Long Past and Other Stories (Anthology)
Counterfeit Viscount—Devil Take Me (Anthology)

Short Stories

"Shy Hunter"—Queer Wolf
"Blood Beneath the Throne"—Icarus Magazine
"The Hollow History of Professor Perfectus"—The Long Past and Other Stories
"Seed Stitch Solution"—Once Upon A Fact
"Treasured Island"—Scourges of the Seas of Time (and Space)

Fei'suul
Scepter

A battered, second-hand book purchased at the Palace Complex.

Master Tam often made notes from scrap paper and posted them near places stray cats slept on the temple grounds.